THE WILY O'REILLY

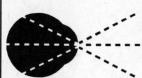

This Large Print Book carries the
Seal of Approval of N.A.V.H.

IRISH COUNTRY STORIES

THE WILY O'REILLY

PATRICK TAYLOR

THORNDIKE PRESS
A part of Gale, Cengage Learning

GALE
CENGAGE Learning·

Detroit • New York • San Francisco • New Haven, Conn • Waterville, Maine • London

GALE
CENGAGE Learning·

LIBRARY OF CONGRESS CATALOGING-IN-PUBLICATION DATA

Taylor, Patrick, 1941-
  The Wily O'Reilly : Irish Country stories / by Patrick Taylor. — Large print edition.
    pages ; cm. — (Thorndike Press large print core)
  ISBN-13: 978-1-4104-6648-8 (hardcover)
  ISBN-10: 1-4104-6648-5 (hardcover)
  1. O'Reilly, Fingal Flahertie (Fictitious character)—Fiction. 2. Physicians (General practice)—Fiction. 3. Country life—Northern Ireland—Fiction. 4. Ulster (Northern Ireland and Ireland)—Fiction. 5. Large type books. I. Title.
  PR9199.3.T36W55 2014b
  813'.52—dc23
                                                                2013047806

Published in 2014 by arrangement with Tom Doherty Associates, LLC.

To Simon Hally
who first let me develop Doctor Fingal
O'Reilly and with a gentle editorial hand
guided the eccentric GP from early
beginnings to the maturity that finally
became the Irish Country Doctor novels

CONTENTS

8

AUTHOR'S NOTE

I have written all my life, or at least since an essay of mine phrased in the style of Sir Francis Bacon was published in my school magazine when I was sixteen. It seems so long ago now that I wonder if the task came easily to me because the old seventeenth-century statesman, jurist, scientist, and author and I were practically contemporaries.

Whenever I give readings from my later works, all novels, someone invariably asks a two-part question, the first part of which is, "Where did Doctors O'Reilly and Laverty come from?" It'll take me a page or two to answer that.

The whole process was a lengthy evolution of a writer and his characters. Much of it seemed to come by chance, a strange admixture of who you know and luck. The short stories included between these covers are the proof of that and I hope you enjoy them.

The second part of the question will have to await the fuller explanation of part one, but I promise I'll tell you what the query was and answer it before the end of this introduction.

During most of my medical research career any literary efforts were confined to the production of scientific papers and, in collaboration with colleagues, half a dozen textbooks. Dull, I can assure you. Very, very dull.

That changed in 1989. My longtime friend and medical school classmate Doctor Tom Baskett had been appointed editor in chief of the *Journal of Obstetrics and Gynaecology Canada (JSOGC)*. To lighten its otherwise dry content he invited me to contribute a regular page of tongue-in-cheek observations about the world of then modern medicine. "En Passant" began appearing monthly and lasted for nearly ten years.

To my surprise the associate editor of the *Canadian Medical Association Journal (CMAJ)* noticed the early efforts and commissioned a six-weekly column, "Medicine Chest," for his publication. An idea had begun to germinate and I asked permission to devote five hundred words in each episode to the doings of a fictional Ulster GP, Doctor Reilly — please note Reilly, not yet O'Reilly — and the suggestion was accepted. Unfortunately the electronic records of these stories are lost, but I had fun with the character.

Simon Hally, who over the years has become my friend, was then editor of *Punch Digest for Canadian Doctors,* which subsequently became *Stitches: The Journal of Medical Humour.* He'd read the Reilly stories in the *CMAJ* and wondered if I'd consider doing a regular piece for him, to be called "Taylor's Twist." He also mentioned a dollar sum that would keep me in paper, ink, and the high technology of the time, floppy discs. I agreed, but asked that rather than doing short, one-paragraph observations I could devote each column to a single, I hoped humorous, anecdote. The first of these stories appeared in 1991, and until 1995 chronicled the vagaries of the life of a medical undergraduate in Belfast in the '50s and '60s, and yes, they were autobiographical, if exaggerated and a bit twisted.

But old Doctor Reilly, whose antics had ceased with the discontinuation of "Medicine Chest" somewhere in 1991, kept muttering to me that he felt he should be resurrected. After four years of undergraduate stories I was running out of steam, and with Simon's permission switched to the recounting of the misadventures of a newly qualified medical graduate who innocently accepts a position of assistant to an irascible, blasphemous, hard-drinking, rural Ulster GP who by now had adopted the name Fingal Flahertie O'Reilly. I think you probably know him. Those columns ran until 2001. Like the undergraduate stories they were based on my own and my friends' experiences in Ulster general practice. Some come from good stories heard in pubs.

Forgive me if I now digress into some technical aspects of writing fiction, but I needs must if I am going to explain why in these columns I cast myself, Patrick Taylor, as the straight man and narrator in this Hippocratic Laurel and Hardy double act.

The best modern stories are written in "point of view." The author must slip into the background and let the reader experience the action through the eyes of the "point of view character." This means that, for example, a subsidiary character in a scene cannot comment as an aside on what the main character is thinking or doing. Such asides, while properly called "authorial intrusion" in literary fiction, can be the guts of good comedy. And there is a way to use them so they are not intrusive.

If the point of view character is the narrator, they can make as many asides as they like, and this is even easier if the storytelling character is the first-person "I," as in, "I saw O'Reilly lift Donal Donnelly by gripping the little man's shoulder in one vast paw and as God is my witness I swear I heard the victim's bones creak. O'Reilly never seemed to know his own strength."

To tell the *Stitches* stories my own character became the narrator, the butt of many of the jokes, and I had a useful technique to work with. I am frequently asked, "In the novels are you Doctor Barry Laverty?" O'Reilly's fictional junior. For structural reasons I did indeed use myself in these columns, but I do not translate into Barry in the Irish Country series.

So those were the first stumbling steps. I'm afraid they don't quite answer the question of how did the Country Series evolve. That is also the story of my journey to become a novelist.

Shortly after graduation from medical school in my twenties I tried my hand as a short-story writer. W. Somerset Maugham had been my teenage hero. The Belfast Troubles had broken out and I tried to set

15

human drama against that background. I am the proud possessor of rejection slips from several magazines of the period, including one from *The New Yorker*.

By the mid-'90s I had been appointed editor of the *JSOGC*. The various humour columns were doing well, and as a sideline I was also selling sailing humour. (I think it's genetic. When an Ulsterman goes to sea, strange things can happen. We, after all, built the RMS *Titanic*.) In a fit of chutzpah I dug out some of the short stories I'd written back in the '60s and a few more I'd started to experiment with, and sought an opinion from the publisher of the *JSOGC* and his wife, Adrian and Olga Stein, two people whose interest in the written word is vast. They in turn persuaded Anna Porter, then of Key Porter Books, to take a look, and to my delight she agreed that with editorial help from Carolyn Bateman, who is now my friend and highly valued editor to this day, a short story collection, *Only Wounded: Ulster Stories,* should be produced. It will be rereleased by Forge in 2015.

Another remarkable man, Jack Whyte, author of the Dream of Eagles series and more novels, suggested I try writing a novel. Emboldened by having had my short stories accepted, I took his advice. Thank you, Jack. To cut a long story short, after numerous rejections a psycho-thriller, *Pray for Us Sinners,* was published in 2000 in Canada. Flushed with pride I suggested to my house editor, Adrienne Weiss, "Why don't we take all my Doctor O'Reilly columns, clap on covers, and make a buck or two?"

She said, "If your name was Garrison Keillor I'd say, 'Let's call it *Lake Wobegon Days* and go for it, but . . .' "

Her implication that no one had heard of Patrick Taylor was not lost. She was, however, kind enough to suggest that she liked the character of Doctor O'Reilly. "Perhaps with the confidence gained from one published novel under my belt I might consider . . . ?"

The Apprenticeship of Doctor Laverty, the first novel about O'Reilly, appeared in Canada in 2004 and, thanks to the efforts of Jack Whyte, as well as Natalia Aponte, then acquiring editor for Forge Books, it was republished in the United States in 2007 as *An Irish Country Doctor.* It was the beginning of the Irish Country series.

And so with the support of you, the readers, the continuing story of Doctor Fingal Flahertie O'Reilly has continued to grow.

I started this introduction by quoting the

first part of a two-part question: "Where did Doctors O'Reilly and Laverty come from?" and I promised after a long-winded answer to tell you what the second part was. "You've told us that they came from your humour columns," I can hear you say. "So, when are we going to get to see those old columns?" And that of course is the second part of the question.

The answer is that while I have released a few on my Web page as blogs, now through the generosity of Tom Doherty and Forge Books you can have the lot, warts and all, between these covers. The cover illustration was conceived and brought to life by Irene Gallo and beautifully painted by Gregory Manchess. They have been responsible for all the Irish Country dust-jacket art.

In addition, last March we published a short O'Reilly story, "Home Is the Sailor," in e-format only. You can see how in part it was derived from a column entitled "The Lazarus Manoeuvre" first created in late 1995. I now know that many readers who did not have access to the e-reader technology were disappointed. For them, that story, written much later than the columns, is appended in hard copy in this work.

I have had a lot of fun revisiting these long-ago-written friends. I sincerely hope you enjoy them. If you compare them with the Irish Country novels you will see how characters changed and grew, and simple story lines were twisted and embellished.

And perhaps having had a glimpse into the origins you will see how a writer and his characters can grow from small beginnings.

With my best wishes,

Patrick Taylor
Salt Spring Island,
British Columbia,
Canada

Introducing O'Reilly

IN WHICH WE MAKE THE ACQUAINTANCE OF A RATHER REMARKABLE GP

"Taylor's Twist" first appeared in *Stitches: The Journal of Medical Humour* in September 1991, as a chronicle of the experiences of a medical student in Belfast in the '50s and '60s. By 1995 I'd written about the life of a medical undergraduate for almost as long as I was one. The editor, Simon Hally, was a generous man and allowed me to switch my attention, and I trust yours, to events of postgraduate life in the North of Ireland in the late '60s. To anyone with the intestinal fortitude actually to want more undergraduate stories, I can only apologize. To the rest, who have followed me thus far, let us boldly go where no sentient entity has gone before — and I don't mean the Canadian House of Commons or the Congress of the United States. Come back with me to Ulster and meet my old tutor, Doctor O'Reilly, ex-navy boxing champion, classical scholar, unregenerate poacher, hard drinker, cryptophilanthropist, foul-mouthed widower, and country GP.

He was a big man, about six foot fourteen in his socks and weighing twenty stone or, if you prefer, 280 pounds. His complexion might be charitably called florid, the delicate roseate hue of his cheeks having all the softness of an overheated blast furnace. His nose, once perhaps a thing of beauty and a joy forever, had acquired a distinct personality of its own. The tip was squashed and sat at a rakish forty-five degrees to port of the bridge. Boxing, or as it was once known, the manly art of self-defence, carried its own costs. The tip of O'Reilly's nose had one other important characteristic: when he became enraged it turned white.

I stumbled, all unsuspecting, into his clutches after I'd finished my houseman's (intern's) year and was eking out a meagre existence demonstrating anatomy. Weekend and evening locums for GPs helped me make ends if not exactly meet, then at least come within calling distance of each other. I simply answered a newspaper advertisement.

In the years that I knew O'Reilly, years

that encompassed a series of horribly under-paid registrar's (resident's) jobs, he never ceased to astound me. Sometimes my surprise was a result of his absolutely cavalier treatment of a malingerer; on other occasions his encyclopaedic knowledge of his patients astounded me. He had an uncanny sense of clinical smell, and I would still bet O'Reilly's diagnostic acumen against a battery of CT scans, MRI pictures, and the entire arsenal of the biochemistry laboratory.

He detested bureaucracy with the vitriolic hatred of Torquemada for unrepentant heretics, was kind to widows and small children, and ate public health officers for breakfast. He was stubborn to the point of mulishness when his mind was made up, had a tongue that when aroused would have made Adolf Hitler on a bad day at a Nuremberg rally sound like a cooing dove, yet he'd sit for hours in the dark of the night with a dying patient and still be ready for work as soon as morning surgery, the term for office over there, opened.

I learned more about the art of medicine from that man, and some of the humour of it too, than from a faculty of professors. I wish I could have him with me today when I'm faced with some of the array of meaningful, interactive, holistic, client-centred healthcare providers who want to invade my turf as a physician. You know the kind: the ones who believe that medicine is too important to be left to the doctors (a brilliantly original paraphrasing of old Georges Clemenceau's crack about war and generals, although others would attribute it to Talleyrand) and who, bless their trusting little souls, are convinced that if enough wellness clinics are opened, nasty old diseases will vanish and we'll all live forever.

To be fair to O'Reilly, in some matters he was well ahead of his time. I thought of him the other day while watching a demonstration in which a healthcare provider held her hands over the sufferer and by concentrating, focused vital healing energies. I saw O'Reilly using a similar approach thirty years ago.

He'd asked me to join him for morning surgery, which he conducted in the converted front room of his home, sitting in a swivel chair in front of a great rolltop desk. Beside him was a hard-backed chair for the sufferer. One of O'Reilly's ploys was to have sawn off the last inch of the front legs of this seat so the customer would keep sliding forward, be uncomfortable, and thus not be tempted to stay too long.

I occupied the other piece of furniture in the room, a battered examination couch, swinging my legs and wishing that the incessant flow of coughs, colds, and sniffles would dry up, both figuratively and literally.

The last patient came in. I'd seen her before, twice actually, with vague but time-consuming symptoms. She took one look at me and sniffed. "The young lad's not helping me, Doctor."

O'Reilly rose, and waited until she was seated. He sat and took one of her hands in his, peered over a set of half-moon spectacles, which he affected when he wanted to look particularly wise, and asked, "What seems to be the trouble, Maggie?"

She fired one aggrieved glance in my direction and said in a voice that would have softened Pharaoh's heart if, like Moses, she'd been discussing the holiday plans of the Children of Israel with Ramses, "It's the headaches, Doctor."

"Um," said O'Reilly, leaning forward, left elbow on his knee, chin cupped in his hand, index finger crushing past the side of his bent schnozzle. "Where are they?"

She sighed deeply. "About two inches above my crown."

O'Reilly didn't bat an eyelid. "Tut-tut." He positively oozed solicitousness. "Tut.

Tut!" He released her hand, swivelled in his chair, grabbed a bottle of some new vitamins that a drug rep had left as a sample, swung back, and handed them to her. He stood, signalling that the consultation was nearly over. She stood. He took her arm, piloting her to the door. "Now, Maggie," he said. "You must take two of these for the ache over your head . . ." he looked at me, one upper eyelid drooping in a slow wink ". . . ten minutes before the pain starts."

She thanked him profusely and left.

I saw her a week later. She lost no time telling me what a useless physician I was and how Doctor O'Reilly had effected another miracle cure. I'm sure he would have been a great practitioner of therapeutic touch.

Now you've met Doctor O'Reilly. Next time I'll tell you how he started in practice.

THE LAZARUS MANOEUVRE

HOW THE YOUNG DOCTOR O'REILLY EARNED THE RESPECT OF HIS COMMUNITY

We were sitting in the upstairs lounge of Doctor O'Reilly's house at the end of the day. Himself was tucking contentedly into his second large whiskey. "So," he demanded, "how do you like it?"

Being a little uncertain whether he was asking about the spectacular view through the bay window to Belfast Lough, the small sherry I was sipping, or the general status of the universe, I countered with an erudite, "What?"

He fished in the external auditory canal of one thickened, pugilist's ear with the tip of his right little finger and echoed my sentiments: "What?"

I thought this conversation could become mildly repetitive and decided to broaden the horizons. "How do I like what, Doctor

27

O'Reilly?"

He extracted his digit and examined the end with all the concentration and knitting of brows of a gorilla evaluating a choice morsel. "Practice here, you idiot. How do you like it?"

My lights went on. "Fine," I said, as convincingly as possible. "Just fine."

My reply seemed to satisfy him. He grinned, grunted, hauled his twenty stone erect, wandered over to the sideboard, and returned carrying the sherry decanter. He topped up my glass. "A bird can't fly on one wing," he remarked.

I refrained from observing that if he kept putting away the whiskey at his usual rate he'd soon be giving a pretty fair imitation of a mono-winged albatross in a high gale, accepted my fresh drink, and waited.

He returned the decanter, ambled to the window, and took in the scenery with one all-encompassing wave of his arm. "I'd not want to live anywhere else," he said. "Mind you, it was touch and go at the start."

He was losing me again. "What was, Doctor O'Reilly?"

"Fingal, my boy. Fingal. For Oscar." He gave me one of his most avuncular smiles.

I couldn't for the life of me see him having been named for a small, gilded statuette

28

given annually to movie stars. "Oscar, er, Fingal?" I asked.

He shook his head. "No. Not Oscar Fingal. Wilde."

He did this to me. Every time I thought I was following him he'd change tack, leaving me in a state of confusion bordering on that usually felt by people recovering from an overdose of chloroform. "Oscar Fingal Wilde, Fingal?"

I should have stuck with "Doctor O'Reilly." I could tell by the way the tip of his bent nose was beginning to whiten that he was becoming exasperated. He shook his head. "Oscar . . . Fingal . . . O'Flahertie . . . Wills . . . Wilde."

I stifled the urge to remark that if you put an air to it you could sing it.

He must have seen my look of bewilderment. The ischaemia left his nose. "I was named for him. For Oscar Wilde."

The scales fell from my eyes. "I see."

"Good. Now where was I?"

"You said, 'It was touch and go at the start.' "

"Oh yes. Getting the practice going. Touch and go." He sat again in the big comfortable armchair, picked up his glass of whiskey, and looked at me over the brim. "Did I ever tell you how I got started?"

"No," I said, settling back in my own chair, preparing myself for another of his reminiscences, for another meander down the byways of O'Reilly's life.

"I came here in the early '40s. Took over from Doctor Finnegan."

I hoped fervently that we weren't about to embark on the genealogy of James Joyce, and was relieved to hear O'Reilly continue, "He was a funny old bird."

Never, I thought, but kept the thought to myself.

O'Reilly was warming up now. "Just before he left, Finnegan warned me about a local condition of cold groin abscesses. He didn't understand them." O'Reilly took a mouthful of Irish, savoured it, and swallowed. "He explained to me that when he lanced them he either got wind or shit, but the patient invariably died." O'Reilly chuckled.

I was horrified. My mentor's predecessor had been incising inguinal hernias.

"That's why it was touch and go," said O'Reilly. "My first patient had the biggest hernia I've ever seen. When I refused to lance it, like good old Doctor Finnegan, the patient spread the word that I didn't know my business." He sat back and crossed one leg over the other. "Did you ever hear of Lazarus?"

"Oscar Fingal O'Flahertie Wills Lazarus?" I asked.

"Don't be impertinent." He grabbed my by-now-empty glass and headed back to the sideboard. The delivery of a fresh libation, and one for himself, signalled that he hadn't been offended. "No, the biblical fellow that Jesus raised from the dead." He sat.

"Yes."

"That's how I got my start."

Was it the sherry or was I really losing my mind? Whatever his skills, I doubted that Doctor O'Reilly had actually effected a resurrection. "Go on," I asked for it.

"I was in church one Sunday, hoping that if the citizens saw that I was a good Christian they might look upon me more favourably."

The thought of a pious O'Reilly seemed a trifle incongruous.

"There I was when a farmer in the front pew let out a yell like a banshee, grabbed his chest, and keeled over." To add drama to his words O'Reilly stood, arms wide. "I took out of my pew like a whippet. Examined him. Mutton. Dead as mutton."

I knew that CPR hadn't been invented in the '40s. "What did you do?"

O'Reilly lowered his arms and winked. "I got my bag, told everyone to stand back,

31

and gave the poor corpse an injection of whatever came handy. I listened to his heart. 'He's back,' says I. You should have heard the gasp from the congregation."

He sat down. "I listened again. 'God,' says I, 'he's going again,' and gave the poor bugger another shot." O'Reilly sipped his drink. "I brought him back three times before I finally confessed defeat."

Innocence is a remarkable thing. "Did you really get his heart started?"

O'Reilly guffawed. "Not at all, but the poor benighted audience didn't know that. Do you know I actually heard one woman say to her neighbour, 'The Lord only brought Lazarus back once and the new doctor did it three times.' " He headed for the sideboard again. "I told you it was touch and go at the start, but the customers started rolling in after that — will you have another?"

GALVIN'S DUCKS

HOW DOCTOR O'REILLY MENDED A BROKEN HEART

"That man Galvin's a bloody idiot!" Thus spake Doctor Fingal Flahertie O'Reilly. He was standing in his favourite corner of the bar of the Black Swan Inn, or, as it was known to the locals, the Mucky Duck. O'Reilly's normally florid cheeks glowed crimson and the tip of his bent nose paled. Somehow rage seemed to divert the blood flow from his hooter to his face. I thought it politic to remain silent. I'd seen the redoubtable Doctor O'Reilly like this before.

He hadn't seemed to be his usual self when we'd repaired to the hostelry after evening surgery, and now, after his fourth pint, whatever had been bothering him was beginning to surface. "Raving bloody idiot," he muttered, taking a generous swallow of his drink and slamming the empty glass on the counter.

After six months as his weekend locum and part-time assistant, I'd learned my place in O'Reilly's universe. I nodded to Brendan the barman, who rapidly replaced O'Reilly's empty glass with another full of the velvet liquid product of Mister Arthur Guinness and Sons, St. James's Gate, Dublin.

"Ta," said O'Reilly, the straight glass almost hidden by his big hand. "I could kill Seamus Galvin." He rummaged in the pocket of his rumpled jacket, produced a briar, stoked it with the enthusiasm of Beëlzebub preparing the coals for an unrepentant sinner, and fired up the tobacco, making a smokescreen that would have hidden the entire British North Sea fleet from the attentions of the Panzerschiff *Bismarck*.

I sipped my shandy and waited, trying to remember if I'd seen the patient in question.

"Do you know what that benighted apology for a man has done?"

From the tone of O'Reilly's voice, I assumed it must have been some petty misdemeanour — like mass murder perhaps. "No," I said, helpfully.

O'Reilly sighed. "He has Mary's heart broken."

Now I remembered. Seamus Galvin and

his wife Mary lived in a cottage at the end of one of the lanes just outside the small Ulster town where O'Reilly practised. Galvin was a carpenter by trade and a would-be entrepreneur. I'd seen him once or twice, usually because he'd managed to hit his thumb with one of his hammers. I said the man was a carpenter; I didn't say he was a good carpenter.

"Broken," said O'Reilly mournfully, "utterly smashed."

This intelligence came as no great surprise. Mary Galvin was the sheet anchor of the marriage, bringing in extra money by selling her baking, eggs from her hens, and the produce of her vegetable garden. Galvin himself was a complete waster.

O'Reilly prodded my chest with the end of his pipe. "I should have known a few weeks ago when I saw him and he was telling me about his latest get-rich scheme." The big man grunted derisively. "That one couldn't make money in the Royal Mint."

I could only agree, remembering Galvin's previous failed endeavours. His "Happy Nappy Diaper Service" had folded. No one in a small town could afford the luxury of having someone else wash their babies' diapers. Only the most sublime optimist could have thought that a landscaping company would have much custom in a predominantly agricultural community. Galvin had soon been banished from his "Garden of Eden" lawn care business — presumably because his encounters with the fruit of the tree of knowledge had been limited. I wondered what fresh catastrophe had befallen him.

O'Reilly beat carelessly at an ember that had fallen from the bowl of his pipe onto the lapel of his tweed jacket. "Mary's the one with sense. She was in to see me a couple of weeks ago. She's pregnant." He inspected the charred cloth. "I've known her since she was a wee girl. I've never seen her so happy." His craggy features softened for a moment. "She told me her secret. She'd been saving her money and had enough for Seamus and herself to emigrate to California."

"Oh," I said.

"Aye," said O'Reilly, "she has a brother out there. He was going to find Seamus a job with a construction company."

I'd read somewhere that California was prone to earthquakes and for a moment thought that this unfortunate geological propensity had been transmitted to Ulster before I realized that the pub's attempt to shimmy like my sister Kate was due to

O'Reilly banging his fist on the bar top.

"That bloody idiot and his bright ideas." O'Reilly's nose tip was ashen. "He's gone into toy making. He thinks he can sell rocking ducks — rocking ducks." He shook his head ponderously. "Mary was in tonight. The wee lass was in tears. He'd taken the money she'd saved and went and bought the lumber to make his damn ducks. That man Galvin's a bloody idiot."

O'Reilly finished his pint, set the glass on the counter, shrugged, and said just one more word, "Home."

About a month later, I met Mary Galvin in the High Street. She stopped me and I could see she was bubbling with excitement.

"How are you, Mary?"

"Doctor, you'll never believe it!" She had wonderfully green eyes and they were sparkling. "A big company in Belfast has bought all of Seamus's rocking ducks, lock, stock, and barrel." She patted her expanding waistline. "The three of us are off to California next week."

I wished her well, genuinely pleased for her good fortune. It wasn't until I'd returned to O'Reilly's house that I began to wonder. He was out making a house call. For the last week he'd taken to parking his car on the street. No. No, he wouldn't have . . . ? When I opened the garage door, a bizarre creature toppled out from a heap of its fellows. The entire space was filled to the rafters with garishly painted ducks — rocking ducks. It only took a moment to stow the one that had made a bid for freedom and close the door. When I introduced Doctor O'Reilly, I described him as, among other things, a cryptophilanthropist. Now you know why.

KINKY

EVERY PRACTICE SHOULD HAVE A TRIAGE SPECIALIST LIKE HER

Doctor Fingal Flahertie O'Reilly wasn't the only character in the practice. Mrs. Kincaid, widow, native of County Kerry, known to one and all as "Kinky," functioned as his housekeeper-cum-receptionist-cum-nurse. She was a big woman, middle-aged, with big hands and blue eyes that could twinkle like the dew on the grass in the morning sun when she was in an expansive mood — or flash like lightning when she was enraged. She treated Doctor O'Reilly with due deference when he behaved himself and sub-Arctic frigidity when he didn't. She was the only person I knew who could bring him to heel. In her native county she would have been known as "a powerful woman."

When she was acting in her nursing role, Kinky's speciality was triage. Cerberus at the gates to Hades might have done a fair to middling job keeping the unworthy in the underworld, but when it came to protecting her doctors' time from the malingerers of the town, Kinky made the fabled dog look like an edentulous pussycat. Not only did she get rid of them, she did so with diplomatic skills that would have been the envy of the American ambassador to the Court of St. James.

I began to appreciate her talents one January evening. It had been a tough week. We were in the middle of a 'flu epidemic and O'Reilly, who'd been without much sleep for about four days, had prevailed upon me to come and help him out. By the week's end both of us were knackered. We were sitting in the surgery, me on the examination couch, O'Reilly slumped in the swivel chair. The last patient had left and as far as I knew no emergency calls had come in. O'Reilly's usually ruddy complexion was pallid and his eyes red-rimmed, the whole face looking like two tomatoes in a snowbank. I didn't like to think about my own appearance. He massaged his right shoulder with his left hand. "God," he said, "I hope that's the last of it for tonight." As he spoke the front doorbell rang. "Bugger!" said O'Reilly.

I started to rise but he shook his head. "Leave it. Kinky will see who it is."

The door to the surgery was ajar. I could hear the conversation quite clearly, Kinky's soft Kerry brogue contrasting sharply with harsher female tones. I thought I recognized the second speaker, and when I heard Kinky refer to her as "Maggie," I realized that the caller was the woman who'd come to see O'Reilly complaining of headaches that were located about two inches above the crown of her head. She was in and out of the surgery on a weekly basis. The prospect of having to see her was not pleasant. I needn't have worried.

"The back, is it, Maggie?" Kinky's inquiry was dulcet.

"Something chronic," came the reply.

"Oh dear. And how long has it been bothering you?"

"For weeks."

"Weeks, is it?" The concern never wavered. "Well, we'll have to get you seen as soon as we can."

I shuddered, for it was my turn to see the next patient, but O'Reilly simply smiled, shook his head, and held one index finger in front of his lips.

"Pity you'll have to wait. The young doctor's out on an emergency. He shouldn't be more than two or three hours. You will wait, won't you?"

I heard the sibilant indrawing of breath and could picture Maggie's frustration. I heard her harrumph. "It's the proper doctor that I want to see, not that young lad."

So much for the undying respect of the citizens for their medical advisors. I glanced at O'Reilly and was rewarded with a smug grin.

"Ah," said Kinky. "Ah, well now, that's the difficulty of it. Doctor O'Reilly's giving a pint of his own blood this very minute, the darling man."

"Mrs. Kincaid" — Maggie didn't sound as if she was going to be taken in — "that has to be the fifth pint of blood you've told me about him giving this month."

I waited to see how Kinky would wriggle out of that one. I needn't have worried, as I heard her say with completely convincing sincerity, "And is that not what you'd expect from Doctor O'Reilly, him the biggest-hearted man in the town. Goodnight, Maggie." I heard the door close. As I told you, O'Reilly wasn't the only character in the practice.

TROUBLES AT THE TABLE

O'REILLY EXPOUNDS ON THE GREAT WALL OF ULSTER

Doctor Fingal Flahertie O'Reilly was rarely lost for an opinion, and not only on matters medical. Now it's just possible that you've noticed during the last twenty-five years that there has been a touch of internecine unpleasantness going on in the North of Ireland. Although at this time of writing peace seems to have broken out over there, when I was working for O'Reilly there were nights when I began to wonder when they were going to issue the civil war with a number, like WW1 or WW2. Many great minds had done their collective best to try to come up with a solution. Alas, in vain.

After another huge bomb had remodelled another chunk of Belfast, I foolishly asked O'Reilly, over supper one evening, what he thought could be done about the Troubles.

He paused from disarticulating the roast

43

fowl, stared at me over his half-moon spectacles, and waved vaguely in my general direction with a slice of breast that was impaled on the carving fork. "Which troubles?"

I toyed with my napkin, feeling a great urge to have bitten my tongue out — before I'd asked the question. It had been a busy day and Mrs. Kincaid's roast chicken would have gone a long way to easing the hunger pangs. By the way O'Reilly had asked his question in reply, I could tell that he was ready to expound at some length, and I had a horrible suspicion that he might forget that he was meant to be carving.

"Come on, man." He laid the fork and its toothsome burden back on the plate. "Which troubles?"

I sighed. Dinner, it seemed, was going to be late. "The Troubles. The civil war."

He picked up the fork and expertly dislodged the slice of meat with the carving knife — dislodged it onto his own, already heaped plate. "Oh. *Those* troubles."

No, Fingal. The outbreak of foot and mouth disease on Paddy Murnaghan's farm, the civil war in Biafra, or the fact that you seem to have forgotten that locums, like gun dogs, need to be fed at least once a day. I kept my thoughts to myself. Captain Bligh

44

and his few loyal crew members had rowed a longboat about two thousand miles to East Timor existing on one ship's biscuit. Perhaps if I let O'Reilly expound for a while he might eventually see fit to toss me the odd crumb of nourishment.

A spoon disappeared into the nether end of the bird and reappeared full of steaming sage-and-onion stuffing.

"Those troubles." O'Reilly hesitated, trying to find room on his plate between the slices of breast and the roast potatoes before deciding to dump the stuffing at random on top of the pile. He replaced the spoon in the bird with the finesse of a proctologist. "Those troubles. I reckon there's a pretty simple solution. Pass the gravy."

I did so. "Fingal . . ." I tried, hoping at least to encourage him to start serving me as he held forth. Try interrupting the incoming tide in the Bay of Fundy.

"Simple. Now. You tell me: What are the three most pressing problems in Northern Ireland?" He ingested a forkful and masticated happily while waiting for my reply.

How about pellagra, scurvy, and beri-beri in underpaid, underfed junior doctors?

"Come om, come om . . ." His words were a little garbled. He swallowed. "Right, I'll tell you. Unemployment, falling tourism,

45

and the brave lads who like to make things go bang."

I was drowning in my own saliva, watching him tuck in. He pointed at me with his fork. "The solution is a Great Wall of Ulster."

"A what?"

"Great Wall of Ulster." He pulled the half-carved chicken toward himself, stood, expertly dissected the remaining drumstick, and laid three roast potatoes between the severed limb and the rest of the carcass. "Now look. The thigh there's Ulster and the tatties are my wall."

Brilliantly pictorial, I had to admit, but I really would have forgone this lesson in political science if a bit of his improvised Ulster or the rest of Ireland, if that was what the breast was meant to represent, could somehow have been transported to my still-empty plate.

"Now. Tourism. The tourists would come for miles to see the Great Wall." He used the carving knife to line the tubers up more straightly. "The unemployed would have had to build it in the first place, of course."

My unemployed stomach let go with a gurgle like the boiling mud pits of New Zealand.

"You're excused," said O'Reilly. "Finally"

46

— he squashed one of the potatoes with the spoon he'd used to help himself to stuffing — "the brave banging lads could blow it up to their hearts' content and" — he paused and replaced the mashed spud with a fresh one — "the unemployed could be kept occupied rebuilding." He sat beaming at me. "Told you it was simple."

I hastened to agree, hoping that now he'd finished I might finally get something to eat.

The door opened and Mrs. Kincaid stuck her head into the dining room. "Can you come at once, Doctor Taylor? There's been an accident."

ANATOMY LESSON

THE THINGS YOU LEARN ON
A DUBLIN PUB CRAWL

Doctor O'Reilly was a keen sportsman. I think I've remarked previously that he was an ex–boxing champion. He'd also played a fair bit of rugby football in his youth. I found out about his interest in rugby one weekend in January. Ireland was to play Scotland at Lansdowne Road in Dublin. To my great pleasure, O'Reilly invited me to accompany him to the match. He would provide the transportation and tickets, and would pay for my hotel room on the night before the match.

The drive to Dublin was uneventful and we checked into the Gresham Hotel. I'd barely begun to unpack my bag when there was a knocking at my door. I opened it. There stood O'Reilly, grinning from ear to ear. "Do you fancy a jar?"

It is, I'm told, possible, just possible, for

an entertainer to decline the Royal Command to appear at the London Palladium. It was not possible, not remotely possible, for anyone to turn down O'Reilly's invitation for a drink.

"Right," I said, with all the enthusiasm that must be evinced by the prisoner on death row when the chaplain sticks his head round the cell door. I'll say one thing for convicted American murderers: the electric chair is reputed to be very fast. Their suffering is over quickly. I'd been with Doctor Fingal Flahertie O'Reilly in full cry on his home turf and had lived, barely, to regret it. What he might be like when he was truly off the leash didn't bear thinking about. Oh well. My life insurance was paid up. "I'd love one. Where to?"

He winked, a great conspiratorial wink. "Usually the rugby crowd goes to Davy Byrnes, but I thought we might take a wee wander to The Stag's Head at the back of Grafton Street."

"Do you know how to get there?" I asked, knowing that when O'Reilly was ready for his tot, depriving him of it for long could produce the same effects as poking an alligator in the eye with a blunt stick.

"Of course. Didn't I go to medical school here, at Trinity College?"

That was something I hadn't known. Those of us who were graduates of Queen's University Belfast referred disdainfully to Trinity as "that veterinary college in Dublin." It was unfair to a fine school, but there was a rivalry between Queen's and the other place. The picture of the enraged alligator popped into my mind and I decided not to mention my lack of respect for his old alma mater. "Silly of me," I said. "Lead on, Fingal."

And away we went, just like the caissons, over hill, over dale.

Now Dublin isn't that big a city, it just seemed big after about two hours of walking. O'Reilly was becoming just a tad irritable if the pallor of his nose tip was anything to go by.

"Jasus," he remarked, as we found ourselves at the end of yet another publess cul-de-sac, "I'd have sworn it was down here."

I coughed. "Should we maybe ask directions?"

I imagine Captain Oates would have received the same kind of look from Robert Scott that O'Reilly hurled at me if the gallant gentleman had asked the same question on the way back from the South Pole. Frosty — very frosty.

"Not at all," O'Reilly countered, making

an about-turn on the march and heading back toward the main thoroughfare. "I know this place like the back of my hand." I took little comfort from that statement. He had both hands in his trouser pockets.

Dusk was falling as we trudged along Grafton Street for the umpteenth time. O'Reilly was never one to admit defeat gracefully, but his internal drought, which by then was probably on a par with the drier reaches of the Sahara, finally got the better of him.

A grubby youth was washing a shop-front window or, to be more accurate, redistributing the streaks of city grime. O'Reilly tapped him on the shoulder. The youth turned. "My good man," O'Reilly asked in the tones that he reserved for lesser mortals, "do you know where The Stag's Head is?"

The Dubliner wasn't one bit overawed, neither by O'Reilly's size nor his overweening manner. He gave O'Reilly a pitying look and said with an absolutely straight face, "Do I know where The Stag's Head is? Of course I do — it's about six feet from its arse."

I thought O'Reilly was going to explode, but instead he collapsed in peals of helpless laughter.

We did eventually find the pub in question. The irony was that just kitty-corner from it was another pub, The Vincent Van Gogh, which, believe it or not, is known to the locals as The Stag's Arse. The Dublin lad hadn't even been trying to be funny.

Sunny Disposition

The O'Reilly Method of Social and Preventive Medicine

Doctor O'Reilly was fond of extolling the virtues of general practice. He reckoned that a good GP should be the master of what he called "all branches of the medical arts." Once I thought I'd caught him out, but as usual he managed to get the better of me. It all came about because Sunny disappeared. O'Reilly was very fond of Sunny and by chance couldn't stand Councillor Bishop.

If you're feeling confused, don't worry, any association with O'Reilly will do that to you. If you can bear with me, I'll try to explain.

Sunny lived in his car — not because he was penurious, far from it; he'd inherited a sizable sum when his father died — and not because he was stupid; he held a Ph.D. He lived in his car because there was no roof on his house.

There was no roof on his house because twenty years before, the roof had needed new slates. Sunny had engaged Mister Bishop, town councillor, building contractor, and property developer, to do the job. For reasons that are lost in the mists of Ulster history, just at the time that the old roof had been removed, Sunny and Bishop had fallen out. Sunny refused to pay and Bishop refused to finish the job. Sunny moved into his car and decided to retire from the rat race.

O'Reilly had introduced me to Sunny shortly after I'd started to work there. One of us would drop by to check on him about every couple of weeks or so. I don't think I've ever known a more contented sixty-year-old man.

His car was parked at the front of what had been the garden. One patch of ground remained uncluttered and there Sunny grew his vegetables, which he sold to the locals. The rest of the place looked like a junkyard that had come into close proximity with a tornado on stimulants. Other old cars, perambulators, washing machines, scrap metal, phonograms, two tractors, and an old caravan were piled hither and yon, vaguely covered by tattered tarpaulins, weeds growing merrily in the interstices.

His treasured possessions did little for local property values but his neighbours tolerated his eccentricity, bought his vegetables, and passed the time of day with him. O'Reilly had mentioned that the caravan had been a gift from Sunny's neighbours, but he'd only lived in it for a week before returning to his car and turning the caravan over to his four dogs, who were his best friends and constant companions.

I was surprised one afternoon when I made a routine call to find that neither Sunny nor his dogs were anywhere to be seen. The woman who lived next door told me that Mister Bishop had taken Sunny away two days earlier and that someone from the animal protection society had come for the dogs yesterday. I thought it seemed strange and raised the matter with O'Reilly during the course of our evening meal.

The progress of a large slice of steak to O'Reilly's mouth halted precipitously. He lunged at me with the meat-covered fork. "What?"

I wondered if the old adage "don't shoot the messenger" could be adapted to "don't skewer him on a dinner fork," and repeated the intelligence.

"Bloody Bishop!" O'Reilly slammed the

meat into his mouth and worried at it like a jackal with a particularly tasty piece of dead zebra. He swallowed, larynx going up and down like an out-of-control U-boat. "Bloody Bishop!" he said again as O'Reilly hunched forward, elbows on the table, shoulders high. "I bet he's found a way to have Sunny put in the home." My mentor sat back, pinioned the remains of his steak, and slashed at it with the fervour of a member of the Light Brigade venting his spleen on a Russian gunner. "He's trying to get his hands on Sunny's land." He scowled at his plate and pushed it away. "Right. You nip round to the home and see if Sunny's there." O'Reilly stood. "I think I'll go and have a chat with Mister Bishop."

By the look in O'Reilly's eyes and the pallor of the tip of his nose, I knew Mister Bishop was shortly going to wish he was spending a relaxing time with a Gestapo interrogator who was suffering from strangulated haemorrhoids.

Sure enough, Sunny was in the home. He was a lost, terrified old man. He told me that the nurses scared him, the other inmates were rude, and he couldn't stop worrying about his dogs. He begged me to take him home and cried when I had to explain to him that I'd discovered he was under a restraining order, for his own good, and that until it was lifted, I was powerless to intervene. I stood beside his bed, looking at a man who'd been reduced in two days from an independent, albeit slightly unusual, individual, to a pathetic institutionalized wretch. I could see that he'd lost weight and indeed looked very ill.

I still had his "Och, please get me out, Doctor" in my ears as I climbed the stairs to O'Reilly's sitting room. Doctor Fingal Flahertie O'Reilly was parked in one of the armchairs, pipe belching like a Pittsburgh steelworks chimney. He didn't bother to turn to see who'd come in. "Well?"

I shrugged. "Sunny's in the home. You were right."

His big head nodded ponderously, acknowledging his rightness, but he said nothing.

I carried on. "If we can't get him out of there, I think he's going to die."

O'Reilly half turned and waved toward the other chair. "Sit yourself down, my boy. God is in his heaven and all is right with the world."

I started to argue but he interrupted. "Sunny should be on his way home now."

"But . . ."

"No buts. I explained things to Mister

Bishop."

The only word I can find to describe the smile on O'Reilly's battered face is demoniacal. "You remember the lass we had to ship off to England a couple of months ago — piffy?"

"Piffy? Right. PFI, pregnant from Ireland." I knew that the Ulster community had about as much tolerance for young women with child, but out of holy wedlock, as a mongoose for a cobra. These unfortunates had to be shipped out. "What about her?"

He blew a smoke ring at the ceiling and stabbed his pipe stem through the hole. "Mister Bishop's maid. I just explained to him that if the order wasn't lifted, I might just have to have a word with Mrs. Bishop — tell her the real reason that the lassie had to visit her sick sister in Liverpool. That cooled him." O'Reilly stood and started heading for the sideboard, remarking over his shoulder, "The last I saw of Bishop, he was on his way to the Town Hall, aye, and to the animal shelter." He poured himself a stiff whiskey. "They don't teach you young fellows medicine like that."

Relieved as I was that Sunny's troubles would soon be over, I thought I might just have a bit of a dig at the self-satisfied Doctor O'Reilly, he who reckoned that good

58

GPs should be masters of all the branches of the healing arts.

"And what branch of the healing arts would you say you were practising?" I asked, guilelessly.

O'Reilly stopped in mid-pour, put one finger alongside his bent nose, and said, as if to a not-too-bright child, "Social and preventive medicine, son. Social and preventive."

WELL SAID, SIR

THE SILENCING OF DOCTOR O'REILLY

"How are the mighty fallen?" David, a biblical king, said something along these lines. I'm sure his sage utterances would have been worth the listen if he'd been in the Mucky Duck the night O'Reilly met his match.

When I introduced you to Doctor Oscar Fingal O'Flahertie Wills O'Reilly, I mentioned some of his attributes. As I recollect, I described him as an ex-navy boxing champion, classical scholar, unregenerate poacher, bagpiper, cryptophilanthropist, foul-mouthed widower, and country GP. I may have neglected to note that in addition, he regarded himself as a bit of a wit, and disliked intensely being bested in any verbal joust. The fact that all of his local potential opponents knew very well that Doctor O. could be a great man for prescribing, and on occasion administering, the soap-suds enema as a panacea for just about any minor complaint, if the complaint was brought by someone in whom the font of medical knowledge wasn't well pleased, may in part have taken the edge off the local competition.

On the particular evening I'm about to describe, Doctor O'Reilly was in full cry. No wonder he was in good voice. He'd just won the local pibroch competition.

The pibroch is said, by those who understand these matters, to be a thing of complex beauty. It's the classical music of the great highland bagpipe. Only the most experienced and skillful piper will even attempt the pibroch in public. (Which, as far as I'm concerned, is a great relief. To me, the thing is interminable, tuneless, repetitive, embellished with incomprehensible grace notes, and an assault to the civilized ear.) The tune, if it can be so called, is played on the chanter and immediately brings to mind the noise that would accompany the simultaneous gutting and emasculating of a particularly bad-tempered tomcat. Over the melody, on and on, thunder the drones, those pipes that stick up from the back of the bag like the remaining three tentacles of some long-fossilized prehistoric squid.

Needless to say, playing pibrochs takes a great deal of breath. I forget exactly how much water is lost per expiration, but judging by the post-pibroch intake of *uisque beatha* by the average exponent of the arcane art, the amount of dehydration suffered must be extensive.

To return to the public bar of the Black Swan. O'Reilly sat at a table in the middle of a circle of admiring fellow pipers, replacing his lack of bodily fluids like one of those desert flowers that only sees rain once every ten years. I was in my customary corner sipping a small sherry and trying to mind my own business. I'm told that some people in Florida try to ignore hurricanes.

O'Reilly was at his pontifical best. His basso voice thundered on. He'd launched into a monologue several minutes previously on the relative merits of plastic versus bamboo reeds for the chanter. The assembled multitude listened in respectful silence, although judging by the glazed expressions on some of the faces their interest had waned. O'Reilly warmed to his subject, brooking no interruption, rolling like a juggernaut over anyone who might try to get a word in edgewise. He was talking on the intake of breath. I watched as a member of the group signalled for a fresh round of drinks. The barman delivered the glasses shortly afterward. O'Reilly was now up to verbal escape velocity, emphasizing his words with staccato jabs of his right index finger on the beer-ring-stained table-top.

He stopped dead — in mid-sentence. A ghastly pallor appeared at the tip of his bent nose. Something had annoyed the great man. I craned forward to see. Catastrophe. Somehow the barman had neglected to deliver a drink for Doctor O.

The silence, now that he'd shut up, was palpable. He fixed the cowering bartender with an agate stare and demanded, pointing at the appropriate orifice, "And haven't I got a mouth too?"

That was when it happened. A voice, from which of the assembled pipers I never discovered, was heard to say clearly, distinctly, and with heart-felt sincerity, "And how could we miss it? All night it's been going up and down between your ears like a bloody skipping rope."

I do believe David Rex went on to say, after his remarks about the precipitous plummeting of the powerful, "Tell it not in Gath, publish it not in the streets of Askelon; lest the daughters of the Philistines rejoice, lest the daughters of the uncircumcised triumph."

Philistines are rare in the North of Ireland. There were no women in the public bar, and it would be a breach of professional confidentiality to tell you who among the party were preputially challenged.

But the rejoicing — if not in the streets, at least in the Mucky Duck — was vast. And for once, O'Reilly was at a complete loss for words.

JULY/AUGUST 1996
A Pregnant Silence

Another Lesson by Doctor O'Reilly, Practical Psychologist

Some therapeutic interventions simply do not appear in the textbooks.

Regular readers will remember Maggie, she of the incessant complaints, the headache two inches above her head, the chronic backache. In her early fifties, she was what the ministers of the time when reading the banns would have referred to as a "spinster of this parish," except that for Maggie the banns had never been called. She remained what the locals charitably described as "one of nature's unclaimed treasures."

Her trials and tribulations, and the way O'Reilly handled them, let him teach me a lesson in practical psychology, a lesson that I'll be happy to pass on to anyone who has the fortitude to stick with this story to the bitter end.

65

(As an aside, "the bitter end" is the part of a ship's anchor cable that's attached to the vessel. This column isn't called "Taylor's Twist," another nautical term, for nothing.)

"Pat, that one's driving me bloody well daft," said Doctor O'Reilly. We were walking along the main street. O'Reilly stopped and pointed with his blackthorn walking stick through the window of the local grocery store. Naturally, when he stopped, so did I.

"The grocer?" I asked, knowing full well that the source of O'Reilly's impending descent into raving lunacy was entirely the fault of the other figure visible through the pane.

"No. Maggie. Maggie MacCorkle."

"Oh?" I wondered what was coming — Maggie had been visiting Doctor O'Reilly on a weekly basis for the last three months, and absolutely refused to see me.

"She's convinced she's pregnant." As he spoke, O'Reilly tapped his temple with one thick index finger. "Nutty. Nutty as a fruitcake." He sighed.

I confess her presenting symptoms caught me off guard. Wishing to demonstrate my encyclopaedic grasp of the physiology of the reproductive process, I immediately wondered aloud, "Would she not have needed a bit of masculine help?"

O'Reilly shook his head ponderously. "She says that it's another immaculate conception, and the responsibility is more than she can bear."

I was beginning to see what he meant about Maggie's resemblance to a filbert-filled Christmas confection. The troubled look on his face rapidly disabused me of any notion of making remarks about' wise men and stars in the East.

"She's a sorry old duck." O'Reilly leant on his stick with one hand, jamming the knuckles of the other under his nose. "I'm damned if I can figure out how to persuade her she's just going through the change of life."

"Have you thought about getting her to see a psychiatrist?" I inquired helpfully. O'Reilly shook his head. "Sure you know by now what these country folk are like about things like that."

I did indeed. The last patient to whom I'd made such a suggestion had bristled like an aggrieved porcupine and stormed out of the surgery. I could imagine Maggie's reaction.

"Anyway," said O'Reilly, "she's no danger to anyone or herself." He produced a large handkerchief from his jacket pocket, buried his battered nose, and made a noise like the

RMS *Queen Elizabeth* undocking.

"If she tells one of our headshrinking colleagues that she's the mother-to-be of the Second Coming, she'd be in the booby hatch as quick as a ferret down a rat hole." He stuffed his 'kerchief back into his pocket. "She'd really lose her marbles in there. No. It's just a matter of getting her to see that she's not up the builder's."

Unable to make any useful suggestions, I began to ruminate about the quaint euphemisms of the day for pregnancy: up the spout, in the family way, up the builder's, bun in the oven, poulticed.

It was clear from the way Fingal kept furrowing his brow that he was also at a loss for a solution and, knowing him as I'd come to, I could tell that he was worried. Fate intervened.

As we stood there silently, Maggie bustled out of the grocer's shop. She was carrying a brown paper bag, presumably her purchases. Her face split into a wide grin when she noticed Doctor O'Reilly and she began to hurry toward him. I could see that she'd failed to notice a young lad wheeling a bicycle.

The resultant collision wasn't quite of the magnitude of the meteor that smacked into planet Earth and, it's rumoured, put paid to the dinosaurs, but the fallout was dramatic.

The lad picked himself and his cycle up and rode off muttering some less-than-complimentary epithets about old bats who should watch where they were going. Maggie sat on the pavement, hair askew, legs wide under her voluminous skirt, surrounded by the wreckage of the contents of her parcel. A shattered ketchup bottle lay at the edge of a spreading scarlet puddle of its contents. Right in the middle of the crimson tide, the yolks and whites of two broken eggs peered malevolently upward.

I saw a look flit across O'Reilly's face, a look the like of which must have been there when Archimedes spilled his bathwater. Fingal didn't exactly yell "Eureka," but he'd clearly thought of something. He stepped over to where Maggie sat, knelt, put one solicitous hand on her shoulder, whipped out his hanky, dried her eyes, peered closely at the crimson clots and their ocular ova, and pronounced in sad, sombre, sonorous sentences, "There, there, Maggie. There, there. No need to grieve." He looked up at me and winked. "It couldn't have lived — its eyes were too close together."

The relief on Maggie's face could only have been matched by the joy of the old boy scout Baden-Powell when the British Army arrived at the outerworks of Mafeking.

Some therapeutic interventions simply do not appear in the textbooks.

WORKING AS EQUALS

O'REILLY FAILS TO MELLOW WITH TIME

From time to time after I'd emigrated to Canada, I would return to my roots in Ulster. When I did so, I'd always make a point of visiting my old friend Doctor Fingal Flahertie O'Reilly to see if he'd mellowed with time. The last time I dropped in to see him, in the early '80s, he was still in harness.

When I called at the house, Mrs. Kincaid answered the door. She told me that for the last week Doctor O'Reilly had been dealing with a particularly rough 'flu epidemic. He'd been summoned the night before to see a little girl who was desperately ill with pneumonia. He'd simply loaded the parents and the child into his own car, driven the forty-odd miles to the Royal Victoria Hospital, and then, because the parents had no phone, brought them back to his own home so they could receive regular progress reports. He was like that. He was very tired, she said, but she was sure he'd be glad to see me.

She knocked on the door. "Come in." I'd have recognized those gravelly tones anywhere. She opened the door. O'Reilly sat at his old rolltop desk. The heavy boxer's shoulders were more bent, his complexion more florid. He was writing a prescription for a young woman. "Just a minute." He didn't look up. "Remember, Annie. One at breakfast time and one at noon."

"Thank you, Doctor O'Reilly." The young woman left.

"Good God." He saw me standing there. "You still alive?"

I could tell by the grin he was pleased to see me. He didn't get up. He arched his back. "I'm buggered. Tell you what: you have a pew" — he motioned toward the examining table — "and I'll finish the surgery."

"Right, Fingal." I went to the couch, remembering vividly that this was exactly how we'd started.

"We'll have lunch at the Black Swan when I've finished stamping out disease," he said, as Mrs. Kincaid ushered in the next supplicant.

I sat there quietly as he saw patient after patient, 'flu case after 'flu case. In the middle of the chaos, a well-dressed man in his early forties entered the room and took a seat.

"Good morning," said O'Reilly. "What seems to be the trouble?"

"Oh, I'm fine," said the man, looking disdainfully at the shabby furnishings. "Perfectly fit."

O'Reilly's bushy brows moved closer to each other, like two hairy caterpillars heading for a choice leaf. "I'm just a bit busy . . ."

"My business will only take a moment. I'm new in this town."

The caterpillars reared their forequarters questioningly. O'Reilly said nothing.

"Yes." The man crossed one immaculately creased trouser leg over the other. "I'm interviewing healthcare providers."

O'Reilly leant forward in his own chair, head cocked to one side. "You're looking for a what?" His question sounded so ingenuous he could have been addressing an American tourist who'd inquired where he might find a leprechaun.

The man shook his head and smiled a pitying smile, the kind he obviously kept for yokels like O'Reilly. "A healthcare provider. One who will be sensitive to my needs as a consumer." He looked down his nose at O'Reilly's rumpled tweed sports jacket. "One with whom I can work as an equal, defining and discussing my options, so that I can identify the optimal approach to a given problem."

O'Reilly sat back. The black brows settled. I saw the tip of his nose begin to whiten, an ominous sign, but his rugged face wrinkled in a vast grin. "I doubt if I'm the man for the job." He shook his head sadly.

The man sat stiffly. "And why's that?"

O'Reilly ran his beefy hands along the lapels of his jacket, like a learned judge about to deliver his opinion, fixed the stranger with a stare that would have been the envy of any passing basilisk, and said, in dulcet tones, "For one thing, I'm only a country doctor, not one of those healthcare what-do-you-ma-callums you were telling me about." An edge had crept into his voice. Any one of O'Reilly's regular patients would have found urgent business elsewhere. "And I don't think we could work as equals."

The stranger shifted in his chair. "And why not?"

"Because," said O'Reilly, rising to his feet, "you'd be a very old man. You'd need six years of medical school, two years' postgraduate work, and forty-two years in practice."

The man rose, sniffed haughtily and said, "I don't like your attitude."

O'Reilly's smile was beatific. "I was wrong. We are equals. I don't like yours either." He held the door open and waited for the man to leave.

Doctor Fingal Flahertie O'Reilly, I'm glad to say, definitely had not mellowed with time.

MURPHY'S LAW

DOCTOR O'REILLY
HAS THE LAST LAUGH

I have characterized Doctor Fingal Flahertie O'Reilly as an ex-navy boxing champion, classical scholar, unregenerate poacher, hard drinker, cryptophilanthropist, foulmouthed bachelor, and country GP. This, I believe, is called a thumbnail sketch. There was nothing thumbnail-sized about O'Reilly, however; not his physical dimensions, not his personality, and certainly not his ability to hold a grudge. He could, on occasion, be the perfectly balanced Irishman — a man with a chip on both shoulders.

Someone described revenge as a "dish best eaten cold." For the life of me I cannot remember if it was that well-known Scots-Italian, Mac E. Avelli, or some other dead white male. No matter. O'Reilly had certainly heard of the concept but as usual had improved on it to suit his own requirements. In O'Reilly's world, revenge wasn't best eaten cold. It should be consumed deep-frozen, preferably at about absolute zero. Job, it's rumoured, was possessed of a modicum of patience, but when it came to waiting for just the right moment to deflate a swollen ego or right a perceived wrong, O'Reilly made Job look like a hyperactive child who'd been fed a sugar-enhanced diet and stimulated with an electric cattle prod.

I first became aware of this attribute when O'Reilly arrived home after making a house call. The barometer of his temper, his bent nose, was pallid from tip to bridge, and his eyes flashed sparks. He helped himself to a rigid whiskey (stiff would have been an understatement) hurled himself into an armchair, and snarled, "I'll kill the bloody man!"

I tried to hide behind a copy of the *British Medical Journal.* King Kong tried the same thing on top of the Empire State Building. At least O'Reilly didn't shoot at me.

"That *#@##** Doctor Murphy! He's a menace." O'Reilly inhaled his drink. "Put down that comic and listen."

Hardly respectful of the organ of organized medicine in the U.K., but I felt, given O'Reilly's *#@##*** mood — and please remember that I did describe him as "foul-mouthed" — it might be better to say nothing. Besides, I dearly wanted to know what Murphy had done to raise my colleague's ire, temperature, and, judging by the colour of O'Reilly's naturally florid cheeks, blood pressure.

"Bah," said O'Reilly.

"Humbug?" I inquired.

"Exactly," he agreed, devouring yet more of the potent potable product of Paddy pot-still Distillery.

A modicum of colour was returning to O'Reilly's schnozzle, so either the ethyl alcohol was having its recognized vasodilatory effect — probable — or O'Reilly was beginning to calm down — unlikely.

"That Murphy. I'll get the &#@**. Do you know what he's just done?" Definitely vasodilatation. "Do you remember Maggie MacCorkle?"

This was an easier question than its predecessor relating to Doctor Murphy's doings. The answer to the first question required second sight; for the latter, simple recall was all that was needed.

"Oh, yes, Fingal. The woman with the headaches two inches above her head. The one who thought she was pregnant with the second coming?"

"Exactly," he said. "The silly old biddy decided to consult that well-known veterinarian, Doctor Murphy."

Oops. I had a fair idea of what was coming next. Doctor Murphy and Doctor O'Reilly existed at opposite ends of the spectrum, not only of visible light but of electromagnetic waves not yet discovered by physical science. As O'Reilly was rough and ready, Murphy was devious. O'Reilly's clothes tended to fit him where they touched and Murphy always dressed immaculately. O'Reilly would walk on hot coals for his patients; Murphy might venture onto ashes, but only in very stout, highly polished boots. And O'Reilly had a soft spot for Maggie MacCorkle.

"Poor old duck," he said, "Murphy told her she needed to see a psychiatrist." He snorted like a warthog with severe sinusitis. "It took me two hours to calm her down." I knew he didn't begrudge the two hours but did resent the trauma caused to a simple, if somewhat eccentric, woman.

"Oh dear," I said, and waited.

"Do you know what else he said to her?"

The second sight thing again. I shook my head. "He said, 'Doctor O'Reilly should know better than to play God.'"

I maintained a diplomatic silence.

"Play God! Me? That bloody man doesn't play at being God. Murphy works at it. Pour me another."

I did as I was told, handed the glass to O'Reilly, and tried to change the subject. "What did you think of the Irish rugby team's showing last Saturday?"

His reply was unprintable. I began to suspect that it was entirely my fault that they'd been beaten by Scotland by a substantial margin, but at least I was able to get him off the subject of Doctor Murphy.

I forgot about the whole thing until about three months later. There was a meeting of the local medical society. Doctor Murphy was there, immaculate in a three-piece suit. As usual, he took a pontifical stance on most issues and on one occasion, in public, in front of our peers, admonished Doctor Fingal Flahertie O'Reilly about the dangers of doctors in general and O'Reilly in particular of playing God.

I'm told that the Manhattan Project scientists hid before they made a little bang at the Alamogordo test site. I looked round for the nearest bunker, but to my surprise O'Reilly said nothing. Absolutely nothing. A nuclear blast would have been preferable. Just imagine the feelings of Doctor Oppenheimer if the switch had been thrown, nothing had happened, and it had been remarked that somebody really ought to nip outside and see what was the matter. Now what?

I found out just as we were about to leave.

Doctor Murphy had slipped into his overcoat but seemed to be having some difficulty adjusting his shiny bowler hat.

"Bit of trouble with the hat, Murphy?" O'Reilly inquired solicitously. "Not surprising, really."

The rest of the company waited expectantly, all knowing full well the lack of brotherly love between the two men.

"And why not?" asked Murphy.

"Ah," said O'Reilly. "It's the playing God thing. A fellah's head must hurt when he's spent most of his life wearing a crown of thorns."

The biblical allusion wasn't lost on those assembled. Poor old Doctor Murphy from that day was known locally as "Thorny Murphy," to his great discomfort and O'Reilly's great joy.

And Doctor Murphy never again accused Doctor O'Reilly of playing God.

THE LAW OF HOLES

O'REILLY'S NEAR-DEATH EXPERIENCE

I was surprised one day when, after evening "surgery," I retired to the upstairs sitting room to find my senior colleague, Doctor Fingal Flahertie O'Reilly, sitting in his usual armchair sipping what appeared to be a gin and tonic rather than his usually preferred whiskey. He ignored my entrance and my polite inquiry about whether he'd like me to refurbish his drink.

Do remember that such suggestions were usually greeted with the enthusiasm toward an impending monsoon of those peculiar toads that live in states of total dehydration in certain deserts, only coming to full animation when the rains appear.

"Sure?" I said, helping myself to a very small sherry.

"No," he replied lugubriously, pulling out his old briar and stoking the infernal device until the smoke clouds gave a fair impression of the aftereffects of the combined weight of the attentions of the RAF and the USAAF on the hapless town of Dresden.

"No/yes or no/no?" I said brightly.

"What are you on about, Taylor?"

As far as I could tell through the industrial haze, his nose wasn't pallid, yet his use of my surname was an indicator of his general state of displeasure. Foolishly, I ploughed on.

"Er, no you're not sure you don't want another, which is a way of saying yes you do, because if you had been sure that you wanted no more to drink your answer should have been yes and . . ."

"Sit down," he said, "and shut up."

Which actually seemed like a very sensible thing to do. I sat and said, self-effacingly, "Right. First law of holes: when you find yourself in a hole, stop digging."

The thought struck me as, if not original, at least comical.

"How," he said, peering over his half-moon spectacles, "did you know?"

"How did I know about what?"

"The hole, you idiot."

"I read it somewhere," I confessed.

He grunted. "Couldn't have. It only happened last night."

I was becoming confused. Truth to tell, my being in a fuddled state around O'Reilly was closer to the norm than his drinking gin and tonic. I felt a sense of relief, the kind of feeling that comes with knowing that God is indeed in His Heaven and all is right with the world.

"And," he said, "no one knows about it except Seamus Galvin and me."

My confusion was now as dense as the tobacco fog that surrounded us.

O'Reilly sighed heavily. "Would you like to hear my side?"

It almost seemed a shame to be enlightened. "Please."

He gestured with the glass in his hand. "I'll have to give it up."

Enlightenment was going to be some time coming. I'd thought we were discussing holes. "Digging holes?"

"No." He shuddered like a wounded water buffalo. "The drink."

Oops. I thought for a moment that I was having an auditory hallucination. Fingal O'Reilly? Give up the drink?

"All because of the hole, you see."

"Of course," I said. They'd taught us in psychiatry to humour certain types of raving lunatics. I saw not at all but had no intention of enraging O'Reilly.

He pointed at his glass. "Just tonic water," he said in tones that would have done a professional mourner great credit. "Bloody Galvin," he added, and lapsed into silence.

Tonic water. Holes. Galvin. I had some difficulty seeing any logical connection. Then I remembered. Seamus Galvin and his wife Mary were the ones who were going to emigrate because O'Reilly had restored their family fortunes by clandestinely purchasing a garage full of rocking ducks.

The Galvins were leaving tomorrow, and last night there had been a send-off at the Mucky Duck. I'd missed it because of a long confinement in an outlying cottage, but O'Reilly had attended. Something Fingal had said earlier came back to me: "It only happened last night." Now, Galvin's party was last night and something concerning a hole had happened, something sufficiently catastrophic as to make O'Reilly decide to take the pledge. I was beginning to feel I merely needed a magnifying glass and a deerstalker to be able to change my name to Sherlock. I might even ask Fingal if I could borrow his pipe. Only one question. What was the "something"?

O'Reilly's rumbling interrupted my attempt to reason things out. "Should never have let Galvin leave by himself."

So it was at the party.

"I should never have taken a shortcut through the churchyard, but it was pouring, you see." He peered over his spectacles.

"Quite," I said solicitously.

O'Reilly took a deep swallow of his tonic water and regarded the glass with a look of total disgust before fixing me with a stony glare and saying, "No harm telling you, seeing you already know."

I merely nodded.

"I fell into a freshly dug grave."

The — or more accurately, my — mind boggled.

"I couldn't get out. It was raining, you see," he said by way of an explanation. His nose tip was now becoming pallid.

I seem to remember that when stout Horatio made it across the foaming Tiber, his enemies "could scarce forbear to cheer." Being attached to my teeth I felt that despite the mental image of O'Reilly scrabbling like a demented hamster against the slick sides of a muddy six-foot hole, I definitely should forbear to laugh. "Oh dear."

"Yes," he said aggrievedly. "Bloody Galvin. How was I to know he'd fallen into the same grave? It was black as half a yard up a chimney down there. And cold. What was I to do?"

"Stop digging? First law of holes," I said.

"Don't be so bloody silly. I huddled against a corner and like an eejit said aloud to myself, 'Fingal Flahertie O'Reilly, you're not going to get out of here tonight.' Galvin, who must have been lurking in another corner, tapped me on the shoulder and said, 'By God you won't.' But . . ." O'Reilly shrugged. "By God, I did."

"Must have given you an awful shock," I remarked, wandering over to the sideboard and pouring a stiff Paddy.

"It did. Oh, indeed it did. Got the strength of ten men."

I handed him the glass. "I believe shock can be treated with spirits."

"Are you sure?" he asked, swallowing a large measure, "and none of your no/yes, no/no rubbish."

Men of the Cloth (1)

How the Minister
Learned about Sex

In today's egalitarian society it may be hard to believe that once upon a time some members of a community were held in greater respect than the rest of the common herd. In rural Ulster the possession of a higher education was thought to confer exalted status. The pecking order among the upper echelons wasn't always clear, but it was fair to say that the local teachers, physicians, and men of the cloth were somewhere at the top of the heap.

In his own eyes at least, Doctor Fingal Flahertie O'Reilly stood at the apex. Mind you, the challengers for top spot were a motley crew.

Mister Featherstonehaugh, the teacher, besides having a name that could strangle a pig, was as tall and skinny as a yard of pump water and suffered from what was known

charitably as a "terrible strong weakness."
(Which is to say that any pupil foolish
enough to come within two feet of Mister
F. was at some danger of suffering skin
burns from the whiskey fumes of the permanently pissed pedagogue's pulmonary prod-
ucts.)

Father Fitzmurphy was a quiet man who'd
taken his vows of humility so seriously that
his presence was scarcely noticed. Compared to Father Fitz., Uriah Heep would
have looked like a blatant self-promoter.

On the other side of the sectarian divide,
the Presbyterian church was represented by
a senior and a junior minister. The senior
minister, Reverend Manton Basket, was
middle-aged and very tall across, an allusion to the fact that he was in no danger of
being suspected of suffering from any form
of anorexia. The junior, Mister Angus Mc-
Wheezle, was of Scottish descent. Actually
he hadn't so much descended as plummeted — the kind of man who would have
given Charles Darwin some very difficult
times wondering if he hadn't got things
quite right and perhaps the apes were in
fact offspring of the clan McWheezle.

O'Reilly, while nominally of the Protestant
persuasion, could not have been described
as devout. Well, he could, but it would have

been like attributing feelings of piety and love for all mankind to that well-known philanthropist, A. Hitler. Business, however, was business, and O'Reilly did attend morning services on Sundays, if only to try to persuade his potential customers that he was a worthy physician.

You may well wonder why I'm telling you all this. Bear with me. O'Reilly's relationships with both of the Presbyterian ministers are worth the relating.

"Good to see you, Doctors." Reverend Manton Basket beamed at O'Reilly and me over his chins as he stood outside the church door greeting the departing members of his flock. He had a paternal arm draped over the shoulder of his eldest son, a spherical boy of about twelve. The rest of the tribe, all five of them, were lined up in a row, tallest on the right, shortest on the left, like a set of those chubby Russian dolls.

O'Reilly nodded as he passed the Baskets. "Powerful sermon, your reverence," he said, but he kept hurrying on. I was well aware that he found old Basket dry and, as you know, Fingal Flahertie O'Reilly's preferences tended more to the wet — the wet that even now was waiting for him in the upstairs sitting room over the surgery.

"You should have heard his sermons when

he came here first," O'Reilly said to me. "I'll tell you all about them when we get home."

I had to lengthen my stride to keep up with O'Reilly, who moved from a walk to a canter to practically a full-blown gallop as he neared the source of his sustenance. He relaxed once he was ensconced in his favourite armchair, briar belching, fist clutching a glass of what he'd referred to as his communion wine.

"Where was I?"

I settled into the chair opposite and prepared for another of O'Reilly's reminiscences.

"When?" I asked.

"Not 'when,' where."

"What?"

"Not 'what,' not 'when' . . . where."

"No," I said, feeling the inexorable tug of yet another of those moments with O'Reilly when the circuitousness of the conversation began to feel like the Maelstrom. I knew how old Captain Nemo must have felt as the *Nautilus* sank lower and lower. "I meant what did you mean when you asked, 'Where?' "

"Silly question." He exhaled in his best Puff the Magic Dragon fashion. "I should have asked, 'Who?' "

"When?" It just slipped out.

"Don't you start."

"What?" Oops.

Fortunately he was in one of his expansive moods. He laughed and handed me his empty glass. "Who do you think Manton was?"

"Why?" The sight of the tip of O'Reilly's nose beginning to pale pulled me up short. I refilled his glass and waited.

"Manton was a minor prophet." He accepted the tumbler. "That's who his reverence is named after."

I admit I was pleased to be so informed. It was a name I'd never heard before.

"Came from a very strict family. That's why you should have heard his sermons when he first came here."

"Fire and brimstone?"

"And how." O'Reilly chuckled. "You could have felt the spits of him five pews back." O'Reilly sipped his drink. "He's a decent man, Manton Basket. Unworldly, of course."

I was about to ask what that meant when O'Reilly continued. "When he first came here he put an awful amount of effort into denouncing the sins of the flesh."

"Including gluttony?" I inquired, thinking of Dumbo, Jumbo, and the Reverend Manton Basket.

"No. Just the sexual kind." O'Reilly made a sucking noise through his pipe. The gurgling was like the sound of the runoff through a partially clogged bath drain. "Pity was, he hadn't a clue what he was talking about."

"Oh."

O'Reilly rose and stretched and ambled to the big bay window. "Aye. He'd been here about two years when he came to see me professionally. Seemed he and the wife couldn't get pregnant." O'Reilly turned away from the view of Belfast Lough. "Bit tricky asking a man of the cloth about his procreative efforts. Even worse, his sermon the week before had been about the sin of Onan."

"Onan?"

"Yeah. The bloke who spilled his seed on the ground and got clobbered by a thunder-bolt for his pains."

The "bit tricky" became clearer.

"Fingal, how did you persuade Reverend Basket to provide a sperm sample? Bottle in one hand, lightning conductor in the other?"

"Didn't have to." O'Reilly looked smug. "That's the advantage of a bit of local knowledge. I just asked him to describe exactly what he and his wife did."

"And?"

"Every night for two years they'd knelt together by the bed and prayed for offspring."

"That was all?"

"Aye. I had to put his stumbling feet on the paths of righteousness, so to speak."

"Good Lord. How did he take that?"

O'Reilly chuckled. "Frostily. Very frostily at first."

I had a quick mental picture of the six little Baskets.

"Ice must have thawed a bit when he got home."

"And he was a big enough man to thank me. He is a decent man." A cloud passed over O'Reilly's sunny countenance. "Not like that weasel McWheezle."

"The assistant minister?"

Before O'Reilly could reply, Mrs. Kincaid stuck her head round the door. "Dinner's ready, Doctors."

"Come on," said O'Reilly, "grub. I'll tell you about McWheezle over dinner."

To be continued.

MEN OF THE CLOTH (2)

O'REILLY EXACTS A HEAVY PRICE

"Aye," said Doctor Fingal Flahertie O'Reilly, helping himself to a liberal dollop of horseradish dressing, "old Basket's a decent enough chap for a Presbyterian minister." Fingal was continuing the conversation that had begun upstairs, a conversation that had been interrupted by Mrs. Kincaid's summons to Sunday dinner. I watched in awe as he spread the white concoction over a slice of roast beef prior to transferring the morsel to his mouth.

The horse in Mrs. Kincaid's horseradish was not a Shetland pony. It tended more to the Clydesdale: big, muscular, and very, very strong. Strong enough to have stripped paint. I'd been foolish enough to try it once before. I think it took about three weeks for the mucous membrane inside my mouth to regenerate. I watched O'Reilly's happy mastication, expecting steam to appear from his ears. For all the apparent effect, he might as well have been eating ice cream.

"Here," he said, spreading some of the incendiary condiment on my beef, "spice yours up a bit, young fellow."

I smiled weakly and settled for a piece of Yorkshire pudding.

"Aye," said O'Reilly, "Basket's not a bit like his assistant. That McWheezle. That man has a smile like last year's rhubarb. Mrs. Kincaid reckons that anyone who reared him would drown nothing."

I thought it fair to surmise that Doctor O. didn't exactly hold the Reverend Angus McWheezle in high regard.

"Pass the gravy."

I complied, nibbling on a roast potato and avoiding the fifty-megaton meat.

"Not one of your favourite people, Fingal?"

"Him? He's a sanctimonious, mean-spirited, mealy-mouthed, narrow-minded, hypocritical, Bible-thumping little toad. That man has as much Christian charity in him as Vlad the Impaler." O'Reilly harrumphed and attacked another slice of beef. "Bah."

"So you don't like him very much?" Sometimes my powers of observation astounded even me.

96

"How could anyone like a man like that? Do you know what he used to do?"

I hoped the question was rhetorical. I think I've remarked previously that O'Reilly seemed to think I was blessed with some kind of extrasensory perceptive powers. I simply munched on another piece of Yorkshire pudding and shook my head, both to signify that indeed I didn't know what the Reverend Angus McWheezle had done to draw O'Reilly's ire and to distract him while I tried to hide the horseradish-beef time bomb under a small pile of broccoli.

"Do you know" — I continued to shake my head — "that if there were an Olympic event for smugness and self-satisfaction, the man could represent Ireland?" O'Reilly helped himself to another roast potato. "But I fixed the bugger."

"Oh?"

"Aye. You remember I told you how Mister Basket used to preach against the sins of the flesh?"

I nodded.

"Well, McWheezle went one better. He used to hound unmarried women who'd fallen pregnant. Humiliate them from his pulpit. Name them. That little @#$&*! didn't think that their being pregnant out of wedlock was hurt enough."

O'Reilly's florid cheeks positively glowed — and it wasn't the horseradish. It was his genuine concern for the feelings of his patients, most of whom would have had to leave the village, such was their disgrace.

"I see what you mean."

"Right. I asked him to stop, but he refused." O'Reilly paused from his gustatory endeavours, laid his knife and fork aside for a moment, folded his arms on the tabletop, leant forward, and said, "But I stopped him anyway."

"How?"

O'Reilly chuckled, in much the same way that I imagine Beëlzebub must chortle when a fresh sinner arrives on the griddle. I couldn't prevent a small, involuntary shudder.

"Ah," he said, "pride cometh . . . McWheezle showed up in the surgery one day.

" 'It's a very private matter,' says he.

" 'Oh?' says I.

" 'Yes,' says he. 'I seem to have caught a cold on my gentiles.'

"Threw me for a moment, that. 'Your gentiles?' says I.

"He waved a limp hand toward his trouser front.

" 'Aha,' says I. 'A cold on your genitals.'

" 'Yes.'

" 'Let's have a look.' "

O'Reilly's chuckle moved from the Beël-zebubbian to the Satanic.

I knew what was coming next. I knew the story had done the rounds of every medical school in the world, and yet Fingal Flahertie O'Reilly was the most honest man I've ever met. If he said what I thought he was going to say had actually happened, I'd believe him.

"Mister McWheezle unzips. He has the biggest syphillitic chancre on his 'gentiles' that I've ever seen.

" 'It's a bad cold right enough,' says I, handing him a hanky. 'See if you can blow it.' "

O'Reilly picked up his knife and fork. "Good thing we had penicillin. Poor old McW. was so terrified that I wrung a promise out of him there and then to leave the wee pregnant girls alone." Fingal O'Reilly started to eat. "Tuck in," he ordered.

I was still chuckling at his tale when I suddenly realized that I'd just filled my mouth with enough of Mrs. Kincaid's horseradish sauce to start the second great fire of London.

O'Reilly must have noticed the tears pouring from my eyes. It's hard to miss something with the flow rate of the Horseshoe Falls.

"Ah, come on now, Pat," he said solicitously. "It's a funny story — but it's not that funny."

O'Reilly Finds His Way

"Doctor Gangrene" Is No Match for the Rural GP

"You'd think I'd know my way about up here," said Doctor Fingal Flahertie O'Reilly, looking puzzled as he stood in the middle of the long echoing corridor of the Royal Victoria Hospital in Belfast.

I'd bumped into him on my way to the X-ray department from the ward where I was working. If you remember, I was employed as a registrar at the Royal, my day job so to speak, my other source of revenue and a smattering of post-graduate training, when I wasn't functioning as O'Reilly's part-time locum.

I had a moment of smugness. I did know my way about. Not surprising really; I worked in the place. But O'Reilly hadn't specifically asked for directions. He'd simply made a slightly self-deprecatory statement:

"You'd think I'd know my way about up here."

The smug feeling passed. The burning question was, what was I going to do? Offering unsolicited advice to Doctor O. could provoke a minor seismic event. Neglecting to give the necessary directions, and perhaps allowing him to make an idiot of himself, could result in a major tectonic shift with all the resultant unpleasant fallout — usually on me.

It's a fundamental law of politics and diplomacy that when one is faced with two equally unpalatable options — prevaricate.

"How long has it been since you worked here?" I asked.

"Years."

"Perhaps they've moved the ward you're looking for?"

He scratched his head. "Do you think so? I just popped in to see one of my customers who was admitted here last night."

"It's possible."

"Rubbish. Nothing possible about it."

"But, Fingal, the administrators do it, you know."

"Admit my patients?"

"No. Move wards."

"Oh, that."

I felt relieved. He and I had nearly set off

102

on another of our tortuous verbal peregrina-
tions and to be honest I was a bit pushed
for time. I was supposed to be assisting the
senior gynaecologist Sir Gervaise Grant, a
man who was obsessional about time. Lord
help any assistant who was late in the
operating room.

Sir Gervaise was renowned for the speed
with which he could perform vaginal hyster-
ectomies. "Watch me like a hawk," he would
instruct his assistant, the knife flashing, scis-
sors snipping, ligatures going on like trusses
in a turkey-plucking factory.

O'Reilly was saying something but I'm
afraid I wasn't paying attention. Coming
down the hall, white coat flying, minions
scurrying in pursuit, was Sir Gervaise
himself. I had to get away from O'Reilly.

"Good God," he boomed, in a voice that
echoed from the tiled walls, "there's 'Green
Fingers' Grant."

The "Green Fingers" soubriquet referred
to the fact that Sir Gervaise's wound infection rate was triple that of anyone else. But
while he might be called "Green Fingers"
behind his back, it was a braver man than I
who would call him that to his granite-
jawed, bristling, silver-mustachioed face.
And judging by the scowl on Sir G.'s
countenance — the sort that Medusa re-

served for those passing Argonauts she *really* wanted to fix — he'd overheard O'Reilly's remark.

I closed my eyes and adopted the hunch-shouldered crouch favoured by bomb-disposal experts when something unexpectedly goes "tick."

"To whom are you alluding, O'Reilly?" Sir Gervaise's treacly voice held all the warmth of a Winnipeg winter.

"Yourself."

I opened one eye.

O'Reilly stood his ground, legs apart, chin tucked in. I could see his meaty fists starting to clench and remembered that the man had been a Royal Navy boxing champion. If a bell rang anywhere in those hallowed halls of healing, Doctor O. was going to come out swinging. One wallop would have re-arranged Sir Gervaise's immaculately coiffed hair, his nose, and his teeth as far back as his molars.

The two men stood scowling at each other like a pair of Rottweilers who've met suddenly and unexpectedly over a raw steak.

Discretion is the better part of valour. I knew that I should have found some excuse to slink away, but some idiotic impulse led me to step between the two and say, "Excuse me, Sir Gervaise, but I think we're going to be late."

The great man looked at me with all the condescension of Louis XIV for a grovelling peasant. "Indeed, Taylor. I don't believe I sought your opinion. Indeed when I do want it, I'll tell you what it is."

Oh, Lord. I wished I had the tortoise's ability to tuck its head into its carapace.

"Still. We can't be late. Can't be late. Don't have time to waste on underqualified country quacks." He strode off, courtiers following in his wake, with me bringing up the rear.

To my surprise, the eruption I'd been expecting from Doctor O'Reilly failed to materialize. All I heard him say to our departing backs was, "And good day to you too, Sir Gangrene."

As we sped down the corridor it began to dawn on me why O'Reilly didn't think highly of Sir Gervaise. I remembered the case quite vividly. The man with the Mach 1 scalpel had whipped her uterus out in something under fifteen minutes. Surgical time, that was. The victim took three months to recover from her postoperative abscess. And she'd been one of O'Reilly's patients.

Sir Gervaise seemed to have regained his icy equilibrium as we stood side by side scrubbing for the impending surgery. I wondered if he had any idea what he might have wrought. Recall how Fingal Flahertie O'Reilly lay in wait for Doctor "Thorny" Murphy. I could still hear the words "under-qualified country quack" and picture the malevolence under O'Reilly's grin as he bade Sir Gervaise "good day."

When I was a boy I used to delight in a firecracker called a Thunderbomb. The instructions on the side read, "Light blue touchpaper and retire immediately." Whether he knew it or not, Sir G. had lit O'Reilly's touchpaper. There was a phone message waiting for me when I left the theatre. Would Doctor Taylor please report to the Pathology Department and see Professor Callaghan?

I imagine an altar boy would feel much as I did had he been summoned unexpectedly by the Pope. Awe, fear, and trembling. Professor Callaghan was the dean of the faculty and, in the eyes of us junior doctors, outranked the Pope. There was even some suspicion that he outranked God.

I ran to his office and knocked on the door.

"Enter."

Oh, Lord. I opened the door and to my surprise saw his exalted magnificence sitting at his desk, head bowed over a piece of paper, which also seemed to be fascinating none other than Doctor Fingal Flahertie O'Reilly.

"That should do it, Fingal."

"Thanks, Snotty."

Snotty! Snotty? O'Reilly's familiarity was on a par with that of the young American naval officer who, at some embassy function, asked Queen Elizabeth II, Fid. Def., Ind. Imp., "How's your mum?"

"Ah, Taylor." O'Reilly took the piece of paper from Professor Callaghan. "You know my old classmate, Professor Callaghan?"

I nodded. Yes, and I was on first-name terms with President Nixon and the British prime minister too.

"He and I played rugby together. He's just done me a little favour." O'Reilly rose. "We won't detain you any longer, Snotty."

"My pleasure, Fingal."

I felt a bit like the Emperor's new clothes: not there, as far as Professor Callaghan was concerned.

"Now," said O'Reilly, "let's get a cup of tea."

He headed for the cafeteria with the unerring accuracy of a Nike missile, and this was the man who'd started today by remarking, "You'd think I'd know my way about up here."

He refused to show me the paper until we were seated, teacups on the plastic tabletop. "Here," he said, "take a look at this."

I could see immediately that it was a copy of a pathology report form. Three pages of detailed description of a uterus that had been removed by — I flipped back to the first page — Sir Gervaise Grant. The sting was in the tail. Just one line, which read, "The specimen of ureter submitted showed no abnormalities."

Dear God. The complication most feared by gynaecological surgeons. Damage to the tube that carried urine from the kidney to the bladder. "Is it true?" I asked in a whisper.

O'Reilly guffawed then said, "Not at all, but it should give old 'Green Fingers' pause for thought, possibly a cardiac arrest when he reads it, before he realises that the patient is fine and the report must be wrong," said O'Reilly. He sipped his tea. "Decent chap, Snotty Callaghan, to fudge the report. He can't stand Sir Gangrene either."

He smiled beatifically. "And you thought I didn't know my way round up here."

POWERS OF OBSERVATION

O'REILLY ACCEPTS A BET

"Powers of observation," O'Reilly mumbled through a mouthful of breakfast kipper.

"Pardon?"

"Why? You didn't do anything. Did you?" He pulled a thicker than usual piece of fish-bone from between his teeth and smiled at me. "Good kippers."

"Yes. That was my observation."

You would have thought that after working for Doctor Fingal Flahertie O'Reilly as a part-time locum for almost two years, I would have learned not to play the one-upmanship game with the redoubtable man. I had about as much chance of beating him as Tiny Tim had of wresting the world heavyweight championship from a Mister Muhammad Ali.

"What was?"

"What was what?"

"Your observation."

"That the kippers were rather good."

"No," he said, after some thought. "That was my observation."

"Well yes, I suppose so. But that's why I said, 'Pardon?' "

"Because I had observed that the kippers were good?"

"Er, not exactly."

"They're bad?"

"Not the kippers."

"Sometimes, Taylor," he shook his great head ponderously, "sometimes I wonder about you."

He was not alone. Sometimes I had a similar feeling of confusion, usually at a time like this when our conversation seemed to be taking one of those wandering paths that inevitably led to my utter loss of the thread. Still, something lost, something gained: I usually ended up with a pounding headache.

"Fingal, you said, 'Powers of observation.' "

"Of the quality of the kippers?"

"No. Not the kippers. I asked, 'Pardon?' because I wondered what you meant by the remark."

"Haven't the faintest idea. Pass the marmalade." He rose from the table and wandered off, happily munching a slice of toast.

"Don't be late for the surgery. It's antenatal clinic today." He stopped in the doorway. "I'll teach you about my powers of observation. Mark of a good physician, you know."

"Now," said O'Reilly, some time later, leaning forward from his swivel chair, "I'm going to teach you something you didn't learn at medical school."

"Oh?"

"Yes." His craggy face split into a great, conspiratorial grin. "I bet you didn't know that you can tell what underwear a pregnant woman is wearing just by observing her urine sample."

Sure, and you could pick the winner at Goodwood racetrack by consulting the entrails of chickens. I smiled a skeptical little smile. "A pound says you can't."

"You're on." He stretched out his hand and we shook. "Seems a shame to take your money."

We'll see, Fingal Flahertie O'Reilly. We'll see.

The door opened and Mrs. Kincaid ushered in our first patient, dressed in her Dior creation with a split down the back. So he wasn't going to be able to fool me by making an intelligent guess by looking at each woman's outer garments.

"Mrs. Robertson," said Kinky, handing

111

O'Reilly the chart and a small glass bottle containing the patient's urine sample.

"Good morning, Mrs. Robertson."

O'Reilly rose from his chair and took the sample. "Doctor Taylor here will just take you behind the screens and examine you."

"Thank you, Doctor O'Reilly."

I ushered the patient behind the screens, rapidly took her blood pressure, and then examined her abdomen. She was wearing black silk underpants. "Everything looks fine," I said in my best professional manner. She left.

"Black silk," said O'Reilly.

Dammit. He must have caught a glimpse through the split in the back of the gown. I hoped that was the explanation. I could feel my hard-earned pound slipping away.

"Jeannie Neely," said Mrs. Kincaid.

"Sample," said O'Reilly. "Morning, Jeannie."

"Morning, Doctor."

He nodded toward the screens. I escorted the woman to the examining couch, taking great care to place myself between her retreating back and Fingal. I stole a surreptitious glance in his direction. He couldn't have cared less. He was bending over the sink, urine-testing stick in one hand, the specimen in the other, and a look on his face of sublime confidence.

"Red flannel drawers," he said when she left. He was right again. I swallowed. This was getting serious. That pound was meant to be taking me and my girlfriend to the cinema on Saturday night.

"Annie O'Rourke," said Mrs. Kincaid, ushering in a woman who either was carrying quintuplets or had single-handedly by her eating habits almost caused the second great potato famine. She had, I think, a singleton, vertex, and probably had inherited some genes from old Ahab's mate, the great white whale. More importantly, her complete lack of underwear was going to be O'Reilly's downfall.

"Off you go, Annie."

She left.

"None," said O'Reilly with the absolute confidence of a master.

I saw eighteen women that morning. He was wrong just once. I could only hope that the light of my life would be happy to settle for a long walk on Saturday.

O'Reilly leaned back in his chair and stretched out his hand. "I believe you owe me a pound."

I grudgingly handed it over.

"Ta." He stuffed the note into his trouser pocket.

I gritted my teeth. "Fingal, how did you do it?"

"Powers of observation, my boy." His expression wasn't that of the cat who'd got the cream. His face had the felicity of the feline that had feasted on the fermented foaming of an entire dairy.

I was actually thinking of another "F" word, but delicacy forbids its use.

He must have noted my chagrin. "Come over here, lad." He rose and ambled to the sink. There in neat array stood the containers in which the patients had brought their samples. In those days, the niceties of little plastic bottles hadn't yet been introduced. He picked up the first receptacle. "Here. Mrs. Robertson — Chanel No. 5 — black satin; Jeannie Neely — jam jar — red flannel; Annie O'Rourke — Guinness bottle — none."

The old devil.

He swept the assorted glassware into a wastepaper basket. "First thing I said this morning, 'powers of observation,' and not of the quality of the kippers."

Blast him and blast his powers of observation. My promise to take a certain nurse to see *Lawrence of Arabia* had gone down the pipe as the urine bottles had been chucked into the rubbish.

114

"By the way," said O'Reilly, pulling something from his pocket, "here's the two quid I owe you for staying late the other week." He chuckled. "I was looking at your face, Pat. Amazing what I observed."

STRESS OF THE MOMENT

THE TALE OF MISTER BROWN AND MISS GILL

I think I've mentioned that Doctor Fingal Flahertie O'Reilly, among his other attributes, was kind to widows and small children. He had a knack of talking to youngsters as if they were adults, taking their concerns with grave sincerity.

Please remember this was the man who'd crushed Doctor "Thorny" Murphy with a single sentence, had given Sir Gervaise Grant enough nightmares to make Edgar Allan Poe look like a beautiful dreamer, yet around the chisslers of the small town he was, in his own quotation of the Bard, "Naught but a cooing dove."

A long afternoon surgery had just finished, and I was perched on the examining table. Mrs. Kincaid knocked on the door.

"Come in," said O'Reilly, eyebrows rising as he looked up from his seat at the rolltop desk. "Jasus, not more of the sick and suffering?"

Mrs. Kincaid appeared, followed by a little lad of about six who peered out from behind her skirts. He held firmly to the hand of a girl who must have been a couple of years his senior.

"Mister Brown and Miss Gill would like to have a wee word, Doctor." Kinky looked solemn.

O'Reilly's great eyebrows slid back from their attempt to meet his hairline. "Come right in."

Kinky ushered the pair forward to stand in front of O'Reilly. I was immediately put in mind of the carollers who visited Rat and Mole in *The Wind in the Willows*. The boy's short pants almost reached his skinned knees and while one sock was firmly held in place, the other was wrinkled round his ankle. He stood with his toes turned in. He clung to the hand of his companion.

The girl, clean in a patched grey dress, kept her cornflower blue eyes demurely fixed on the threadbare rug.

"Well," said O'Reilly, "what can I do for you?"

I sat quietly watching.

The little girl looked up at him and said, quite clearly, "Mister Brown and I are going

117

to get married."

O'Reilly didn't bat an eyelid.

"Married, is it?" He pushed his half-moon glasses up the bridge of his bent nose, sat back, and steepled his fingers. "There's a thing now."

The little boy scuffed his toes along the carpet, sniffed, and dragged the back of one forearm across his nostrils.

"Yes," she said. "Mister Brown proposed to me yesterday."

"Did he now?"

"I did," said Mister Brown.

I couldn't recollect how my textbook of the diseases of children suggested how one dealt with a paediatric premarital counselling visit, but was quite willing to learn. Besides, I wanted to see how O'Reilly managed to extricate himself from this one. I would probably have laughed and sent them packing.

Not O'Reilly.

"Well," he said, " 'Marriage is an honourable estate, not one to be entered upon lightly.' "

I flinched. I couldn't believe he was going to get to the bits about the comforts of the flesh.

Mister Brown nodded very seriously. He seemed to be uncomfortable and stood pressing his knees together.

"Good," said O'Reilly, "that's clear then."

Mister Brown tugged at the front of his pants.

O'Reilly stood. "I tell you what. I think we should continue these discussions over a cup of tea. Would you like that, Miss Gill?"

"Yes, please."

"Good."

"Doctor Taylor, would you be kind enough to ask Mrs. Kincaid to put the kettle on and set a tray for four?"

I thought I might as well go along. I might also have the opportunity to ask Kinky who the children belonged to. I left the room, hearing Fingal say, "And have you found a nice place to live?"

He was standing at the front door when I returned, his big shoulders shaking with suppressed mirth. I could see past him to where the betrothed were scurrying down the front path, Mister Brown still clinging to Miss Gill's hand.

He called after them. "Are you sure you won't stay for tea?"

But Miss Gill called back over her shoulder. "We can't, Doctor O'Reilly — Mister Brown's just wet himself."

O'REILLY'S SURPRISE

THE FLOWERS THAT BLOOMED IN THE SPRING

"Begod, I'm famished," announced Doctor Fingal Flahertie O'Reilly, helping himself to a canapé. The morsel vanished with the rapidity of a small insect trapped on a chameleon's tongue. "There's not enough on these things to keep a flea from starvation. Come back here, you."

The red-jacketed waiter to whom these words were addressed did a quick one-eighty like one of those figure skaters winding up for a death spiral. Donal Donnelly, mostly unemployed, occasional waiter at catered functions, proffered the tray of nibblers to O'Reilly with the subservience of a minion offering John the Baptist's head to Salome on a silver platter.

Now I wouldn't want you to think that Donal was scared of Doctor O'Reilly. Just because Donnelly was a patient of long standing and once upon a time Doctor O. had reduced Donal's dislocated shoulder — without the benefit of anaesthesia — was no reason for the youth to be scared of my mentor. Absolutely, totally, and utterly petrified is probably a better description.

"Good lad," said O'Reilly, grabbing a shrimp and a chippolata on a cocktail stick. "Run along."

Donal scuttled away.

"So?" O'Reilly asked, picking a tooth with the chippolata stick. "What do you think of this hooley?"

"Very nice," I replied, slightly overawed by my surroundings. I should tell you that in the late '60s, the concept of elitism hadn't been invented yet by the perpetually dissatisfied — those whose only claim to any degree of status is the volume with which they can whinge about perceived wrongs and who reckon because they always came last in the egg-and-spoon race that there's a conspiracy afoot to keep them in their places. The ones who have a personality with a specific gravity that would match that of lead, who feel they should have floated to the top by dint of no other effort than the fact of their existence.

Lord Fitzgurgle, twentieth Earl Hurtle-toot, hereditary master of the lands surrounding our small village, had no doubts about who was elite and who wasn't. The medical profession, represented by Doctor Fingal O'Reilly, Doctor Murphy (he of the crown of thorns), and myself, were. Just. We'd been invited to the annual "show the peasants a bit of condescension" evening at his lordship's stately home.

"Very nice," I said once again.

"Stop repeating yourself," O'Reilly grunted, swallowing a dollop of Black Bush whiskey. "His lordship keeps a good drop." He smacked his lips with the appreciatory enthusiasm of a satisfied orangutan. "Where the hell's young Donnelly?"

"I think he went back to the kitchen."

"Keep an eye out for him." O'Reilly adopted the tone he usually reserved for when he was imparting one of his pearls of wisdom. "I've been to these dos before. Takes forever to get the grub on the table. Take my advice." He waved an admonitory finger. "Stock up now."

"Right, Fingal." I cast an eye about for our waiter and hoped he would shortly hove into view. A hungry O'Reilly could become a tad irritable. Like a viper with its tail caught in a vice-grip.

"Don't go away," said O'Reilly. "I see our esteemed colleague Doctor Murphy over there. I'll just nip over and inquire after his health." Fingal had that look in his eye. I deemed it safer to stay where I was.

I stood looking around me. The room was a fine example of the kind of decayed gentility to be found in the houses of the remnants of the nobility in Ireland. Lord Fitzgurgle's ancestors scowled down from the walls. Ranks of oil paintings of peers of the realm. The First Earl looked like a brigand. He'd probably been ennobled for nicking a few sheep for his liege lord or stamping on a few Irish peasants. There was no sitting on your duff in the sixteenth century if you fancied a bit of swift promotion.

Between the pictures hung assorted trophies. Wicked-looking knobkerries, assegais, a horribly serrated spear, one or two moth-eaten zebra-skin shields. Hunting trophies abounded. Fox heads, stags' heads, and a mounted cape buffalo stared down.

"That fellow must have come through the wall at a hell of a tilt." I turned to see the returned O'Reilly squinting up at the buffalo. "Faster than that bloody Donnelly."

I saw O'Reilly's eyes light up. I followed the direction of his gaze. It was fixed on a large ceramic bowl that sat on a heavily carved sideboard.

"Peanuts," he muttered and set off at a trot.

"Evening, Doctor." His lordship stood at my side. Stiff military bearing, bushy white moustache, and a bulbous nose the colour of raw beef. The quinine in tonic water is prophylactic against malaria. And it had been effective — in all the seventy-six years he'd lived in Ulster he had not contracted malignant quartan. Not once. The brandy with which the duke had for years fortified his tonic accounted for the nose.

"My lord."

It's difficult to express in writing what my expression actually meant. At first glance you may think it was a greeting appropriate to my host's station. I can only hope he took it that way. In fact it was an exclamation of serious concern.

Out of the corner of my eye I could see O'Reilly. His eyeballs bulged, his face was redder than his lordship's nose. Much redder. And the tip of O'Reilly's nose, the marker of his anger level, was white as driven snow. His cheeks bulged and he was tugging at his collar. This display of facial gymnastics had clearly upset the very attractive woman to whom he'd been talking. She was hastening away, occasionally casting a backward glance at Fingal.

124

"Good. Good," said Lord Fitzgurgle. "Enjoy yourself, my boy."

"Thank you, my lord. Excuse me." I thought I was witnessing my first case of apoplexy, but as I neared O'Reilly his complexion cleared slightly. He managed an enormous swallow.

"You all right, Fingal?"

He made a gurgling noise for all the world like water running out of a bath and pointed at the bowl of peanuts. Now, it's said that when Horatio swam the swollen Tiber, Lars Porsena of Clusium could scarce forbear to cheer. I had a similar bad attack of the scarce forbearances. In my case, it was laughter I had to suppress.

Doctor O'Reilly, momentarily distracted by the charms of his companion, had seized and stuffed his mouth with an enormous handful, not of peanuts, but of the dried flower petals that had lurked in a potpourri.

He didn't complain of being hungry for the rest of the evening.

Shock Therapy

The Astonishingly Rapid Cure of Agatha Arbuckle

I may have alluded to the fact that my old tutor, Doctor Fingal Flahertie O'Reilly, could, on occasion, be a little unorthodox. I believe the early Catholic Church regarded Martin Luther in roughly the same light. I do, however, suspect there was a difference between the two men. There's not a shred of published evidence to suggest that the hero of the Reformation had much of a sense of humour. Certainly in any of the woodcuts, lithographs, and other sundry reproductions of the old cleric he looks to have been remarkably po-faced.

O'Reilly could be accused of many things (and frequently was, after the Mucky Duck had closed for the night), but lacking a well-developed sense of the ho-ho-hos was never one of them.

It has been said that laughter is the best

medicine. It could be back then. I'm not so sure today. A well-meaning one-liner may be greeted with a polite titter. It can also lead to a frolicsome chat with the disciplinary committee of your provincial college or a visit from those merry minions of mirth, the harassment police.

Doctor O'Reilly suffered from no such constraints.

Just before Friday-morning surgery was to start, he peered through a crack in the door to the waiting room.

"Would you look at that lot?" he said. "The weary, wilting, woesome, walking wounded wanting our wisdom before the weekend. The scabrous sick searchers after solace for their scorched souls. Jasus." He stepped back from the door. "See for yourself."

I chanced a glance.

The waiting room was full. Four local farmers; three housewives; Donal Donnelly, who I'd last seen waiting at Lord Fitzgurgle's soiree; and Maggie, looking suspiciously as if the pain above her head had returned, sat on benches arranged round the walls of the room. Two small boys ran around the remaining open space, arms outstretched, banking and weaving and making machine-gun noises.

127

A single wooden chair occupied one corner. Whoever took that seat would be first into the sanctum sanctorum when O'Reilly opened the surgery. This morning's winner was a woman with a smile like last week's rhubarb. Her lips were set at a permanent twenty to four. Her upper body, thin as a rake handle, twitched up and down at about two-second intervals. A series of faint "hics" could be heard over the racket of the simulated dogfight.

"Ha," said O'Reilly as he let the door close. "You'd need the diagnostic skills of a Galen to sort out that lot. Piles, sniffles, backaches, a couple of ruptures. Donnelly'll be looking for another doctor's letter so he can draw his sick pay, and God only knows what Maggie has for us today. And to top it off there's Agatha Arbuckle with her chest going up and down like a hoor on hinges."

He got that glint in his eye and a coercive tone to his voice. "I don't suppose you'd like to take the surgery today?"

He was right. If for no other reason than I had no wish to tend to Maggie or Agatha Arbuckle, I know the oath of a certain classic quack from the isle of Cos has some kind of codicil about ministering unto the sick. Old Hippocrates didn't practise in Ulster. Nor did he have to sort out Maggie or Aggie on a regular basis. "Sorry, Fingal. Lots of house calls." I began to sidle toward the front door.

O'Reilly heaved an enormous sigh, the kind of noise a beached right whale makes just before expiring. "All right. But I could do without Agatha today."

"Sorry about that," I lied. I could do without her too. Agatha Arbuckle, fifty, spinster of this parish, secretary-treasurer of the Presbyterian Women's Union, was not one of my favourite people. Nor one of O'Reilly's. Somewhere in the woman's soul lurked a pool of acid. Not your regular sulphuric or nitric. Oh, no. Agatha's psyche was fuelled by aqua regia, an acid so powerful that one drop can dissolve the armour of a main battle tank.

"I'll have to be getting on," I said. "Just going to nip upstairs and get my bag."

I'd been wrong about the whale. It wasn't one. From O'Reilly's expiratory rumblings it sounded as if a whole school of cetaceans had taken up permanent residence in the hall. As I headed up I heard him say, "Come in, Agatha. What seems to be the trouble?" Just as I came back into the hall, doctor's black bag clutched in one hand, the door to the surgery opened and Agatha rushed past me to the front door. The look of shock on her face would have suited the mayor of Hiroshima just after the big bang. What had Fingal said to her? From somewhere I remembered that hiccups could be a sign of terminal ureamia.

O'Reilly sat in his swivel chair at the roll-top desk. He looked enormously self-satisfied. "Thought you were off doing house calls."

"I'm just going, but I saw Aggie a minute ago. Is she all right?"

"Right as rain."

"But . . ."

"No 'buts' about it. I fixed her."

"How?"

Certain cats, I believe from the county of Cheshire, are reputed to grin. O'Reilly's vast smirk would have shamed them into expressionlessness. "Told her she was pregnant."

"You what?"

He nodded. "Told her she's up the builder's."

Aggie? Impossible. "She couldn't be."

"I know," he said, rising to his feet and pausing for dramatic effect, "but it cured her hiccups."

HAPPY AS A PIG IN . . .

DIAGNOSING PORCINE PREGNANCY

"What do you know about pigs?" O'Reilly inquired.

I paused, a small sherry halfway to my lips. "Pigs?"

"Mmm," said O'Reilly, wiping Guinness froth from his upper lip. "Pigs."

I glanced round the snug of the Mucky Duck, but the landlord was nowhere in sight. Erroneously, as it turned out, I'd assumed that O'Reilly was about to make some disparaging remark about mine host, Arthur Turloch Osbaldiston, purveyor of strong drink, intoxicating liquors, and fine tobaccos. A man of substantial proportions, a complexion of a pinkness to match the hue of a hog, and a squashed nose of similar configuration.

"Pigs?"

"Yes. Pigs, man," said O'Reilly, his nose tip paling.

What the hell was he on about? Male chauvinists, lumps of cast iron, the Saracen armoured personnel carriers of the British Army, or cloven-hoofed mammals? All could legitimately be called pigs. Certainly the APCs were by the citizens of Belfast. "Pigs, Fingal?"

O'Reilly's brows knitted. Actually they moved up and down so rapidly it might have been said "O'Reilly's brows crocheted," but it wasn't. Not by me anyway.

"They say," he remarked, idly using an index finger to draw a smile in the white head of his stout, "that perseveration is an early sign of mental disease. Why do you keep mumbling 'pigs'?"

"You asked the question."

"What question?"

"Pigs. You asked, 'What do you know about pigs?' "

"Did I?"

"You did."

"Oh."

That seemed to put an end to a rather aimless conversation. I wasn't disappointed, but of course I was wrong. O'Reilly heaved himself vertically, carried his empty glass to the counter, leaned over, and yelled, "Nurse!" He wasn't ill. This was his standard summons for anyone with the power to pour him a drink. Arthur Turloch Osbaldiston hove weightily into view, glass in one hand, dishrag in the other. "Yes, Doctor O'Reilly?"

"Two more."

"Right, sir." Osbaldiston busied himself seeing to Doctor O'Reilly's next pint. As he ran the black brew into the glass he asked, anxiously, "Well?"

O'Reilly shook his head. "Doctor Taylor doesn't know anything about pigs."

Arthur Turloch was so upset he allowed some of the beer to spill. "Ah, dear," he said, handing O'Reilly his pint and a small sherry for me. "I'll just have to carry on with your advice then, Doctor O'Reilly."

"You will," said O'Reilly, neglecting to pay, as he headed back toward our table. He sat, set my second drink beside the unfinished first, and took a deep pull of his own.

"Pigs," he said, mournfully.

I flinched. This, more or less, was where I'd come in. I thought it wiser to agree.

"Yes, indeed," I said. "Pigs."

"Bloody animals. Pity you don't know more about them."

"Yes, indeed."

He rummaged round in his jacket pocket, hauled out his briar, stoked the bowl, and

133

lit up. At least it gave me time to see if I could offer any solace on the subject that was troubling him. I could not.

"Fat and very rotund," he said.

I nodded. Did he mean Osbaldiston or the subject of the moment?

"Bloody difficult to tell if they're pregnant."

Pigs. Definitely not Arthur Turloch.

"And Arthur there needs to know."

"If he's pregnant?" I asked.

"Not him. His sow."

Light began to dawn. Our landlord ran a smallholding on the side. He'd bought a sow last year. She would have been ready for breeding this year, and every visit to the boar cost money.

"Yes," said O'Reilly, "and he asked me how he could tell if the boar had scored a winner."

"Yes," I said, "I know."

"What do you know?"

"About pigs? Nothing."

O'Reilly growled, stabbed the stem of his briar in my general direction and said, "How did you know I'd given him advice?"

"Because he said, a moment ago, that he'd just have to go on taking it."

"Damn silly advice too." The man had the decency to look slightly embarrassed. "Do you know how the farmers round here breed pigs?" he asked.

It seemed not the most opportune time to remind him that we'd established beyond reasonable doubt that the sum of my knowledge on that subject was zero. I merely shook my head.

"The usual procedure is to load the sow in a wheelbarrow and trundle her off to the boar."

"Seems sensible."

"Not," said O'Reilly, "if you have to keep repeating the exercise. Gets expensive."

"Oh."

"And you know Arthur would wrestle a bear for a farthing."

I nodded, thinking to myself that Doctor Fingal Flahertie O'Reilly could probably give Osbaldiston a few pointers in the sport of ursine mat-grappling — certainly if there was any prospect of a pecuniary payoff.

O'Reilly sighed. "The best I could think of was an old farmer's tale that I'd heard years ago."

I listened.

"Seems there was a local belief that recently pregnant sows, if given a choice between mud and grass, would always roll in the mud, so after you'd bred her you waited to see if she'd go to the mud."

"Well," I said, "that makes sense."

"What?"

"Oh yes. The raised progesterone levels of pregnancy would put the animal's temperature up. Naturally she'd prefer the mud. Help her cool off."

O'Reilly looked at me suspiciously. "You're not pulling my leg?"

"Me, Fingal? Never."

He brightened up. "Perhaps I did give him good advice after all. I just hope the wee sow gets into the mud soon." O'Reilly chuckled. "It's a sight every evening to see Arthur toiling up the hill, pushing the barrow with the pig in it."

Before I could reply I became aware that Arthur Turloch had reappeared. He didn't look happy.

"Ah," said O'Reilly, grandiloquently. "You'll be glad to hear that young Doctor Taylor has applied his understanding of basic science to our problem. He concurs with my opinion." O'Reilly held up his now-empty glass and looked hopeful. "I'll bet your sow will be rolling in the mud already."

"No," said Arthur, lugubriously. "She's not. She's sitting in my wheel-barrow with a smile on her face."

BAROMETER FALLING

FLYING WOULD BE MORE ACCURATE

There's an anaeroid barometer hanging in
the hall of the house of Doctor Fingal Flahertie O'Reilly. Barometers, as you know,
measure atmospheric pressure. This one no
longer does. It's battered, the glass is
broken, and the needle is stuck permanently
indicating "fair." Let me tell you why.

"I think . . ." said Doctor O'Reilly, and
paused.

"Therefore I am?" I suggested.

He scowled at me as a gouty retired
colonel might regard a scruffy teenager
who'd just run a skateboard over the ex-
military man's bandaged foot.

"*Cogito ergo sum.* I think, therefore I am,"
I mumbled rapidly, citing my source for
good measure. "Descartes."

"Idiot," said O'Reilly. "Dostoyevsky."

I was relieved that Doctor Fingal O'Reilly
hadn't dipped further into his encyclopaedic

catalogue of the classics. I shuddered to think what he might have called me if he'd taken his riposte from the works of D. H. Lawrence.

"Sorry," I said.

O'Reilly harrumphed then said, "Should bloody well think so."

I wondered why O'Reilly's mood, which had been so high earlier in the morning, was now giving a good impression of a pint of milk left out in the sun too long. Sour. Very sour. Morning surgery was over and he'd announced with a broad grin that this afternoon he would take a half-day holiday.

This, I should tell you, was somewhat out of character. O'Reilly, and indeed most of his generation, took it as a matter of course that single-handed country GPs were on call twenty-four hours a day, seven days a week, twelve months a year. What was even more curious, he'd made the statement immediately after consulting a heavy mahogany-and-brass barometer that hung in the hall. "Wonderful," he'd remarked. "Barometer's rising and it's already at 'fair.' "

Pestered as I'd been for most of the pre-noon by a passing parade of perambulatory paediatric problems produced for my perusal by their painfully prolix progenitors, I'd forgotten that my senior colleague had some thoughts of recreation after lunch. And in some way the barometer's cheerful prognostication had, in the fore part of the day, lifted O'Reilly's spirits. Now he stood and scowled at the thing. "I think . . ." he began again.

Discretion is always the better part of valour. I stood like the middle one of the three monkeys, speaking no evil, and wondering what weighty pronouncement was going to fall from O'Reilly's lips.

"I think . . ." he peered at the needle on the face of the anaeroid, "that sometimes the marvels of modern science could have been somewhat improved."

A glance through the window served to confirm his observations. The heavens hadn't so much opened as gaped. I confidently expected to behold a bearded gentleman wearing a burnoose, muttering about cubits and spans, the tardy delivery of gopher wood, and the difficulty of housing diverse animal species two by two.

"It's raining," I said.

The look he gave me over the pallid tip of his nose would have induced Medusa's serpentine hairs to shed their scaly skins simultaneously. "You should give up medicine," he said. "You missed your calling. You'd have made a great meteorologist."

Some might call that remark brilliant repartee, others biting sarcasm, given the force of the deluge outside. I chose to remember that he who fights and runs away lives to be sworn at another day.

"Sorry," I said.

"I was going golfing," O'Reilly said mournfully. He pointed an accusatory finger at the barometer. "I trusted that bloody thing this morning and phoned an old friend, Charlie Elphinstone. He's coming down from Belfast." O'Reilly tapped the instrument's glass with the gentility of a caress from King Kong and scowled at the needle. The pointer, presumably terrified, swung farther into the "fair."

O'Reilly's nose moved from ashen to ivory. His neck veins bulged. "Fair? Fair?" He ripped the insultingly inaccurate instrument from the wall and with the powerful grace of a caber tosser hurled it straight through the glass of the window and out into the downpour. "See for your stupid self!" O'Reilly yelled, as he set the Irish and all comers' open record for anaeroid barometer throwing. "Bah," he added, but the colour was returning to his proboscis. I could only surmise that his outburst had served the same purpose as one of those vents in the side of an active volcano and

140

that O'Reilly's internal pressure was beginning to subside.

I ventured a query: "So what will you do?"

"Do?"

"With your friend from Belfast?"

It might have been pouring outside, but the sun came up in O'Reilly's personal heaven. "Charlie? Play golf, of course."

"Play golf? In this?"

"No, you idiot. In the nineteenth hole." He turned to leave. "Be a good lad," he said. "Nip out and collect the barometer."

THE FLYING DOCTOR

O'REILLY TAKES THE WHEEL

"Did you ever see the likes of that chase?" Doctor O'Reilly asked, fist curled round his second John Jameson's, elbow nestled in its accustomed groove in the bar of the Mucky Duck.

"Impressive," I remarked, cuddling a small sherry and trying to make it last.

"That Steve McQueen must be a powerful driver." He was clearly in awe. I should tell you that he and I had just returned from the local cinema's screening of the film *Bullitt*. The one with the classic car chase through the hills of San Francisco. It dawned on me, vaguely, that the good Doctor O. might be tempted to emulate McQueen's driving. The prospect of the carnage that would be wrought among the local livestock and itinerant rustic cyclists hardly bore contemplation. Even with his present style of procession in his long-bonnetted

Rover he was a force to be reckoned with.

When they teach you about side effects at medical school, no mention is ever made of the fact that emergency house calls lead to an increase in the incidence of minor sprains and abrasions.

If he truly believed that life or limb of one of his patients was at risk, O'Reilly would hurl his motorcar through the streets and byways of our district with all the enthusiasm of Toad of Toad Hall. In fairness, Doctor O. was able to refrain from yelling "poop poop" at the top of his voice. If Fingal Flahertie O'Reilly had been driving a panzer for Heinz Guderian in May 1940, the Battle of France would have been finished in two weeks flat.

The natives, many of whom went about their lawful (and in the case of Turlough Tweezlethumbs the local poacher, unlawful) pursuits mounted on fixed-wheel bicycles, had evolved their own method of dealing with O'Reilly in one of his Charge-of-the-Light-Brigade moments. The fixed-wheel bicycle has no brakes. You stop it by standing on the pedals. It is a slow method of arrest. Too slow for O'Reilly avoidance. I can only assume it was some kind of Darwinian genetics at work. To a man, and the three lady cyclists of the townland, standard operating procedure was to recognize O'Reilly's chariot, flinch, tuck in the head, and deliberately fall off into the ditch. Thus the abrasions and sprains.

"I hope you'll not be trying to drive like Bullitt," I remarked.

Doctor O. was in an expansive mood. He chuckled, swallowed his whiskey, and clapped an avuncular hand on my shoulder. (The bruise faded in four days.) "Don't worry your head about that, Pat."

His grin bothered me. So did his next words: "The hills aren't steep enough round here."

I forgot about the film and our conversation until about three weeks later. O'Reilly had gone off for the afternoon to visit his brother, Lars Porsena Fabius Cunctator O'Reilly, in the small town of Portaferry, which lies at the mouth of Strangford Lough. It's connected to the village of Strangford on the other shore by a car ferry. By the way, the short road ending at the ferry loading ramp lies at the foot of a steep hill.

I was enjoying the last scraps of one of Mrs. Kincaid's steak-and-kidney puddings and wondering casually where Doctor O. might be. It was most unlike him to be late for supper. His head appeared round the door and his expression could only be described as sheepish.

"Um," he said in a small, very un-O'Reilly voice. "Um, Pat, could I borrow your car?"

"Why?" I inquired with approximately the same degree of trust as would be evinced by a lamb that has been invited over by a starving lion.

"It's embarrassing."

It might have been emotionally upsetting for O'Reilly, but more so for me was the thought of what he might do to my poor secondhand Volkswagen — or, to be more precise, the Bank of Ireland's Volkswagen. (They let me drive it while exacting their pound of flesh, two pounds of sinew, and one molar a month.) For once, facing the prospect of financial ruin if he wrecked the thing, I straightened my shoulders, emulated Pharaoh, and hardened my heart. "Why?" I demanded.

He flinched, took a deep breath, and said, "If you were late and had to get back here from Portaferry, which way would you come?"

"Take the ferry to Strangford."

"Right. Cuts a good ten miles off the journey."

I couldn't quite grasp what this had to do with borrowing my car, and said so.

"What would you do if you were at the top of the Portaferry hill and the ferry was just going to leave?"

"Wait," I said.

"I didn't." O'Reilly's eyes flashed. "I went down the hill like Ben Hur in the Circus Maximus. There was only about ten feet between the ferry and the dock and the ferry was half-empty. There was as much space on the car deck as on the flight deck of the USS *Enterprise.* It would be like landing on a carrier with her forward speed making the runway seem even longer."

"You didn't!" I asked, immediately regretting my superfluous use of words.

"I did," he said. His eyes adopted that glazed look of satisfaction only seen in the orbs of committed opium smokers after a full and satisfying pipeful. "And it was wonderful. My Rover flew like Bullitt's Mustang."

"So why do you want to borrow my car?"

"Because," he said, "the bloody ferry was coming in."

FORTY SHADES OF GREEN

ANOTHER O'REILLY
DRIVING ADVENTURE

You may remember Doctor O'Reilly's attempts to emulate Wilbur and Orville Wright. As memory serves, and no, I was not a spectator on that memorable day at Kitty Hawk, the "Wright Flyer" successfully conquered gravity and landed in one piece. O'Reilly had managed, albeit briefly, the first part of the daring aviator's feat. He'd defied gravity in a Rover car. His landing on the deck of the Portaferry ferry had been less of a three-point job than a full-blown kamikaze attack on the unfortunate vessel. I'm told the *Hesperus* after being wrecked was in better shape than the ferry after O'Reilly.

I'd stuck to my guns and refused to lend him my Volkswagen, and until his own motor was returned from the body shop, a repair that made the raising of Lazarus seem like prescribing two aspirins for a cold, he'd been forced to make his way round on a bicycle. This had worked wonders for his figure and his wind, but had reduced his tolerance of delays to somewhere on the southern side of absolute zero. Which was unfortunate for Donal Donnelly.

Donal, you will recall, was last seen handing out canapés at Lord Fitzgurgle's annual "be nice to the peasants" evening. He was a gangly youth, as lacking in self-confidence as Uriah Heep, as unprepossessing as a sack of cold porridge, and to say he was as thick as two short planks was to do disservice to the local woodworking industry. Donal's density made a couple of short planks look like a piece of microfilm. And he was terrified of Doctor Fingal Flahertie O'Reilly.

I should tell you that our town had a traffic light. (I know that stories are meant to have an internal logic and a sequential flow. You should recognize by now, however, that "logic" and "O'Reilly" are not two words with the happy congruence of, say, "love" and "marriage" or "peaches" and "cream." Try "oil" and "water" or "Hatfield" and "McCoy." Please accept that the town had a traffic light.)

O'Reilly had asked me to accompany him by train to Belfast to collect his refurbished automobile. The old Rover, which must have been rebuilt from scratch, gleamed. The engine purred. O'Reilly beamed. O'Reilly purred. When the prodigal son returned, his father killed the fatted calf. When O'Reilly took possession of his motorcar, it was a good thing he did so in Belfast, not the countryside. In a more bucolic setting, herds of fatted cows, and probably several chubby sheep, would have been slaughtered, so great was Doctor O.'s rejoicing.

"Come on, Pat," he said, "let's get her home."

"You'll drive carefully?"

"Of course." I believe a piecrust promise is one that is made to be broken. O'Reilly's pie that day was made of the transparent caramel used for special effects in the cinema. The ones where bad cowboys are hurled through windows to the accompaniment of shattering glass.

I understand that once Mach 1 is exceeded, the pilot can no longer hear the engine of the plane. Either the mechanics had fixed the Rover's motor to the specifications of Rolls-Royce or we were a tad above the speed limit for most of the journey. There were moments, usually in heavier traffic, when I could perceive a high-pitched keening noise. It took me a while before I recognized that I was making it.

"Got to get home for the match," O'Reilly said.

I'd forgotten that Ireland was playing England in a rugby game. Actually, I didn't care. I just wanted to get home in one piece.

Now I made a point of mentioning our town's traffic light and Donal Donnelly. On rare occasions planets line up in conjunction and astrologers foretell the coming of the apocalypse. Donal was driving his father's tractor and was stopped at the light. O'Reilly's home was visible not a hundred yards away, kickoff was in two minutes, and the Rover was stopped behind the tractor as we waited for the light to change.

Green went the light. O'Reilly, presumably wishing to encourage young Donal, blew his horn.

Donal may have been suffering from grand mal, the battery of the tractor may have shorted and hurled a shock through his scrawny body, or it may just have been abject terror brought on by peering astern to discover that the horn blower was Doctor O. Whatever the cause, he began to tremble uncontrollably and stalled the engine of the tractor.

Red went the light.

"#@$~#!" went O'Reilly.

Green went the light.

"Nurgley-nurgley-nurgley," went the tractor's engine, but failed to start.

Red went the light.

White went the tip of O'Reilly's nose.

Green went the light.

"Nurgley-nurgley-phtang!" went the tractor's engine as the exhaust billowed clouds of fumes as dense as the rock dust fallout from the explosion of Krakatoa.

Light red, O'Reilly's nose ivory, smoke black, Donal's face puce. Colourful. Very colourful. O'Reilly swore once more, opened the door of the Rover, and dismounted. I followed. Just as the light turned green for the fourth time, I distinctly heard him say to Donal Donnelly, "Was there a particular shade of green you were waiting for?"

I did not hear Donal's reply.

A G(H)ASTLY MISTAKE

O'REILLY CHRISTENS
HIS PROPANE BARBECUE

I believe I may have mentioned that Doctor Fingal Flahertie O'Reilly was an ex-naval man. He hadn't been personally responsible for sinking the *Bismark* or winning the Battle of the Atlantic single-handed, but he claimed to have seen more cases of crab lice than Pharaoh after one of the plagues of Egypt.

He'd maintained his contact with the sea as the owner of a twenty-six-foot sloop. Apart from washing, this was as close as he was prepared to let H_20 come to his body. I once had the temerity to ask for a glass of water and was soundly chastised with the admonishment that if I knew what the stuff did to the outsides of boats, I'd never let it past my lips.

From time to time he'd invite me to act as his crew. Perhaps "invite" would be rendered better as "shanghai." Dana's *Two Years Before the Mast* described a pleasure cruise compared to a nautical outing with O'Reilly. His style of skippering, taken straight from Captain Bligh's manual of how to win friends and influence people, left a certain amount to be desired.

"I need a hand on the boat today," he said.

I flinched and sought around for an excuse to run. I imagine French aristocrats had the same impulse when invited to try Doctor Guillotine's new invention — and with about as much success.

"Come on," he said.

My spirits rose when we reached the dock. He didn't intend to put to sea. Instead he wanted my help to install a propane barbecue on the taffrail.

"Propane?" I inquired.

"Marvellous stuff," he said, unpacking the grill from a cardboard box. "Clean-burning, safe as houses, and these new barbecues are idiot-proof. I've had propane in the galley for years."

The propane that fuels a boat's stove is isolated from belowdecks by a series of solenoids, cut-off valves, and taps. NASA's rockets have similar arrangements. Both systems are designed to prevent the payload, which may be a multimillion-dollar satellite or a small sailboat, from leaving the confines of Earth's gravitational pull prematurely.

Clever things, these safety devices. Teams of highly skilled engineers, bomb-disposal experts, and, for all I know, pardoned arsonists have toiled long to ensure the safety of seagoing propane, and O'Reilly was right: the system was idiot-proof. There was no guarantee it was O'Reilly-proof.

It was a warm day and it took us several hours of fiddling, screwing, unscrewing, re-screwing, bolting, unbolting, rebolting, massaging skinned knuckles, and misplacing screwdrivers and wrenches before the barbecue was fixed in place. I'd thought my vocabulary was fairly complete in the scatological department. O'Reilly would have been an instant nominee for a Nobel if the inventor of dynamite had seen fit to award a prize for blasphemy.

"That's it," he said, sweat streaming down his face with the volume and velocity of the Horseshoe Falls. "Fixed the @~&**# thing."

"Mmm."

"Now, let's give it a try."

He lifted a locker lid and extracted a squat metal bottle of liquefied gas.

"Gimme that hose."

I handed him a black rubber pipe and

watched as he fitted screw couplings to the grill and the bottle. "Perfect," he announced. "Hang on."

He disappeared below for a moment, only to reappear in the hatchway clutching two bottles of beer. "Time to christen it." He handed me one bottle.

"I think I'll just go up on the foredeck," I said, sidling away as he produced a box of matches. I believe that the men who dispose of unexploded bombs are supposed to keep a distance of four hundred metres between themselves and the device. O'Reilly's twenty-six-foot boat fell a little short, but I had no intention of standing right beside the infernal machine when O'Reilly struck the match.

He joined me for'ard a minute later. "It's going like a bomb," he said, grinning from ear to ear.

I thought he might have used a different simile.

"What the hell's that?" O'Reilly inquired.

From aft came a roaring like Mount Vesuvius on one of its more active afternoons. A jet of flame tore across the cockpit and scared the daylights out of a passing gull. It looked as though a leftover storm-trooper from WWII was firing a *flammenwerfer* (flame thrower for those of you too young to remember).

"Jasus," said O'Reilly.

"Abandon ship?" I asked, having no wish to emulate the boy standing on the burning deck.

"Holy thundering Jasus," O'Reilly said, heading aft.

Call me boastful if you wish. Feeble-minded is probably a better description. I actually followed him, feeling horribly like one of the "Noble Six Hundred." Into the jaws of death and all that.

As soon as we reached the boat's cockpit, the source of the conflagration became apparent. When O'Reilly had hooked up the hose he'd managed to let it lie against the barbecue. The flames from the grill had melted the rubber and ignited the escaping propane, which even then howled and flared like something only Red Adair should be asked to tackle.

I watched in awe as O'Reilly bent and turned off the valve on the propane tank. The roaring subsided. The flames died. The only sounds that broke the stillness were the chattering of my teeth and the rattling of my knees.

And I stifled my desire to remind O'Reilly of his earlier remarks that propane was as safe as houses and that gas barbecues were idiot-proof.

Blessed Are the Meek

The O'Reillys, Alas, are Not Among Them

"It's not fair, Uncle Fingal." Thus spake a tear-stained William Butler Yeats O'Reilly, Fingal Flahertie O'Reilly's nephew. Willy, aged ten, was the son of O'Reilly's brother, Lars Porsena Fabius Cunctator O'Reilly, the one who lived in Portaferry. That's the place, you'll remember, where Doctor O. tried to emulate Steve McQueen and nearly sank the ferry when he hurled his motorcar at the incoming vessel.

On this occasion, O'Reilly had been invited to his brother's for the pre-Christmas festivities and had dragged me along.

"Cheer up, Willy. It's not as bad as that," said O'Reilly at his avuncular best.

"It is." Willy sniffed and O'Reilly handed him a handkerchief.

"Blow," said O'Reilly.

Willy honked. He was an unprepossessing child, snub-nosed, freckled, and with a shock of ginger hair that stood up from his crown like the crest of an indignant cockatoo. His damp eyes were full of the unspoiled innocence of childhood. I didn't know then that beneath this apparent gentility lurked the O'Reilly propensity for bearing a grudge and that Willy, like his uncle, wasn't one to let a wrong go unpunished. I didn't know that then — but I was going to find out.

"It's not fair," he repeated. "I've been Joseph twice. I know all the lines."

"And you were a grand Joseph," O'Reilly said, retrieving his hanky. "You'll be a great innkeeper."

"Don't wanna be an innkeeper. Wanna be Joseph."

I stood there, both legs the same length, in a state of utter confusion. This was my usual condition when in the company of Doctor O.

He must have noticed my dazed look. "Willy was Joseph for the last two years," he said.

I'd already grasped that piece of intelligence. "I see."

"No, you don't."

"Don't what?"

"See."

"True."

"Then why did you say you did?"

"I wanna be Joseph," quoth Willy.

"Doctor Taylor doesn't see," said O'Reilly.

"Don't care," said Willy. "It's not fair."

I was beginning to feel a vague pounding at the temples. "Would somebody please explain," I asked.

"Willy wants to be Joseph," O'Reilly said. "See?"

"I see." The pounding intensified. I had an overwhelming urge to go and lie down.

"No, you bloody well don't," said O'Reilly.

"Wanna be Joseph."

"Willy's to be the innkeeper this year," O'Reilly explained.

"I . . ." I strangled the word "see" in mid-utterance and waited.

"In the school Christmas pageant," O'Reilly said.

The pieces were beginning to come together. "You mean Willy played Joseph in the pageant for the last two years?"

"Now you see," said O'Reilly, and indeed I did.

"And Johnny Fagan gets to be Joseph this year and I've to be the innkeeper." Willy had added the last piece to the puzzle. "He's a little s*#*! I'll get him."

160

There was a fire in Willy's eyes that made me look closely at his nose tip to see if like his uncle's in moments of great passion it too paled. It did.

Picture now the parish hall. Serried rows of parents, teachers, older and younger brothers and sisters, half a dozen nuns, itinerant rubberneckers with no attachment to the school but who have nowhere else to go until the pubs open, the O'Reilly clan, and myself. The stage is divided by a wall so the audience can see the courtyard on one side and the interior of the inn, stable, and manger on the other. The innkeeper, known to his friends and family as William Butler Yeats O'Reilly, waits in the inn with sundry shepherds, wise men, angels, cherubim, and seraphim.

Enter stage left Mary, dressed in one of her mother's cut-down dresses. Mary is astride a small, moth-eaten donkey. Joseph, a.k.a. Johnny Fagan, wearing a nightshirt, head wrapped in a tea towel held in place with a piece of rope, leads the donkey. The gum arabic holding his flowing beard has given way and the beard straggles down his chest.

Mary. "Is this the inn, Joseph?"

Joseph. "It is. I'll knock and see if the

161

innkeeper's in."

Joseph knocks.

The innkeeper opens the door. (Perhaps I'm the only one in the audience who notices the pallor of his nose.)

Innkeeper. "Is that you, Mary and Joseph?"

Joseph. "It is, innkeeper." He gives a sneering inflection to the word "innkeeper."

Joseph. "All right. Come on in, Mary."

Mary dismounts and enters.

Innkeeper, glowering at Joseph. "And you, Joseph" — the innkeeper pushes Joseph in the chest — "Joseph, you can just feck off."

I swear two nuns fainted.

A Matter of Tact

Or Lack of It

"Tactless," Doctor Fingal Flahertie O'Reilly remarked. "Utterly bloody tactless."

This observation was not so much a question of the pot calling the kettle black as referring to it as stygian. O'Reilly could be described as possessing many attributes, indeed he has been, but, and feel free to correct me if you think I err, tact was not among his own most sterling qualities. In most social and professional encounters, O'Reilly was as tactful as a regimental sergeant major discussing the inadvisability of a new recruit's recent unfortunate dropping of his rifle in the middle of a ceremonial parade.

I was puzzled. I'd said nothing. I couldn't have. I'd just entered his surgery as his last patient of the morning left. Nevertheless I automatically assumed a defensive crouch and wondered what sin of social ineptness I

163

was about to be accused of committing.

"Sorry," I said. I believe in criminal circles this is known as "copping a plea."

"Why?" asked O'Reilly.

"Why what?"

"Why are you sorry?"

"For being tactless."

"You weren't."

"Sorry?" I asked.

"No, you idiot, tactless."

"Oh," I said. "Sorry."

"Stop apologizing." Just a hint of paleness brightened the tip of his nose.

I decided it was time to beat a retreat. "I'm sor . . . so glad I wasn't."

"Yes, you were."

"Tactless?"

"No. Apologizing."

"Sorry."

"Do not say 'Sorry' again. Sometimes I wonder about you, Taylor," said O'Reilly, staring into the distance and clearly letting his mind wander. "I really wonder."

He was not alone. Sometimes, in fact frequently since I had fallen into his clutches, I wondered about myself.

I thought it was probably time to give a slight course correction to the conversation — the kind lunar astronauts make to ensure a safe return to Earth rather than a trip to the Oort Cloud.

"You were saying something about 'tactless,' " I remarked.

His gaze focused and he turned to face me. "Sorry?" he asked.

I think in cardiovascular circles this is known as a reversal of shunt. I ignored the temptation to tell him there was no need to apologize, and gave the lateral thrusters a little more liquid oxygen: "You said someone was 'bloody tactless.' "

"I did, didn't I?"

"Yes, Fingal."

"Sean Millington O'Casey," he said.

I knew that Doctor O. had been named for Oscar Wilde, had a nephew yclept William Butler Yeats O'Reilly, but who the blue blazes had been given a combination of Synge and O'Casey?

"Man's totally lacking in social graces," said O'Reilly. "O'Casey's the bloke that left as you came in."

"Oh," I said.

"Just had a hell of a row with his wife. He wanted some marital counselling." O'Reilly rummaged in his pocket and produced his briar. "More like martial counselling the way the pair of them go at it."

I remembered Mrs. O'Casey. I'd seen her last week for an antenatal visit.

"They must talk to each other occasionally," I observed. "His wife's pregnant with their fourth."

"Um," said O'Reilly, lighting up. "And that's another miracle. He's a travelling salesman. Away from home a lot."

"Perhaps he writes passionate letters."

"He does more than that. He makes stupid remarks on the telephone. Tactless remarks." O'Reilly paused to tamp the tobacco more firmly into his portable blast furnace. " 'What'll I say, Doctor?' says he to me.

" 'What did you say?' says I.

" 'Well,' says he, 'I was in England last week. Staying in a hotel. The phone rings and I picks it up. A woman's voice says, "You bastard." I knew it was the wife.'

"I told him to go on." O'Reilly exhaled. I confidently expected to see Sherlock Holmes and Doctor Watson appear from the pea-soup fog that poured from O'Reilly's pipe.

" 'I said nothing,' says O'Casey." O'Reilly exhaled again. The miasma was thick enough to conceal a hansom cab.

"Tactful of him," I remarked, "to say nothing."

"He should have kept his mouth shut," said O'Reilly. "Apparently the next thing

166

his wife said was, 'You've gone on the road and you've left me pregnant,' and the daft eejit, quick as a flash, replies, 'And who is this I'm speaking to?' "

"Definitely not tactful," I observed.

"So," asked O'Reilly, "if you were advising O'Casey, what would you tell him to say to his wife?"

It slipped out before I could help myself. "Sorry?"

THE CAT'S MEOW

ONE WAY OF DEALING WITH FELINE FRIENDS

I sucked my lacerated finger. In the fullness of time you'll find out what had caused the trauma. Suffice it to say for the moment, finger notwithstanding, on the day in question O'Reilly and I had finished our house calls, tending to the bedridden, the bewildered, and those too bloody bolshie to come to the surgery.

"Maggie's next," he said. "I need her advice about the new kitten."

I felt the throbbing in my wounded digit and thought unkindly of cats and with some affection of Maggie, spinster of this parish, one of nature's unclaimed treasures, the old duck with, as we say in the mind-healing trade, a bolt loose. Maggie was definitely one stook short of a stack, but she was a gentle soul and O'Reilly had a soft spot for her.

"I'm sure she'll know what to do." He fired up his briar inside the car, the clouds of smoke giving me a fair impression of the last minutes of the poor benighted in one of the humanitarian American states that still favour the gas chamber. I opened the window and as the sulphurous fumes escaped, hauled in a lungful of clean air. I swear rows of barley withered.

"Haven't seen her for a few weeks," he remarked cheerfully, accelerating and paying no attention to a cycling peasant taking refuge in the ditch.

I should tell you that about once a month, if we'd had an easy afternoon making house calls, Doctor O. would drop by to see how Maggie was getting on. The vitamin pills that he'd told her to swallow ten minutes before the start of the headaches two inches above the top of her head had cured that particular problem.

She rarely needed medical attention. It was simply a mark of the man. He actually cared about his patients, although to have suggested such a thing to his face would have produced a rumble like Vesuvius on an off day and a pallid hue to his nose tip that would have made Greenland's icy mountains look like ebony.

We arrived at her cottage and left the car.

O'Reilly knocked on the door. Maggie answered, smiled, and asked us in.

"How are you, Maggie?" he inquired.

"Grand, Doctor."

"And how's Montgomery?"

I knew from previous visits that he was referring to Maggie's ginger tomcat. She'd named the animal "General Montgomery" in deference to Sir Bernard Law of the same name, victor of El Alamein, the man who Churchill described as being "In defeat — indefatigable; in victory — insufferable."

The pussy in question appeared from behind a sofa. He rubbed against O'Reilly's leg. Doctor O. bent and tickled the animal's head.

"He's pleased to see you, Doctor O'Reilly."

Maggie's Montgomery looked as though he'd also taken part in the desert triumph of British arms and had been as badly used by the Afrika Korps as a Sherman tank after a debate with one of the Wehrmacht's antitank 88s. His left ear was a fragment of cartilage and his right eye scarred and shut. Some contenders who'd had encounters with Joe Louis had similar miens.

"He's looking well, Maggie," O'Reilly said.

I confess I've never been able to find any particular enthusiasm for moggies, particularly — my finger ached — at that moment, but O'Reilly doted on them and his rambling old house was a regular Doctor Barnardo's for waifs and strays of the feline persuasion.

"I wanted to ask you about that," O'Reilly said.

"What, Doctor?"

"I've a new kitten."

Indeed he had. A cross between a Siamese and a rabid tiger. If anything moved in the house, like an unsuspecting finger, the kitten would pounce. The damn animal had nailed me this morning and cost me so much blood I suspected I was suffering from anaemia.

"It claws the furniture," Doctor O'Reilly said.

I felt somewhat resentful to be considered part of the furniture. (This was before the days when heads of committees were called "chairs.") I also had a clear image of O'Reilly's sofa leaking kapok stuffing stained with my gore.

"Ah sure that's no problem, Doctor." Maggie smiled. "Montgomery had the same habit. Hang on." She trotted off and returned carrying a strange device. "Get him one of these scratching posts."

It was a cylinder of wood, five inches in

diameter, two feet tall, swathed in a strip of old carpet and mounted on a square plywood base.

O'Reilly stared at the device. "That thing worked for Montgomery?"

I looked around. General Montgomery cowered under the table, one paw over his tattered ear. He made a whining noise that clearly belied his warlike appellation. His good eye was fixed on the post.

"Indeed it did, Doctor. The first time he clawed my chair I got this post, didn't I, Montgomery?"

Montgomery's whining went up two octaves.

"And you put it by the chair and the wee pussy clawed it instead of the chair?" O'Reilly was clearly impressed by the simplicity of the solution.

Maggie chortled. "Not at all, Doctor." She looked at the cat and waved the post in his direction. "I belted him on the head with it."

Montgomery fled. And my finger felt much better.

O'Reilly at the Helm

Things That Go
Bump in the Daytime

"Like the back of my hand," O'Reilly remarked as he sat comfortably on the weather side of his sloop, tiller held loosely. "Been sailing these seas for years."

I was tempted to remark that Captain John Smith had made many crossings of the Atlantic before he had a close encounter of the lethal kind with a large lump of solidified water. His tiny navigational oversight did little for the hull of the RMS *Titanic* or for the reputation of the Belfast shipbuilders who'd constructed the ocean-going leviathan. I comforted myself with the thoughts that O'Reilly's vessel was a tad smaller than the great liner and that icebergs were passing rare in Strangford Lough. Nevertheless I did offer him the chart.

"Don't be daft," he said. "I don't need that thing."

173

I stowed the results of years of painstaking depth sounding by the survey crews of Her Majesty's cartographers and let myself be lulled by the day.

I confess that as usual I'd agreed with reluctance to crew for the twentieth century's answer to that old Irish seaman, Saint Brendan the Navigator. If you remember, Saint B. had nipped out for a day's boating in a craft constructed of tarred cowhides, taken a wrong turn at St. Kilda, and but for fortuitously running into Newfoundland might have beaten Marco Polo to China by nipping round the back way.

It did seem that my reluctance had been ill-founded. It was a perfect afternoon. The sun shone from an azure sky. A ten-knot breeze filled O'Reilly's sails and pushed the boat along at a steady five knots. The multitude of islands that dotted the lough were like green jewels in a porcelain sea. God was in his heaven, all was right with the world, O'Reilly was at the helm and, as he'd recently remarked, he knew these seas like the back of his hand. I hoped.

"Warm," he said, inclining his head toward the companionway.

A wink is as good as a nod to a visually challenged equine.

"Beer?" I asked.

"Um," he said.

"Aye aye, Skipper." Nautical, I thought, very nautical. I rose and surveyed the lough. Open water for miles. Not a hazard to navigation in sight — except — I noticed a tower close on the lee bow. It was just visible round the corner of the headsail. I'd seen pictures of the seventh wonder of the ancient world, Ptolemy's lighthouse at Alexandria. The local construction in question seemed to be of roughly similar dimensions. It stood out in splendid isolation miles from any other indication of shallows. "Fingal, there seems to be a marker ahead."

" 'Course there bloody well is. It's the light on Danger Reef."

"Sorry." I'd forgotten that he knew these waters like the dorsal surface of his paw.

"It's warm!" he growled.

I knew that when O'Reilly had his mind set on liquid refreshment, those who kept him from his heart's desire ashore could become the recipients of a tongue-lashing. Afloat, keelhauling would probably be the order of the day. The lighthouse seemed to be drawing nearer. It cast a long dark shadow over the surface. Still, he knew these waters . . . but you already know that.

I slipped below, opened the icebox, and was deafened by a crash like the opening salvo at the away game on the Somme in 1916. I was still travelling at five knots. Apparently the boat wasn't.

After I'd disentangled myself from the forward berth and looked with some amazement at the bruise that was rapidly growing on my left shin, I noticed that our gentle heel to starboard had become alarmingly acute. For reasons that I cannot quite explain, a line or two from a poem I'd had to learn at school came into my head:

The vessel strikes with a shivering shock.
Oh, heavens, 'tis the Inchcape rock.

I struggled up the companionway. O'Reilly must have learned the same ode, which, as I recollect, continued:

Sir Ralph the Rover tore his hair
And cursed himself in his despair.

Doctor O. was giving a pretty fair Sir Ralph impersonation: "#**@**#ing Danger Reef."

We were hard aground, and O'Reilly's pride, like my shin, was badly bruised. I thought it might be impolitic to inquire whether some local magnetic anomaly had jinxed his retro-manual aid to navigation, and instead sought for words of comfort.

Off our bow the lighthouse towered.

"I see," I ventured. "The lighthouse blocked your view of the shoals."

Concern for younger and more sensitive readers prohibits me from printing his reply.

O'Reilly Strikes Back

It Was Worth the Wait

I was back home in the North of Ireland a few summers ago, and I paid a visit to my old mentor, Doctor Fingal Flahertie O'Reilly. I rang the brass front-door bell of his home-cum-surgery. You'll remember that the very first time I'd depressed that particular bell push the door had flown open and a giant of a man had hurled a small supplicant into a rosebush and roared, "Next time you want me to look at your ankle, wash your bloody feet."

This time I reflexively stepped back. I had no wish to be thumped by a human projectile. You may think I was overreacting. Lightning, it's said, never strikes twice. I wasn't worried about lightning. Those of you who study proverbs, saws, adages, and assorted folk wisdom won't have encountered the gem "O'Reilly never strikes twice." That's because he does. Bear with me and

I'll explain.

The door opened.

"Good God," he said. "You?"

"Me," I replied. I wasn't going to claim to be the benevolent deity.

"Good God."

"I'm not exactly."

"You're not exactly what?"

"God."

"Taylor, I was well aware of what you were not when you worked with me." He looked me up and down with a gaze as piercing as an oversensitive metal detector in a Canadian airport. "I see no reason to alter that opinion."

Nor had O'Reilly changed. Tweed sports jacket that fitted his massive frame only where it touched, pipe ashes on his badly knotted tie, florid cheeks, and, heavens be praised, not a trace of pallor in the tip of his boxer's bent proboscis.

"Don't stand there with both legs the same length," he rumbled. "Come in." He grasped my hand and exerted the kind of pressure that will ultimately cause the San Andreas Fault to let go. I felt a personal tectonic shift of metacarpals and comforted myself with the thought that now my right hand was two inches wide and more than a foot long there could be no doubt that my future as a gynaecologist was assured.

"How are you, Fingal?"

He grunted and made his way into the dining room.

I followed.

"What time is it?" he asked.

"Eleven."

"Not in Moscow."

"Moscow?"

"Moscow."

Perhaps I'd misjudged him. Perhaps he had changed. Perhaps he was starting to dote.

"Why Moscow, Fingal?"

"Because, you idiot, I never take a drop until the sun's over the yardarm."

"I didn't know Moscow had yardarms."

By the look in his eyes, if chez O'Reilly had been so equipped I'd have been dangling from it. "It hasn't but it's after noon there. No reason why we shouldn't have a tot here. Sherry?" He handed me a cut-glass version of a fire bucket. "Better," he said, demolishing half his own whiskey in one swallow and lowering his frame onto a chair. "Have a pew."

I obeyed.

"Now," he said. "Tell me what you've been up to."

I was happy to ramble on about my life in

what I thought of as Canada and he kept dismissing as "the colonies." We must have chatted for twenty minutes before I was able to inquire about his doings. For the first time in all the years I'd known O'Reilly I saw a genuine sadness in his eyes.

He sighed. "I'm retired. Have been for two years."

To think of medicine without O'Reilly was difficult. The thought of O'Reilly without his practising medicine verged on the incomprehensible.

"Good God," I said.

"Not exactly."

"Not exactly what?"

"God," he said, and chuckled.

He'd not lost his sense of humour. I found myself laughing with him.

"So what are you up to?"

He leaned back in his chair, cocked his head on one side, and said, "I'm a student."

"Good God!"

"Don't start."

"Sorry. It just slipped out. What are you studying?" I'd forgotten that he was a self-taught classical scholar.

There was a pride in his voice when he said, "I'm finishing my second year. Doing a BA in classical literature."

I was impressed. "I don't suppose there

are many retired doctors in your faculty?"

O'Reilly guffawed. "You're wrong. Remember Sir Gervaise Grant?"

I had to delve back, but it came to me. Sir Gervaise had, years ago, called O'Reilly "an underqualified country quack." With the connivance of the dean, an old rugby-playing friend, O'Reilly had spoiled the senior gynaecologist's week by arranging for him to receive a pathology report in which appeared the line, "The specimen of ureter submitted showed no sign of abnormality."

"I do indeed. I had a half-notion you weren't too fond of Sir Gervaise."

"Stuck-up bugger. I got him with the path report." O'Reilly gazed happily into the middle distance. "He's retired and reading classics too. In his first year."

"Good . . . gracious."

"Mmm," said O'Reilly, sipping at his Jameson's. "I hadn't forgotten what he called me but I don't have to worry about that now."

"Because you're both retired?"

O'Reilly shook his head and said with deep sincerity, "You remember what a class-conscious snob he was?"

I nodded.

"I've put him in his box."

"How?"

"He came up to me all sweetness and light on the first day of term this year. 'Splendid to see you, O'Reilly,' says he. I gave him a cold look. 'Go away,' says I. 'Second-year students never — never — *never* speak to mere freshmen.' "

Lightning may only strike twice. In top form O'Reilly could strike and go on striking with all the venom of a rattlesnake with grand mal.

"Good God," I said.

"No," said O'Reilly, "but I outrank Sir Gervaise."

A WORD TO THE WISE

O'REILLY WAITS FOR A BUS

You may remember that Doctor Fingal Flahertie O'Reilly's method of practising medicine was a trifle unorthodox. But I'm indulging in understatement. Doctor O'Reilly's approach to life, the world, and the entire cosmos was unorthodox — and there was nothing trifling about him. He didn't suffer fools gladly and detested being bested in any verbal joust. He rarely was.

When affronted by a lesser mortal, and that definition as far as he was concerned encompassed the rest of the human race, he could use his words with the force of one of King Arthur's boiler-plate-encased knights. I'm sure you've seen them on the cinema screen, happily delivering caresses with a spiked cannonball on a chain to the helmeted dome of an opponent.

One of O'Reilly's ripostes was less of a rapier thrust than the spoken equivalent of being hit with a mace and trampled by a war-horse simultaneously. The fundamental difference between Good King A.'s round-table mob and O'Reilly was that the former lived by a chivalrous code of honour while O'Reilly belonged to the head-butt, knee-him-in-the-groin, pull-his-lungs-out-through-his-nose school of combat.

He had to. The citizens of Northern Ireland, and particularly the denizens of Belfast, are no mean contestants when it comes to a bit of the old jocular thrust and parry. The "Good Book" says, "The gentle word turneth away the blow." Judging by the number of victims of grievous bodily harm I used to encounter in the ER on Saturday nights after chucking-out time from the pubs, either the Belfast men hadn't appreciated the scriptures or were a bit short in the "gentle word" department.

I ask that you try to recall this informa-tion while I illustrate how O'Reilly could with one carefully chosen sentence demol-ish a self-styled humorist who tried to raise a giggle at O'Reilly's expense.

For reasons that are lost to me I found myself in the Belfast city centre in the company of O'Reilly. We seemed to have walked for miles. He was slightly in the lead and for that I was grateful. I'm small and dislike being jostled by passersby. O'Reilly's progress, in a beeline, parted the throng with all the efficiency of Moses at the Red Sea. Of course both the well-known old Israelite and O'Reilly were highly motivated. Moses had Pharaoh's seventh cavalry hot on his heels. O'Reilly wanted a drink.

"Get a move on, Taylor."

I hurried to keep up.

"Not far now." O'Reilly stopped at a bus stop. A queue of would-be passengers stood waiting to be granted admission to the red omnibus parked at the curb. "We'll take the bus back to where I left the car."

I had mixed feelings. Relief that we wouldn't have to walk back mixed with some minor concerns — the kind of vague worries experienced by the mayor of Hiroshima when he heard the *Enola Gay* was on its way — about being driven home by a somewhat befuddled O'Reilly.

"Now?" I said, hope springing eternal that he might forgo his libation.

"No, you idiot. After we've had a tot."

"Oh," I said, bowing to the inevitable. "When does the bus go?"

"No idea. I'll ask." With that he strode to the head of the queue. Line jumping was frowned upon in Belfast. O'Reilly ignored the insubordinate chorus of muttering that arose from the line jumpees, who began to form a scrum around the jumper.

"My good man," he roared at the blue-uniformed bus conductor, "how long is the next bus?"

O'Reilly's syntax left a certain amount to be desired. I knew he wished to inquire, "How long will it be until the departure of the next public-transport vehicle?"

So, clearly, did the bus conductor, but he'd been given an opportunity that none of his ilk could ignore: an unpopular line jumper, a potentially appreciative crowd, and an ambiguous question. He grasped the metal pole that ran from the floor to the ceiling of the bus's rear platform, swung slightly outward, grinned, looked out over the waiting mob, and said, scorn dripping from his lips like oil from a cracked crankcase, "Fifty-two feet. Same as this one."

I believe the expression used by sports commentators when a goal has been scored is "The crowd roared." It did.

O'Reilly's nose paled. He let the laughter subside, fixed the conductor with a glare the intensity of one of those laser lances that safe-crackers use to cut through tungsten-carbide-toughened steel, and said, "Thank you."

I was amazed. I'd expected bile laced with

sulphuric acid.

He half-turned away, hesitated, turned back, and said in a deceptively level voice that could be heard all the way to the back of the waiting passengers, "And will that one have a monkey in a blue uniform swinging round the pole too?"

DOG DAYS OF WINTER

THE CASE OF THE LEG-LOVING LABRADOR

Normally I like dogs, but I'm prepared to make exceptions. Let me explain — but first let me give you the background. Did I tell you that Doctor Fingal Flahertie O'Reilly was a keen shot? I found it difficult to approve of his pastime. After all, what had a duck ever done to him? Besides, I often found myself taking call at peculiar hours on my days off — either pre- and post-dawn or before and after dusk — so he could slip away to fire feverishly at his feathered friends.

Ducks, it seems, are creatures of habit and fly inland to feed at night and back out to sea during the day. They reverse the process in the gloaming. At these times wildfowlers park themselves on the shoreline, like the heavy flak of occupied Europe during the last global unpleasantness, and blaze away at the unsuspecting avians with all the enthusiasm of a regiment of Luftwaffe anti-aircraft gunners at a squadron of Lancaster bombers. The only difference is that the ducks can't shoot back.

I'm giving you this information because his hobby was the reason O'Reilly had another member of his household. One I've neglected to tell you about before. Arthur Guinness wasn't the patriarch of the famous family of Dublin brewers but a large black Labrador dog, O'Reilly's constant companion on his murky missions of mayhem against mild-mannered mallard.

Arthur had all the attributes of his breed: gentleness, playfulness, boundless enthusiasm, and, I suspected, a willingness to be trained, if O'Reilly had had the slightest notion of how to teach an animal. He didn't. One word from Fingal and Arthur did exactly as he pleased.

One thing that pleased him enormously was my trousered leg. No matter where we were, as soon as I hove into view Arthur would greet me with a joyful "Arf," rear up, and clasp me to him. Front paws round my thigh, grinning as only Labradors can, he would bash away at my shin like one of those automatic rivet guns. It was a miracle that I didn't give birth to a litter of Labrador puppies with corduroy coats.

I did say I could make exceptions to my generally pleasant feelings toward the genus Canis.

Another of Arthur's little pleasures was his pint. It seemed that some years previously he'd accompanied O'Reilly into the Mucky Duck, his usual stop for a glass of revivification after huddling on the chilled foreshore. On that particular post-hunting foray, someone had spilled a glass of bitter on the floor and Arthur had lapped it up with the speed of a commercial vacuum cleaner. From that moment the dog had been hooked.

I apologize for taking so long filling in the background, but bear with me. It's all germane.

I was sitting in the surgery at nine o'clock on a December evening. I wasn't in the best of moods but was in my best suit. I was dressed up because I'd planned to take a certain young nurse out to dinner. I was cast down because O'Reilly had pleaded with me to look after the shop.

It seemed that the wind and tide conditions were so ideal that he might have the best evening's shooting of his life. To deprive him of the opportunity would have been more cruel than Pharaoh's refusal to let the

Israelites set off on a package tour of the Sinai Desert. He promised he'd be back by eight. I hadn't had the heart to refuse his entreaties and I could still see my nurse if he kept his word.

By nine, having just sewn up a lacerated finger when I might have been gazing over a glass of Beaujolais into a pair of marvellously brown eyes, I hoped that his bloody shotgun had exploded.

It hadn't.

The door opened. O'Reilly stuck his head round.

"I'm back."

I grunted.

"Sorry I'm a bit late."

"Very late."

"Come on, Pat, I had a flat tire."

I let a silence hang, the kind that psychology research workers achieve in sensory-deprivation chambers.

He had the good grace to look sheepish. "Look. I really am sorry. I came straight home. I didn't even stop for a drop in the Duck."

Perhaps it wasn't his fault and his sacrifice of his usual post-wildfowling tot was a measure of his contrition.

"All right, Fingal." I managed a weak smile.

"Good lad." He beamed. "I'll make it up to you. Come on, I'll buy you a jar."

Why not? I had no other plans for the evening now.

"Fine." I rose and followed O'Reilly into the hall.

"Arf." A muddy Arthur Guinness, who must have accompanied his master, greeted me with enthusiasm.

I watched him eying my brand-new trouser legs and prepared to fend off his amatory advances.

"Hang on to Arthur, Fingal."

"What? Right." O'Reilly grabbed the dog by the collar and the three of us set off for the Duck.

Osbaldiston was behind the bar and what's known in Ireland as "the usual suspects" were in their accustomed places.

"Evening, Doctors," mine host remarked. "The usual?"

"Aye," said O'Reilly and planked himself down at a vacant table. I followed suit and Arthur Guinness tucked himself in by O'Reilly's feet. At least he seemed to have lost interest in my pants.

Osbaldiston waddled over, put a whiskey in front of O'Reilly, a small sherry before me, and set a bowl of best bitter on the floor. Arthur Guinness gave a fair impression of the tattered cartoon character leaving the desert and arriving at the oasis. He was the only living creature that could sink a pint faster than Fingal or who had a similar capacity.

By my count Arthur had consumed half a gallon before we left. He was only a bit shaky on his pins but his perpetual grin was even more lopsided. I was heartily relieved that his inebriation had definitely dampened his amorous ardour. My new pants were safe.

At least they were until we stopped and waited to cross the road. Arthur must have mistaken my leg for a lamppost. I could have killed him.

IN A PIG'S EAR

WHAT A BOAR

"What," inquired Doctor Fingal Flahertie
O'Reilly, "do you know about pigs?"

I stopped in my tracks. *Déjà vu.* We'd had
this conversation before, six months previously, when the question had reared its ugly
head about the fecundity of the publican
Arthur Osbaldiston's sow.

"Absolutely nothing. Don't you remember?"

"Pity."

"I agree. It is a pity you don't remember."

He grimaced. "No, idiot. It's a pity you
don't know anything about pigs."

"Why is it a pity, for God's sake?" I was
feeling a tad exasperated.

"Because," he said, pointing vaguely
across the field we were crossing, "there's
one coming."

I glanced over my shoulder. He was right.

I should tell you that we were making a

house call. One of his patients, Dermot Kennedy by name, lived on a small farm on the outskirts of the village. The lane was so rutted that O'Reilly had simply abandoned the car, opened a five-barred gate, and announced, "We'll take a shortcut through the fields." And so we did.

The grass was knee-deep, dew-bespangled, and absolutely perfect for ensuring that my remaining pair of trousers was sodden. (My other pair was at the dry cleaner's after O'Reilly's alcoholic Labrador, Arthur Guinness, had mistaken me for a lamppost.) The joys, I thought, of rural practice.

And it seemed that those joys were to be multiplied.

"It's coming this way," O'Reilly muttered, lengthening his stride.

I chanced another look. I wasn't even sure that the brute in question was a pig. It seemed to me to be about the size of a well-nourished hippopotamus, moved with the same rolling gait, and was indeed heading in our direction. It was a healthy pink colour, except for a pair of very red and rather malevolent-looking eyes, and hippopotami were exceeding rare in the fields of Ulster.

"It is a pig," I said, more to myself.

196

"Brilliant. I didn't realize you were an experienced zoologist." O'Reilly's walk changed to a canter and I modified my steps to match his, wondering what all the unseemly hurry was about.

"I read somewhere that domesticated boars can turn ugly," he said. He seemed rather short of breath.

I chanced another glance behind, forgetting that such errors have been known to cost Olympic sprinters the gold medal. Our porcine pursuer had no distance to go to live up to O'Reilly's description if my mentor had been alluding to physical appearance. It also had narrowed the gap between two perspiring physicians and itself.

"Ugly?" I asked.

"Right." Puff. "Bloody big teeth." O'Reilly's canter moved through the gears to a fully developed gallop.

He was right about boars' teeth and, more to the point, O'Reilly was opening a respectable distance between me and his rapidly departing back. It dawned on me that if the boar astern had any intentions of using its "bloody big teeth" on the intruders in its territory it would settle for the closest to hand — and that was me.

I've heard that a small man, in the heat of adrenaline-driven action, can single-handedly lift an overturned motorcar. As I passed O'Reilly I was covering the turf at a rate that would have beaten Roger Bannister to the four-minute mile. The boar's hoof-beats drew nearer. My only consolation was that O'Reilly was a big man and it would take the animal some time to devour him. I imagine early Christians felt much the same about plumper members of their groups when the lions entered the Circus Maximus.

I was even luckier than a skinny Christian. I had a way out. I was drawing nearer to the far side of the field. I went over the gate like a steeple-chaser at the Grand National and nearly collided with a man who stood in the farmyard. I just had time to notice that the onlooker wore a flat tweed cap on his head and a bemused grin, confused by a ferocious squint on his face.

The quiet of the afternoon was broken only by my heavy breathing and a crashing, rending noise as O'Reilly burst through the blackthorn hedge like a Sherman tank in the Bocage country of Normandy.

I watched as he took several deep breaths, examined the rents in his jacket, and made an heroic effort to regain his dignity. He stumped over to the cloth-capped stranger. Despite his recent exertions, O'Reilly's nose tip was ivory. "Dermot Kennedy," O'Reilly bellowed, "what the hell is so funny?"

Mister Kennedy was unable to answer. He was doubled over and laughing like a drain.

"Jasus, Kennedy." I thought O'Reilly was going to burst. "Jasus, Kennedy, you've a man-eating boar in that field. We've just escaped by the skin of our teeth. How in the name of the wee man can you laugh?"

Mister Kennedy straightened up, gathered himself, and said, "She's not a boar. That's Gertrude, the kids' pet sow. She just wanted her snout scratched."

I made a quick preemptive strike. "I told you, Fingal. I don't know anything about pigs."

ARTHUR AND THE GENERAL

"I'M AS HELPLESS AS A KITTEN UP A TREE"

"Quick, Pat," said O'Reilly. "Take Arthur Guinness inside the house."

"Why?" I asked, looking at O'Reilly's black Labrador, who was making a peculiar ululation and staring intently upward into the boughs of the big sycamore tree that grew at the bottom of O'Reilly's back garden.

"Don't ask, just do it like a good lad. Maggie's coming."

"Oh," I said, reaching for Arthur's collar and wondering why O'Reilly wouldn't want Maggie MacCorkle, she of the supracranial headaches, to see his dog. "Right." I'd been impressed as a child when shown a picture of a statue of the Greek mythological figure Lacoön wrestling with two enormous snakes. I achieved a deeper understanding of the old boy's difficulties when I tried to persuade Arthur Guinness to go where he did not wish. Little boys may be made of "snaps and snails and puppy dogs' tails," but adolescent Labradors are constructed from high-tensile steel springs. I pulled in the general direction of the back door to O'Reilly's house. Arthur dug in his heels, cranked up the volume of his yodelling, and stared straight up.

My gaze followed his and I wondered what up the tree had captured the dog's undivided attention. There was something just visible in a fork of a high branch. The something was orange-coloured and bore a striking resemblance to — Maggie's ginger tomcat, General Montgomery.

All was revealed unto me. With the exception of O'Reilly's furniture-clawing kitten, all cats were anathema to Arthur G. It was almost certainly his fault that General Montgomery was up the tree, and that would explain why O'Reilly wanted the dog out of sight when Maggie arrived.

The least I could do was accommodate my mentor. Besides, I wanted to see what would happen when Maggie discovered the whereabouts of her perpendicularly placed pussycat.

"Come on, Guinness." By dint of super-human effort I managed to haul the black dog along the path and shove him inside the house. He wasn't happy to be incarcerated and expressed his dissatisfaction by hurling himself against the closed door.

I ignored the dog and headed back. My return to the scene of the action coincided with Maggie's arrival. Now that Guinness was offstage, a semblance of quiet had returned, punctuated only by an intermittent yowling from above.

"Evening, Maggie," I heard O'Reilly say.

"Evening, Doctor," Maggie replied, craning her neck and staring upward. "Jesus, Mary, and Joseph. Is that you, General? Is that where you are? I've been looking for you. How did you ever get up there?"

I saw O'Reilly blush and was convinced that my original supposition that the General had been chased up the tree by Arthur Guinness was correct. Fortunately the cat didn't speak English and couldn't give O'Reilly away.

"Will you not come down now?" Maggie said and made "push-wushing" noises. O'Reilly said nothing and the General gave a fair impression of an air-raid siren. He budged not an inch. In both his colour and his lack of locomotion he could have passed for an Ulster Orangeman whose motto is "Not an Inch."

"What'll we do, Doctor?" Maggie implored.

I saw what was coming next and launched a preemptive strike. "It's a pity about my acrophobia, Maggie," I said gravely, adding both for her benefit and for O'Reilly's, "I've a terrible fear of high places."

I could see by the pallor creeping into O'Reilly's nose tip that I'd been right again. He had been going to suggest that I climb the tree. It was his dog that had put the cat there. As far as I was concerned, natural justice demanded that O'Reilly get it down.

General Montgomery yowled. Maggie sniffed. I waited.

"All right now, Maggie." O'Reilly shrugged off his jacket and handed it to me. "Don't you fret." He hauled himself onto the lowest bough. His upward progress reminded me of a nature film I'd once seen of a three-toed sloth as it made its hesitant, ponderous way through the jungle. All O'Reilly needed was a bit more hair.

His nose drew level with the General's perch. I heard the cat spit and O'Reilly's expletive as claws raked his schnozzle. Perhaps my moving well away from the base of the tree reflected a degree of cowardice but I had no desire to be underneath if O'Reilly lost his hold.

I was impressed by his skilful descent, the General tucked like a rugby ball under one arm. He reached the ground, offered the cat to Maggie, shot me a look of utter disdain, and rubbed the back of his hand over his bloody nose. "Here you are, Maggie. Now don't let General Montgomery go up any more trees."

"I won't, Doctor."

I'm sure Maggie meant it. It was a pity that at that moment Mrs. Kincaid opened the back door to yell, "There's a phone call for you, Doctor Taylor."

My last picture as I went inside to take the call was of a happy Arthur Guinness at the tree's foot and the tweed-covered backside of O'Reilly as he ascended on his second mission of mercy.

SOMETHING HAPPENED

ARTHUR GUINNESS HAS
A RUN-IN WITH THE LAW

I'd been away from the practice for a week and had returned just in time to help O'Reilly with a busy morning's surgery. I didn't have the opportunity to ask him to bring me up to date on the doings in the village of Ballybucklebo. I hoped he'd fill me in over lunch, but after the last patient of the morning departed, O'Reilly wanted to make a house call, on foot, to a nearby cottage. I decided to accompany him.

It was a glorious June mid-morning, a grand day for a walk, and after the bustle of Belfast I was enjoying the relative tranquillity of Ballybucklebo's only street. As we walked I surmised that it was unlikely that gold had been found in Jimmy Ferguson's manure heap or that Maggie MacCorkle had won the Miss Ireland beauty pageant during my absence. Nothing much ever happened in the place. I knew that.

As usual, I was wrong.

"Jasus," said O'Reilly, staring straight ahead.

My gaze followed his and I saw approaching us the portly figure of Police Constable Michael McGillicuddy, Royal Ulster Constabulary, sole uniformed upholder of *Lex Britannicus* in the village and the surrounding townlands.

I knew that O'Reilly's opinion of PC McGillicuddy, RUC, was rather to the south of contempt. As I remembered, there was something about one of Lord Fitzgurgle's pheasants that had found its way into the backseat of O'Reilly's car — all unknown to his lordship or his gamekeeper — and a debate between the chubby arm of the law and the local representative of *Hygeiea* and *Panacea* surrounding the ownership of that deceased member of the family *Phaisanus versicolour.*

My musing was interrupted by O'Reilly muttering, "Bloody dog."

I assumed he was referring to Arthur Guinness, but before I had time to inquire, O'Reilly stopped walking and I was forced to follow suit. Our progress was blocked by PC M. McG., RUC.

"Morning, Doctors."

206

"Morning, Officer," I replied. It has always struck me as sensible to keep on the good sides of policemen, parking wardens, gamekeepers, water bailiffs, and such. I didn't expect O'Reilly to do more than grunt, given his known opinion of the constable in particular and the rest of the human race in general. As you well know, Doctor Fingal Flahertie O'Reilly treated few people with respect, let alone deference.

I imagine Catherine the Great, or "Big Katy" as she would have been called in Northern Ireland, had a similar approach to the citizens of Mother Russia. *"Rodina,"* I believe, is the correct term in Russian for the place — but you probably didn't want to know that. Anyway, Big Katy would condescend to peasant and archduke alike. They in turn would grovel to her.

She had a bit of an edge over O'Reilly. Although almost every citizen of Ballybucklebo and its environs did metaphorically tug their forelocks to their physician, he didn't have the right to order them shot if they did not. And I know that in his heart he believed he should have that prerogative.

It was with those thoughts running through my mind that I watched in amazement as he smiled, inclined his head, touched the peak of his cap with the fingers

of his right hand, wished Constable McGillicuddy a very good morning, and inquired
about his health.

"I'm grand, Doctor," replied the constable. "Grand altogether."

"Good," said O'Reilly. "Very good. Well.
Must be off. Duty calls." He sidled past
McGillicuddy and I followed. What on earth
could have happened to reduce O'Reilly to
such a pacific state?

"Bloody dog," he grunted as he strode
along.

"Arthur?"

"Arthur."

"More cats in trees?"

O'Reilly shook his head. "Worse." He
stopped dead. I halted. Fingal turned to
face me. "I had a burglar."

"My God." Something had happened in
my absence.

"Indeed. Some misbegotten nitwit broke
into my place. Arthur's meant to be a
watchdog." O'Reilly snorted. "Bloody animal must have nearly beaten the intruder to
death with his tail. Flaming dog didn't even
bark, never mind tear the man's throat out."

I had no difficulty believing that. Arthur
Guinness, apart from an unrequited passion
for my trouser leg, was the gentlest dog in
Ireland.

"What was taken?" I asked.

O'Reilly shrugged. "Couple of bottles of whiskey. Not much, but I thought I should at least make our local Sherlock Holmes earn his wages, so I telephoned him."

Aha, I thought, and McGillicuddy had apprehended the villain and recovered O'Reilly's whiskey. That would explain his recent civility.

"Bloody dog," he said.

"Why?" I asked. "Arthur's a retriever, not a Rottweiler. You can hardly blame him for not going for the burglar."

"Burglar? Burglar?" O'Reilly shook his head. "I would forgive him that, but just now you saw me being nice to McGillicuddy."

"Because he got your whiskey back."

"I wish," said O'Reilly. "I have to be nice to the constable because, after neglecting to deal with my burglar, do you know what was the first thing Arthur-bloody-Guinness did when McGillicuddy arrived?"

I shook my head and saw O'Reilly's brows knit and his nose tip pale. "Arthur-bloody-Guinness bit McGillicuddy."

I had difficulty stifling a laugh, which, if the look on O'Reilly's face was anything to go by, would have been as appropriate as a snigger at a funeral.

To my surprise O'Reilly himself was starting to smile. "Still," he said, turning to stare at the constable's retreating back, "old Arthur G. does have impeccable taste."

HELL ON WHEELS

DONAL DONNELLY AND HIS
VENERABLE VELOCIPEDE

I was walking along the street on my way to make a house call. O'Reilly was taking morning surgery. My forward progress was blocked by Donal Donnelly, who clearly wanted my opinion. "It's a beauty, isn't it, Doctor Taylor, sir?" he asked.

You'll recall Donal, a gangly youth who occasionally worked as an itinerant barman at Lord Fitzgurgle's soirees. You can't place him? Not surprising, really. Donal had once been described by Kinky — O'Reilly's housekeeper — as "an unpredisposing sort of a kind of a man." He was. Utterly unpredisposing. There's no reason why you should remember him.

Cast your mind back to the time Donal stalled his father's tractor at the village's only traffic light. That was when O'Reilly, stuck behind as the light kept changing col-

211

ours, left his car, walked up to the tractor, and asked a terrified Donal if he was waiting for a particular shade of green.

Got him now? Right. Twenty-three, four foot ten, ninety-one pounds, ginger hair, a squint, buck teeth that were the envy of the local hares, and a tendency to acneiform eruptions.

You're probably wondering why I'm spending so long getting you up to speed on the physical characteristics of Donal Donnelly. You may even have forgotten his opening remarks: "It's a beauty, isn't it, Doctor Taylor, sir?"

The "it" in question was a Raleigh bicycle. Donal stood beside it holding on to the handlebars, beaming at the elderly velocipede with all the pride of a new mother looking into her pram.

"Indeed, Donal." The white lie was invented for these situations. "Beauty" and Donal's 'cycle could only occupy the same sentence when ice skates are sold in Hades, but Donal was a gentle soul and if he wanted me to admire his new possession I saw no reason not to.

I gazed at the machine. Once it had been black. There were flakes of enamel scattered over the uniform patina of rust that covered the frame. It was the woman's model. Men's bikes had a crossbar that ran horizontally from the front wheel-forks to the saddle post. On the woman's model, the bars dipped from the fork to the bit where the pedals are attached. The arrangement was a hangover from the time women wore voluminous skirts. Real men — the non-quiche-eating types — wouldn't have been caught dead on a woman's bike.

"It only cost me thirty bob," Donal said.

"You stole it." I couldn't bring myself to tell Donal that he might have made a reasonable bargain if the previous owner had paid him thirty shillings to take the thing away.

"Just you wait until I've fixed her up a bit, Doctor." He pushed the lever that should have activated the handlebar-mounted bell. There was no "ting," just a rusty grinding noise. "Just you wait."

"I'll do that," I said, glancing at my watch, "but I'd best be getting on now, Donal."

He touched the peak of his cloth cap and we parted. I confess I thought little of Donal Donnelly and his bike for several months.

The next time I saw the bike it was propped against the side of O'Reilly's house. I didn't recognize it at first as Donal's. He had indeed "fixed it up a bit." The rust had been sandpapered away and the frame painted a screaming primrose yellow. A chrome-plated bell was fixed to the right handlebar. The mudguards' lime green shone in the morning sunlight. Every spoke had been tinted scarlet. This, it must be remembered, was before LSD and the psychedelic movement. I was so engrossed I didn't notice Donal and O'Reilly approaching.

"Morning, Doctor Taylor." I turned and saw Donal grinning from ear to ear. "Told you I'd fix her up." He laid one hand on the saddle. "And Doctor O'Reilly says I can keep her." The relief in his voice was palpable. "That's right, isn't it, sir?"

"Indeed it is, Donal." I could see O'Reilly was struggling to keep a straight face.

"That's good," I mumbled, wondering what that last remark meant. I watched Donal cycle away with all the dignity of the maharajah of Ponderistan in his state barouche, then turned to O'Reilly, who was now laughing openly.

"Oh, dear," he said, "poor Donal." A frown crossed O'Reilly's craggy visage. "That bloody man the Reverend McWheezle should have known better."

"Pardon?"

"Donal's getting married."

"Never. Who to?"

"Maggie MacCorkle's niece, Martha, and the pair of them went to McWheezle for a bit of a rehearsal."

I was having some difficulty understanding what this had to do with Donal keeping his bicycle.

O'Reilly explained. "They got to the bit, 'With all my worldly goods I thee endow.' Donal asks what 'endow' means. McWheezle tells him Martha gets all Donal's possessions."

"He didn't."

"He did, and poor old Donal's been stewing for a week about whether to give up Martha or his bike."

"And that's why you told him he could keep the bike."

"It is," said O'Reilly.

"But how could you outrank McWheezle on a theological question?"

"Easy," he said, pulling out his briar. "I told Donal that endowments were made after a man dies. Martha gets the bike in Donal's will."

I had to laugh. "You're a crafty old devil, Fingal. The Wily O'Reilly."

"I am," he said, "and you can buy me a pint."

WHAT'S IN A NAME?

O'REILLY CHECKS IN

Some ethnic expressions suffer in the translation and yet if left untranslated are well understood. Take the Yiddish "chutzpa." There's no English equivalent nor does there need to be. I know I need not expound further, at least to those of you who know my old mentor, Doctor Fingal Flahertie O'Reilly, when I tell you that he had "a good conceit of himself." And you know he didn't "suffer fools gladly."

This combination could lead to misunderstandings, pallor of the O'Reilly schnozzle, and as much heat generated as in one of those bizarre chemistry experiments we were forced to conduct as first-year medical students.

I was present when O'Reilly's unwillingness to condescend to lesser mortals led to such an inevitable outcome. To add spice, it was one of those rare situations when

216

O'Reilly was bested in a verbal joust. The reagents in the reaction were Fingal Flahertie and a desk clerk at the Gresham Hotel in Dublin. The catalyst was a suitcase.

It had been a present to O'Reilly from Lord Fitzgurgle. Fingal was inordinately proud of the buffed pigskin and his name, Doctor F. F. O'Reilly, inscribed on a small brass plaque.

How the clerk and O'Reilly came into contact requires a few words of explanation. The occasion was one of those annual exercises of legalized thuggery. I refer of course to the sport of rugby football. According to tradition, the game was invented at the English school Rugby, when during a soccer game one young lad picked up the ball and ran with it. I favour an earlier explanation that the modern game is a watered-down version of a contest invented by the Visigoths, who used a human head for a ball.

O'Reilly had been a keen player in his youth. (I believe that if gladiatorial contests had been legal in his salad days he would have taken an active role. He was, as you'll recall, a former boxing champion of Her Majesty's Royal Navy.) He always went to Dublin to cheer on the Irish rugby team. And this was the second time he'd asked me to come as his guest.

"It'll be a grand trip," he announced. "And we'll stay at the Gresham again."

"Terrific." I almost meant it. The internationally recognized luxury of the Gresham Hotel would almost make up for being driven to Dublin by O'Reilly. I won't bore you with an account of the journey. I will take you directly to the Gresham.

O'Reilly strode up the front steps with the force of the Bolshevik Army at the St. Petersburg Winter Palace. He brushed aside the efforts of the uniformed doorman to carry the pigskin portmanteau. "Jasus, Gallagher. You know I always carry my own luggage."

The doorman tugged at his forelock. "Sorry, Doctor, sir. I didn't recognize you for a minute."

"You what? Haven't I been coming here for twenty years now?"

"Sorry, sir."

O'Reilly grunted. "Come on, Taylor. I want to get us registered and go for a jar." He shouldered his way through the crowd in the lobby. "This won't take long. All the staff know me here."

I refrained from remarking that that had not been initially obvious from the way the doorman had behaved, and followed in

O'Reilly's footsteps.

He halted at the registration desk, set his case on the plushly carpeted floor, and leant forward, arms folded on the counter.

The desk clerk was filing papers in pigeon-holes behind the counter. As was the custom in those days, he wore a full morning suit, tail coat and pinstripes.

I heard a low rumbling coming from O'Reilly and knew how much he disliked being ignored.

"Oi," he said.

Either he was not overheard or the clerk chose to overlook the less than polite remark.

"OI!"

The clerk half-turned, looked over a pair of spectacles at O'Reilly, and returned to his filing.

O'Reilly's nose tip paled. I knew he was going to go ballistic. (As an aside, if you believe you've found an anachronism because the expression "going ballistic" belongs to the '90s, not the '60s, let me remind you that the original *ballista,* a Roman artillery piece, predated even O'Reilly by the odd millennium.) He lifted a hand and smashed it down on a bell that adorned the counter. Quasimodo would have been proud of the clangour.

"OI, YOU!"

The clerk turned. "Is sir addressing me?"

"Sir bloody well is. I want to register."

"Indeed." The clerk pulled a ledger along the countertop.

"What name, sir?"

"Jasus, not you too," said O'Reilly. "How many years have I been coming here?"

"I haven't the faintest idea, sir. I started working here two weeks ago." The clerk sniffed. "Now. What name, sir?"

"Use your eyes, you thick bastard." O'Reilly pointed at his suitcase. "My name's on the case."

"Certainly, sir." The clerk scrutinized the luggage. "I see," he said. "Silly of me."

"I should think so," said O'Reilly, calming a little, at least until the clerk remarked in unctuous tones, "And how long will Mister Genuine Pigskin be staying with us?"

FILL 'ER UP

DONAL DONNELLY MAKES A FUEL OF O'REILLY

When I told you about Fingal Flahertie
O'Reilly and the desk clerk at the Gresham
Hotel in Dublin, I remarked that I wouldn't
weary you with an account of our drive
there from Belfast. There was no promise,
overt or implied, not to tell you about our
drive back.

Motorcars were to O'Reilly as explosive-
laden bombers were to kamikaze pilots. The
only difference between the "Divine Wind"
fliers in their Mitsubishis and O'Reilly in
his long-nosed Rover car was that he confidently expected to return from each mission. In our small village and the environs
all the locals were well aware of his propen-
sities and were as adept at taking avoiding
action as U.S. warships in Leyte Gulf. Well,
most U.S. warships.

Like some of the smaller aircraft carriers

in the Philippines, Donal Donnelly was an exception. In his last vehicular encounter with Fingal Flahertie — when Donal's tractor had stalled at a red light — the unfortunate youth had been the subject of a tongue-lashing of ferocious intensity.

This fact is germane to the rest of the story. I hadn't realized at the time that Donal could harbour a grudge and, like the mills of God, he ground slowly, but he ground exceeding small. I probably would never have known if O'Reilly hadn't told me the story on the drive back from Dublin.

We left the Gresham on Sunday morning. Ireland had beaten England the day before and we'd celebrated with some of Fingal's old classmates from Trinity College. I had a very sore head, O'Reilly looked as if he might bleed to death from his eyeballs, and I had a distinct impression I'd be better to go home by train.

Certain mystic sects believe the gods are especially protective of small children and idiots. The same deities must also have held a watching brief for O'Reilly when he was behind the wheel — and I leave it to you to decide under which category. If, as O'Reilly's passenger, I qualified for attention from the deities, it was definitely because I was an idiot. There was a perfectly good train service from Dublin to the North of Ireland.

"Hop in," he said, climbing into the driver's seat. "Great day."

As I boarded I couldn't help but agree. It was one of those crisp February mornings — sun bright, sky eggshell-blue, clouds puffy and white — that God makes in Ireland to ensure that never more than half the population can bring themselves to emigrate.

"Right," said O'Reilly, grinding the Rover into gear and pulling away from the curb in a series of jerks that would have made a spastic kangaroo proud, "won't take us long to get home."

"Good." I crossed my fingers and hunched down in my seat.

We managed to leave the city of Dublin more or less intact. I didn't count the dray horse that was last seen disappearing along O'Connell Street at Mach 0.5 or the two dustbins that were bowled over. I was heartily relieved when the Rover hurtled along the country roads, if for no other reason than there were fewer impediments to forward progress.

"We'll be across the border in no time," said O'Reilly, swerving to avoid a chicken.

I glanced at the dashboard instruments. The speedometer read seventy miles per hour and — oops — the petrol gauge read empty.

"Er, Fingal. I think we're going to run out of petrol." I hoped he'd take my word for it and not feel constrained to take his eyes off the road.

He glanced down at the gauge. The car wobbled across the white line and back to O'Reilly's side, missing a gypsy caravan by the width of a coat of paint.

"You're right," he said. "We'll stop at the next petrol pump."

I was surprised. O'Reilly always mistrusted instruments that didn't show him what he wanted to see. And petrol was at that time considerably cheaper in the North of our divided country.

"You believe the gauge?" I asked.

He laughed like a drain. "I do now," he said, "ever since that Donal Donnelly gave me my come-uppance."

"What — ?" I was momentarily interrupted as the car crested a small rise and for several seconds was airborne. The crash of our yielding to Earth's gravitational field muffled O'Reilly's chuckles, then he said, "A while back there I was very interested in the petrol consumption of this motorcar."

224

"I remember." I did indeed. He'd been extremely boring on the subject and then inexplicably had lost interest.

"Do you recall the week I thought I was going to get a hundred miles to the gallon?"

"Watch the sheep, Fingal."

I swear he drove the only vehicle that could go from seventy to zero in less than a microsecond. The halted Rover oscillated on its springs while two black-faced ewes ambled across the road. The gears ground and the Rover continued on its way.

"Can you imagine I really thought this car would do a hundred miles on one gallon of petrol?" O'Reilly snorted. "Boy, was I the right eejit."

I was relieved that we were travelling rather more sedately. I was also surprised that Fingal would admit to having been wrong — and smile about it.

"I'd spent all week telling the lads at the Mucky Duck I'd got her up to forty, then fifty. They started taking bets when I'd hit seventy."

In those days, thirty miles to the gallon was pretty impressive. "So you're telling me the instruments were wrong?" I asked.

"Not at all. They were spot on. I might have believed I'd made the hundred if I hadn't caught him."

Are you a bit lost? Don't worry. I was often confused and confounded by O'Reilly.

"Him?" I inquired as O'Reilly pulled the car off the road beside a single petrol pump.

"Him," he said. "Donal Donnelly."

"Right," I agreed, happy that the car had stopped. I watched a red-faced gentleman, presumably the owner of the pump, amble toward our car.

"Aye," said O'Reilly, rolling down the window. "Donal had heard about the whole business. Every night he'd been slipping into my garage, and do you know what he'd done?"

I shook my head.

O'Reilly nodded at the pump's proprietor. "Fill her up, please." He turned back to me. "Just like Donal. Just to make a goat of me, Donal Donnelly had been topping up my petrol tank."

A Curious Affair

Things That Go "Yeeow" in the Night

"Riven" is a word that has slipped from common usage, but I can't think of a better one to describe the effects of the shriek that tore through the fabric of the early morning hours chez O'Reilly. Believe me, the night was riven — positively riven — by a caterwauling like the death throes of a banshee.

I sat up in bed. I didn't have goose bumps; I had ostrich wens. My *erector pilae* were in spasm. I silently begged the Deity to ensure that whatever was making the noise would find the slumbering O'Reilly in his bedroom on the floor below before it came after me. I hauled the blankets up round my chin and listened.

"Thumpity-thump" came from below, drowning the chattering of my teeth. That would be O'Reilly's feet hitting the floor.

"Stop making that **#**#@!* noise!"

Three miles offshore the lighthouse keepers must have heard O'Reilly's dulcet tones.

The creature ignored his blandishments and went up and down the scale like an air-raid siren with operatic pretensions.

Judging by the clumping on the stairs, O'Reilly was heading down.

"Shut up!" O'Reilly's command made the glasses on my nightstand rattle. The eldritch howling ceased as if the sound waves had been sliced with a razor. The front door opened and was slammed. I heard O'Reilly climbing the stairs muttering, "Bloody cat."

When O'Reilly appeared for breakfast, my initial thought was to avoid any mention of the mysterious events of the earlier part of the morning. I'd slept badly and was not in the mood for conversation.

"Did you hear all that row?" he asked, helping himself to a pair of Mrs. Kincaid's poached kippers from a steamer on the sideboard.

I could imagine the mayor of Hiroshima asking a passing citizen, "Did you notice that bang?"

"Indeed," I said, waiting for O'Reilly to be seated at the table. "Most curious." I hoped my uninterested tone would stifle any further discussion. "Some tea?"

He ignored my offer to pour. "Curiosity,

my boy. Curiosity. You've said it." His speech was muffled by a mouthful of kipper.

"Actually, I said, 'Most curious,' but it's probably the same thing."

"It's not," he said. " 'Most curious' describes your appreciation of the events. 'Curiosity' is the property that was responsible for the row."

"Curiouser and curiouser," I remarked.

"Do not," he said, "try to confuse matters by quoting Lewis Carroll. The issue is one of curiosity."

"Killed the cat, I believe." I hoped that might put an end to the discussion. I was unprepared for the effects of that remark.

He guffawed — loudly — almost choked on a kipper bone, and slapped himself on the chest. "Absolutely right. It damn nearly did."

I remembered his "bloody cat" remark.

"This morning?" I inquired.

"Umm," he said, holding out his teacup. "Pour."

I did as I was told. "Lady Macbeth couldn't contain hers." He shovelled sugar into his cup.

You may remember an episode with a kitten that had savaged my finger. She'd grown into a massive moggie and rejoiced in the name of Lady Macbeth. It sounded as though something untoward had happened to my feline nemesis. "Go on," I said.

"Piqued your curiosity, have I?"

I let the remark pass, although the frustrating thing was that he had.

"Thought so." O'Reilly reached for the milk jug. "Well, the old curiosity piqued Lady Macbeth last night. Mrs. Kincaid must have set a couple of mouse traps."

Mouse traps. Little wooden devices with bait and a spring-loaded bar. Mouse took the bait, dislodged a lock, and released the bar, which snapped over with enough force to break the mouse's neck.

"Lady MacB must have decided to investigate." He poured milk into his tea. "Stupid animal had one stuck on the end of her nose."

Despite my dislike of the beast I couldn't help feeling a certain sympathy for her plight.

"No real harm done, in spite of the row she was making," said O'Reilly. "More a matter of hurt pride." He lifted a forkful of kipper. "She can have the leftover kippers for her breakfast. That'll cheer her up." He masticated slowly and swallowed. "It might teach her a lesson. Like the one I taught Donal Donnelly."

"Donal?"

"Um. He was most curious."

I confess so was I, until O'Reilly glanced at his watch and said, "Come on. Eat up. We're going to be late for morning surgery. I'll tell you that story at lunchtime."

To be continued.

CURIOUSER AND CURIOUSER

THINGS THAT GO
"AARGH" IN THE DAY

"I'll tell you that story at lunchtime." That had been O'Reilly's parting remark as we finished our breakfasts and headed off to our morning tasks. He'd gone to visit Lord Fitzgurgle to make comforting noises about his lordship's gout — and probably spend the rest of the morning sampling the baronial sherry.

I'd not had much time to wonder about the story that was meant to be forthcoming at lunchtime. The question of Donal Donnelly's curiosity had been pushed aside by the demands of a busy morning.

I ushered Maggie MacCorkle, my last patient, into the surgery. She'd come in for a fresh supply of the vitamin pills that, if taken ten minutes before the onset, prevented the recurrence of headaches two inches above the crown of her head.

I reached into the cubbyhole of the roll-top desk where O'Reilly kept his free samples and produced the magic placebo.

"Ah, thanks, Doctor," said Maggie, stuffing the bottle into her handbag.

I hoped she was going to leave, as it was now half an hour past lunchtime, but she was anxious to tell me about the doings of her cat, General Montgomery.

I listened — I hope patiently. Perhaps it was my empty stomach's quite believable impression of those boiling mud pits in New Zealand that prompted her to remark, "Ah sure but I've taken up enough of your time, Doctor sir."

"That's all right, Maggie." I held the door, waiting for her to leave. "Glad to hear the General's still bright as a bee."

She sniffed. "He is that — and it's more than I can say for that buck-eejit Donal."

Donal Donnelly, you'll remember — he of the psychedelic bicycle — was married to Maggie's niece, Martha. "You'll not need me to be telling you about that one," she said. "Away on, Doctor dear, and get your lunch."

"Right, Maggie."

As I watched her go, I began to wonder about a strange series of coincidences. Maggie's chat about her cat had led her admit-

233

tedly sometimes off-centre thoughts to Donal Donnelly. Last night O'Reilly's cat, Lady Macbeth, had suffered a misfortune. It had led his usually convoluted intellectual processes to Donal Donnelly.

Somewhere in the back of my invariably muddled mind I started to hear the theme music of an American TV program that was starting to gain some notoriety even in Ireland. A little subconscious voice said, "Welcome to the Twilight Zone" — although in Ballybucklebo it would more likely be the "Early Evening Environs."

Comforting myself with the thought that whatever supernatural events had befallen Donal were more likely to have been the result of too long a stay in the Mucky Duck rather than a close encounter of the third kind, I left the surgery, crossed the hall, and went into the dining room.

"Busy?" O'Reilly muttered through a mouthful of chicken pot pie. I could see the congealed remnants of what half an hour ago would have been another of Mrs. Kincaid's culinary gems.

I nodded, helped myself to a glutinous plateful, and sat at the big table. "I've just been having a chat with Maggie."

He hiccupped. So he had been at the sherry.

"She mentioned Donal. You said you were going to tell me a story about him."

"Did I?"

"You did. About curiosity."

"That's right," he said, and hiccupped. "Poor old Donal."

I chewed my chilled chicken.

"Do you know what a polecat is?" he asked, and before I could answer, continued, "It's a member of the ferret family — but bigger. More teeth, more claws."

I knew as much about overgrown weasels as I did about pigs. Nothing. I'd conveniently forgotten that years ago, when I introduced you to O'Reilly, I may have remarked that among his many attributes he was an unregenerate poacher — and in Ireland ferrets were as much tools of that particular trade as scalpels are to surgeons.

"That's nice," I said.

"Donal didn't think so."

I swallowed. "Fingal, it's been a long morning. I've a list of home visits as long as your arm to do after my late and thus nearly inedible lunch. If you want me to say I'm curious, consider it said, but please get to the point."

"What point?" He footered about lighting his briar. I swear O'Reilly did it simply to irritate.

235

I pushed my half-finished plate away. "This morning you said that Donal was curious, you taught him a lesson, and that you would explain at lunch."

"I am explaining."

"Then what does my state of knowledge about stickcats have to do with Donal?"

"Polecats, son. Polecats. They bite."

"Fingal."

He hiccupped, exhaled smoke, and chuckled. "All right. Donal used to do odd jobs for me, but apart from his congenital dimness he had a fatal flaw."

"Let me guess. Curiosity?"

"Right. He couldn't keep his nose out of things that didn't concern him." O'Reilly's brow wrinkled. "I didn't really mind him rummaging about in the drinks cabinet, but I drew the line when I caught him reading patients' charts."

My immediate thought was that under those circumstances Doctor O. would have been less likely to draw a line than dig an enormous trench. "What did you do?"

"I spoke to Fergal McGillicutty and borrowed something from him."

McGillicutty was a farm labourer who, for a price and no questions asked, was always able to produce a brace of pheasants or a fat hare for Mrs. Kincaid.

"And?"

"I put it in a box in the back garden just before Donal came over to cut the grass. I told him that under no circumstances was he to open the box."

"He opened the box, didn't he, Fingal?"

"Curiosity killed the cat." O'Reilly could barely contain himself. "But Donal survived. He only needed six stitches."

"Good God. What was in the box?"

"I told you," said O'Reilly. "Polecats bite."

My involuntary laughter was cut short when he looked pointedly at his watch and said, "Isn't it about time you were off to see your customers?"

"Right," I said, rising.

"Don't you want to know what I'm going to be up to this afternoon?"

I knew very well he'd go to sleep off this morning's load of sherry, but I said, and I meant it, "I'm not curious, Fingal. Not in the least."

A Matter of Time

O'Reilly Bends the Law

There's a difference between broken and bent. If you don't believe me, I'll explain. As with anything vaguely related to Doctor Fingal Flahertie O'Reilly, you may find the explanation convoluted.

When I worked for Doctor O'Reilly, Ireland had returned to daylight saving time, but during the second great numbered unpleasantness we'd had a peculiar system of "double summer time" when the clocks were advanced not one but two hours.

This, it was widely believed, had been introduced to foil the Luftwaffe's night bombing raids. How, the denizens of Ballybucklebo reasoned, could the German air force indulge itself in a touch of nocturnal bombing when there was no longer such a thing as night, and the sun, literally, shone at midnight? (It was this kind of reasoning that allowed the Irish to plan a manned mis-

238

sion to the sun. They'd avoid the heat by going after dark.) The Germans short-circuited the defensive ploy by resorting to what was, according to the new clock settings, very early morning bombing raids. This upset that sense of fairness so dear to the hearts of the average Ulsterman; the Germans were regarded as no longer playing by the rules.

Doctor Fingal Flahertie O'Reilly would never have failed to play by the rules. Never. He was, or at least as far as Her Majesty's Royal Navy had been concerned, he had been, an officer *and* a gentleman. I can categorically assure you I never saw him break a single rule during all the time I spent with him.

Bending was another matter. It's said the first pretzel was designed by O'Reilly when he mistook a straight biscuit for a statute of which he disapproved.

You may be wondering what the vagaries of springing forward, falling back, and O'Reilly's disdain for the laws of mere mortals have in common. To help you see the connection let me add the catalyst — alcohol. Still confused? Bear with me.

You do know that O'Reilly enjoyed a shot, both in the "of whiskey" sense and at the occasional unsuspecting duck. It might help if I explained that the months for molesting migratory mallard ran from September to February. You also are aware, because I've been at some pains to tell you, that when the omens were propitious on any given autumn or winter Saturday, Doctor O. would stick me with being on call, summon Arthur Guinness, and vanish in the pre-dawn blackness to bang and blaze barrel after barrel at the bewildered birds.

On the third Saturday of October in the year of our Lord I don't remember exactly, O'Reilly and the faithful hound had been somewhere on the foreshore of Strangford Lough since well before dawn. I'd been ministering to the medical emergencies: one cut finger, one marble up a nostril, and one hangover — Donal Donnelly's — that could have been mistaken for the symptoms of a brain tumour in anyone who actually possessed such an organ. I'd eaten a splendid late supper — slices of one of Mrs. Kincaid's roast hams — and for once feeling like a bit of company had wandered over to the Mucky Duck.

By this stage of my apprenticeship with Doctor O. I was well known to the locals and they to me. The snug was full of the usual suspects — Arthur Osbaldiston behind the bar, Fergal McGillicutty, Donal

Donnelly "having a hair of the dog," as the English call it, or, as the Irish say, "taking the cure" — in front. The local constable leant against the bar, straight glass of stout clutched in one hand.

"Evening, Doc. Sherry?" Arthur asked.

"Thanks."

He poured, handed it to me, and glanced over to where a large clock hung high up on the opposite wall. It was eight minutes to ten. "Himself's late the night."

"The ducks," I remarked, sipping from my glass.

"Oh aye," said Arthur, polishing a glass with a grubby dishcloth, "Doctor O'Reilly's a terrible man for the ducks." He glanced back at the clock and his head made an almost indiscernible twitch toward the rotund arm of the law. "The doctor'd better get himself in soon if he wants a wee hot whiskey to keep away the dew. I've to close in five minutes." He smiled obsequiously at the constable. "Isn't that right, officer?"

"It is, Mister Osbaldiston. The licensing laws are very strict. Very strict." He held out his now-empty glass. "I've just the time for the one more."

"Time, gentlemen," called Arthur as he started to build the policeman's pint.

At precisely 9:55 the door flew open and

O'Reilly, pursued by Arthur Guinness, entered. His cheeks were a slate grey, his nose a screaming red. He blew on his hands, rubbed the palms vigorously together, and blew on them again.

"Jasus, it's cold as a witch's tit out there," he remarked to the bar in general, and, "Hot Irish. Double," to Arthur Osbaldiston in particular.

The constable turned and glared first at O'Reilly then at Arthur Guinness. I suspected the episode when Arthur had mistaken the man for a burglar and had bitten him still rankled.

"Last shout's been called. It's nearly ten o'clock, Doctor."

O'Reilly looked at the clock, then back to the officer. I may have been the only one in the place to notice the change in the colour of O'Reilly's nose tip, but he hid his anger well.

"True, officer, true," he said, "and I know you're just doing your job."

The constable hurried to finish his pint within the five minutes drinking-up time permitted by the law. "True, sir."

"But," said O'Reilly, "if I could prove you're wrong about the time could I buy you a pint and have a wee warmer myself?"

Every eye was on the peeler. The silence

was such that the dropping of a single pin might have resulted in a bang of sufficient magnitude to rupture eardrums.

"Well . . ."

"Walking stick, Arthur," said O'Reilly in his best quarterdeck voice.

The stick was produced.

O'Reilly stepped over to the clock, pushed open the glass front with the stick's rubber-tipped ferrule, and with great concentration used the thing to turn the minute hand back. It was now, local Mucky Duck time, 8:58.

"But," spluttered the constable, "you can't just do that."

"You're right," said O'Reilly, "I can't, but Her Majesty's government can." He glared round the room. "Today is the third Saturday of October, and what happens tonight?"

To give him credit, Donal Donnelly saw it first. "Jasus, Doctor. The clocks go back."

"They do," said O'Reilly.

The constable began, "But not until two . . ."

"Drinks have been poured, officer. One for you and, Arthur, a hot double John Jameson for me."

The constable laughed. "All right, Doctor. I'll allow that you're not breaking the law — only bending it."

"Right," said O'Reilly, lifting his steaming glass. "Cheers."

JUNE 1999
THE LAST LAUGH

MRS. BISHOP'S WILL

"We'd better be off," said O'Reilly.

The temptation to suggest that he'd been going off for quite some time was firmly resisted. It was after all a solemn occasion, and in deference to the solemnity O'Reilly, as was the local expression, had cleaned up well. He wore black shoes that gleamed like the Koh-i-Noor diamond and pinstriped trousers with creases that would have cut tungsten-strengthened steel. His rusty black jacket covered an immaculately starched white shirt. His tie, as befitted the occasion, was black — except where a stubborn egg stain marred its ebony sheen. The entire ensemble was topped — literally — by a top hat made of velvety beaver pelt.

Funerals were taken seriously in Ballybucklebo.

"Sad day," said O'Reilly. "The place will miss Mrs. Bishop."

"True," I said, shifting uncomfortably in my best dark suit. The waistband of my seldom-worn trousers had shrunk since I'd encountered Mrs. Kincaid's cooking. "Mrs. Bishop was a decent woman. We will miss her."

"Not as much as Councillor Bishop." O'Reilly let one eyelid droop in a slow-motion wink that would have done justice to a voyeur at a strip club. "I was the witness to her will. I'd to deal with one of her bequests yesterday. And I'd to tell her husband."

"Oh?" When O'Reilly grinned the way he grinned then, I knew there was more to tell.

"I'll tell you after the service," he said. "Come on or we'll be late." He was unusually quiet as he piloted the long-nosed Rover out to the main Belfast road. Mrs. Bishop was to be cremated and the crematorium was in the big city. I contented myself watching the hedgerows rush by and the occasional cyclist take to the ditch. I tried to puzzle out what he could mean by, "Not as much as Councillor Bishop."

You may remember he was a man who would wrestle a bear for a farthing. Several years ago he'd arranged for a harmless old eccentric, Sunny, to be put in a home so that Bishop could acquire Sunny's land.

O'Reilly had resorted to some absolutely ethical blackmail then. He'd suggested to the good Councillor, with all the subtlety of the blow of a battering ram on a castle gate, that unless Sunny was returned to his land and his dogs forthwith, Mrs. Bishop might have to find out about why their maid had left so abruptly for England. In those days being single and pregnant was not regarded enthusiastically in rural Ireland.

Neither was divorce.

I recalled that by means other than O'Reilly, Mrs. Bishop had found out about her husband's little peccadillo. (It's an awful example of authorial intrusion but I can't resist the temptation to remark that no, Viagra would not have helped the man.) Matters in the Bishop household had attained the state of diplomatic relations that existed between England and Denmark when Admiral Nelson won the battle of Copenhagen — armed neutrality. This must have had some effect on the late Mrs. B.'s will — but what? Given that the pair of them shared a house only to avoid the shame of divorce proceedings I would have thought that Bishop might have felt a certain relief when his wife joined the choir invisible. Why would he miss her?

"Come on, Fingal," I paused as he

screeched past a cow that had somehow wandered onto the road, "what was the bequest?"

"Later, my boy." He grunted, shifted down, and accelerated over one of those little hills in the roads of Ireland which, if taken at the right speed, have the same effect on the motorcar as did the launching ramps of V1 flying bombs in the second numbered unpleasantness. Touchdown came with a ferocious crash.

My teeth were still chattering when he parked the Rover in the lot at the crematorium.

It was, as funerals go, a pleasant one. A couple of hymns, prayers for the departed. The Reverend McWheezle gave the eulogy — and for once kept his words short and to the point.

O'Reilly, as befitted his station, and I, as O'Reilly's minion, had been given pews at the front of the chapel. It was from this vantage point that I was able to observe Mister Bishop's reactions to the proceedings. The portly gentleman seemed to have his emotions reasonably well under control. Occasionally a tear — which even then I regarded as the essence of hypocrisy — leaked from one pallid eye when he glanced at the bier where his late wife's coffin lay.

The organ began to play "Nearer my God to Thee," and by whatever mechanical miracles make these things happen, the coffin sank slowly from view. The gears of the device were almost soundless, the organ music subdued, but the air was rent with the keening coming from Councillor Bishop. The man was as grief-stricken as Orpheus when he discovered that Eurydice had fallen off the perch. I stole a glance at O'Reilly. His features were composed, his hands folded primly before him, and his eyes held that sparkle that I only saw when God was definitely in his Heaven and all was very right with O'Reilly's world.

"Fingal," I whispered, "tell me."

He bent his head and said, sotto voce, "She had the money in the family. Inherited it from her people." O'Reilly nodded toward the hapless Bishop. "Her last bequest — and I had the pleasure of telling him last night — was that all her — hang on —"

Bishop's wailing had reached epic proportions. I looked at one of the glass chandeliers to satisfy myself it had not shattered. I had a last glimpse as the coffin vanished and the lid of the bier slid back into place.

I heard O'Reilly try to stifle a snigger "— that all her money was to be put into ten-pound notes and used to line her coffin."

I wondered how I was going to explain my unseemly guffaws to the rest of the mourners. My struggling to compose myself wasn't helped by O'Reilly's next suggestion: "Maybe Bishop could put the ashes in an egg timer — after all, time is money."

Author's note: *A friend who read this manuscript before it was submitted has pointed out that the money-in-the-coffin ploy was used in a Frank Sinatra and the Rat Pack movie,* Ocean's Eleven. *Unfortunately Ol' Blue Eyes himself has shuffled off this mortal coil — otherwise he'd be hearing from me on the subject of plagiarism.*

EASY COME, EASY GO

O'REILLY TRIUMPHS AGAIN

"Would you fancy a day at Loughbrick-land?"

O'Reilly wandered into the surgery just as Maggie left. I barely heard his question, thinking as I was about Maggie Mac-Corkle's sore back that had failed to respond to everything I'd tried. I'd even used his vitamin-pill trick, telling her to take the placebo exactly seventeen minutes before the pain started. O'Reilly had cured the aches above her head that way. Why were my ministrations not working?

"Have you gone deaf?" he asked.

"What?"

"You have — either deaf or stupid. I just offered you one of the best days out you'll ever have." He fired up his briar. "Of course if you don't want to go to the races maybe Lord Fitzgurgle would enjoy the trip."

"Sorry, Fingal. I was thinking about Maggie."

"Oh? Headaches or backaches?"

"Back."

"What have you tried?"

I sighed. "Everything."

He laughed, a deep throaty rumbling noise, the sort of sound you might hear when one tectonic plate shifts over its neighbour. "No, you haven't."

I sniffed. "I bloody well have." My professional pride had been stung by my failure.

I should have seen the glint in his eye, heeded the warning signals. It's said that a leaden hue to the sky, humid air that's almost drinkable, and an oily calm on a breathless sea is a sure harbinger of a tropical hurricane. That glint in O'Reilly's baby-blues was as accurate a predictor of squalls. I ignored it when he said, "Bet you I can fix her."

"Don't be daft. I've done everything."

His eyebrows knitted and he said, slowly and deliberately, "I believe I remarked, 'Bet you.' Would you like to chance five pounds?"

That stopped me. Five pounds was a lot of money. I hesitated.

"What's that business about 'money' and 'mouth'?" he asked.

"All right, Fingal. You're on."

He grinned like an open drainpipe as he shook my hand. "We'll see her together the day after tomorrow."

"Why not tomorrow?"

"Because," he said, shaking his head, "tomorrow you and me are going to Lough-brickland."

And, on the morrow, go we did. Lough-brickland is the site of one of those peculiarly Irish events, point-to-point horse racing. The English aristocracy may turn out in their ducal splendour in the paddock at Royal Ascot or Epsom Downs. Tame affairs. The horses there are true thoroughbreds that run round a level track. An Irish point-to-point is a cross between Ben Hur's endeavours in the Circus Maximus, without the chariots, of course, and a ride on the "Sky Demon" roller coaster. The horses and jockeys thunder round a course that's interrupted at intervals by hedges, gates, ditches, and sometimes combinations of hedges and ditches. At least they try to. Most horses finish but a goodly number of riders part company with their mounts before journey's end. The spectators aren't usually drawn from the ranks of those whose names appear in Burke's Peerage, but the *craic,* as they say in Ireland, is powerful.

Tis there you'll see the fiddlers and the
   pipers all competing,
The nimble footed dancers and they trippin'
   on the daisies,
And others crying cigars and lights and bills
   for all the races,
With the colours of the jockeys and the
   price and horses' ages.

That stanza from a song called "The Gal-
way Races" puts the point-to-point in a
nutshell — particularly the bit about the
horses' prices. At one end of the track the
bookmakers, who in Ireland rejoice in the
title of "Turf Accountant," set up their
stands, cry the odds, and happily take the
punters' money.

We'd parked the old Rover in an adjacent
field.

"Come on," said O'Reilly, as eager to get
down to the track as any one of the horses
awaiting the start of the first race.

I trotted along in his wake, trying not to
step in too many cow-claps or twist an ankle
in one of the ruts in the ground. I was
breathing heavily as he shouldered his way
through the crowd of farmers and towns-
folk, stopping at last in front of a stand that
bore the slogan "Honest Bobby Greer."

"Is it yourself, Doctor dear?" enquired a

florid-faced gentleman standing on a raised platform beneath the sign. This, I assumed, was Trustworthy Robert. He wore a yellow-checked waistcoat beneath a Donegal tweed jacket, moleskin trousers, and a bowler hat tipped forward over his brow. He clearly knew O'Reilly of old and, judging by the huge smile on Greer's face, had lightened O'Reilly's wallet more than once in the past.

"Good day, Bobby," said O'Reilly. He handed over a ten-shilling note. "Finnegan's Fancy both ways in the first." I watched as he accepted a ticket.

"Are you not having a flutter, Pat?" he inquired. I shook my head. I'd let him put his ten bob on a horse in the hopes that it would finish in the first three. I'd be quite happy to follow its progress vicariously. Besides, there was the small matter of tomorrow's wager.

"Come on then," he called over his shoulder as he forced his way to the fence near the finish line. I followed.

"They're off!" cried the starter. The faint pounding of hooves grew louder. The ground trembled. The punters yelled encouragement. The mass of equine bodies hurtled past. No wonder, I thought, caught up by the moment, no wonder Liza Doolittle encouraged the horse she'd backed to

"Move your bleeding arse."

"Bugger," said O'Reilly, tearing up his ticket. "Come on."

Off we went back to Honest Bobby. Ten shillings changed hands. Next race. Steaming horses, crouching jockeys, turf clods flying from hooves.

"Bugger," said O'Reilly, tearing up his ticket.

He said that word seven times all told.

The eighth and final race would start in ten minutes. Off we went back to a now happily grinning Bobby Greer.

"So what's your fancy, Doctor dear?"

"I've got you now," said O'Reilly. I saw a five-pound note. "That on Butcher's Boy to win." He took the ticket.

I hadn't placed a bet all day but the name of a filly took my eye: Strangford Sally. The current love of my life was a young woman from Strangford and, yes, you've guessed her name. The odds were twenty to one, but I thought there might be an omen so I risked five shillings.

As we walked back to our places at the finish, O'Reilly said, "I've got Greer on this one. Donal Donnelly's father owns Butcher's Boy. He's never been out before. I've seen him jump." He rubbed his hands. "That horse loves hedges like Orpheus loved Eurydice. Just goes at the nearest one as if his legs were springs."

"They're off!" I waited, fingers crossed, peering up the track, wondering what the commotion was near the start. A horse with its jockey clinging on to its neck had left the track and was charging up a hill like Lord Cardigan's mount at Balaclava. I was so intrigued I nearly missed the finish and that would have been a shame.

I was feeling rather smug the next morning as I sat in the surgery beside a chastened O'Reilly. Strangford Sally had come in at twenty to one, which made me five pounds better off. Butcher's Boy had lived up to expectations and had, like winged Pegasus, soared over the nearest hedge. Unfortunately, it had been the one marking the boundary of the track. As O'Reilly had remarked yesterday, "At the rate the bloody thing was going up that hill it's probably in County Antrim by now." Only one tiny matter remained to be resolved.

"Come in, Maggie," said O'Reilly as she hobbled in. "It's the back again?"

"Yes, Doctor."

"Let's have a look."

I watched as O'Reilly palpated her sides. He didn't even ask her to take off her dress. He bent and whispered something to her.

She nodded and moved behind the screens. I heard the rustling of material. Maggie reappeared, smiling to beat the band. Her limp had gone.

"Thank you, Doctor O'Reilly," she said. "Oh, that's better."

"Go on with you now, Maggie," he said.

She left. He turned to me. "I believe you owe me a fiver."

I fished in my pocket for yesterday's winnings. "What did you do?"

He chuckled. "Her corset stays were too tight. I told her to loosen them."

I handed him the bank note. Easy come, easy go.

LATERAL THINKING

OR SHOULD THAT BE VERTICAL?

"I wonder what it is about my family?" muttered Doctor Fingal Flahertie O'Reilly, sipping his whiskey as he sat comfortably ensconced in the armchair in the upstairs sitting room of his home.

I had a pretty fair idea of some of the peculiarities of the clan O'Reilly, but as my sage old father had often remarked, "Some questions are better not answered." I sat in my armchair, peered through the big bay window, and feigned interest in a fishing boat drifting on the rippled waters of Belfast Lough.

"Sometimes they can be a bit odd," he said.

As two left feet, I thought, but left the thought unsaid.

"Do you remember Lars Porsena?" he asked.

" '. . . of Clusium,' " I countered, " 'by

the nine gods he swore, that the great house of Tarquin should suffer wrong no more.' Macaulay's *Lays of Ancient Rome.*"

O'Reilly grunted. "So you're not altogether unread. At least you recognize the source." He shook his head. "No. I was thinking of my brother. The one in Portaferry."

I had one of those flashbacks that are only supposed to come to patients with recovery of suppressed memories. I pictured Lars Porsena O'Reilly's youngest son devastating the school Christmas pageant by venting his wrath, very publicly, on the boy who'd replaced O'Reilly Minor in the part of Joseph.

"That Lars Porsena," I said.

"Himself," said O'Reilly. "It's his oldest lad, Liam."

"Who can be a bit odd," I prompted.

"As two left feet," said O'Reilly.

I started. Could O'Reilly have read my mind just a few seconds ago?

"Do you know what he's just done?" O'Reilly asked.

"No," I replied, taking some comfort that if O'Reilly could have delved into my thoughts he wouldn't have needed to ask the question.

"Daft bugger," he continued, then, noticing my hurt look, added, "Not you, Pat. Liam."

"Oh," I said.

"He's just passed his final examination for his B.Sc. up at Queen's University."

"I wouldn't have thought that qualified him for what you just called him."

O'Reilly shook his head. "He should have had a first-class honours but he managed to upset one of his professors."

"Never."

"Oh, aye," said Fingal. "Daft B." He busied himself lighting his pipe. "I got the story from Frothelbottom."

"Frothelbottom?"

"Professor John Stout — known to his old school friends as Frothelbottom. Froth for short."

I waited.

"Seems Froth had Liam in an oral. Asked him a question about barometers and a block of flats."

I remembered the same question from my own undergraduate days. "If you had a barometer, how could you tell the height of a tall building?"

"Do you know what Liam said? 'Go to the top, let down the barometer on a piece of string, and measure the length of the string.'"

I confess I'd considered a different approach, but Liam's solution would have worked.

"Froth told Liam he could do it that way, but could he suggest another. 'Sure,' says Liam. 'Go to the top, chuck the barometer off, and time its descent. Then use the acceleration formula to calculate the distance fallen.'

" 'Um,' says Froth, 'but is there another way?'

" 'Yes. Measure the barometer and walk up the stairwell. Turn the barometer end over end and multiply the length by the number of revolutions.' "

At this point I was quite intrigued. Fingal's nephew must have been possessed of a keen mind to come up with these original approaches. "Seems that he should have got his pass mark by this point," I observed.

"I agree," said O'Reilly, "but as Froth admitted to me, by this time he wasn't getting the answer he wanted, and was beginning to take a dislike to young Liam."

"Oh, dear."

"Indeed. Oh dear. 'Try again,' says Froth. 'Measure the barometer, stand it vertically on the ground, and at noon measure the lengths of the shadows cast by the barometer and the building. Now you'd have a ratio and could calculate the height from that.' "

For the life of me I could see nothing wrong with that answer.

O'Reilly sighed, blew out a cloud of tobacco smoke, and muttered, "I wish old Froth had packed it up after that, but he told me that by then he was determined to wring the real correct answer out of young Liam. 'Mister O'Reilly,' says Froth, 'there's only one more way and if you tell it to me I'll give you a pass with honours.' "

"Seems to me that was a pretty fair offer."

"It was," said O'Reilly, "but Froth hadn't allowed for the O'Reilly oddness."

Neither had I when I joined his practice, but you already know that.

Fingal shrugged. "I thought I understood a bit of physics, and I tell you, Pat, by that time I could only think of one more way to skin that particular cat. When old Froth started the last of the story he had me rightly flummoxed."

I waited.

" 'Only one way?' says Liam. 'Rubbish.' " O'Reilly sighed. "Students don't say 'rubbish' to senior professors."

"Liam did."

"I know," said O'Reilly, "and do you know what? He was right. He finally allowed that if he measured the difference in barometric pressure between the ground and the roof he'd be able to calculate the height of the building."

That was the very answer I'd given some years before. But apparently Liam had known another way. "He should have called it a day right then," I said.

"I know. I know. But he didn't. 'Right,' says Froth, and as he admitted to me, he was just about ready to forgive the young fellow his impertinence when Liam says, 'Do you not want to know the other way?' 'I do,' says Froth. You'll never guess what Liam said."

He was right.

"Says Liam, 'I'd go to the caretaker's flat, knock on the door, and when he opened it, I'd say, 'Mister, if you tell me the height of the building, I'll give you this bloody barometer.' "

I couldn't stop laughing.

"It's all very well for you to cackle like a broody hen, Pat Taylor. You don't have to wonder what it is about your family."

FLIGHT OF FANCY

THE DOG WHO LOVED PLANES

When I introduced you to Doctor Fingal
Flahertie O'Reilly, I numbered among his
attributes his propensity for kindness to
small children and animals. There is of
course an adage that "the exception proves
the rule," and loyal readers will remember
that even O'Reilly's faunophilia didn't
extend to *Sus scrofa,* the domesticated pig.
Perhaps it was to compensate for his mis-
trust of all things porcine — unless roasted,
glazed, or served in thick rashers by Mrs.
Kincaid — that he was especially attached
to members of the tribe *Canis familiaris,*
defined in the *Oxford English Dictionary* as a
"domesticated carnivore." Arthur Guinness,
O'Reilly's Labrador retriever, was assuredly
carnivorous. His domesticity was another
matter. One word from O'Reilly and the
brute did exactly as he pleased. The merest
sight of my corduroy trousers either drove

him into a state of sexual arousal previously recorded only at some of Nero's classier Roman orgies or reminded him that his bladder was full. In my opinion he was as domesticated as a rabid Tasmanian devil.

But O'Reilly doted on Arthur G., and showed his adoration in some of the most peculiar ways. (Please do not misinterpret that last remark. Remember, *Honi soit qui mal 'y pense.*) On reflection, perhaps a few words of explanation are warranted. Bear with me and I'll give you an example.

It was a perfect late-summer evening. O'Reilly and I had retired to his spacious back garden to ruminate on the state of the universe in general and the vagaries of medical practice in Ballybucklebo in particular. The air was soft, rose-perfumed, and drowsy with humming bees. O'Reilly sat on a wooden chair clutching his John Jameson, sucking contentedly on his briar. I squatted on the grass at his feet. We must have looked like the setup for an early Edwardian photograph. All I needed was an Eton jacket and a tasselled cap. Even Arthur Guinness, lolling under O'Reilly's chair, seemed hypnotized by the tranquillity.

I thought, occasionally God really is in his heaven and all is right with the world. I became aware of a distant droning, but before I could turn to try to identify the source of the increasingly loud noise, Arthur Guinness crawled out from under O'Reilly's chair, sat erect, and stared at the sky.

I knew that Labradors owed their retrieving ability to remarkably accurate vision so I followed his line of sight and saw on the horizon a small monoplane coming our way. Probably going to the Belfast airport, which at that time rejoiced in the name of Nutt's Corner. Honestly.

As the aircraft approached, Arthur began to ululate. I'd never heard him make the noise before. It fell somewhere between the falsetto keening of professional mourners at an Irish wake and the harsh wailing attributed to the banshee. And its volume increased until, as the plane passed overhead, I glanced hurriedly at the kitchen windows to assure myself that Arthur's yodelling hadn't cracked them.

I had only enough time to note the panes' integrity when I caught a blur of movement. Guinness's wailing had changed to a bark that would have been the envy of a California sea lion, and I swear he was already approaching Mach 1 as he raced the length of the garden, staring upward and roaring his battle cry. Only the distant hedge stopped his career, and his ranting didn't cease until the aircraft was out of view.

O'Reilly was on his feet. "Come in here, sir."

Arthur looked over his shoulder, his view interrupted by his still-raised hackles.

"Come here, I say."

Presumably misinterpreting this command for one to "sit," Arthur planted his glossy behind, wagged his tail, but kept his back to O'Reilly.

"Daft bloody dog," O'Reilly rumbled in my general direction.

Daft? Arthur's recent display had been, at least to my mind, closer to raving lunacy than mere daftness. If the Baskerville canine had ever needed a stand-in, I could have pointed it in the right direction.

"What on earth," I asked, "was that all about?"

"Ducks," said O'Reilly, shaking his head. "He thinks they're ducks."

I thought O'Reilly was finally beginning to assume some of the less balanced attributes of his gun dog but said, with a gently interrogative inflection, "Ducks?"

"He keeps mistaking aeroplanes for ducks. You saw how happy he was chasing that one."

"That was happiness?"

"Oh yes. Just look at him."

Arthur must have meandered back. O'Reilly bent and patted the dog's head. "Who's a good lad?" he inquired.

Arthur's tail moved so rapidly it seemed to stand still. The fact that it was in action was given away by the frenetic shimmy of his backside. His face wore a grin and his pink tongue dripped. In the fullness of time, disdaining even a sideways glance at my trouser leg, Arthur subsided under O'Reilly's chair. Even I was convinced that the pursuit of the aircraft had in some inexplicable way brought great joy to the dimmer recesses of Arthur's brain.

It was then that I first glimpsed O'Reilly's peculiar ways of demonstrating his adoration.

"Um," he said, a beginning I'd learned always prefaced his asking for a favour, "um, Pat, I don't suppose you'd consider working this Saturday? I'd pay you a bit extra."

"Why, Fingal?"

He hesitated. "It's special or I wouldn't ask."

"What's special, Fingal?"

"It's Arthur's birthday. I want to give him a treat."

I had to laugh. "I suppose you're going to take him to the airport so he can really get

269

close to some of those big 'ducks.' "

O'Reilly's jaw dropped. "How in the hell did you know that? And keep your voice down." He glanced at the black dog under the chair. "It's meant to be a surprise."

I agreed to work on O'Reilly's behalf. How could I be so unfeeling as to keep the pair of them from a trip they so clearly warranted? To Nutt's Corner.

FUEL FOR THOUGHT

O'REILLY AND THE TEXAN

"Curious people, Americans," observed O'Reilly as he helped himself to a plateful of Mrs. Kincaid's devilled kidneys.

It was suppertime chez O'Reilly and the pair of us was ensconced at the big mahogany dining table. I'd finished the afternoon surgery and Fingal, now masticating with the fervour of a cud-chewing yak, had come back from what I assumed must have been a successful confinement of Mrs. McGillicutty's fourth. Certainly if the grin on his craggy face was anything to go by, something had pleased him enormously. Of course, what Americans had to do with the labour of a farmer's wife was anyone's guess.

Forgetting the old adage about the impetuous entry of idiots into environs where the winged denizens of the celestial sphere would not venture, I decided to find out.

"Curious, Fingal?"

"Curious." He mumbled, mouth full, fist-held fork on its way to deposit another load.

"Do you mean they, like the ancient Greeks, are possessed of inquiring minds, or was that a comment about certain ethnic peculiarities?"

He stopped in mid-chew. "What the hell are you on about, Taylor?"

It was not an unreasonable question. I flinched. "Sorry, Fingal. Just — I was wondering aloud about what kind of curiousness the Americans had."

He grunted. "Odd bunch, the Yanks." And lapsed into a digestive silence.

I thought it better to follow suit, and let my mind wander on the subject under discussion. Americans. They'd started coming to our corner of Ireland in the late '50s. They came by the coach-load — friendly, large people who dressed in baseball caps, tartan sports jackets, and Bermuda shorts and spoke loudly about "finding our roots in li'l ol' Ireland."

The natives regarded their transatlantic cousins with gentle amusement and, ever with an eye to the main chance, grasping avarice. Prices in the Mucky Duck soared. Bed-and-breakfasts blossomed. Donal Donnelly had shown remarkable enterprise. He'd fashioned a leprechaun costume, complete with buckled brogues, knee britches, waistcoat, and stovepipe hat, equipped himself with a shillelagh, and parked himself on a stool outside the Duck. A hand-lettered sign beside him announced, "Will say 'Begorrah' for $1." He'd done very well.

My mental meanderings were interrupted.

"Well, do you want to know why I think Americans are curious?"

I glanced across the table. No sign of nasal pallor. The grin was back. "Oh, indeed."

He chuckled. "What do you know about petrol tanks?"

"Nothing." I was about to add that I didn't see the connection between petrol — what Americans would call gasoline — and Americans themselves, when O'Reilly charged on.

"There's a funny arrangement in my Rover car."

"Oh?"

"Aye. The outflow pipe is an inch above the bottom of the tank."

His line of reasoning was like Maggie MacCorkle's headaches — at least two inches above my head.

"It's to stop dirt in the bottom of the tank getting into the carburettor and clogging it," he explained.

"That's nice."

His brows knitted. "It can be a bloody nuisance when you're low on petrol and the engine stops."

"I can see that."

"But there's a way round it."

"Go on." I tried to sound enraptured.

"I had to use it this afternoon."

I could only hope that O'Reilly, like Roald Amundsen, who, as you'll remember, announced that he was setting off for the North Pole but arrived at the South to the disgust of one Robert Falcon Scott, would eventually come back onto his true course.

"Bloody car conked out on the way to the McGillicuttys, and you know how fast her labours are."

Indeed I did. I'd confined her last year. The term "precipitate" when applied to Jean McGillicutty's second stage was about as descriptive as calling the then-recent puncturing of the sound barrier as "a wee bit fast, like."

O'Reilly mopped up his gravy with a slice of bread. "Do you know what I did?"

I shook my head.

"I'd no time to walk to the garage. I had to get the car to go, so I got out and peed in the petrol tank."

"You what?"

"Peed in the tank. The petrol floats on the pee, is able to get into the feed pipe, and the engine'll run for a while longer —"

I sat in awe of his ingenuity.

"— trouble was, I'd been in such a rush I hadn't noticed the American tour bus parked at the side of the road —"

Aha. Perhaps Amundsen was going to head north.

"— one of the Yanks had been watching me. 'Watcha doin', buddy?' says he." O'Reilly gave a very creditable imitation of John Wayne. " 'Refuelling, pilgrim,' I told him. 'Is that a fact,' says he. 'Ah never heard of using that fer fuel — and ah'm from Texas and that's oil country.' 'I've heard that,' says I, 'but this is Ireland — and this is Guinness country. Now if you'll excuse me, I'm in a bit of a rush.' 'Mighty fine,' says he, 'do you think it would work with Budweiser?' "

I had no doubt that O'Reilly had assured the innocent that such indeed would be the case. My mental image of some poor bewildered Texan shaking his head over a stalled Lincoln Continental was too much. I had what was known locally as "a fit of the giggles."

O'Reilly's guffaws drowned my strangled squeaks.

"Told you," he gasped, "they're a curious people. And, by the way, I made it to the McGillicuttys in time."

Times Are A-Changing

Or Are They?

The smell in O'Reilly's surgery would have gagged a maggot. He stood at the sink, test tube grasped in one hand, oblivious to the acrid fumes spewing forth with all the fervour of a genie who has been in his bottle for centuries too long.

Maggie MacCorkle sat expectantly, awaiting the pronouncement from her oracle.

"No sugar in that, Maggie." O'Reilly looked pontifically over his half-moon spectacles. "Run along, now. And leave the door open."

"Thank you, Doctor." Maggie rose, gave me her usual look of disdain, and left. Her departure allowed a modicum of fresh air to penetrate the fug.

"God's strewth, Fingal, what were you about?" My eyes watered and my words were muffled by a series of involuntary constrictions of my throat.

"Fehling's test, my boy." He waved the noisome vessel under my nose.

For readers who didn't attend a medical school that boasted either Hippocrates or Galen as members of its faculty, Fehling's test involved boiling one test tube of the mystical Fehling's solution and another of the patient's urine. The two were mixed. If nothing exploded, the appearance of a blue tinge indicated the presence of glycosuria. Maggie may not have had glucose in her specimen, but something had managed to slip through her glomeruli — probably, I thought, burnt Wellington boots.

It was always tricky — as in trying to remove a piece of well-decayed cow from a starving alligator — to suggest to O'Reilly that he might not be entirely up to date. It was going to be even more so because I did remember the hypochondriac who'd insisted on calling O'Reilly in the middle of the night. Doctor O. had instructed the victim to pass urine every hour on the hour until morning and use dipsticks on every specimen. So he couldn't have been entirely unfamiliar with the things.

In the spirit of scientific inquiry, and with a precautionary glance to assure myself that the door was still open, I began.

"Er," I asked, "er, Fingal, would it not

have been easier to use a dipstick?"

"Of course," he said benignly, dumping the fuming mixture down the drain, "but remember, there's art to medicine as well as science." He chuckled. "Maggie would never have believed the results of a wee bit of cardboard but she's absolutely convinced by my pyrotechnics."

Lord help us, I thought, if he ever decides she needs leeching, but although I kept the sentiments to myself, my cynical look must have betrayed me.

"You don't believe me?" he asked.

I have difficulty with the concepts that the Earth is flat, the moon is made of green cheese, and Darwin and armies of palaeontologists are wrong. "Well . . ."

"There's nobody — I mean nobody," he shook his head, "absolutely nobody as resistant to change as Ulsterfolk."

There was some truth to that. Half of us were still fighting a battle that officially ended in 1690 — with no need for a couple of periods of overtime, never mind three centuries of rematches. There was, however, an increasing subset of the inhabitants of the northeastern corner of the Emerald Isle who had moved with the times. Instead of pikes and muskets, they used Semtex. "Yes, but . . ." I tried, but he rolled over me.

"I'll prove it. Do you remember Sunny?"

"Sunny? The chap who lives in his car?"

"The very one."

Of course I remembered Sunny and his run-in with Councillor Bishop, he whose wife had had herself cremated, with the family wealth in ten-pound notes in the coffin.

"I should remember him. Don't I call to see him and his dogs every week or so?"

"Still living in his car?"

"Yes." I was having some difficulty following Fingal's line of reasoning — but that was something that would never change. As is a corkscrew to a ruler, so was O'Reilly's convoluted logic to linear cogitation. I suspected he was probably the originator of divergent thinking.

"But," I said, "I don't see what that has to do with the inflexibility of the average Ulsterman."

"Huh. Do you know what Sunny's chief delight was — other than his dogs?"

I had to admit I did not.

"His car had a wireless. He'd listen to it for hours."

"And I suppose you're going to tell me that when the BBC added new stations he refused to listen to them because he's an Ulsterman and Ulsterfolk are resistant to change."

"Not at all. He took to them like a duck to water."

"So he did change."

"Up to a point," said O'Reilly. His face softened. I knew he had a warm spot for his eccentric patient. "But the car was 1940s vintage and eventually the radio stopped working."

I'm sure that on occasions in darkest Africa Stanley must have despaired of ever finding Doctor Livingstone.

"I don't see . . ."

" 'Course you don't." A smile played round O'Reilly's lips. "But somebody bought Sunny a television set and ran an electrical cable from his deserted house to the car."

Archimedes is reputed to have leapt from his bathtub yelling, *"Eureka."* I had an urge to mutter the same Hellenic expletive — not because I had the faintest idea what this piece of intelligence had to do with O'Reilly's thesis about stubbornness, but because I was certain who the "somebody" had been.

To accuse O'Reilly of anything resembling kindness would have upset the big man. Like the Good Lord, Fingal liked to "move in mysterious ways his wonders to perform."

Lest my expression give me away for a second time, I tried to steer O'Reilly back to his original argument.

"So," I said, "Sunny did change. He switched from listening to the radio to watching television." Adopting my best Perry Mason manner, I remarked, "I rest my case."

"Almost," said O'Reilly. "You're almost right."

"Oh?" The argument seemed pretty solid to me.

"He used the set. No doubt about that — but do you know what he said to me after he'd had the thing for a month?"

I shook my head.

O'Reilly's big frame quivered. "Sunny said — Sunny said, 'Do you know, Doctor dear, but thon TV's the powerful thing. All you have to do is watch it with your eyes shut and it's near as good as my old wireless.'"

I had to laugh.

"Change an Ulsterman?" said O'Reilly. "You'd have a better chance getting Niagara Falls to run uphill."

Now, after thirty years, I can look back and laugh at myself, and O'Reilly was wrong. Some Ulstermen do change. If they didn't, I'd be writing this with a quill pen instead of my trusty Underwood typewriter.

THE STING

O'REILLY BAGS A WASPS' NEST

"Holy thundering mother of Jasus," O'Reilly roared, springing from his deck chair, dousing me with the contents of his glass, and clapping a hand to the back of his neck with enough force to have decapitated a lesser mortal.

I leapt to my feet, simultaneously dabbing at the large John Jameson stain on my pants and wondering what could have provoked the big man's outburst.

"Little bugger," O'Reilly growled.

I thought he was addressing me — he was prone to using such terms of endearment — but he wasn't looking at me. Instead he glowered at an insectoidal remnant clutched between his finger and thumb. It was a very wide, very flat, very dead wasp. One of the kamikaze breed. Only an insect with no desire to continue its existence would have had the temerity to sting Doctor Fingal Fla-

283

hertie O'Reilly, MB, BCh, BAO.

He discarded the corpse and rubbed the back of his neck. I could see the red weal. "Blue bag," he grunted as he galloped from the garden and into the house.

When he reappeared — fresh whiskey in one hand — a deep blue splodge covered his nuchal lump. I hadn't the faintest idea what resided within the famous blue bag, but I did know that its application to insect stings was soothing. Certainly it seemed to have calmed O'Reilly.

"Wouldn't be summer without the odd wasp," he said mildly.

I nodded. The beasts were pests in late August and — I watched one as it clung to the edge of my sherry glass — there seemed to be more of them on that particular evening. Lots more. Two had joined the original sherry seeker and five were having a go at O'Reilly's whiskey.

I've neglected to tell you that we'd set our deck chairs under the shade of the sycamore tree at the bottom of O'Reilly's garden. It was a magnificent specimen, tall, leafy, ancient, and from among its branches squadrons of the brutes buzzed in close formation. They made beelines, or perhaps that should be wasp-lines, for our drinks.

I dislike physical pain and it seemed to

me that the odds against my being stung were going down dramatically. There were so many yellow-and-black bodies on the wing that I began to wonder if Pharaoh and Moses had taken up residence in Bally-bucklebo and that the old patriarch had given up on locusts and moved on to wasps as a method of softening Ramses' ossified cardiac organ.

"I think we should go in, Fingal."

He ignored me and stared up into the leafy canopy overhead.

"C'mere, Pat." He pointed upward.

I moved beside him and followed the line of his outstretched finger.

"What do you make of that?"

High in the tree, suspended from a branch, was a grey thing, narrow at the bottom, wide at the top, and about the size of the ill-fated *Hindenburg* dirigible.

"It's the biggest wasps' nest I've ever seen, Fingal." One settled on my ear. "I really do think we should be going in," I remarked, sidling toward the house, leaving my drink on a garden table, hoping the wasps would be distracted long enough for me to make my getaway unscathed.

He grabbed my arm.

"It's got to go," he said. "Got to."

"I agree," I said, and instantly regretted

my words. Someone was going to have to make the nest go, and from the look on O'Reilly's face I realized that he thought he'd found his volunteer. I imagine Lord Wellington's eyes took on the same steely glare when he selected the poor devils to be first to storm the breach in the walls of a French-held fort. The term for those wretches was "the forlorn hope."

"Sorry, Fingal, but remember when Maggie MacCorkle's cat got stuck up this tree?"

"Right," he said, "right. I'd forgotten you had acrophobia." And a highly developed sense of self-preservation, I thought.

"Donal," he said. "Donal Donnelly's the man for the job."

Writers of tales of darkest Africa often mentioned the jungle telegraph, as in ". . . the heat, the heat, and the native drums." Plains Indians reputedly communicated using smoke signals. How messages were transmitted in Ballybucklebo, where few of the natives possessed telephones, was a mystery to me, but communicate they did. I called this phenomenon the bog telegraph. It had worked with its usual celerity.

Half an hour after O'Reilly's pronouncement, Donal Donnelly showed up at the house, wheeling his psychedelic bicycle and

286

wearing his simple smile.

"Hear you've a wee job for me, Doctor, sir," he said, knuckling his forehead — a very thin strip between his eyebrows and hairline — and bending to remove his bicycle clips, strange metallic devices worn around the ankles to prevent the 'cycle's chain from devouring the wearer's trousers.

"Indeed I do," said an avuncular O'Reilly, draping a fond arm round Donal's narrow shoulders and regarding the victim with the expression I've always imagined Lewis Carroll's walrus used when talking to a group of oysters. "Just a wee one. Come on in," he said, "and I'll show you."

Donal trotted in O'Reilly's wake and I brought up the rear. Once in the back garden, O'Reilly started to explain the nature of the "wee job."

"Here's your ladder, Donal." O'Reilly bent, picked up a wooden extending ladder, and loaded it onto Donal's shoulder.

"Painting, is it, Doctor?"

O'Reilly shook his head.

"Here's your sack." Fingal handed Donal a large potato sack.

Donal frowned as he accepted the thing.

"There's the tree."

Donal's face lightened. "Another wee pussycat up your tree, Doctor, sir?"

287

"Not exactly."

The frown came back.

"It's a wasps' nest, Donal."

Donal froze. I believe his eyeballs swole in their sockets. "Jasus, Mary, and Joseph and all the little saints," he whispered.

"Nothing to it, Donal. Nip up the ladder, whip the sack round the nest, snap off its stalk, and hold the mouth of the sack tight shut."

Donal's head nodded like one of those big-beaked, globular-bodied, feather-tailed toy birds which if clipped to the rim of a water glass would oscillate back and forth for hours.

"There's a good lad," said O'Reilly, pushing Donal in the direction of the elm. "By the time you bring the nest down in the sack, I'll have a bonfire lit. We can cremate the whole bloody lot of them." This last was said with a leer that would have looked well on the face of a Roman emperor giving the thumbs down to an army of defeated gladiators.

I retreated inside the kitchen doorway. Donal went to the tree. My last glimpse was of his legs disappearing up through the leaves. O'Reilly bent to his work making a heap of dried leaves and twigs, his ample behind pointing straight at the old elm.

I heard Donal yelling from his leafy aerie, "I've got them, Doctor, sir. It's going to be all right."

And it would have been — if the bottom hadn't fallen out of the mouldy old sack and the nest's infuriated occupants hadn't been released when the nest hit the ground.

PIPES OF WRATH

THE MAN WHO SILENCED O'REILLY

Very few people ever told that medical gentleman, Doctor Fingal Flahertie O'Reilly, what to do, but it could be done. I saw it happen. By the way, please remember that a gentleman may be defined as "a man who can play the bagpipes — but doesn't." By this account Doctor Fingal Flahertie O'Reilly was certainly no gentleman. His weekly practices with the local pipe band were one thing. They took place in an old barn sufficiently far from Ballybucklebo that the natives were scarcely if ever disturbed. I could even find it in my heart to forgive his solitary warbling on his miniature chanter.

Chanter? For those unfamiliar with the great highland bagpipe and wondering what on Earth I'm on about, let me explain the arcane workings of the things. The bits that stick up over the player's shoulder are the drones. There are no prizes for guessing why. The tube that connects the apparently apoplectic puffer's mouth to the tartan-covered bag is the blowstick. The chanter is the perforated pipe up and down which the musician's fingers ripple as though the digits' owner had forgotten to take his anti-convulsants for at least a week. It's from the chanter that the tune is wrung.

Pipers with consciences can exercise their chanter fingering on a miniature version. The full-sized job roars like the booming of some long-dead dinosaur. A regimental pipe band can re-create the noises of the entire Jurassic period. Massed bands, like those at the Annual Edinburgh Tattoo, for example, can emulate the racket of the Mesozoic Era. The miniature version produces a gentler note — somewhere between an oboe and a ruptured duck — and is barely audible at a range of a spear's throw, the average distance used by Sassenachs to decide whether to flee from the noise or try to show their disapproval in a more pointed way. No, I had little cause for complaint when O'Reilly confined himself to the mini version.

Life only became auditorily awful when himself would fire up the whole set and march up and down the back garden playing something called a pibroch. According to O'Reilly, the pibroch was the classical music of the pipes. I didn't seem to recognize the names of Beethoven or Brahms among the composers of these works but I'm sure it was due to an oversight. Mozart's rarely if ever played K1007 1/2 was probably a concerto for pibroch and orchestra.

Picture if you will, O'Reilly, bag under left arm, drones on left shoulder, face florid, nose flashing from scarlet to white (the latter when he missed a note, although how anyone but him could tell was beyond me), pacing up and down the back garden, pipes roaring, birds fleeing from the trees in panic, and the faithful Arthur Guinness marching at his master's side, gazing with the eyes of a besotted fool at the Labrador's version of God and lending his not inconsiderable howling in counterpoint.

The natives of Ballybucklebo tolerated these outbursts, less because of any great affection for their medical advisor, but rather from a deep-seated local belief that so awful was the wailing that the indigenous banshees fled in terror. And as everyone knew, no one could die in Ballybucklebo without a preliminary hullabaloo from the banshee.

On the night in question I was cowering in the upstairs sitting room, praying that the row would stop, beseeching the Almighty with all the fervour of one of Custer's cavalrymen asking that the Indians go away. Somewhere in my pounded ears I became aware of an insistent ringing. I knew that tinnitus could be provoked by too many decibels. For a happy moment I hoped it might be the harbinger of a merciful deafness, then I realized it was the front doorbell — and it was Mrs. Kincaid's night off.

When I answered the door, a small, bekilted man stood there. He looked like a Scottish garden gnome that had climbed down from its concrete plinth. His face was as weathered as if he'd spent his entire life — which must have been at least seventy winters — in the open air.

"Good evening," I remarked, expecting to be addressed in the almost incomprehensible burr of the Glaswegian.

"Aye. Chust so." His speech was soft, melodious. I was conversing with a highlander or a man from the Western Isles.

"It will be the Doctor himself that I am hearing?"

No, I thought, it's the wrath of God. But I nodded.

"Chust so. And could I be speaking with himself?"

"Actually I'm on call tonight, Mister . . . er . . ."

"MacKay of the Island MacKays." He offered his hand as a laird would to a peasant.

I shook it gravely. "Come into the surgery.
Please." I ushered him in. Even with the
heavy door closed behind us the awful
ululation thundered on.

"What can I do for you, Mister MacKay?"

"Well . . ." His face contorted into a ric-
tus of such anguish that I thought the little
man was having a heart attack.

"Are you all right?"

His features softened. "Fine. Ah'm grand.
It's himself." He inclined his bald pate in
the direction of the piping. "The Doctor
cannae get the grace notes right."

"And is that why you wanted to see him?"
I asked.

He nodded.

"Right," I said. "I'll go and get him." At
last, I thought, someone who can tell
O'Reilly to shut up. Then a thought struck
me. "Mister McKay, if he's making mis-
takes, does that mean he'll have to practise
harder?"

"Chust so."

"Could you do me a favour? Could you
suggest he uses the practice chanter?"

A very knowing look spread across the old
Scotsman's face. "Aye, son. Chust so."

My heart soared as I sped to the back

294

garden. It took about five minutes to attract O'Reilly's attention. He lowered the bag and the moaning ceased slowly. The noise would have been described locally as "the tune the old cow died to."

"What do you want?" he roared.

Do not try to take a raw steak from a pit bull. Do not interrupt O'Reilly's pibroch.

"There's a Mister MacKay to see you, Fingal."

O'Reilly flinched. "Lord," he muttered.

"He says something about your not getting your grace notes right."

O'Reilly looked as if he had been struck by lightning. His voice fell to a whisper — the first bit of peace and quiet I'd had for what seemed like hours. "Did he?"

I nodded.

"Jasus. Do you know who he is?"

I shook my head.

"Angus MacKay was the Lord of the Isles piper before he moved here to Bally-bucklebo." By the look on Fingal's face the position must have been on a par with the Archangel Gabriel's in a more elevated sphere. "He taught me to play."

"And," I said, "he says you need a lot more practice. On the little chanter."

O'Reilly hung his head.

And for a while, I thought, blessing the

name of Angus MacKay, there will be peace in the valley.

SAM SLITHER

WHAT NOISE ANNOYS AN OYSTER?

Doctor Fingal Flahertie O'Reilly was a man of definite likes — you know about his terrible strong weakness for the product of John Jameson's distillery — and his share of well-formulated dislikes.

When it came to certain members of the species *Homo sapiens* — Councillor Bishop immediately springs to mind — O'Reilly regarded them with the distaste of a South Seas cannibal for banana fritters. Nor did he confine his animus to specified individuals. Certain subspecies — district health officials, a well-defined breed of Presbyterian minister (the Angus McWheezles of this world) and lawyers, for example — he would condemn to perdition en bloc. Not that he ever let his general disgust stand in the way if the opportunity to attack a particular member of one of the subsets presented itself.

297

Take the case of Samuel P. Shaughnessy, LLB, known to the citizens of Ballybucklebo as "Sam Slither." The "slither" part was an allusion to the man's slippery courtroom carryings-on.

The legal eagle in question had visited us because he was troubled by a persistent cough. Shaughnessy was a little man, birdlike. He had beady eyes and a hooked nose that wouldn't have been out of place on the face of a peregrine falcon. He strutted into the surgery, breast thrust out like a pouter pigeon — and a particularly haughty pouter at that.

From his opening, "Well, O'Reilly?" — not, you will note, "Doctor O'Reilly" — he treated my senior colleague as a duke would treat a scullion. He simply ignored me. He left without as much as a thank you.

O'Reilly had dealt with the man in an entirely professional manner — and about as much warmth as the blizzard that finally saw off Scott of the Antarctic.

"Jasus," said O'Reilly as soon as Slither, S., had left the surgery, "I can't abide that man. He'd better not go swimming."

"Because it would be bad for his cough?" I asked naively.

O'Reilly snorted. "Not at all. If he ever went in the water, the whole of the coast guard would be out to clean up the oil slick."

I knew of Shaughnessy's reputation. "You're right, Fingal," I said, but contained my desire to laugh. O'Reilly's nose tip was pure alabaster.

"I don't like Mister Shaughnessy," growled O'Reilly. "Not one bit."

It seemed superfluous to remark that I could have guessed that. I assumed that Mister S. was in O'Reilly's bad books as a side effect of the little lawyer's profession. As usual when it came to guessing why Doctor O. behaved the way he did, I wasn't entirely right.

O'Reilly rummaged in his pocket and produced and lit up his briar. "Come to think of it, keeping him away from the water's another good reason that he should never be let loose on the deck of a yacht."

Aha, I thought, there's more to this than immediately collides with the contents of the eye-socket.

You'll remember that O'Reilly was a keen sailor. So was Shaughnessy. Indeed he was commodore of the local yacht club, and to add insult to injury, his boat and O'Reilly's were tied at four wins each in the biweekly race series.

"It's your day off on Saturday," O'Reilly remarked, catching me quite off guard.

"What are you up to?"

With my unerring ability to fabricate a plausible excuse on the spur of the moment, I answered, "Um . . ."

"Good," said O'Reilly. "It's the last race in the series and I . . ."

"Need a crew?"

"Exactly, my boy." He beamed and exhaled a cloud of tobacco smoke that would have cleared the first two lines of enemy trenches in World War I. "I'm sure we can get a locum down from Belfast. You'll have a wonderful sail."

I wondered if Mister Christian had offered similar comforting words as he cast Captain Bligh adrift on the start of his two-thousand-mile journey in an open longboat.

I won't weary you with the details of the great yacht race. I'll merely remark that O'Reilly's boat and Shaughnessy's crossed the start line bow to bow and immediately engaged in what I'm told is referred to as a tacking duel. The shining hours passed with tacks, gybes, luffing ups, and sundry other arcane manoeuvres, all accompanied by roars of command to the crew — me — and abusive bellows of "Starboard!" and "Water!" hurled from vessel to vessel. I believe if O'Reilly's boat had been armed he'd have given Shaughnessy a broadside and ordered me to "board him in the smoke."

The ferocity of the competition would have made an America's Cup race look like the endeavours of two model boats on a duck pond. O'Reilly's boat crossed the finishing line a mere two feet ahead of the competition.

I was soaked, frozen, and felt as though single-handedly I'd hauled a grand piano to the summit of Mount Everest. Pulling on ropes on a yacht isn't called grinding for nothing. But I confess there was a sense of satisfaction. Not only had O'Reilly beaten Shaughnessy, he had, as far as I understood these things, won the series.

I glanced at Shaughnessy's boat and noticed a red flag flying from the piece of string that ran from the blunt end to the top of the mast. Assuming this signal to be some kind of gracious concession of defeat, I happily drew the matter to O'Reilly's attention.

He erupted. "Bloody lawyers! Bloody Sam Slither. Trust him to hoist a protest flag."

"Protest?"

"Protest. He's saying that somewhere we broke one of the rules." Given the ferocity of the recent competition, I couldn't help remarking, "The Marquess of Queensberry Rules?"

"No, you nitwit. Racing rules. We'll have to meet with the race committee. He'll present his case — bloody lawyer — and we'll have to try to defend ourself. That little weasel knows the laws of sailing better than a Talmudic scholar knows the Torah." The sound of O'Reilly grinding his teeth was so intense that I thought we'd run aground — again.

The atmosphere at the post-race buffet was frosty. The committee had met. Shaughnessy had presented his case, and to the obvious disappointment of the committee members and the huge chagrin of O'Reilly, they'd had to find, purely on some abstruse point of maritime law, in Slippery Sam's favour. It wouldn't be entirely accurate to describe O'Reilly as crushed, but he was distinctly subdued.

I believe revenge has been described as "a dish best eaten cold." If the originator of the remark had been at the buffet he might have changed the remark to "a dish not eaten at all," but then its author Joseph Marie Eugène Sue couldn't have known O'Reilly.

He stood at the table, pint in one hand,

plate in the other. He was accepting the condolences of his many cronies.

Shaughnessy pushed his way through the little throng. He carried a plate of raw oysters.

I listened as he addressed O'Reilly.

"To make up for my victory," I saw the man's chest puff out farther than usual, "let me buy you a drink."

O'Reilly did not speak.

Nor did any other member of the yacht club. A dropping pin would have sounded like the eruption of Krakatoa, so deep was the silence.

"Well, at least have an oyster. Quite delicious."

I saw O'Reilly's grin start and steeled myself.

"Shaughnessy," Fingal said in gentle tones, "you're a quare dab hand at the law." Sam Slither's pullover nearly burst.

"But my trade's medicine, and you know . . . so I'll pass on the oysters." His pause wasn't merely pregnant. It was carrying triplets. He inclined his head to the plate of slithery bivalves and said in gentle but very widely audible tones, "I always advise my patients never — never — to eat anything as slimy as a lawyer."

A MATCHLESS EXPERIENCE

PITY THE STRANGER
VISITING BALLYBUCKLEBO

Occasionally, outsiders wandered into Bally-bucklebo. Some of them, when confronted with the likes of Maggie MacCorkle, Donal Donnelly, the Reverend Angus McWheezle, and indeed the redoubtable Doctor Fingal Flahertie O'Reilly himself, must have wondered if they'd stumbled into a dress rehearsal for one of the more bizarre efforts of *Le Théâtre du Grand-Guignol.*

I'm sure that collectively the denizens of our little village could have kept teams of geneticists happily employed for years. Behavioural psychologists could have filled countless journal pages with arcane articles with titles like, "The Immediate Onset of Incomprehensible Gibbering Among Strangers on First Being Introduced to Maggie MacCorkle" or "The Impact of Entering the Mucky Duck on the Cognitive

Processes of Otherwise Well-Balanced Persons."

Usually, the poor benighted who stumbled into our little backwater had arrived there by mistake. Most had taken a wrong turning on the Belfast-to-Donaghadee Road. Even the mere act of seeking directions to return a wayward traveller on their merry way could lead to nervous exhaustion. Such clearly stated navigational tips as, "Go down the road 'til you come to a red barn, sir. Now don't turn right there," or, "When you've not turned at the red barn, go on three more fields. There'll be a black-and-white cow there unless Willy John has her in the red barn for milking. Go two fields past and follow your nose."

I once heard Donal Donnelly at his most helpful reduce a bewildered-looking city gent to a state bordering on hysteria. The party in question halted his Rolls-Royce, wound down the window, and said to the passing Donal, "My good man, how would I get from here to Donaghadee?"

Donal, as you'll remember, was a bit slow. Indeed snails had been known to cover vast distances while Donal puzzled out the answer to a question.

"Come on, man. I haven't got all day."

"It's Donaghadee you want, sir?"

"I just told you that."

"Donaghadee? Aye, indeed. Donaghadee."

"Yes. Donaghadee." There was a great deal of drumming of fingers on the steering wheel.

"That's a hard one, sir. That's a very hard one. You know" — here Donal paused and a beautiful smile plastered itself across his normally bland face — "if I was you I wouldn't have tried to get to Donaghadee from here in the first place."

You can understand why few non-natives, apart from impecunious assistants to established general practitioners, would decide to let their caravans rest in that rural loony bin. And yet once in a navy blue moon someone would appear from the great world outside, sample the village, and decide to stay. They usually didn't last long unless they were able to adapt to the aboriginal ways and, more importantly, gain acceptance into the Ballybucklebo social circle. In Ireland such recent arrivals are known as "blow-ins."

It might have been his acknowledged virtuosity on the great highland bagpipe — after all, the man had been piper to the Lord of the Isles — that led to the initial acceptance of Angus MacKay.

The fact that he'd had the temerity to point out to O'Reilly his inability to master certain grace notes as he throttled a thing called a pibroch from his tartan-clad octopus would have raised MacKay's stock further with the locals. His complete bringing into the fold was assured on the night when MacKay simultaneously reaffirmed his Scotsness and succeeded in discomfiting a visiting Sassenach.

Angus worked as a shepherd. He lived in a cottage about ten miles from the village and it had become his wont to walk into Ballybucklebo on a Saturday, stop at the Mucky Duck for a wee dram, purchase one bottle of single malt, and hike back to his cottage.

O'Reilly had hauled me into the Duck. The place was relatively quiet. Only one or two of the usual suspects held up the far end of the bar. A stranger leaned dispiritedly, alone as a heron on a mudflat, toying with a half-pint. The poor man had probably popped in to ask directions.

O'Reilly and I were sitting at a table when Angus came in. As usual he wore a tam-o'-shanter and was bekilted and besporranned.

"Good evening, Doctors," said Angus.

"Evening, Angus."

He propped his cromach, the long crook

beloved by Scottish shepherds, in a corner and walked over to the bar. He was so short his nose barely reached the countertop.

"Evening, Angus." Arthur Osbaldiston, our red-faced, spherical host, beamed over the bar. "The usual?"

"Chust so, and a packet of Woodbines."

"Twenty?"

Angus rummaged in his sporran, produced a handful of coins, consulted them with the concentration of a Viking warlock examining his runes, shook his head, and said, "No. Ten will be chust fine."

Spendthrift and Angus MacKay did not have quite the happy relationship of say, peaches and cream.

Arthur delivered the cheap cigarettes and a glass of whisky.

"There you are, Angus."

"Thank you, Arthur," he said, lifting his tam-o'-shanter with the courtesy of a Spanish grandee. He pulled out and lit one cigarette, leaving the packet on the counter, said, "*Slainte,*" and sipped his drink.

Perhaps it was his accent, so different from those of the locals, that persuaded the stranger to sidle along the bar and try to strike up a conversation.

"Hello, old chap," the man said by way of introduction. Immediately I recognized the plummy, marbles-in-the-mouth tones of an English ex–public schoolboy. No wonder, I thought, that he'd been ignored by the others in the place.

Angus inclined his head, but said nothing.

"Couldn't help noticing you're having a smoke."

Angus nodded, but kept his counsel.

The Englishman's voice was louder than those usually heard in the Duck and I could see that the others in the place were now paying avid attention to the little drama unfolding at the other end of the bar.

"Um . . . don't suppose you could spare a match?"

Aha, I thought, the ask-for-a-match gambit as a way of striking up a conversation. I wondered how successful the Englishman would be.

Silently Angus opened his sporran, fumbled in its depths, produced one single match, and gravely offered it to his new-found acquaintance, who accepted the match and said, "One is terribly grateful. Live round here, do you?"

Angus's nod was barely perceptible.

"Nice place, what?"

I began to rise as the man spoke. His hands were moving rapidly over his body, patting himself here and there. I thought I was witnessing my first case of Saint Vitus's dance.

"Do you know" — the man's hands stilled and he nodded his head toward the packet of Woodbines on the bar counter — "terribly stupid of me. I seem to have come out without my cigarettes."

Every eye in the place was focused with the pinpoint accuracy of radar sets on the pair at the bar.

The stranger finally succeeded in getting Angus to say something. He probably wished he hadn't.

The little Scotsman's usually soft speech was softer yet, but not a word was lost on his audience.

He held out one hand and said, "In that case, sir, you'll no' be needing my match."

A HUMBLE APOLOGY

O'REILLY COMES TO
THE RESCUE ONCE AGAIN

I'd last seen Angus MacKay, shepherd and piper extraordinaire, in the company of the Reverend McWheezle. The man of the cloth had tried to suggest that the splendour of Angus's garden was largely attributable to the work of the Almighty. Angus, and I must say I'd thought he'd been pretty diplomatic, had simply asked the Lord's local representative if he could recall what the garden had looked like when the Celestial Being had been left in sole charge of the then-weed-infested plot.

The Reverend McWheezle took to being bested verbally with all the enthusiasm of a man having a fingernail yanked out, and from that day had gone out of his way to belittle Angus MacKay. The schism between them had developed into a chasm that would have made the Grand Canyon look like an irrigation ditch.

Mister McWheezle took every opportunity, usually thinly veiled as prim pastoral piety, to take a verbal swipe at Angus. The old Scot bore this vituperation with apparent sangfroid, although unknown to all of us in Ballybucklebo, the sang that ran in the little Scot's veins was coursing at about absolute zero.

I confess that from time to time I wondered when Angus would stop turning the other cheek and turn the other set of knuckles — as in a right cross or jab and uppercut. But no matter how hard the reverend pushed, Angus would mutter a civil, "Chust so," and walk away. He kept his counsel until the day McWheezle moved from Angus-baiting to a direct frontal assault upon Angus's nation — an attack as forceful as the one that delivered Badajoz into the hands of the Iron Duke.

"Ah," said McWheezle, in front of a small crowd of his congregation outside the kirk at the end of morning service, "been praying, MacKay?"

"Chust so, your reverence." Angus tipped his caubeen most civilly.

"Just like the Scots," said McWheezle, vinegar oozing through the honey of his words. "Pray on their knees on a Sunday —

and their neighbours for the rest of the week."

Angus stopped dead. His kilt shuddered like an electrocuted jellyfish. He turned, faced the reverend gentleman, and said in low but measured tones, "Mister Mc-Wheezle, sir?"

"Yes, Angus?"

"It would be a cause of great pleasure to me, sir — with all due deference to your station — it would be a cause of great pleasure to me, sir, if you would kindly bugger off."

The words were clear, deliberate, and greeted with the kind of stunned silence that would have marked a royal wedding if the answer to the question, "Do you take this prince . . ." had been "Sod this for a game of soldiers." Every mouth gaped. Lips pursed. The members of the audience looked like a school of expiring codfish.

"Aye," said Angus — in fencing circles his original remark had been a parry; now came the riposte — "and as soon and as fast as possible." He spun on his heel and strode off, cromac clattering on the pavement.

From the look on the Reverend McWheezle's face he'd been taken off guard as much as a certain King Edward at a spot called Bannockburn. It was a good thing the old church was built of granite, so great was the huffing and puffing of the practically paralyzed Presbyterian.

The only sound that could be heard over the reverend's respiratory rasping was a gargantuan grumbling — the kind of noise an antiquated steam boiler with a stuck safety valve might make if the internal pressure was reaching a critical point. I turned and realized it was O'Reilly trying to control himself.

We didn't see Angus for several weeks, then he resurfaced as the very last patient of a busy morning's surgery. O'Reilly ushered him in. O'Reilly seated himself at the rolltop desk and, as usual, I parked myself on the examining couch.

"Have a seat, Angus." O'Reilly gestured toward a chair.

The little Scot shook his head. He stood silently, holding his caubeen in both hands.

I waited. O'Reilly waited. Angus said nothing. The silence stretched like a piece of knicker elastic caught in the spokes of a bicycle wheel.

"Well," said O'Reilly, at last, "what seems to be the trouble?"

"It is that man," said Angus. "Himself. The dominie."

Domino? I thought. Whatever was he on about?

"Mister McWheezle?" asked O'Reilly.

"Chust so. It was a terrible thing."

"What he said to you?" O'Reilly probed.

"No," said Angus with a mighty shake of his head. "What I said to him."

"Come on, Angus. He was asking for it."

Angus drew himself up — well to half-mast; remember he was less than five feet tall. "It was not a thing to be forgiven. A shentleman" — I realized he meant gentleman — "from the Isles should never lose his temper." The little Scot was clearly distressed.

"Um," said O'Reilly, "um, I don't suppose you'd consider apologizing?"

From the look on the little man's face I guessed that he would rather have eaten his haggis raw.

"This is upsetting you, Angus, isn't it?" said O'Reilly.

"Chust so, Doctor. It is what you might call a dilemma."

Right, I thought. Come on, O'Reilly, let's see you solve this one.

O'Reilly bent his head over to Angus, whispered something I couldn't hear, and straightened up. The thunderclouds fled from Angus's wrinkled face. The sun gleamed on the hills and valleys of his cheeks. His deep blue eyes twinkled.

"Chust so. Sunday then, Doctor . . . Thank you, sir." He turned and left.

"What . . . ?" I began.

"The power of authority," said O'Reilly, and that was all he would say.

After service that Sunday, a larger congregation than usual gathered on the church steps. O'Reilly and I kept our places at the front of the crowd as Angus MacKay approached the Reverend McWheezle.

"It is a word I would like, your reverence."

"Yes," said McWheezle with the inflated dignity of a Doge of Venice and all the warmth of an Atlantic northeaster.

"Well," said Angus mildly, "well, you'll no' have forgotten that I told ye tae bugger off?"

"Indeed," said McWheezle.

"Aye, and soon."

McWheezle sniffed.

"Well," said Angus slowly, "after giving the matter consideration, and after consultation with Doctor O'Reilly, I have come to the conclusion that . . ."

The reverend's chest puffed up like the *Hindenburg* before her final flight. "You must apologize?" he sneered.

"Oh no," said Angus, "no, it's chust that

Doctor O'Reilly says you need nae bother — but if you must, you'll no' be needing tae rush."

The Patient Who Broke the Rules

And Why O'Reilly Didn't Mind

Devotees of Ray Bradbury, and indeed many students of physics, know that paper bursts into flame at a temperature of 451°F. Devotees of Doctor Fingal Flahertie O'Reilly know that his flashpoint was considerably lower. If he'd been a volcano, teams of vulcanologists would have set up permanent encampments in his garden, ever ready to be on hand for his next inevitable eruption. Living in his house, as I did, was akin to dwelling on the lower slopes of Mount Vesuvius.

Ever since the first report of the dangers of secondhand smoke — written, I believe, by one of the Plinys, describing the minor upset that engulfed Pompeii — Neapolitans have developed a kind of early warning system. They rely on the behaviour of animals, their own ability to sense earth tremors, and any release of smoke from the

318

summit of their local planetary safety vent.

Ever since I'd witnessed the ejection of Donal Donnelly by my mentor, I'd developed my own early warning system. I relied on the rapid disappearance of Arthur Guinness, O'Reilly's cerebrally challenged Labrador, my own ability to see the great man tremble, and any suggestion of pallor in the tip of his nose.

Neapolitans are always prepared to beat hasty retreats at the slightest sign of instability. Removing myself from the great man's presence wasn't always possible but at least I'd evolved a pretty acute idea of when to keep my mouth shut and look the other way.

I also kept a mental checklist of people and circumstances likely to provoke one of his outbursts. Councillor Bishop, the Reverend McWheezle, and Doctor "Thorny" Murphy, unkindness to widows or eccentrics who lived in old cars, hypocrisy, and shoddy medical practice . . . but if we take the list of characters I've just mentioned, I repeat myself.

Malingerers with sore backs weren't high on O'Reilly's list of preferred patients. Slow historians — you know the type, the ones who in response to the question "Does anyone in your family suffer from anything similar?" will start with the utterly unrelated complaint of a distant ancestor whose name was recorded in the Domesday Book, and ramble glacially through the generations — slow historians would get shrift of such shortness from O'Reilly that it couldn't have been measured with a micrometer. At least that had been my experience until the day I sat in on a consultation with a local fisherman.

Declan O'Tomelty was a large man. He sat in the chair, boots firmly planted on the floor, knees apart, gnarled hands resting on his thighs. He wore moleskin trousers held up at the knee by those leather thongs that the Scots call knicky-tams.

O'Reilly sat before his rolltop desk, half-moon spectacles perched on the end of his nose, elbow on knee, chin resting on the back of his hand. He looked like a rustic version of Rodin's *Thinker*.

I kept a close eye on O'Reilly's schnozzle. By all the usual indicators, it should have borne an even closer resemblance to old Auguste R.'s lump of bronze on a marble pedestal — glanced at my watch — at least ten minutes ago. The history of O'Tomelty's sore back seemed to be going on forever, but O'Reilly simply sat, immobile, only occasionally making a sympathetic grunt.

O'Tomelty's epic expostulation eventually ended.

O'Reilly rose and gestured to me to get down from my perch on the examining table. He asked O'Tomelty to undress and lie on the table, and once the man had painfully climbed up, O'Reilly examined his patient's back with a thoroughness and gentleness that surprised me.

"Right," he said, "hop down, Declan. I've just to make a phone call."

O'Reilly lifted the receiver and dialed. "Hello? Royal Victoria? Orthopaedics, please." His fingers drummed on the desktop. "Professor Muldoon, please." Just a hint of nasal pallor. "I don't give a tinker's damn who he's busy with. This is Doctor Fingal O'Reilly. What? I should bloody well think so."

I wondered if the recipient's receiver was melting.

"Hello? Monkey Nuts?"

Good Lord, I thought. Professor Michael Muldoon had been the terror of all of us when we were students, and O'Reilly has the temerity to call the old fire-eater "Monkey Nuts"?

"No, sorry, I can't make it for golf on Saturday. No, I need a favour. Patient of mine. You'll see him at five? Splendid."

O'Reilly put down the phone and spoke quietly to the now fully dressed O'Tomelty. "Have a pew in the waiting room, Declan. Doctor Taylor here won't mind finishing the surgery. I'll run you up to Belfast."

"Thank you, Doctor, sir," O'Tomelty said as he left.

My mouth hung open. The man had broken at least two of O'Reilly's rules — thou shalt not have a sore back nor give a rambling history — as effectively as a murderer and an adulterer would have bent a couple of the Ten Interesting Suggestions that Moses brought down from the Mount, numbers five and ten by the Augustinian method of reckoning if memory serves, and yet O'Reilly had listened patiently and . . .

"I know what you're thinking, Taylor," he said, "so stop it."

"I promise," I replied. The Neapolitans, when in doubt, run.

"You don't know Declan O'Tomelty the way I do." O'Reilly's hazel eyes had a faraway look. "Don't suppose you know much naval history either."

I was about to remark that I wasn't entirely ignorant of the fate of the Spanish Armada when I remembered that O'Reilly had had a distinguished career in His Majesty's floating forces in the last great nastiness. He continued, "I hadn't been in practice here for long when Declan showed up, quite late at night. His back was sore. I wasn't too pleased."

Nor was King Charles I when Olly Cromwell decided that the royal locks needed a bit of a trim — permanently.

"Maybe," said O'Reilly pensively, "maybe I was a bit easier in those days. I listened to the man."

You *what*? I thought.

"Just showed me the value of a well-taken history. 'All right,' says I, 'how did you hurt your back?' 'Wasn't me that hurt it, Doc,' says he, 'it was them Germans.' 'Pardon,' says I. 'Well,' says he, 'I was in the navy.' I suppose because he and I had something in common I paid a bit more attention. 'Go on,' says I. 'I was minding my own business, strapped to my antiaircraft gun. Then there was a bloody great bang and me and the gun is heading up — right up. God knows what happened to the gun, but I headed down, and I'll tell you, Doc, that water was bloody cold, so it was.' 'Right,' says I, and I'll tell you, Pat, I was tired and not too pleased with his story. I only asked him one more question."

" 'Are you going to get out of here?' " I suggested.

O'Reilly shook his head. "No. I asked him, 'What ship were you on?' 'I don't suppose, Doc,' says he, 'that you ever heard of the *Hood*?' "

"The *Hood*?" I said, "but there were only three survivors."

"I know," said O'Reilly. "Declan really is one of them."

O'Reilly strode to the door. "His back has given him gip ever since. I think he's earned a ride to the hospital."

Author's note: I usually make up these stories but this is a retelling of an actual episode of my own early years in practice, although the name Declan O'Tomelty and his occupation are fictitious. I had no reason to doubt O'Reilly.

GOING TO THE DOGS

O'REILLY PLACES A BET

"Good Lord," said O'Reilly, "I wonder if he'll paint it the same colours as his bicycle."

We were strolling along the main, indeed the only, street of the humming metropolis of Ballybucklebo. Approaching us was Donal Donnelly, who was being tailed by something vaguely canine. After closer inspection, as our respective paths converged, I noticed that the beast was attached to Donal by a piece of frayed rope.

Donal, you will remember, wasn't overly bright — in the way that Mount Everest isn't overly short — and definitely belonged to the Charles Atlas School of Bodybuilding, Class of '61 — Failures. Anyone who'd ever seen Donal stripped for action was immediately reminded of some poor shipwrecked wretch who'd survived for several months on the boilings of his leather shoes and the smell of a greasy rag. Donal's visage would have been a geometrician's dream, pointed as it was both vertically and fore and aft.

I tell you this because the greyhound, for such it was, bore a striking resemblance to its master. There was nothing of the creature but a muzzle like a weasel's, ribs that only needed little paper chef's hats to pass muster as a rack of lamb, and a tail that the animal carried between its legs.

The last attribute was Donal's normal demeanour when addressing Doctor O'Reilly, but on that particular morning Donal was distinctly cocky. "She's a beauty, isn't she, Doctor O'Reilly?" Donal wasn't bursting with pride — he was exploding.

"Mmm," said O'Reilly noncommittally as he bent to examine the dog.

"You should see her run," said Donal. "Greased lightning wouldn't get a look in."

I thought back to my classes in nutrition and some arcane formula concerning rate of caloric expenditure and weight loss. Looking at Donal's greyhound, it seemed to me that the mere effort of standing was probably generating a calorific deficit. Running might make the animal disappear completely.

"What do you call her?" O'Reilly inquired,

diplomatically.

"Bluebird," said Donal, smugly.

"Bluebird. Would that be after Sir Malcolm Campbell's speedboat?" asked O'Reilly.

"Aye, Doctor. Boys-a-dear, you should see that thing go."

"Donal," said O'Reilly, "That *Bluebird* runs on water."

Donal held one finger alongside his nose. His left upper eyelid drooped like a sagging theatre curtain — the nearest Donal could manage to a wink — and he inclined his head to the dog. "So does she, Doctor."

For the life of me I couldn't understand why O'Reilly guffawed, slapped Donal on the shoulder, and said, "You'll tell me when she runs dry, won't you, Donal?"

"Indeed, Doctor. Indeed I will." Donal took his leave, pursued by the faithful Bluebird.

"Smart lad, that Donal," said O'Reilly. "That dog will bear watching."

O'Reilly's attribution of smartness to a man whose thickness was an affront to all short planks so dumbfounded me that I neglected to ask why Bluebird would bear scrutiny. I didn't find out for several months — and, as usual, I found out to my cost. I found out when O'Reilly and I went to the dogs — literally.

I may have neglected to mention that in the rural Ulster communities, working dogs were the order of the day — haughty police Alsatians, super-intelligent border collies, gentle guide dogs, and, oh yes, the dimwitted, boozing, look-there's-Taylor's-trouser-leg-let's-have-a-go-at-it, so-called gun dog, Arthur Guinness.

Bluebird was nominally a worker. Her task was to charge round an oval track in pursuit of a mechanical hare, beat all the other dogs, and by so doing enrich those who'd seen fit to wager on the outcome.

I'd learned from O'Reilly that those who chanced a flutter on Donal's dog were forming a line on the left for admittance to the local poorhouse. It was locally supposed that the only chance the animal would ever have of coming in first was to be almost overtaken by the dogs entered in the next race after the one she'd come last in.

The seasons followed their preordained paths in Ballybucklebo. O'Reilly swore at Councillor Bishop, practised his bagpipe grace notes (almost to the satisfaction of Angus MacKay), increased the share values of both the Guinness brewery and John Jameson's distillery, and allowed the practice of medicine to interfere with his busy schedule as little as possible. He had, after all, acquired the services of a junior assistant — me — and, as he was fond of remarking, "There's no sense buying a dog and barking yourself." Perhaps his allusion to dogs was what eventually made me inquire about the celerity of a certain Bluebird, the dog that ran on water.

"Tell you what," he said, "let's find out. We'll go and watch her run on Saturday."

And so we did.

On the appointed day, O'Reilly took me to the stadium. You may remember the Loughbrickland horse racing. The greyhound races bore a striking resemblance to their equestrian counterpart. A low fence surrounded the track. Between the fence and the spectators, the "turf accountants" had their stands. Florid-faced men in loud tweeds stood on their daises calling the odds and turning the purses of the punters to penury. Bluebird, it seemed, was to appear in the third race.

Donal materialized like a genie from a bottle. As he passed O'Reilly, his eyelid managed its slow descent and all he murmured was, "Very dry today, Doctor."

O'Reilly brightened considerably.

"Come on," he said, pushing his way through the crowd with all the gentility of a

Tiger tank. He clattered to a halt before "Honest" Joe Johnston's stand and examined the odds chalked on a board above the platform.

"Bluebird's at one hundred to one," he remarked. "Take my advice, Pat, put a couple of quid on her." He muttered this as he proffered five pounds to Honest Joe.

"Bluebird on the nose," O'Reilly said.

Honest Joe hesitated. Perhaps, I thought, even a bookie has a sense of decency. Taking O'Reilly's money seemed about as ethical as selling London Bridge to an unsuspecting antipodean.

"Bluebird," said O'Reilly. "To win."

The bookie shrugged, took the note, and gave O'Reilly a ticket.

"Well?" O'Reilly said, looking straight at me.

I shook my head. Given Bluebird's dismal record, I'd decided it would have been less painful simply to tear up one of my hard-earned pounds.

"You'll be sorry," O'Reilly growled.

I won't weary you with the details of the race. I'll simply remark that Bluebird, the slowest dog in all Ballybucklebo, obeying Einstein's laws of relativity, actually lengthened by a good two inches, so close did she come to the speed of light. If I'd taken

O'Reilly's advice I'd have been a hundred pounds better off.

He chuckled all the way home and made me wait until we were safely ensconced in his upstairs sitting room before he deigned to explain the day's proceedings.

"You see, Pat," he said, "Bluebird really did run on water."

I was mystified.

"Look, the dog fancy aren't above helping their animals along."

"I don't . . ."

"They give the poor things stimulants."

"Never."

"Oh, aye. That's why all winners have a dope test."

"But if Donal gave Bluebird something, that'll show up — and you'll have to give back the money."

The aspidistra that adorned the corner of the room grew a good two inches before he stopped laughing.

"They'll not find a thing," he said when he'd finally collected himself. "Donal's been stopping the dog."

"How?"

"Water," said O'Reilly. "Good old H_2O. Donal's been keeping the animal dry for a day before every race and then he's given her a bucket of water just before the start.

331

Slows the dog down — and no one ever tests the losers. Dog finishes last time after time, up go the odds, and then . . ."

"Lord," I said, "that's what Donal meant by 'It's a dry day.' He didn't give her the water today."

"Bingo," said O'Reilly. "They can test the wee bitch 'til hell freezes over."

"Dry day," I muttered, thinking of the hundred quid I hadn't collected.

"Never mind," said O'Reilly smugly, heading for the decanter on the sideboard, "we can always have our own wee wet."

A Meeting of the Minds

The First Lesson
of General Practice

"Old men forget." For the life of me I can't remember the originator of that quotation, but I can recall my first meeting with Doctor Fingal Flahertie O'Reilly — classical scholar, bagpiper, poacher, hard drinker, and foul-mouthed country GP — as if it were yesterday.

Parenthetically, I also do know that loss of short-term memory and clarity of long-term recall characterize dementia, but with regards to dumuntia — I reckon if I can still spell it I ain't got it.

Nor had Doctor Fingal Flahertie O. When I met him, and in subsequent years when I returned to Ulster to visit him, his cortical processes would have made the workings of a Pentium chip look like the slow grinding of an unwound grandfather clock. He coupled his mental acuity with an unshakable belief that actions spoke louder than words — which was often just as well. While his actions could be precipitate, his words, when he was riled, could be as cutting as the obsidian knives so beloved by the ancient Aztecs for slicing the hearts out of living victims. Add to that his propensity for salting his vituperations with a lexicon of blasphemy that would have made a sailor blush, and you can understand why Fingal Flahertie O'Reilly was as much a force to be reckoned with as a supercharged bulldozer.

And yet his patients loved him, and I suppose in time, so did I — although when I first met him, love at first sight seemed about as likely as the survival of a woodlouse under the front cylinder of a steamroller.

I'd just graduated from the Queen's University of Belfast. The ink on my diploma where the dean, one Hippocrates of Kos, had made his mark, had barely had time to dry. I was young, idealistic, determined to carry healing to darkest Ulster, wet behind the ears, sanctimonious — in short an inexperienced, opinionated pain in the arse. I had more rough edges than a piece of Precambrian rock. O'Reilly was responsible for smoothing the more jagged bits to something that more closely resembled a piece of emery paper. I will forever be in his debt — but had I followed my instincts when we first met, I would have fled from his village of Ballybucklebo with the single-mindedness of the Israelites on their package trip out of Egypt.

I'd driven down from Belfast, parked my elderly Volkswagen, and walked along a gravel path flanked by rosebushes to the front door of an imposing three-storey granite block house. I stood on the front doorstep, brand-new black bag clutched in one hand, and read the brass plate affixed to the door frame: "Doctor F. F. O'Reilly, MB, BCh, BAO, Physician and Surgeon."

Two bell pushes resided in their recesses in the plate. One was labelled "Day Bell," the other, "Night Bell." Above the plate, the mouthpiece of a speaking tube glistened dully in the summer sunlight. As I later learned, O'Reilly had been in practice since before the telephone had reached Ballybucklebo. Patients needing to consult the great man were expected to whisper their complaints along the tube as Pyramus and Thisbe spoke to each other through the crack in the wall in *A Midsummer Night's Dream*.

I was wondering whether to apply my own

mouth to the orifice when the front door opened, much as I imagine the jaws of hell gape for an unregenerate sinner. I took a step backward.

A large man, a man who stood about six foot thirteen and had the shoulders of Atlas, stood on the front steps. His face was as wrinkled as dried-out chamois leather, his cheeks florid, and his nose tip an alabaster white. His right hand grasped the coat collar and his left the seat of a pair of moleskin trousers on a much smaller man. I noticed that the grabee's left foot was bare and not altogether clean. The victim wriggled and whimpered, "Ah, Jesus, no, Doctor . . ."

Whatever the rest of his sentiments might have been, they were cut off by a high-pitched keening as he was hurled bodily into one of the rosebushes.

The ogre bent, picked up a shoe and a sock, and hurled the footwear after the now-crash-landed chap. I'll never forget Doctor O'Reilly's words, delivered in a voice that would have made old Stentor sound like a sufferer from laryngitis.

"Next time, Donal Donnelly, next time you want me to look at a sore ankle . . . wash your bloody feet!"

He spun on me. "Who are you and what the hell do you want?"

336

Immediate transportation to a place of sanctuary seemed like a good idea, but I was so numbed, all I could think of was to hold my black bag in front of me. I suppose I thought it might have offered some protection. The captain of H.M.S. *Hood* probably felt the same way about his ship's armour plating — before the *Bismark* let go.

"I said," he roared, "what the hell do you want?" As he spoke he advanced toward me.

"Doctor O'Reilly?"

"No. John — bloody — Wayne."

I wondered why I didn't simply mutter, "My mistake," and make tracks. Instead I swallowed, took my black bag and my courage in both hands, and said, "I'm Taylor. Your locum."

He guffawed. "Then why didn't you say so?"

Because I'd been feeling like a rabbit confronted by a boa constrictor. Because it wasn't the cat that had got my tongue, it was a pride of rabid lions. Because . . .

"Never mind," he said, "come on in."

His handshake would have done justice to a gravel crusher. Before turning to go into the house, he pointed an admonitory finger at the heap of human wreckage that was still struggling to disentangle itself from a mass of floribunda. "Go on home now,

Donal, do what I said." Doctor O'Reilly consulted his watch. "Surgery hours are over but if you're back within an hour I'll wait for you and Doctor — what did you say your name was?"

"Taylor."

"Doctor Taylor and I will have a look at your hind leg." He didn't wait for a reply, but turned and went in. I followed, closing the door behind me. He stood in a spacious hall, beaming from ear to ear, the tip of his nose now the colour of the rest of his face. "Let that be your first lesson, Taylor. If you want to succeed in practice, never — never, never, never — let the customers get the upper hand."

IT'S IN THE CAN

O'REILLY TAKES THE BAIT

My loyal reader stopped me in the corridor of the hospital yesterday and remarked that he still enjoyed his monthly dose of O'Reilly. He asked how I'd developed the ability to conjure up such farfetched pieces of fiction. I could have explained to him too, poor chap, if he hadn't been running late for his appointment with his psychiatrist.

My answer would have been that many lower species — and no, I don't mean Donal Donnelly — have developed remarkable survival strategies. Certain sea slugs, when threatened, eviscerate themselves. In my case, rather than performing repeated seppuku — the Samurai warrior's do-it-yourself total colectomy — I'd learned to be pretty quick off the mark with plausible excuses when in the company of Doctor Fingal Flahertie O'Reilly.

The need to do so was never more pressing than when Admiral Lord Horatio O'Reilly tried to inveigle me into accompanying him for a day's outing on the briny deep. You'll remember that he was the proud owner of a twenty-six-foot sloop. I believe he'd bought the wretched vessel after she'd failed the admittedly low entrance standards to qualify her as a coffin ship during the great Irish potato challenge of the 1840s.

Once O'Reilly had taken the helm, he seemed to think he was a direct descendant of Vasco da Gama, Christopher Columbus, and James Cook. In fact, his navigational skills were such that if Noah had signed O'Reilly on as navigator, given the reproductive rates among animals, the old patriarch would have been skipper of a pretty crowded Ark and might be looking for Mount Ararat to this very day.

Since the day when Fingal had piled his craft up on a reef — a reef that was clearly marked by a lighthouse — it had been my avowed intent never again to set foot on his decks. I often amazed myself with my rapid creativity when there was the slightest hint of an oceangoing jaunt. O'Reilly more often amazed me with his uncanny ability to beat me to the punch.

"What," he asked, one sunny August Saturday, "do you know about crabs?"

My mind was elsewhere — probably on a permanent leave of absence. "Not much," I said. "They walk sideways, have dirty great claws, and live on the bottom of the sea." The mention of the crustaceans' natural habitat should have set my alarm bells ringing, but you already know that I wasn't concentrating properly.

"Very tasty," he observed with a faraway look on his face. "Fancy some for tea?"

I nodded.

"Come on, then," he said, heading for the door.

I followed, neglecting to pay attention to the fact that he was wearing a Guernsey sweater and a pair of corduroy trousers — his favoured seagoing rig.

It was a short walk to the shops. He surprised me by turning into the grocery store instead of the fishmonger's.

"Cat food," he announced, paying for a can. "Nothing like it."

"For supper for us — or for the cat?"

He shook his head. "No. For the crabs."

Somewhere deep in the recesses of my mind a tiny red light glowed weakly.

"Cat food for crabs?"

"Bait, my boy. They love it."

My cortical red light flashed on and off like the Eddystone Lighthouse. Sirens howled. "Er, Fingal, did I mention I had plans to . . ."

"Nonsense, my boy. We'll have a wonderful time."

My heart plummeted like a U-boat in a crash dive.

"Not on your boat, Fingal?" My hopes were about as valid as those of an early Christian martyr who has tried to persuade himself that the lions in the Coliseum were of a peculiarly vegetarian breed.

He draped an avuncular arm round my shoulder and, with the gentility of a hydraulic ram, propelled me toward the door. "Where else, my boy? Where else?"

To have suggested that the innermost circle of Dante's Inferno held a certain appeal would have been churlish. Besides, his hand gripped my arm the way Godzilla caressed one of his foes.

For once, the seagoing day turned out to be more pleasant than I'd anticipated. I suffered only a minor concussion when the boom and my head came into immediate juxtaposition during a manouevre he referred to as a gibe. When we dropped anchor in the lee of a small island, I was comforted by the thought that the ground tackle's ability to hold us in position was no doubt augmented by the extra weight it was carrying from the pounds of flesh the chain had ripped from my hands.

"Marvellous," said O'Reilly. "Absolutely marvellous. Now. Crabs."

He opened a locker and hauled out a Heath-Robinson device of netting and metal struts.

"Cat food," he demanded.

I handed him the tin. He wrestled it into the infernal machine, lifted the thing, and tossed it over the side.

"Er, Fingal . . ."

"Not now, boy. I'm busy." He was. He was paying out fathoms of rope that I assumed were attached to the crab pot.

I waited until he'd made the rope fast to the taffrail.

"Er, Fingal . . ."

"Not now, boy. Beer," he ordered.

I'd noticed something about the tinned cat food that was surely going to spoil his afternoon, but in the confusion of falling down the companionway, dropping the lid of the ice chest on my fingers, and hitting my head on the hatch cover as I returned to the deck, whatever it was must have slipped my mind — or perhaps I decided to let it slip. I handed him his beer and sat beside him.

"If you listen carefully," he said, "you'll hear the scrabbling of crustacean claws as the little darlins fight to get at the bait. They do love it, you know."

I remembered what had bothered me, but said nothing.

"Mrs. Kincaid will do them a treat. Boiled. Melted butter." O'Reilly was salivating so heavily at the thought of his upcoming feast that if he hadn't been consuming beer at his usual rate he would probably have suffered dehydration.

For one hour he extolled the virtues of boiled crab. I would have been bored by the monologue had I not been given periodic respite by being sent below for more beer.

"Right," he finally announced, "let's get at 'em." He rose and began hauling in the rope. The bay must have been on the edge of the Marianas Trench. I watched as coils of manila filled the cockpit. O'Reilly's fluid deprivation was mightily increased by the rivulets of sweat pouring from his brow.

Finally the crab pot broke the surface.

"Gotcha," he roared in triumph, hauling it into the boat.

The device was as empty as Donal Donnelly's mind. Not a single crab, not even a shrimp. The cat food can sparkled in the sunlight.

344

"Can't understand it," said O'Reilly. "Cat food usually works a treat."

"I'm sure it does, Fingal," I observed as gently as I could, "but I think you're meant to open the can."

"What?" he roared, reaching into the trap and pulling out the can, pristine in all its unpunctured glory. "Well, I'll be damned."

"Never mind," I said, probably less than tactfully, "I'm sure Mrs. Kincaid can work wonders with cat food."

NOVEMBER 2000
A Very Pheasant
Evening . . .

. . . And Another Pain in the
Arse for His Lordship

"Thank you, Fingal," said the only denizen
of Ballybucklebo — other than myself — to
be accorded the privilege of addressing
Doctor Fingal Flahertie O'Reilly, MB, BCh,
BAO, without using the great healer's title.

The patient buttoned up his tweed trousers.

"My pleasure, John," O'Reilly said, dropping a rubber glove into a disposal bin.

O'Reilly had just finished examining the
fat, feudal fundament of John Fitzgurgle,
DSO, MC, and bar, Viscount Ballybucklebo.
Under the circumstances, Doctor O. was in
the position to call the great man just about
anything he chose.

"Haemorrhoids, I'm afraid. Sorry, John,"
O'Reilly said, his half-hidden smile giving
the lie to his spoken regrets. "Here."
O'Reilly sat at his desk and scribbled out a

prescription. "Twice a day. Should clear them up in about a week."

"Damn," said his lordship, "today's Tuesday. Had rather hoped they'd be gone by Saturday. I'm having a shoot. Won't possibly be able to walk the coverts."

"Lots of birds this year, John?" asked O'Reilly with the innocence of a choirboy inquiring after the health of a beloved choirmaster.

"Rather," said his lordship. "Mostly in the Leprechauns' Wood."

I saw O'Reilly smile. Mata Hari must have had the same look on her face after she'd extracted some juicy tidbit from a member of the French high command.

"Lots of time in the season left for you to get a shot or two, John," O'Reilly said helpfully as he showed his lordship to the door.

"Isn't that interesting, Pat?" O'Reilly asked, after the pathetically piles-pained peer had perambulated through the portal.

"Oh, yes," I said, trying frantically to guess which night O'Reilly had in mind for using his recently acquired intelligence. I knew I had to have an ironclad excuse for being somewhere else — anywhere else.

Perhaps the reason for my panic-stricken preemptive planning requires a word of elaboration. For those unfamiliar with sporting life in Ulster or with one of Doctor F. F. O'Reilly's eccentricities, let me offer an explanatory note.

The landed gentry stocked their estates with large numbers of *Phaisanus versicolour* — the ring-necked pheasant. The birds were raised from chicks, and during their formative months were given the kind of loving care usually reserved for tiny premature infants. The pampered pheasants were fed, kept warm, and thoroughly coddled. Coddled, that was, until the start of the shooting season. Then the bewildered birds were rousted from their avian Eden. Flapping fearfully in full flight, they were set upon by hordes of happy hunters who blazed away with all the enthusiasm of Montgomery's artillery during the warm-up to the away match at El Alamein.

Being a pheasant was no bed of roses. Lord Fitzgurgle's guests, poltroons who paid for the privilege of joining in the awful avicide, weren't the only ones the birds should have feared. Several of Ballybucklebo's citizens, in the spirit of Danton, Marat, Robespierre, and the rest of the French revolutionaries, saw no reason not to indulge in a bit of egalitarian free enterprise.

Lesser mortals had practised poaching for years. This activity was mightily frowned upon by the upper crust. In days of yore they spent considerable resources to ensure that vast tracts of Australia were populated by platoons of penurious peasants who'd purloined or pilfered privately purchased pheasants.

And I hope you'll remember that when I first introduced you to my mentor, I described him as, among other things, an unregenerate poacher. Well, he might fancy a night in the woods. I did not.

As usual, my wishes and my fate were on widely divergent courses.

"Whiskey," said O'Reilly. "Whiskey and oatmeal."

"Yes, indeed." I wondered what on Earth he was talking about, and quite lost track of my search for a self-preserving alibi.

"Come on," said O'Reilly, leaving the surgery and heading for the kitchen. I followed.

He opened a cupboard and removed a bottle of a well-known Scotch brand's Red Label, not one of his favoured Irish whiskeys.

"Cooking whisky's good enough," he remarked, producing a bag of oatmeal.

A bucket came next, the oatmeal was dumped into the bucket, and the spirits poured in. O'Reilly left just enough in the bottom of the bottle to allow him to take a healthy swallow as he stirred the soggy mess. "No need to let it all go to waste," he remarked, and burped.

I was lost. Oatmeal was used to make porridge. If Mrs. Kincaid decided to boil some up from the contents of the bucket, my performance at morning surgery would certainly not be up to scratch. "What . . . ?"

"You'll see, my boy. You'll see." And so I did — but not until Friday night.

We were sitting in the upstairs room. The curtains were open and I was admiring the effects of the full moon on the waters of Belfast Lough. In the distance, the Hills of Antrim stood dark against a darker sky. A single coal boat ploughed a dark furrow through a sea like burnished silver. From somewhere inland, the liquid call of a barn owl was the only sound to disturb the velvet silence. The evening was idyllic, peaceful . . .

"Right," said O'Reilly, "go and put on some dark clothes."

"What?"

"Get a move on. I'll get the oatmeal and I'll meet you at the car."

The oatmeal. I'd forgotten about it and was curious to know its purpose. Utterly forgetting the catastrophic consequences of curiosity to the cat — who became a cadaver with a certain degree of celerity — I went and changed.

It was a short drive through the darkened countryside. I wondered why O'Reilly switched off the engine and let the car glide silently for the last part of our journey — until I realized that we'd stopped by a large copse. A copse that I instantly recognized as Leprechauns' Wood.

"Oh no, Fingal . . ."

"Oh yes," he said. "Out, and keep very quiet."

Together we wriggled through a barbed-wire fence and went on our way. O'Reilly carried the bucket of whisky-soaked oatmeal. I merely bore a two-inch laceration of my left hand. He made his way through the dimly lit undergrowth as silently as Daniel Boone might have approached a hostile Indian encampment. I trailed behind, making only the occasional acquaintance with briars' thorns.

When we arrived in a small clearing, he stopped, held an extended finger to his lips, and began to peer intently up into the trees. My gaze followed his. There, silhouetted against the night sky, I saw the rotund shapes of roosting birds.

O'Reilly grinned at me and silently scattered the oatmeal on the forest floor. He rejoined me and guided me back into the undergrowth. He lay down. I lay down. Among a stand of broad-leafed plants. Pity they were nettles.

O'Reilly cupped his hands to his mouth and produced a most peculiar sound. I clapped my stung hands to my mouth and tried not to whimper.

Something stirred in the branches. One after another the sleeping birds sat bolt upright. One after another they fluttered to the ground. They bent and pecked at the oatmeal with the enthusiasm of a set of small pile-drivers. Sated at last, they fluttered back up to their perches, tucked their heads under their wings and, like a row of dominoes, one after another they lost their grips and tumbled to the ground.

They were a party of profoundly pissed pheasants, beautifically blotto birds, drunk as a lord — to whom, lest we forget, they actually belonged.

O'Reilly rose, walked into the clearing, grabbed two birds, and rapidly dispatched them. At least, I thought, they died happy. I wondered if the birds he left behind would awaken with horrible hangovers.

It struck me quite forcibly as we made our way back to the car that for Lord Fitzgurgle, haemorrhoids were not the only pains in the arse.

'TIS THE SEASON TO BE JOLLY

O'REILLY AND THE TURKEY

Sir Stamford Raffles was an empire builder. He gave his name to a magnificent hotel in Singapore where, if the works of W. Somerset Maugham are to be believed, the tuans and memsa'bs would sit at tiffin sipping their chota pegs — and a good thing too. There's quinine in tonic water, without which gin and tonic would be merely gin, the despised tot of the "other ranks" of His Majesty's armed nitwits. Without the quinine, G&T would have absolutely no anti-malarial powers whatsoever. It would be like Christmas without the presents.

And what, you may be wondering, does this have to do with the Machiavellian machinations of one Fingal Flahertie O'Reilly, MB, BCh, BAO? Those who have come to know and love the old reprobate would immediately assume there might be some connection with alcoholic consumption. A logical, almost Holmesian piece of deductive reasoning, but of course putting logic and O'Reilly in the same sentence is about as sensible as mixing water and sodium and chucking in a dose of gasoline for good measure. No, the link is rather more obscure. I'll explain.

Please picture his surgery. It was mid-December. As I entered, his last patient of the day — Finnula Finucane, widowed mother of three — pushed past me. I could see the swelling beneath her usually lively green eyes and the silver tracks on her cheeks that spoke sadly of recent tears. "Finnula . . ." I began, but she hustled by without speaking. O'Reilly sat in his swivel chair staring over his half-moons at her departing back. I don't think he even knew I was there. "Bugger it," he muttered to himself, then, looking up, scowled at me.

"What's wrong with her?" I asked, knowing full well that for all his bluster O'Reilly could care deeply for his patients.

"Bloody Santa Claus."

"What?" For the life of me I failed to see how old Saint Nick could be the cause of Finnula's grief.

He ignored me, hunched forward, clearly lost in his thoughts, then straightened, pointed one finger at me, and said, "We'll just have to fix it. It'll be Christmas in a week."

"Yes. Right," I said, utterly at sea, but it seemed simpler to agree.

He rose, strode to the door, and roared, "Mrs. Kincaid!"

I heard her coming along the corridor.

"Yes, Doctor O'Reilly?"

"Kinky, have you bought our turkey yet?"

"No, sir."

"Well, buy two."

She nodded.

I was trying to make sense of all of this. Finnula in tears. O'Reilly's strange outbursts: "Bloody Santa Claus," "It'll be Christmas in a week," "Buy two turkeys." Good Lord, was O'Reilly going to cast himself as the reformed Ebenezer Scrooge, somehow hoping that Finnula or one of her youngsters would greet his gift of a turkey with a "God bless us each and every one"? I couldn't quite see Finnula's youngest — a carrot-haired six-year-old whose mischief was legend in Ballybucklebo — as a latter-day Tiny Tim.

O'Reilly grunted, then scratched his bent nose and continued, "Do you have any of those tickets you used for the parish dance left?"

"Yes, Doctor."

"Get them, please."

She left.

"Fingal, I . . ."

"Not now, Taylor. I need to think."

Mrs. Kincaid reappeared and handed O'Reilly a roll of paper tickets.

"Thanks, Kinky." O'Reilly ripped one free.

"I want you, Taylor, to buy a raffle ticket."

"What for?" I think he detected the hint of suspicion in my voice. My tones were ones I imagined were used by flies following an invitation to visit a spider's domicile.

"What for? A pound."

"No, Fingal. I mean . . ."

"You might win a turkey."

"No, Fingal. I mean what's the draw in aid of?"

His face split into a grin of heroic proportions. "Santa Claus," he muttered conspiratorially. "Now give." He held out his hand.

I surrendered a note with all the enthusiasm of a Chicago South Side speakeasy owner who has just assured a large gentleman in a trench coat and a bulge under one armpit that nothing would be more gratifying than to buy beer from Mister Alphonsus Capone's brewery — and, yes, an assurance that nothing nasty would go "bang" on the premises would be appreciated.

"Here." He gave me my ticket. "It's for a

good cause."

The departure of some of my hard-earned cash drove away any charitable thoughts I might have been harbouring about O'Reilly giving a turkey to Finnula Finucane. I had a horrible suspicion that I'd just contributed to the F. F. O'Reilly Christmas festivities fund. As P. G. Wodehouse remarked, I was suffering from a distinct lack of gruntle.

"Come on," he bellowed, heading for the door, "the Mucky Duck's open."

I swallowed. Could he actually have the temerity to take my money and immediately go and spend it?

I followed in his wake like a very small dinghy being dragged along by a very large motorboat.

The Duck was packed. O'Reilly accosted the usual suspects. All, including Arthur Osbaldiston, Donal Donnelly, and even the notoriously tight-fisted Angus MacKay, were given a ticket and relieved of their pounds with a skill and apparent ease of a London pickpocket divesting his prey of their wallets and fob-watches. The rapine and pillage was over before it had sunk in to the befuddled mob that they'd been fleeced. I noticed that Angus MacKay looked as though he might be going to object. O'Reilly must have read the signs.

358

"Home," he roared before any of the recently shorn could object.

And he hadn't even stopped for a drink.

When we were once more ensconced in his surgery, O'Reilly pulled out a wad of notes and counted them with a well-licked thumb.

"Sixty-four quid," he remarked, "less one for the cost of the prize." He shoved a note into his trousers pocket. "Leaves sixty-three. That should do it." His smile was like a morning sunrise.

"Fingal . . . ?"

"Yes, my boy."

"What exactly was that all about?"

He stuffed the notes into an envelope.

"Finnula," he said, "and bloody Santa Claus. Didn't I explain?"

It was my turn to grunt.

It must have been the imminence of the "season to be jolly." His next words were ones I'd never — not in a month of Sundays — expected to hear pass O'Reilly's lips: "Sorry about that, but it would have been a catastrophe of the first magnitude. We had to do something."

I tried to ignore the "we." My contribution had been a grudgingly given pound. And I was no closer to getting an explanation.

"Fingal . . ."

"You see, Pat," his voice softened, "Finnula has been having a hard time making a go of it since her husband died. But she wanted her kids to enjoy Christmas. Do you know, she saved her egg money every week to buy them little treats."

"Was she robbed?"

He shook his head. "Worse. Remember when you were a kid you'd write a letter to Santa, tell him what you wanted, and send it up the chimney?"

"Yes."

"Her wee ones did — but the things they asked for were away beyond her budget. She did her best to explain to them that Santa was a bit hard up this year."

"Sensible."

"You'd have thought so, but she hadn't counted on the wee redheaded one. She told me today that she'd gone out and when she'd come home she'd just been in time to see the lad send the last of her hard-saved pounds up the chimney because, 'Santa could use a bit of help.' She hadn't the heart to chastise him."

"So that's what the money's for."

"Aye," he said. "We just have to work out how to get her to accept it. She's a very proud woman."

"You'll think of something, Fingal," I said, and I meant it.

"I will," he fixed me with a steely glare, "and you'll keep your mouth shut about it — or I'll kill you."

And what has all this to do with one of the Founders of Empire? I believe the selling of tickets to a group of unwilling punters in the hope that one will win a prize — and somehow the turkey found its way to the table of Angus MacKay — is called a raffle.

And with that, nothing remains but for me to wish my reader — I can't believe that there's actually more than one — a Merry Christmas and a Happy New Year.

Just a Wee Deoch an' Dorris

With Apologies to Sir Harry Lauder

O'Reilly paused, shook the water from his tweed coat, and shouldered his way to the bar of the Mucky Duck. His words would have been audible from the quarterdeck to the main-top-gallant mast of HMS *Victory* in a Force 10 gale, and indeed, given the state of the weather that night, with the rain pelting off the roof like bursts of Maxim gunfire and the wind rattling the pub's shutters, there was some justification for his raising his voice. Of course he had another, more pressing reason to make himself heard. "I believe your estate can sue the landlord if you die of thirst in a public house," he roared.

Patience, you'll recall, was not in his catalogue of virtues, particularly when the thirst was on him.

I watched as other patrons sidled away

along the bar, studiously avoided his gaze, found fascinating areas of exploration under their fingernails, and otherwise tried, like a child who pulls a blanket over his head in the belief that he's now invisible to the outside world, to avoid attracting the attention of Ballybucklebo's resident ogre. O'Reilly in need of a drink was like a bear with a sore head — a sore head that had been brought on by repeated applications of a heavy blunt instrument to the top of the ursine skull.

Only Angus MacKay, piper, shepherd, Highland gentleman, a man held in enormous esteem by the locals for once daring to point out to O'Reilly that his bagpipe playing needed as much work to clean up his grace notes as the Earth did following Noah's boat trip — only Angus held his ground. I noticed he had no drink in front of him but stood quietly at the bar, apparently waiting for something to arrive.

Arthur Osbaldiston trundled along behind the counter, bowing as much as his three hundred pounds allowed and sweating like a jaunting-car pony after a trip to the summit of Ballybucklebo Hills with Osbaldiston in the trap. He shoved something out of sight under the bar counter and asked,

"Large whiskey and a small sherry, Doctor, sir?"

"Jasus, Arthur," O'Reilly rumbled, "if you ever get out of the pub business you can always get a job in the circus as a mind reader."

"Or as Art the Human Whale," called a voice I didn't recognize, from somewhere in a darker corner of the establishment.

O'Reilly spun like a principal dancer in mid-pirouette, pointed an admonitory finger and, keeping his quarterdeck voice at full decibels, announced, "That was uncalled-for, Paddy Finnegan. Arthur can't help his weight. It's in his genes, and for those who don't know what genes are, they're little small thingies in the cells."

A respectful muttering filled the room. In one sentence O'Reilly had established his sympathy for Arthur Osbaldiston's obesity and his own intellectual preeminence in the Ballybucklebo pecking order.

And I'd recognized an edge creep into his voice — the one that appeared when he was about to cut someone down to size with the finality of a chain saw.

"Cells," he pronounced. "Cells, Paddy — but then you'd know all about that, wouldn't you now?"

Laughter swept the company as a breaker

roars over a shingle beach. Every man there knew that Paddy Finnegan had just returned from six months as a guest of Her Majesty Elizabeth II Regina, Dei Gratia, Fid. Def. A small matter of four salmon from Lord Fitzgurgle's river, as I now recalled.

"Here you are, Doctors," said Osbaldiston, setting the drinks on the counter. "Five shillings, please."

"Thank you," said O'Reilly, ignoring mundane things like money and the look of supplication on the landlord's face. "Better," he said, taking a hefty pull, "much better."

I slipped Arthur the necessary coins, sipped my sherry, and waited.

O'Reilly, placated now by the success of his repartée and the taste of his John Jameson's, turned his attention to his immediate neighbour.

"How are you, Angus?" he asked.

The little Scot pondered his reply with all the gravity of a High Court judge prior to donning the black cap and handing down the death penalty. Finally he vouchsafed, "I am well."

"Grand," said O'Reilly. "Good to see you in town."

Angus nodded.

I remembered. Today was Friday. It was

365

Angus's day to walk the ten miles from his cottage to visit Ballybucklebo. I'd only once made the mistake of offering him a lift. Angus MacKay would be beholden to no one.

"You walk in every Friday, don't you, Angus?" I asked.

"Chust so."

"Indeed," said O'Reilly, waving his now-empty glass in the general direction of Osbaldiston, who'd been hovering at our end of the bar like a waiting peregrine falcon and who now stooped on the glass at roughly the same speed as the world's fastest bird. Parenthetically, for those who think I should have written "swooped" instead of "stooped," the action of a diving peregrine is a "stoop." But to continue.

"Bit of a walk on a day like today," O'Reilly mused. "Ten miles there and ten miles back. Be careful not to catch your death of cold."

"I will, sir. I have my medicine."

"Medicine?" asked O'Reilly, looking at me questioningly.

I shook my head to answer his unasked question.

"So, who has been prescribing for you, Angus?"

The Scot's eyes twinkled. "Doctor Osbaldiston here."

"Who?" asked O'Reilly incredulously.

"Himself there," said Angus, nodding to the landlord who'd set O'Reilly's refilled glass on the counter.

"Arthur? Doctor Arthur?" O'Reilly was clearly baffled.

"Could I trouble you for my parcel?" Angus asked Arthur, who reached beneath the countertop and produced a brown bag.

"Thank you, Mister Osbaldiston." Angus accepted the bag and handed over two pound notes. "My medicine," he remarked, opening the neck of the bag and showing the contents to O'Reilly.

O'Reilly laughed. "Whisky. Is that your medicine, Angus?"

The Scot became very serious. "Chust so, Doctor, chust so. But if you examine the label, sir, this is real whisky — from the highlands."

"So you don't think much of Irish?" O'Reilly inquired, lowering the contents of his glass by a good half.

"It will do very well for the cooking with," Angus allowed, "but should only be drunk by a chentleman in moments of great stress."

I thought O'Reilly might take offence, but he clapped the little Scot on the shoulder. "Would you have an Irish with me, Angus?"

he asked, signalling to Arthur to refill his glass.

"Thank you, no, sir," said Angus, "but it's a handsome offer." He took his change from Arthur, who'd also given O'Reilly his third double whiskey. "I must be getting along now, for it's a fair tramp."

"Hold on," said O'Reilly. "Do you walk twenty miles every Friday to buy one bottle of whisky, Angus?"

Angus nodded. "Chust so."

"But," said O'Reilly, knocking back most of his third double, "why not buy half a dozen bottles and save yourself the long weekly walk?"

"Because," said Angus solemnly, eyeing O'Reilly's nearly empty glass, "as you no doubt will have observed, Doctor O'Reilly, when the whisky is close at hand, it's like butter in summer."

"Why?" I asked.

"Because when it's close by" — Angus nodded at O'Reilly's glass — "it does nae keep very well."

WHAT'S IN A NAME?

YE BANKS AND BRAES
OF BONNIE BALLYBUCKLEBO

Ballybucklebo, home of Doctor Fingal Flahertie O'Reilly and an assorted cast of
characters whose intellects on their communal best days would make the inmates of
the old Bedlam Asylum look like a collection of dons from a Cambridge college.
Ballybucklebo, site of my introduction to
the art and craft of medicine — if not the
science. Ballybucklebo, a name to conjure
with and a name that has led my loyal
reader to inquire, just what the hell does it
mean?

In truth, Irish place names can be a mite
confusing to the foreigner. There's a
plethora of Kil-something-or-others, Drum-
whatchamacallums, and Bally-this-that-and-
the-other-things. A smattering of knowledge
of the origins of the prefixes can cast a little
light on the matter. And as those of you who

369

have accompanied me through the darker reaches of Ballybucklebo well know, illumination of anything pertaining to that particularly peculiar place can only be to our mutual advantage.

T. S. Eliot, who may very well have had Ballybucklebo in mind when he wrote *The Waste Land,* was quite particular in his instructions for *The Naming of Cats.* I, in my turn, will now dilate further on the naming of Irish locales.

"Kil" simply means "the church of," so Kiltoom is the church of the burial mound. "Drum" is "ridge," "bo" is "cow." Drumbo: cow ridge. "Bally" is the "townland" — an old feudal method of establishing the boundaries of the countryside surrounding a particular geographical feature. "Bally" was also used as a polite euphemism for "bloody," leading to a popular verbal play on real place names: "If you hadn't been so Ballymena with your Ballymoney, you'd have a Ballycastle for your Ballyholme." But I digress.

What about Ballybucklebo? All right. Bally, "townland," buckle (or in Irish, *buachaill*), "boy," bo — those with retentive memories will already have learned that "bo" means "cow." Ballybucklebo: the townland of the boy's cow. Quite simple, really.

Well, actually it's not, and I'm sure that comes as no surprise. In fact, the village had grown up on the banks of the River Bucklebo, where legend had it a great calamity had befallen an invading English army, a calamity precipitated by a wandering cow that had magically distracted the Sassenach troops at a crucial point during the statutory clashing of halberds, swords, axes, maces, and other macabre methods of mediaeval mayhem. The date of the awful affray is lost in the mists of Celtic twilight, but in Ireland history has a habit of repeating itself, and it was on the banks of that very Bucklebo that I witnessed the downfall of another English invader — not at the hands of the Irish but from the actions of one Angus MacKay, Scot, shepherd, piper extraordinaire, and Highland gentleman.

I'll tell you about it.

O'Reilly had gone to Belfast, ostensibly to attend a postgraduate course. Knowing him as you do, you'll no doubt have surmised already that while his cerebrum might be mildly stimulated, his tonsils would undoubtedly receive a thorough inundation and his liver a workout of gargantuan proportions. While my mentor was off besporting himself, I'd been left in charge of the practice and, Lord help them, the health of the local citizenry. I stuck my head into the waiting room expecting to summon Angus MacKay. I'd noticed him coming in some time ago and by my reckoning he should have been my last patient of the afternoon.

Instead I was greeted by a stranger who addressed me in the plummy accents of an English public school.

"You must be the local quack, what?"

"I'm Doctor Taylor," I replied, noting his three-piece suit, old school tie, watery eyes, and distinct lack of chin.

"Taylor? Oh. His lordship — I'm Cholmondely, guest of the Fitzgurgles, you know — his lordship said I should consult a Doctor O'Reilly."

"I'm sorry," I said. "Doctor O'Reilly has gone to Belfast. He'll be back tomorrow."

"Blast! Can't wait 'til then." He grimaced. "Oh well, I'll just have to make do. Beggars can't be choosers, what?"

"I'll do what I can," I said as civilly as I could, "but Mister MacKay" — I nodded at Angus, who'd been sitting quietly, and clearly observing the exchange — "has been here for rather a long time. If you'd care to wait, I'll . . ."

"Wait? Don't be ridiculous. This fellow

won't mind hanging on, will you, my good man?"

"Chust so," said Angus quietly, but knowing him as I did I could tell he was remembering Bannockburn, the battle where King Robert of Scotland took the gold, silver, and bronze, and left King Edward of England holding nothing but a few splinters from the wooden spoon. It's generally recommended that blunt sticks not be forcibly inserted into the orbits of rabid dogs, but perhaps the newcomer hadn't learned the parallel between such activities and the act of patronizing a Scot from the Western Isles.

"Come along, Doctor," the newcomer said, then he turned to Angus. "Won't take a jiffy, old boy."

I stole a glance at Angus, who nodded.

So Cholmondely accompanied me into the surgery, where I dealt with his medical difficulties. I have no doubt that Hippocrates wouldn't have approved of my secret delight when I discovered that the man had a case of inflamed haemorrhoids.

"Here you are," I said, handing him a prescription for an anti-inflammatory cream.

He did have the courtesy to thank me. He rose. "One more thing," he said. "Did I by any chance hear you refer to that chappie next door as MacKay?"

"Yes."

"Small world. He must be the laddie his lordship mentioned. I'm over for the fishing, d'you see?"

I did see. Lord Fitzgurgle owned the fishing rights to a large stretch of the Bucklebo, and Angus, when not occupied with his sheep, worked as a ghillie, tending to the waters, the salmon therein, and guiding his lordship's guests.

"Better have a word with him," the Englishman said, heading for the waiting room. I followed. The upcoming conversation could be interesting.

To be continued next month.

WHAT'S IN A NAME? (PART 2)

SCOTLAND 1, ENGLAND 0

Last month, Doctor Taylor treated the inflamed haemorrhoids of a visiting Englishman named Cholmondely, who was less than courteous to Angus MacKay in the waiting room. That was before Cholmondely learned that Angus worked as a ghillie, looking after Lord Fitzgurgle's waters and salmon . . .

"So, MacKay," said Cholmondely. "Hear you're a very fine ghillie."

"Aye." Angus's mien was as expressionless as a Highland tarn in a flat calm.

"Excellent. His lordship says you'll take me on the water tomorrow — at nine."

"Chust so," said Angus, "if that is what the chentleman wants. But the Bucklebo's in spate chust now."

"My good man, I'm here to fish and fish I will. I'll expect you on the bank at nine. Clear?"

"Aye," said Angus. He hesitated. "Doctor, sir, is tomorrow your day off?"

"Yes, Angus."

A twinkle flashed into the steely eyes of the little Scot, an unholy twinkle that would have dimmed the fires of hell.

"You'd not mind, sir, if Doctor Taylor came with us? He enjoys the riverbank."

"Bring who you like," said Cholmondely, "but remember one thing. I'm a very expert fisherman and I do not like being advised unless I ask for information. Is that clear?"

"Och aye, sir," said Angus. "Och aye."

Angus and I arrived at the banks of the Bucklebo promptly at 8:55 A.M. There was no sign of Mister Cholmondely.

"Would you look at that, sir?" Angus pointed at the river. Judging by the way the brown waters tossed and roiled, somewhere upstream there was a large gopher-wood vessel, inhabited by pairs of animals and skippered by an older, bearded gentleman in long flowing robes — a gentleman who'd decided that despite the return of a dove with an olive branch he'd better wait until the very last of the deluge had dissipated down the course of the Bucklebo.

Angus's mien was utterly devoid of gruntle. "He'll no take a fish in yon."

My muttered agreement was interrupted

by the arrival of Mister Cholmondely, dressed as I could only suppose he imagined an expert fisherman should be. His tweed deerstalker was so festooned with flies that it had the appearance of an exotic tropical parrot having a bad feather day in a high wind. His tweed suit — hacking jacket and plus-four pants — was complemented by a pair of tartan socks that could only have been knitted by someone from the very-post-impressionist school. Over his shoulder was slung a wicker creel and he carried a rod with the dimensions of one of those old-growth Canadian pines. "Morning," he said, hefting his rod. "Should do well today."

I watched Angus. I could tell he was wrestling with his conscience. His duty as a ghillie was to do his utmost to provide the guest with the best day's fishing possible. His instructions were not to proffer advice. His ethics won.

"Sir, you see the water. Maybe, at the edge, with the wee rod" — Angus offered a slim fly rod — "you might take a trout or two."

Cholmondely bristled. "When I want your advice, MacKay, I'll ask for it. This" — he struggled to wave his own rod — "this is a double-handed Spey rod."

"Aye," said Angus, "I ken that."

377

"Just you watch." At that, Cholmondely, grasping his angle in a two-handed grip, began hurling casts at the swollen waters. He thrashed at the river with the enthusiasm of a Nelsonic bos'n laying on the cat-o'-nine-tails. His face reddened. Rivulets of sweat coursed from under his deerstalker. His back casts fouled in trees, rushes, and just missed an inquisitive cow that had wandered down to observe.

Angus dutifully untangled the line and kept his counsel — for an hour. Then he ventured, "Perhaps, sir, if you tried this wee fly rod . . ."

"MacKay. I do not . . . not . . . need advice from you."

Then his rod tip flickered. Had he hooked a fish after all?

Cholmondely began to reel in. The rod was definitely under some tension. I looked sympathetically at Angus but was rewarded with a tiny smile and an inclination of the little man's head, which said, more loudly than any words, "Wait and see."

Finally, after much reeling in, a fish broke the surface close to the bank. It was a salmon parr, an immature fish the size of an over-developed minnow. Its ordinarily puny ability to put up a fight had been boosted by the force of the water.

Cholmondely cranked on until all the line was in and the tiddler flapped weakly at the rod tip, some fifteen feet above the breathless Cholmondely's head. "Now, my good man," he huffed, "what shall I do?"

Angus bent slowly, picked up a fair-sized stone from the bank of the Bucklebo, handed it to Cholmondely, and said in dulcet tones, "If I was you, sir, I'd shinny up yon great rod and beat the wee thing to death with this."

Whiskey in a Jar

O'Reilly Goes Fishing

"And what do you think of that?" asked O'Reilly. He stood in the doorway of the surgery, beaming from ear to ear. He held a rod in his right hand and struggled with his left to hold aloft a salmon that was probably, as the horsey set would say, "by Moby Dick out of Leviathan." It was a superlative specimen of the spectacular species *Salmo salar.*

"That's quite a fish," I acknowledged testily. If my words were a little clipped it was because he should have been working that afternoon. It was supposed to have been my half day. Mrs. Kincaid had collared me just as I was about to drive away and had regretfully informed me that himself was nowhere to be found and the waiting room was chockablock. I'd been left with no choice but to cancel my arrangements and see the sufferers, rather to the

380

chagrin of one of the tiny number of members of the opposite sex who would agree to share my company — and she had the most alluring brown eyes. At least, I'd assumed, some medical emergency had delayed him. I hadn't for a moment thought that he'd have gone fishing.

"Sorry it kept you away from the surgery," I said. "You missed some absolutely fascinating head colds."

O'Reilly, like a small boy caught with pockets stuffed with apples in someone else's orchard, hung his head for a brief second and then said, sotto voce, "Sorry."

I started. It was the one word I'd never thought to hear from him. If Beëlzebub himself had appeared in the room, enunciating the Lord's Prayer and gargling with holy water, I couldn't have been more surprised.

"No, really. I should have been here. Thanks for holding the fort."

Old Nick had graduated from gargling with holy water to bathing in the stuff. If the films of the time were to be believed, such activities would have led to a considerable degree of dolour on the part of the Devil's disciple.

O'Reilly's look of childish content belied any suggestion that he was truly remorseful, but as he wiggled the fish and said, "Just look at this beauty," I couldn't find it in me to begrudge him his contentment, particularly when he continued, "I'll make it up to you, Pat. How about I take the calls this Saturday night?"

"Well . . ." There was a dance in Belfast I would enjoy if a certain ebony-eyed nurse happened to be free. "Well . . ."

"All right, and Sunday too."

He who hesitates is lost? Not always. Sometimes he improves his bargaining position. For once I had the upper hand and decided that I might as well use it. "All right, Fingal."

"Great."

"But there's one more condition."

"Oh?" His eyes narrowed. When it came to bargaining, O'Reilly's techniques were of such effectiveness that Romany horse traders had been known to ask him to take their animals away — and accept a small fee for doing so.

"And what's that then?" he asked, smile now replaced by his patented poker face.

I laughed. "I'm finished for the day. Go and get rid of the fish and then you can take me to the Mucky Duck, tell me the story of how you caught that salmon, and . . ."

"Right." He turned to go. You, dear reader, may have forgotten the night in the Duck when he'd been so involved in a discussion with Angus MacKay that I'd been stuck with the cost of the drinks. I had not.

"... and, Fingal?"

"What?"

"You're paying."

The Duck was almost deserted. O'Reilly paid Arthur Osbaldiston, turned from the bar, and carried his own large John Jameson's and my small sherry to our table. "Here," he said, handing me my drink and lowering his bulk into a chair. *"Slainte."* He sipped his whiskey. "Grand drop," he announced, "and a potion with remarkable powers."

"Fingal," I said, "I'm sure you're right about the Irish whiskey, but I believe you promised to tell me about the fish."

"I'm doing that," he said. "The last time we were in here I had a chat with Angus MacKay."

"I know," I said. "I got stuck with the bill."

"Yes, right, but it's my shout tonight."

"Correct." I savoured my sherry.

"Anyway," he continued, "Angus was very much of the opinion that Scotch whisky was greatly superior to Irish."

I thought about this, but the connection between the relative merits of two kinds of ethnic firewater and the catching of a salmon wasn't instantly apparent.

"I showed him," said O'Reilly smugly.

"Fingal," I glanced at my watch, "I'm sure this is intriguing, but what about . . . ?"

"The salmon?" He emptied his glass and roared, "Arthur, two more!" He turned back to me. "Patience, my boy. Patience."

The drinks appeared and once again O'Reilly paid. "Now," he said, "where was I?"

"Search me."

His brows knitted. "Right. The whiskey."

"No, Fingal. The fish."

"Same thing," he said. "Listen and I'll tell you — and don't interrupt."

"I'm all ears." Wondering where this was going to lead, I sat back and waited.

"You know I went fishing today? Well, who should be on the bank of the Bucklebo but Angus MacKay.

" 'Morning, Angus,' says I.

" 'Chust so,' says he." O'Reilly made a fair hand at imitating the little Scot's lilt. "And that was the last we spoke for about four hours." O'Reilly glanced round the room. I presumed he was ensuring that he wasn't being overheard. Apparently satisfied, he bent forward and said quietly, "Angus had six fish on and I hadn't had as

384

much as a nibble."

I understood his reluctance to be over-heard. The man couldn't stand to be bested at anything, and his next words took me as much by surprise as his earlier apology.

"I finally went and asked Angus's advice. I'd noticed that he had a little jar of some brown liquid. He dipped his worms into it before he cast. 'What's that, Angus?' I asked him."

For a moment, O'Reilly asking for guidance seemed to me as likely as Julius Caesar having a quick word with a legionary recruit about the advisability of crossing the Rubicon. Then I remembered that Angus was Lord Fitzgurgle's ghillie — a man of undoubted piscatorial expertise.

" 'The whisky,' Angus told me. 'The Scotch whisky.'

" 'Could you spare a drop?' "

So there was a connection between the drink and the fish. Interesting, I thought.

"Angus looked solemn and peered at his jar. 'I'd like to, Doctor, sir, but there's chust enough for me — and the worms.' I don't need to tell you that I was a wee bit disappointed."

As was a Mister Adolf Hitler when his generals informed him that regrettably his plans to own a large chunk of the city of

Stalingrad would have to be deferred for a week or two.

"So what did you do?" I asked.

"I remembered that I always carry a flask of Irish — for medicinal purposes. I took it out and showed it to Angus. 'Do you think this might work?'

" 'Would that be the Irish, Doctor, sir?' The wee man looked as disdainful as only Angus can. 'I think it would chust upset your worm,' said he.

"I needn't tell you, Pat, I considered that a bit of a challenge."

The code of chivalry called for the armoured antagonist to throw down a galvanized gauntlet. In my opinion, Angus MacKay had chucked the mailed glove and accompanied it with a breastplate, a pair of greaves, and the helmet for good measure.

" 'We'll just have to see, won't we, Angus?' I told him. I gave a worm a good soaking and cast."

O'Reilly's eyes took on a faraway look. "Have you ever seen a depth charge go off?"

"No. They weren't part of our classes," I said, reminding myself that O'Reilly had been in Her Majesty's seagoing forces.

"It's a thing of beauty," he said. "White water everywhere." He chuckled. "The Bucklebo looked just like that. And do you know what?"

"No," I replied innocently.

"When all the spray died down, there on the end of my line was the salmon I brought home, twice as big as anything Angus had caught."

"So you reckon you'd made your point about the superiority of Irish whiskey."

"More than that. When Angus dipped his worms in Scotch, the fish took the bait. It wasn't until I'd landed mine — and fighting him is what kept me away from the surgery — it wasn't until he was on the bank that I saw — and so did Angus, for I called him to see — that my worm had grabbed the fish by the throat."

O'Reilly Puts His Foot in It

Out of the Mouths of Babes . . .

"I'll kill you, Uncle Fingal. I'll kill you bloody well dead, so I will." Thus spake an obviously enraged William Butler Yeats O'Reilly, aged eleven.

I could infer his state of mind by observing the pallor of his nose tip.

When gales were impending in coastal areas around Ireland, the coast guard hoisted south cones as a warning to mariners. This information was broadcast on the radio. Seamen who were familiar with the signalling convention made all speed for safe havens. When an eruption by a member of the clan O'Reilly was imminent, the O'Reilly schnozzles blanched. Those who could read the signs were usually well advised to take avoiding action.

On this particular occasion the wrath of the youngest O'Reilly was directed at Fingal, not me. I decided it might be interesting to stay and observe.

If you're having some difficulty remembering William Butler Yeats O'Reilly — Willy for short — he was the son of Lars Porsena O'Reilly, who was the brother of Doctor Fingal Flahertie O'Reilly. By intensely exercising your genealogical skills you'll be able to ascertain that Willy was Fingal's nephew.

O'Reilly's brother and family dwelt in the town of Portaferry at the mouth of Strangford Lough, and O'Reilly had dragged me along while he paid a familial pre-Christmas visit. When last Doctor O. and I had ventured down there, young Willy had been the cause of a minor upset, much as one Gavrilo Princip had been the source of a certain amount of dissension when his disposal of the Archduke Ferdinand had inexorably led to the first great numbered unpleasantness.

You may remember that I told you about Willy, then aged ten, in the Portaferry school's Christmas pageant. That was when, because he'd been relegated from the starring role of Joseph to that of innkeeper, he had, on stage, in public, in front of six nuns, invited Mary into the inn but told the upstart playing the part of Joseph, in no uncertain and very audible tones, to "feck off!"

When the smoke and dust had died down, Willy's father, Lars Porsena, had taken his son aside and had explained gently that the English language was a precious thing, an instrument of great precision, of beauty, of resonance, not a thing to be taken lightly or profaned. His words, or perhaps his actions, had seemed to make a lasting impression on Willy, who'd stood to take his meals for the next three days.

Certainly since that time Willy's use of profanity, at least within the earshot of potentially offendable adults, had ceased. Until today.

"It's all your bloody fault." Willy spat the words. Some species of cobra have the ability to hurl their venom several feet. They would easily have been outranged by O'Reilly's nephew.

I watched O'Reilly. I could tell by the way he shuffled his feet that he was uncomfortable, and I suspected that although I was completely in the dark about why his nephew should be so irate, O'Reilly might well have some inkling of understanding of the nature of his misdemeanour. He made no attempt to defend himself or to chastise Willy for swearing.

"Would you like to tell me what happened?" he asked.

"Can you not guess?"

"Well . . ."

"Aye. Well. Easy for you to say." Willy shook his head in the kind of pitying way adults use when they notice a small child or someone of strictly limited intellectual ability — a Donal Donnelly, say — commit some unspeakable act of folly.

This was what our old professor of psychiatry used to call "role-reversal" of the very first magnitude. The boot, as Donal Donnelly was frequently heard to observe, was very firmly on the other shoe.

"All right, Willy," said O'Reilly in his most placating voice, "tell me what I did."

"Can you not guess?"

"Was it the words?"

" 'Was it the words?' " Sarcasm dripped from Willy's tongue like gobbets of fat from a tallow candle. "Was it the bloody words?"

"Hah-hm," said O'Reilly in a fair imitation of C. S. Forester's fictional sea captain, Horatio Hornblower. "Hah-hm."

I'd stood quietly, trying not to draw attention to myself as I enjoyed his discomfiture, but some imp drove me to inquire, "What words, Fingal?"

He turned and glowered at me.

"You tell him, Uncle Fingal. Just you tell him," said Willy.

"Well," said O'Reilly uneasily, "Willy here got himself into a little bit of bother at last year's . . ."

"Christmas pageant," I said. "I remember."

"And Dad said he'd marmalize me if he ever caught me swearing again," added Willy.

"He was just right," said O'Reilly.

Willy's look of scorn would have stopped a train in its tracks. "My dad always keeps his promises," he said. "I didn't want that, so I started to use little words."

"Little words?" I asked.

"Aye," said Willy. "I'd not say, 'train,' I'd say, 'choo-choo.' I'd call dogs 'bow-wows,' cats 'kitties.' " He scowled at O'Reilly. "It's very hard to say, 'Look at what that bloody bow-wow's done now.' And it worked. I never once upset my dad — until he took your advice."

"And what would that have been, Fingal?" I asked sweetly.

"Hah-hm," said O'Reilly, hanging his head. "I thought Willy was too old to be using baby talk, so I suggested to Lars Porsena that he should make Willy use proper, adult language."

"And you should have minded your own bloody business," said an aggrieved Willy.

O'Reilly sighed. "All right, Willy," he said resignedly, "perhaps you're right."

"I know I am," said Willy. "Do you know what happened?"

"I can guess," said Fingal.

"No, you can't," snapped Willy. "You and your 'adult language.' Dad kept at me for weeks and weeks." Willy's pause was pregnant, not with a singleton but with triplets at least. I became impatient. "Go on," I prompted.

Willy looked at me. "Dad asked me what books I wanted for Christmas."

As was usual in my dealings with the O'Reilly clan, the waters of my hitherto clear understanding of the problem were beginning to become muddied.

"No," said O'Reilly, "he didn't ask for *Lady Chatterley's Lover,* if that's what you're thinking."

"I did worse," said Willy, "and it's all your fault, Uncle Fingal. You gave me *The House at Pooh Corner* last year." Willy scowled. "Dad had been going on so much about me using grown-up language that I got muddled about what book I wanted this year. So I asked for 'something more about Winnie the Shite.' "

O'Reilly's Cat

"I Must Go Down to the Sea Again . . ."

"You're not serious, Fingal?" I asked the question because his most recent suggestion made about as much sense to me as the thought of climbing into the works of an operating combine harvester.

" 'Course I am. She'll love it. You'll see."

The "she" to whom he referred was at that moment imprisoned in a cat-carrying box, from which emanated a series of low, deep, threatening growls that would have made a banshee blanch.

You may remember that O'Reilly had a cat. Why not? After all, Old MacDonald had a farm. I've told you about the creature — a pure white beast whose ancestors must have come straight from Transylvania if her taste for my blood was anything to go by. I'd earlier given some thought to seeing if a certain Doctor van Helsing was listed in the medical directory.

After all, Maggie MacCorkle's advice to belt the beast with a scratching post to discourage her attempts to reduce O'Reilly's furniture to kindling and me to a walking heap of raw meat had been ignored. O'Reilly had dismissed Mrs. Kincaid's pleas and brushed away my protests with an assurance that Lady Macbeth — that's what he'd named her — would grow out of her repeated and totally unpredictable moments when she apparently believed that since there was definitely some sabre-toothed tiger blood in her past, she had a moral obligation to live up to her heritage.

O'Reilly picked up the cat carrier. "Absolutely love it," he said.

Judging by the increased volume of the caterwauling, her ladyship was not of the same mind, but as you well know, dissenting opinions rarely carried much weight with Doctor Fingal Flahertie O'Reilly. "Come on," he said, "let's get her down to the boat."

That, you see, was what O'Reilly had decided. Lady Macbeth would love, in his decidedly minority opinion, a trip to sea in his twenty-six-foot sailboat.

Ordinarily, as you know, I'd have used any legitimate excuse short of shooting off one of my toes — a habit referred to during the first great numbered unpleasantness as "causing self-inflicted injury" — to avoid another nautical adventure with Ballybucklebo's answer to Captain Ahab. This time, particularly given the dubious outcome for the original old ivory-legged, obsessive-compulsive when he actually caught up with his Moby Dick, nothing would have kept me away. "Just call me Ishmael," I muttered as we headed for the car.

"What are you on about, Taylor?" O'Reilly asked, shoving the cat carrier into the backseat. "Lady Macbeth's a white cat, not a white whale."

"I know. But Ishmael was the only survivor of the *Pequod*'s crew. If it weren't for him the tale would never have been told."

"The only story you'll have to tell will be about how much her ladyship enjoyed herself. Isn't that right, Lady Macbeth?"

Only Doctor Fingal Flahertie O'Reilly, whose self-described ever-open mind had that day clanged shut like a steel trap, could have interpreted the cat's very accurate impression of a hand-cranked air-raid siren with a slipped clutch as an affirmative.

"I'll leave her below in the saloon," O'Reilly announced, squeezing his bulk through the hatch. "We'll let her on deck once we're well away from the dock." He vanished. The cat box vanished. He closed the hatch behind him.

Sound carries at sea, even when a vessel is still moored. From my vantage point in the cockpit I had no difficulty hearing, "Out you come, Lady Macbeth," hissing that could have been forced from an over-inflated and recently perforated rubber dinghy, and then a bellowed, "Yeeeow!"

It took some self-control on my part to refrain from passing any remarks about the four red lines on his face that were very evident the moment his head appeared at the hatchway. Still, I thought, with his almost blue cheeks, red stripes, and very white nose tip, his face would have a certain amount of appeal to any passing Ulster Loyalist.

"It's all a bit strange to her," he remarked. "She'll be all right once we're at sea."

"If you say so, Fingal."

" 'Course I do. Now," he bent and turned on the engine, "you let go the dock lines. I'll take the boat out."

And so it came to pass.

Small-boat diesel engines tend to be somewhat noisy and their exhaust gases malodorous. It's usually a great relief to hoist the sails and turn the motor off. Then, in the normal course of events, if there's a decent breeze, little can be heard but the gentle singing of the wind in the rigging, the swish and lap of the water. Salty scents fill the nostrils.

That's in the normal course. O'Reilly had been adamant that Lady Macbeth would love her first seagoing experience, and as was recognized by no less an expert than Billy Shakespeare, "The course of true love never runs smooth."

"Eldritch" is the only word I can use to describe Lady M.'s commentary on her situation. She sounded like the entire string section of a symphony orchestra when half have been given the score to one of Shostakovich's tone-poems and the rest upside-down copies of a Sousa march. The song of the wind had no hope of competing. And please remember the hatch was shut.

Borne on the sea breeze came a strange aroma. Pungent, acrid, and very definitely feline, it was something an advertising executive might have described, in a last-ditch attempt to save a failing perfume company, as eau de catpiss.

"I don't think she's altogether happy, Fingal."

I could see that it pained him to have to admit that I might just be right.

"Be a good lad," he said. "Nip below and see how she's doing."

Worms, it is said, can turn. My very acute self-preservatory instincts kicked in. In helminthic terms, I positive whirled on my axis.

"No," I said, surprising myself with the vehemence of my reply. I moved some distance away from him, expecting his response to be on a par with the verbal riposte Captain Bligh must surely have hurled at a certain Mister Fletcher Christian, but to my surprise O'Reilly merely shrugged.

"Take the helm. I'll go below," he said, moving forward and opening the hatch.

Something white raced past his shoulder, shrieking like every last one of the Furies. I wouldn't have believed the cat's next actions if I hadn't been there in the flesh to bear witness. She went up the mainsail, close to the mast, at something that must have approached the escape velocity the American space scientists of the time were trying to achieve with their Agena rockets, reached the spreaders that stick out from the mast to support the shrouds, and stopped there. She crouched like one of the exotic gargoyles that ancient monks used to adorn the eaves of their more spectacular cathedrals and hurled noisy and vituperative imprecations down onto the heads of the humans below.

"No," I said, forestalling the inevitable suggestion that as O'Reilly was much bigger and stronger than I, then I would be the logical choice to be swayed aloft to try to effect a rescue. "We'll just have to wait for her to come down."

"I think," said an obviously chastened O'Reilly, "I think we should head back to port."

"Agreed." I put the helm over. "And Fingal?"

"Yes?"

"If she doesn't come down once we've docked, someone's going to have to stay aboard until she decides to budge."

"I know. You wouldn't . . . ?" He must have seen the look on my face. "Thought not."

He sat quietly on the short trip home, docked the vessel, and stared up the mast. "Come on down, sweetie," he crooned in his gentlest voice. "Push-wush. Pushy-wushy."

I've never mastered catspeak but I guessed, judging by the arch in the cat's back, the way her tail fluffed like a semi-electrocuted lavatory brush, and the loudness of her hissing, that she was politely declining his blandishments.

She must have continued to do so for some considerable time, because O'Reilly didn't reappear chez himself until just before my bedtime. I expected him to be somewhat out of sorts, but perhaps the hours of quiet reflection he'd spent on his boat had given him time to mellow.

Mind you, I could be wrong. He never went to sea without enough beer aboard to quench the thirsts of the entire supporters' contingent of the Irish rugby football team, and his breath had a certain hoppy quality.

"Get her down?" I asked.

"Eventually. You know, Pat, I think I know what went wrong."

"Oh?"

"Indeed. It dawned on me while I was waiting for her. Who's ever heard of a sea cat?"

"Right."

"Mind you, 'sea dog' is an expression with a long and honourable history."

"Drake, Frobisher, Nelson."

"How do you think Arthur Guinness would enjoy a day at sea?"

I stared at him, trying to decide if he was being facetious. He wasn't.

And if you want to know how the big

black Labrador fared on the boat, I'm afraid you'll have to wait for next time.

O'REILLY'S DOG

YET ANOTHER SAILING ADVENTURE

"I must down to the sea again / To the lonely sea and the sky / And all I ask is a tall ship / And a star to steer her by . . ." O'Reilly's memory for the words of Johnny Masefield's "Sea Fever" was, as with all things literary, phenomenal. His voice was not. He may have thought he was singing. I'd assumed he was in some late stage of mortal anguish, so doleful was the noise.

Arthur Guinness, who was standing upright in the backseat of the old Rover car, front paws draped over my shoulders, took a break from salivating down my neck and joined in. His "Ooowwlll . . ." did give a certain harmonic counterpoint to O'Reilly's off-key bellowing. When they got to the bit about ". . . for the call of the running tide / Is a wild call and a clear call . . ." I could in all honesty only agree with the first of the sentiments. Clear, in their combined rendition, it definitely was not.

What was clear was that O'Reilly had learned nothing from his disastrous experiences when he'd tried to persuade Lady Macbeth, his demoniacally possessed white cat, to enjoy a short sea voyage. Apparently neither her dousing the saloon's upholstery with liquid high in urea content, nor the rents that had miraculously appeared in the mainsail when she'd gone up the mast like one of Nelson's topmen pursued by a bad-tempered bos'n wielding a knotted rope's end, nor the claw marks that had barely healed on his cheek would convince him that taking animals to sea, unless of course your name happened to be Noah and you were under divine protection, was probably not a very good idea. (Parenthetically, I believe that's the longest sentence I've ever managed to write.)

He'd promised last week, and he was a man who always kept his word, that he intended to retry the nautical experiment, this time with the unsuspecting Arthur Guinness as the subject.

"Dogs," he remarked, pulling the car into the marina's parking lot, "are much more stable creatures than cats."

And certain rural general practitioners, I thought, but naturally kept the idea very much to myself.

"Out," he barked.

Arthur and I complied.

"I think that's where we went wrong with Lady Macbeth last week."

"Not 'we'; you, Fingal. I tried to talk you out of it. Remember?" With, I thought, about as much success as was obtained by a certain King Canute when he commanded the tide to stop coming in.

"Slip of the tongue," he said. "You're absolutely right. Come on, Arthur." And with that he set off across the tarmac, followed by the unsuspecting hound.

I'd learned early in my acquaintance with Doctor Fingal Flahertie O'Reilly that he was always at his most placatory when he wanted something. I knew he wanted me to accompany him on the boat. He didn't know that he need not have been one bit polite to me. After last week's debacle, I wouldn't have missed this Saturday's outing for the world.

And it was one of those glorious summer days that grace Ulster with roughly the frequency of a planetary conjunction, a blue moon, and a total eclipse of the sun — all in one twenty-four-hour period. The sun beamed from an azure sky. Not even the

405

thin, diaphanous wisp of an aircraft's contrail marred the unblemished firmament. Had I not been in the company of O'Reilly and his distinctly ditsy dog, I could easily have been persuaded that God was in his heaven and all was right with the world.

"Are you coming?" he called, as he led Arthur onto the finger where his sloop was moored.

"Right." I trotted down onto the dock and followed the pair of them.

O'Reilly stopped while Arthur investigated the dock's planking, happily trotting from side to side, sniffing here, cocking his leg there, doing the usual doggy things.

"I want to give him time to get used to his new surroundings," O'Reilly said.

That seemed reasonable. I was a bit lost myself. It was only in the last week that the new facility had been opened. Boats had always been moored to buoys out in Ballybucklebo Bay, but now, borrowing from the American experience, a proper marina had been constructed. Several long docks stuck out into the bay. At right angles to each were shorter slips. There was room for two boats to be moored, stern in, between each slip.

"We're out at the very end," said O'Reilly. "It's not far." He'd grabbed Arthur Guinness by the collar. "Get out of there, Arthur."

When I looked to see the nature of the dog's transgression, I noticed that he was standing rigidly, nose thrust forward, tail sticking out astern, staring fixedly at a Siamese cat that lay languidly on a velvet cushion in the cockpit of a very smart yawl that was tied up closest to the shore.

"He's just being inquisitive, Charley," I heard O'Reilly reassure the skipper of the yawl. "I'll get him down to my boat."

"Don't worry about it, Fingal. Cleopatra here can look after herself." Charley stroked the cat's head.

Obviously, I thought, he hadn't been present when Arthur Guinness had treed Maggie MacCorkle's cat, General Sir Bernard Law Montgomery, in O'Reilly's sycamore — twice.

O'Reilly sauntered along, pausing at each moored vessel to exchange pleasantries with other members of the yachting fraternity. It must have been the sunshine that had brought them out in their droves, much as mosquitoes appear in swarms when the sun follows the rain.

Men in shorts, blazers, and Dutch captains' caps, women in short skirts and blue-and-white-striped T-shirts lolled in the cockpit of almost every vessel. I noticed that each member of the nautical set grasped a glass of something, and judging by the sparkling beads of dew on the outsides of the glasses, something cold. If this had been imperial India, it would have been the sahibs and memsa'bs at tiffin.

All terribly civilized, dontcha know? It was a scene of peacefulness, tranquility, and, unbeknownst to anyone, about to be disrupted by a force with the strength of those mild tropical breezes that used to be identified with women's names — like Hurricane Gladys.

O'Reilly hustled the Labrador onward and it seemed that any interspecies unpleasantness had been avoided. Things may not always be what they seem.

I joined O'Reilly as he encouraged Arthur Guinness to clamber aboard his sloop. The big dog jumped into the cockpit, gave one happy "Woof," turned round three times, curled up, and promptly fell asleep.

"Told you," said O'Reilly. "To the manner born. Nothing's going to go wrong this time."

I was just about to agree when something caught my eye. A small feline figure was moving along the dock. Cleopatra must have taken a short shore leave and was exploring her domain.

"We'll just give him a few minutes to settle in," O'Reilly said. "Fancy a beer?"

"Please."

"I'll get them." He vanished below.

Just as O'Reilly appeared in the hatch, a brimming beer glass held in either hand, thus of course breaking the first law of seagoing vessels, "One hand for the ship, one hand for yourself," Cleopatra jumped nimbly aboard.

The Americans of the time had developed a sophisticated early warning system to alert them to the presence of anything slightly antisocial — like several gazillion incoming megatons of nuclear firecrackers. I suspect they pinched some of the technology from our animal friends. Although the cat had landed soundlessly, Arthur was awake in one instant and on his feet in the next. Cleopatra let go the contralto-crossed-with-a-bandsaw howl that the Creator gave only to Siamese cats. On this occasion it was the feline equivalent of the orders, "Dive! Dive! Dive!" screamed from the conning tower of a submarine that has unexpectedly found itself directly in the path of an enemy destroyer.

Cleopatra didn't dive. She took off at maximum revolutions, nimbly leaping from deck to deck of every one of the moored boats as she frantically fled for sanctuary on her own yawl.

Arthur boosted himself from the gunnels with the force of one Dick Fosbury trying for yet another Olympic high-jump record, and, if you remember your physics, "To every action there is an equal and opposite reaction."

O'Reilly's sloop pitched horribly, thrashing from port to starboard like a gazelle caught in the coils of a boa constrictor. I was too busy grabbing the nearest fixture to see what had caused, almost simultaneously, a roar from O'Reilly, a massive "thump" from belowdecks, and the sounds of smashing glass. All I can tell you was that when I did look inboard, he was no longer in the hatchway.

I would have gone to his aid but was distracted by a chorus of screeches, curses, more glass-breaking noises, and the crashing of a series of tsunamis displaced by the rocking hulls of a fleet of wildly tossing yachts. I realized that I could gauge the extent of Arthur's trans-decks progress by the way each mast in succession began to thrash to and fro and the chorus of imprecations increased in volume. The last to be hit was the yawl.

Eventually, I'm told, all good things must come to an end. The churned-up waters returned to their previous calm. In sequence, the masthead gyrations lessened in duration and amplitude. In another sequence, nearest vessel first, farthest boat last, the owners of the battered boats began to form a mob, something akin to the one that I imagine stormed the Bastille, on the dock beside O'Reilly's boat.

The last to arrive was Charley. His blazer was very damp and his yachting cap seemed to have gone missing. He was a big man, much bigger than O'Reilly. The calluses on his knuckles might have been caused by their obvious ability to trail on the ground.

"I'd like a word with your skipper," he said. "Now."

"Oh," I said, wondering if maritime law, as well as giving captains the right to perform marriages, also waived the usual civilities surrounding suspension from the nearest yardarm. "He's below."

"And he'll soon be going aloft," Charley growled.

They were going to hang O'Reilly. I could only hope that there was no such crime as aiding and abetting in the nautical legal lexicon.

"You don't mean . . ." I glanced up and

swallowed.

"I bloody well do," said Charley. "Somebody's going to have to get Cleopatra down from my masthead."

O'Reilly's Rival

Doctor Murphy Feels the Wrath of his Fellow Physician

O'Reilly smacked his empty pint glass on the bar top of the Mucky Duck, nodded at mine host Arthur Osbaldiston, and turned to me. "One day . . ." muttered O'Reilly. The tip of his nose was alabaster. His eyes flashed with the kind of light that must have given the Hamburg fire chief pause for serious thought in July 1943. "One day I'm going to marmalize that monstrous mountebank Murphy."

"Indeed," I remarked, taking a step backward and wondering what Doctor "Thorny" Murphy had done this time to, well, rile O'Reilly.

"He's a qualified quack, a certified charlatan. He's not fit to be a bloody benighted barber-surgeon."

You may recall that deep in hillbilly country there once was a minor misunderstanding between the Hatfield and McCoy families. Their falling-out was an *entente cordiale* compared to Fingal Flahertie O'Reilly's feelings for his medical competitor in the village of Ballybucklebo.

If you remember, it went back to the occasion when Doctor Murphy had publicly accused Doctor O'Reilly of playing God. O'Reilly had not so much bided his time as lurked, setting up an ambush that would have done credit to the skills of a squadron of the SAS hiding in the hills of County Tyrone awaiting the coming of a unit of the PIRA. And when O'Reilly did strike, his verbal assault had been as devastating as the cross fire from half a dozen assault rifles.

Discretion, I decided, was definitely the better part of valour. No doubt he would explain his present agitation in the fullness of time. I merely nodded sympathetically and waited.

"Are you pouring that bloody pint or brewing it, Arthur?" O'Reilly roared down the bar. "A man's estate can sue the publican if he lets a customer die of thirst, you know."

"Sorry, Doctor, sir." Arthur waddled along from the beer pump and set a full pint glass of Guinness before O'Reilly, who grunted, lifted the glass, and sank half of its contents before gracing me with, "The College shouldn't suspend Murphy's licence — they should hoist the bloody thing to the top of the tallest flagpole and burn it." The second half of his pint disappeared. "Arthur!"

I had no doubt that all of the unsuspecting gentlemen named Arthur who lived within a ten-mile radius of the Mucky Duck wondered who was shouting at them.

"Right, Doctor, sir. Coming, Doctor, sir."

"Worms," said O'Reilly to me. "What do you know about worms?"

I wondered if we were going fishing but kept the question unspoken.

"Come on, Taylor."

"Well, they're blind helminthes that burrow around in the soil and turn vegetable matter into humus," I tried, quite proud of remembering something from my first-year zoology class at medical school.

"Not those ones, you ninny. Pinworms. Threadworms."

I was on safer ground now and happily trotted out, "*Oxyuris vermicularis*. Most common parasitic infection of children. Cause pruritis . . ."

"Exactly. Make life bloody miserable for the wee ones. And how would you treat them?"

"Piperazine."

"That's how any self-respecting physician would. I just found out we've got an outbreak here in the Ballybucklebo kindergarten, and do you know what Murphy has been prescribing?"

I shook my head. By the scowl on O'Reilly's face, the answer might be interesting, but I had to contain my curiosity because of the arrival of Arthur and O'Reilly's new pint. He grabbed the glass and muttered, "Lime water."

"Looks like Guinness to me," I ventured.

"Not this." O'Reilly must have been calming down, I thought. His first swallow merely consumed the upper third of his beverage. "Lime water is Murphy's miracle cure for worms."

"But . . ."

"Not just lime water. He's been telling the mothers to write *'Et verbum carum factum est,'* on a piece of paper and make the sign of the cross over the concoction before they make the kiddies drink it."

" 'And the word is made flesh,' " I translated. "Biblical."

"Aye. It's an old country remedy that goes back to a Franciscan friar. A fellow called Father Gregory Dunne."

"Your erudition amazes me, Fingal."

"Never mind amazing you. We've got to

stop that bloody man."

"How?"

O'Reilly shook his head. "Dunno. Yet." I saw something in the depths of O'Reilly's brown eyes that would have given Edgar Allen Poe nightmares. "But I'll think of something."

It took us three weeks to repair the wreckage wrought by Doctor Murphy's hamfisted practices. I confess that I felt rather smug as we basked in the gratitude of the mothers of the youngsters who, now properly treated, no longer had to suffer constant perianal irritation. The only one in the village who still had an itch that needed to be scratched was one Doctor Fingal Flahertie O'Reilly. His opportunity to do so came, as before, at a meeting of the county medical society.

All of the GPs from County Down had assembled in Belfast, nominally to hear a learned address by some imported speaker. The added attraction was of course the splendid dinner and copious amounts of some very excellent claret, courtesy of an international pharmaceutical company.

O'Reilly was in one of his expansive moods. He was a splendid raconteur and, after the lecture and the meal, had surrounded himself with a coterie of his cronies whom he was entertaining with yet another of his stories of naval life. I hovered at the periphery of the crowd. Judging by the gale of laughter that swept through the assembly, they'd fully appreciated his last rendition.

I became aware of a presence at my shoulder, heard a disdainful sniff, and turned to see the tall, angular, black-suited figure of Doctor "Thorny" Murphy.

"I see your senior associate is up to his usual uncouth antics," he remarked in condescending tones. I don't know how he did it, but he always struck me as being arrogantly subservient, a cross between Gilbert and Sullivan's Pooh-Bah and Dickens's Uriah Heep.

"Doctor Murphy." O'Reilly's voice boomed across the room. All heads turned to where we stood.

"Doctor O'Reilly." Murphy inclined his head. His tones were the ones he might have used if he'd stepped into a cesspit.

"How very pleasant to see you." O'Reilly's voice oozed charm.

I glanced round, trying to find cover. Before going anywhere near something that might be a bomb, army bomb-disposal officers don a thing called an "explosive ordnance device suit." It's made of Kevlar. Its protective attributes are of such magnitude that compared with it, a mediaeval suit of armour would offer about as much protection as silk thermal underwear. I knew O'Reilly was going to explode and frankly wished to be well out of range.

"I thought you did a very nice job with the worms," O'Reilly said in his most sincere tones. He addressed the throng. "Doctor Murphy here is our local expert on traditional healing."

O'Reilly had once told me that the secret of being a good physician was sincerity. Once you could fake that, everyone would trust you.

Doctor Murphy inclined his head. "Well, I . . ."

"Now don't be modest," O'Reilly said. "If anyone here needs to know how to make a nettle-leaf decoction or a mustard plaster, Doctor Murphy's the man to ask."

I swear a little blush of pleasure tinged the sere wattles of Murphy's scrawny throat.

"Oh, yes," O'Reilly continued. "Doctor Murphy has been in Ballybucklebo for thirty-five years and the local customers are always talking about his wondrous cures."

Murphy's pink turned to a deeper hue. "Well, I . . ."

"I myself heard, only yesterday, about his

cure for infertility."

"What was that?" a voice asked from the back.

"Gunpowder," O'Reilly said conspiratorially.

"Now, Doctor O'Reilly . . ." Doctor Murphy's brow wrinkled into the beginning of a frown.

A juggernaut was a huge wagon under the wheels of which devotees of Krishna hurled themselves and were crushed to death. It was unstoppable. It was but a wheelbarrow compared with O'Reilly, once he got up a head of steam.

"Gunpowder," O'Reilly continued. "One of Doctor Murphy's first patients, Paddy Finucane, couldn't get his wife pregnant. Our esteemed colleague told the man to substitute one teaspoonful of black powder for the sugar in his cup of tea, the tea to be taken three times daily."

"I did no such . . ."

"Worked like a charm. Do you know that when he died, old Paddy left six children, fourteen grandchildren . . ." O'Reilly's timing was impeccable. He paused and swept his gaze over the clearly enraptured audience before adding, ". . . and a bloody great hole where the crematorium used to stand."

The famous roar of the crowd of soccer

supporters when Manchester United scored a goal would have been a muted whisper if ranked against the gales of laughter that filled the meeting room.

Doctor Murphy flushed scarlet, gobbled like a cock turkey that had just noticed the pre-Christmas axe, spun on his heel, and fled.

"Keep up the good work, 'Thorny,' " O'Reilly roared at the departing back. He lowered his voice and turned to me. "Maybe now he'll think twice before inflicting his rubbish on the poor unsuspecting supplicants," he said.

And do you know? He was right.

The Smoking Gun

A lesson in the
Hazards of Tobacco

"Bah! Rubbish! Fiddlesticks! Unadulterated twaddle. Them eejits in London think they can prove anything with their statistics. This here fellah Vessey's utterly, absolutely, categorically wrong."

I knew it was O'Reilly who was making these ex cathedra statements. No one could have mistaken the gravelly tones or the vehemence with which the words were uttered. And a good thing too, because any hopes of actually seeing the orator were roughly on a par with Captain Robert Falcon Scott's chances of finding a room at the Savoy Hotel for a quick overnight stay on his way back from the South Pole. Fingal Flahertie's dining room was filled with a fug of pipe-tobacco smoke that would have made the impenetrable clouds after the first black-powder broadsides at the Battle of

Trafalgar seem as clear as the pure crystal air of the Mourne Mountains.

I coughed and flapped an ineffective hand in a vain attempt to clear the pea-souper from which I confidently expected Sherlock Holmes and Doctor Watson to emerge at any moment. My efforts were about as useful as those of the cabin boy who thought he could use a teaspoon to bail out the entire Atlantic Ocean from the depths of R.M.S. *Titanic*'s hold.

"I thought the article in the *British Medical Journal* seemed convincing."

"You would," O'Reilly growled, "and you probably believe that duodenal ulcers are caused by some as yet unidentified bacterium."

"Don't be daft. They're caused by stress," I said, wondering about the gnawing sensation in my epigastrium, "but I don't think it's unreasonable to suggest that there might be an association between smoking and ill health. Doctor Vessey's figures looked pretty impressive to me."

"Aye," said O'Reilly, "and if you draw a graph that shows the increase in the rates of purchases of television sets and the rates of heart attacks, they've been roaring upwards at about the same speed. If you want to, you can prove that television is the cause of coronaries."

He laughed at his own razor-sharp repartee. "Don't believe everything you read in the *BMJ*."

"Well, I think . . ."

"Jasus, Pat, you'd better watch yourself. If you're that gullible, somebody's going to try to sell you the Queen's Bridge."

According to the late Jim Croce, "You don't tug on Superman's cape. / You don't spit into the wind." According to the still-living P. J. Taylor, you didn't argue with O'Reilly when it was obvious that his mind on a given subject was firmly made up. This simple rule may account for my continued survival. Deciding that discretion was indeed the better part of valour, I conceded defeat. "You're probably right, Fingal."

" 'Course I am," he said with the finality of the Spanish geographers who took great pains in explaining to Christopher Columbus that when it came to the configuration of this planet, "flat" was the word he was looking for.

Clinging to the one remaining shred of my self-respect, I made a last feeble effort. "Is there anything at all that might convince you?"

"That smoking's bad for you?"

"Yes."

424

"Not a thing, my boy. Not a single thing on God's green Earth."

I sighed, not knowing that he was going to be proven wrong.

The question of any relationship between smoking and disease was forgotten in the general hurly-burly of rural practice. I probably wouldn't have given the matter much more thought — although I confess I was developing an aversion to being bested by my mentor — if, some months later, fate hadn't intervened.

We were standing in the hall of his house.

"Could you do me a favour, Pat?" O'Reilly's voice oozed charm. My internal alarm bells went off.

"What is it?" I asked, with as much trust in my tones as the housefly (order Diptera) must have used when invited into the parlour of a certain arachnid.

"Have you noticed the weather?"

If he'd ever given up the practice of medicine, there would have been a stellar career in elected office for Fingal Flahertie O'Reilly. The first rule for that merry bunch of pilgrims is never, never give a straight answer to a direct question.

"What favour?" He might be trying to divert the conversation. I was going to keep it on course with all the concentration of the master of a square-rigger trying to navigate through the Straits of Magellan down in Cape Horn country.

"There's a gale. From the south," he said.

Perhaps I'd misjudged him. Meteorology might be his avocation. It certainly must have taken an acutely honed weather sense to have noted the shrieking of the wind in the great sycamore tree at the end of his garden, the intermittent crashes as slates were ripped from roofs and hurled to the road, and the rattle of rain on the window-panes.

"It's time Arthur Guinness got out to play, you know," he continued. "You'd be doing him a favour too."

"No, Fingal. I am not going to take him for a walk."

O'Reilly laughed. "Mad dogs and Irishmen go out in the midday rain, and you're not daft, is that it?"

"Badly paraphrased Noel Coward. And right, I'm not going out in that lot."

"I wasn't going to ask you to. But this is the very best weather for the ducks."

I was tempted to remark that if he could see my feathers I'd venture out of doors, but unless such was the case I intended to stay as firmly put as King Arthur's Excalibur in the famous stone.

"They'll have to come in low to the ground at evening flight tonight."

Gale. Arthur Guinness — a gun dog. Low-flying ducks. Somewhere at the back of my mind a series of small synapses went off in sequence. A little red light bulb glowed — dimly, I admit, but it definitely lit up. "And you want me to run the evening surgery so you can take Arthur and go shooting?"

"Jasus," he said, "your powers of deduction would make the Great Detective look like a candidate for a school for the hopelessly muddled." He lit his briar. "I'll make it up to you. I'll do next Saturday and Sunday."

I examined the proposition. It seemed to be decidedly deficient in attached strings. No obvious catches were apparent. "You're on," I said, comforting myself with the thought that given the inclemency of the climate, only the true sufferers would brave the elements and make the trip to the surgery. I might have an easy evening.

"Good man." His craggy face lit up with the inner glow only seen on the countenances of small children who have been given the much-desired train set for Christmas. "I'll be off then." He galloped upstairs.

I wandered to the kitchen to see if perhaps

Mrs. Kincaid had made an afternoon cup of tea. Moments later O'Reilly reappeared, clad for his outing in hip-waders, a waterproof jacket, and a deerstalker hat. He had a game bag slung over one shoulder and a double-barrelled twelve-bore tucked in the crook of one arm.

Mrs. Kincaid looked at him and asked, "Now have you got all that you need, Doctor dear?"

O'Reilly checked in his game bag. "Cartridges. Tobacco. Pipe. Matches." He looked at the teapot. "I don't suppose there's enough of that to fill a thermos."

"Aye." Mrs. Kincaid found a flask, filled it with hot tea, and presented it to an obviously impatient O'Reilly. "Off you go now."

And off he went. He was too big a man to skip, but the lightness of his step was akin to the dances of "The Lordly Ones." You know, the little folk that "dwell in the hills / in the hollow hills."

"I don't know," said Mrs. Kincaid, chuckling after he'd slammed the door, "whether himself or that great lummox of a dog has more fun when he goes out after the ducks."

Neither Mrs. Kincaid nor I could have had the slightest inkling what form O'Reilly's fun would take on that particular evening.

■ ■ ■ ■

Evening surgery was, as I'd predicted, light. I retired to the upstairs sitting room and was well into the new James Bond book when I heard the crash of the back door and a heavy tread on the stairs. O'Reilly entered, stage right, with as much force as the gale that still howled outside and all the drama of the Demon King in a Christmas pantomime. He spoke not one word but headed for the sideboard and helped himself to a large John Jameson.

I simply stared. O'Reilly's usually bushy eyebrows had shrunk as if an American Marine Corps barber had given them the full new-recruit treatment. His hairline had receded like a neap tide and his normally florid cheeks had a roseate hue that only John Turner could have rendered in oils. From him emanated a vague smell of something singed.

"Lord," he said, lowering a very large gulp of Irish, "you and that fellah Vessey were right."

"Pardon?"

"About the smoking. Just look at me."

I did, and by herniating most of my face muscles managed to refrain from grinning.

"What happened?"

"I dropped my matches. Couldn't light my pipe. So I did something a bit silly."

This confession coming from the redoubtable O'Reilly would have been on a par with King Charles I admitting that perhaps he had been a little over-optimistic in his opinion of the Divine Right of Kings.

"Go on," I said.

"Well, I thought it was a brilliant idea at the time."

It had been, I thought, on a par with General Ulysses S. Grant's notion of digging a ditch to divert the entire flow of the mighty Mississippi at the siege of Vicksburg — and obviously O'Reilly had had about as much success.

"Aye. I really wanted a smoke so I split a cartridge and put the powder on top of a rock. Then I stuck the stem of the pipe in my mouth and the bowl in the powder." He finished his whiskey. "Did you ever make sparks from a couple of pieces of flint?"

"No, Fingal, and I never went looking for a gas leak with a lit match either."

"Jasus. It worked a charm. Went off like the crack of doom."

"Worked wonders for your haircut too," I said, peering at his frazzled face. "Do you think maybe we should slap a dab or two of ointment on you?"

"I do," he said, "and I'll tell you something else. Smoking can be dangerous to your health. Bloody dangerous."

I'm sure that Doctor Vessey, who was eventually knighted for his work linking cigarette smoking with lung cancer, would have been delighted to have received such a ringing endorsement of his theories from no less a personage than Doctor Fingal Flahertie O'Reilly, MB, BCh, BAO.

RING AROUND THE ROSIES

O'REILLY'S NEPHEW DEMONSTRATES HIS ENTREPRENEURIAL PROWESS

You may remember O'Reilly's nephew, William Butler Yeats O'Reilly, aged eleven. An enterprising boy. Something of an original thinker in the O'Reilly mould. His main claim to fame, at least in Ballybucklebo circles, had been won by his uttering one unscripted sentence at the infamous Christmas pageant.

He'd been moved from his starring role as Joseph — a part that he'd carried off with dramatic flair in the two previous years — to a supporting spot as the innkeeper, and wasn't one bit happy about his demotion. "Seething" is a descriptor often applied to superheated mud pits in remote parts of New Zealand. It would barely have done justice to the pent-up fury inside one small boy.

It would be unfair to compare Ballybuck-lebo's thespian retelling of the nativity story with the Oberammergau Passion Play or the Wagnerian Ring Cycle at Bayreuth, but it was nevertheless an annual fixture in our little village's social calendar and well attended. Willy had dropped his bombshell on opening night.

The effects of his ad lib on the audience had been on a par with the conflagration started by His Majesty's Royal Air Force (Bomber Command), in February 1945 at a spot called Dresden. Willy's father, Lars Porsena O'Reilly, had found himself at the epicentre of the firestorm. Well, you could hardly have expected Willy's immortal lines when admission was sought to the inn by Joseph and Mary — "You can come in, Mary, but Joseph, you can just feck off!" — to have been greeted with thunderous applause by an audience of teachers, parents, and a convent's worth of blushing nuns.

Willy had eaten his meals standing up for several days after the event and his pocket money had been stopped for three months. The Wall Street Crash of 1929 would have seemed but a minor readjustment of the markets in the impecunious eyes of William Butler Yeats O'Reilly. He was facing fiscal catastrophe. Monetary meltdown. But I did tell you that he was an enterprising boy. Wall Street recovered. So did Willy.

In the process he caused his uncle, Doctor Fingal Flahertie O'Reilly, and Doctor O'Reilly's junior colleague, myself, a great deal of head scratching — and we weren't alone. We had the village schoolmaster and most of the children from Ballybucklebo's primary school to keep us company. In the case of ourselves and our perplexed parish pedagogue, the capital clawing was metaphorical. In the cases of the little learners, it was literal.

At first we were caught off guard, but our initial surprise soon turned to complete consternation. O'Reilly began to look like a U-boat skipper who'd surfaced directly under the fifteen-inch guns of one of His Majesty's larger ironclads.

The first inkling that we might be facing some difficulties came at the end of a busy surgery. The last patient was a small boy — you remember Mister Brown, who once before had come in for prenuptial counselling but had cut the interview short when he'd wet his pants — and his mother. She tugged at his hand and said, "Take off your cap." He removed that peculiar head adornment favoured by the school authorities of the time, a soft, peaked cap embellished with concentric rings in the school colours, which in the case of Ballybucklebo Primary were horribly clashing yellow and orange.

O'Reilly peered at the boy's crown. "What do you make of that, Doctor Taylor?" he asked, pointing to a circular bald spot in the middle of the child's head.

I peered at the lesion in question. The hairs had broken off close to the scalp and the stumps had a frosted appearance. "Tinea capitis?" I suggested.

"Brilliant," growled O'Reilly. "I'd guessed that. But which fungus?"

I shook my head. "Could be anything from *Microsporum audouinii* to *Microsporum canis* to one of the Trichophytons."

O'Reilly pursed his lips. "It's ringworm, Mother, but we'll have to send the wee lad up to the skin clinic in Belfast to find out what's the cause."

She looked worried. Mister Brown sniffled and scratched his head.

"All the way to Belfast, Doctor O'Reilly?" she said, doubtfully. "He'll miss a day of school."

"I'm sorry," said O'Reilly, "but he may miss more than that."

I noticed her frown and her son's grin as O'Reilly continued. "If it's one of the animal fungi that's the cause, it'll not spread, but if it's the human kind it could infect every kiddie in the class. He'll have to stay home until we know the answer to the test, and if it is the human kind he'll be off school until he's cured."

Her mouth rounded into a silent "O." Mister Brown's grin widened.

"And," said O'Reilly, "burn his cap."

"But it's brand-new."

"I'm sorry," said O'Reilly, "the bloody thing gets into the cloth and could be given to another youngster. Now just you wait until I make the arrangements at the Royal Victoria Hospital."

The arrangements were made, the patients dismissed, and O'Reilly fired up his briar. "If it is *Microsporum audouinii,* I hope to God we've caught it in time. Once that one gets into a school it can go through the place like wildfire."

It was, we hadn't, and it did. Within a week, every boy in the school had shown the telltale symptoms and signs. Every boy had been given a prescription for Griseofulvin. Every mother had been given instruction about shaving the affected parts of the scalp. The smoke of the funeral pyres of yellow and orange school caps hung over the village. The streets of Ballybucklebo rang to the sounds of childish laughter, and would continue to do so for at least six more weeks until every child was considered fungus-free. The boys rejoiced in their unexpected holiday. Their mothers wrung their hands and O'Reilly grumbled that unless we could trace the source of the outbreak, the whole epidemic could break out again at any time. He was right and it did. Two days after the last of the lads, who looked like a group of tiny tonsured Trappists, was safely ensconced behind his desk, Mister Brown and his mother were back in the surgery.

"Bugger," said O'Reilly, glowering at the boy's scalp, "here we go again. We've got to find out where it's starting."

I had to agree, but the mystery seemed to be unsolvable — unsolvable, that is, until O'Reilly discovered that he'd run out of Erinmore Flake, his favourite pipe tobacco, a product of Messrs. Gallagher and Sons, who in my opinion added sulphur, Greek fire, and a whiff of the great nineteenth-century fogs of London to their product.

"Come on," he said. "We'll nip down to the shop."

We strolled along the main street to the little store. The door opened and who should appear but William Butler Yeats O'Reilly. His cheeks were bulging. In his left hand he carried a paper bag and in his right a brightly coloured school cap. His eyes widened when he caught sight of his uncle.

"Morning, Willy," said O'Reilly.

Willy's reply was unintelligible. He had difficulty forming the words round an enormous mouthful of peppermint gobstopper.

"Buying sweeties?" O'Reilly inquired as he stared at the paper bag.

Willy nodded.

"Huh," said O'Reilly. "I thought you'd no money."

Willy blushed, and tried to hide the cap behind his back.

O'Reilly struck like a cobra. His big hand shot out and grabbed Willy by the ear.

"Spit out that gobstopper," O'Reilly roared.

Willy spat and a great spherical lump of multi-hued hard candy hit the gutter.

I had no idea what was happening, but of course that was often my state of mind when in the company of Fingal Flahertie.

"Give me that cap."

The item in question was surrendered.

"How long have you been at it?" O'Reilly tugged on his nephew's ear.

At what? I wondered as Willy whimpered.

438

"How long?"

"Six weeks, Uncle Fingal."

"Jasus."

"You won't tell my dad?"

O'Reilly paused, pursed his lips, then said, very slowly, "Not if you tell me how much a rub."

"Sixpence."

"You little . . ."

"Sorry, Uncle Fingal."

O'Reilly pointed an admonitory finger. "No more, do you hear?" He tweaked Willy's ear to add emphasis to his words.

"I promise. Honest."

O'Reilly released his grip. "Go on home, but if I catch you at it again . . ."

Willy fled.

"And that's the end of that," said O'Reilly, clearly pleased with himself. "No wonder we couldn't stop the outbreak."

"What are you talking about?" I was as much at sea as the Ancient Mariner.

"Ach," said O'Reilly, "in the immortal phrase that the great detective never actually uttered, 'Elementary, my dear Watson.' Nephew Willy has restored his exchequer by selling a rub of his cap — his infected cap — at sixpence a pop. The kids get the ringworm and don't have to go to school and Willy . . ." O'Reilly began counting on his fingers, then whistled, ". . . by my reckoning he's made nearly two pounds. Crafty little bugger."

"I wonder where he gets that from," I muttered, but O'Reilly had already gone into the shop.

When we returned to his back garden, I had some difficulty deciding which made the worse stink, O'Reilly's recharged briar or the fumes from the bonfire that consumed Willy's cap. The smoke drifted upward and dissipated, and with it went the great ringworm plague of Ballybucklebo.

"Do you know," said O'Reilly, exuding a certain tangible family pride. "That nephew of mine's going to go far one day. You just watch."

JINGLE BELLS

SAMMY THE SWEEP
RISES TO THE OCCASION

While watching a TV quiz show I fell to pondering how popular these things are. In the Yuletide spirit of giving and, as O'Reilly would remark just before he laid into some miscreant, "It is always more blessed to give than to receive," I thought I'd offer my readers a little quiz.

Translate the following: Airy tipsies, slabbergub, bit of a lig, blether-skite, beelin', boggin', and boke. [Montgomery, M. and F. Montgomery, *Barnish County Antrim Dialect Dictionary* 1993 © Doctor Robert Montgomery. Courtesy Doctor T. F. Baskett.]

Give up? I'm not surprised. You'd not come within a beagle's gowl of the answers unless of course you speak fluent Ulsterese. Please understand, Ulsterese isn't a foreign language but an abstruse form of English embellished with the local expressions used daily in Ballybucklebo and its environs. When rendered at full speed by an upset Ulsterman whose accent would be, in the local parlance, "thick as champ," attempts to comprehend what was being said would have left no less a linguist than Professor Henry Higgins babbling with incomprehension.

Once, at the height of the Ulster Troubles, I saw an NBC documentary filmed in Belfast. Naturally the ubiquitous man-on-the-street had been interviewed. The folks at the network had thoughtfully provided their viewers with English subtitles. And a good thing too. "Beagle's gowl. Thick as champ." Indeed.

Let me instantly explain that failing to "come within a beagle's gowl" is translated as falling short of expectations by the distance from which a howling beagle dog could be heard, and that's a fair stretch of the legs. "Thick as champ" refers to the density of a peculiar Irish dish of potatoes, buttermilk, and scallions. It has the gastronomic qualities of a lump of spent plutonium and, when eaten, "sticks to your ribs like glue." Applied in a descriptive fashion to an accent, this phrase suggests a degree of impenetrability that would make the front armour of a main battle tank seem as thin as tissue paper. When used to describe intellectual capacity — say in the case of Donal Donnelly — well, I'm sure you get my drift.

If you're still wondering about the Airy tipsies list, I'm afraid you'll have to wait until this story is finished before you get the answers, because I really want to explain the expression "thon one has a heart of corn."

"A what?" I hear you ask. That's right. "Thon one has a heart of corn," is precisely how O'Reilly described Samuel St. John (pronounced "sinjin") Slattery, our local chimney sweep, after the man had left the surgery. He'd been in to see about a nasty cough, an occupational hazard of the sweep's trade. I must say I was glad to see him go. It was Christmas Eve and I was going to a dance in Belfast. I really didn't want to be held up by one of O'Reilly's rambling expositions so I merely nodded.

"You can't always tell a book by its cover," said O'Reilly, washing enough soot from his hands to have replenished the entire York, Notts, and Derby coalfields. "Just because your man looks like an escapee from a travelling minstrel show . . ."

"Grunts when you ask him a question and has a perpetual scowl on his face that would make the Medusa on a bad hair day seem as mild as a cooing dove . . ."

"I'm telling you," said O'Reilly. "You can hardly blame him for being covered in soot. He'd come here straight from his work."

I had a mental flashback to the violent ejection of one Donal Donnelly, who'd dared to show O'Reilly an unwashed foot, but decided that it would be wise to make no comment on that matter. I really did want to get away, but foolishly added, "Sammy St. John strikes me as a pretty mean-tempered bloke."

"You'd be wrong," said O'Reilly, dumping himself in his swivel chair and firing up his pipe.

"Prove it."

"All right. I will. Park yourself."

I glanced at my watch, sighed, and hitched myself up onto the examination table. "Go on."

"Do you remember Mister Brown and Miss Gill?"

"The kids that came to see you because they wanted to get married but had to leave because Mister Brown had wet himself?"

"The very ones. Well, I saw Mister Brown on the street today. He was sobbing his wee heart out."

"Fingal, I thought we were discussing Sam

444

Slattery."

"Patience, my boy. All in good time."

I fidgeted.

" 'What's up?' I asked him. It took me a few minutes to understand what was the matter. I tell you, Pat, between the howls of him and his wiping his nose on his sleeve, I thought I was going to be there all day. But you couldn't leave a wee lad that upset. Not on Christmas Eve."

I had to smile. I told you years ago that O'Reilly was kind to widows and small children.

"I finally got it out of him. One of the big boys had told him there was no Santa Claus."

"Ach no."

"Ach yes, and there was no comforting him. I know we all have to find it out sooner or later. I don't think it's right to lie to the wee ones when they hear the truth. But on Christmas Eve?" He shook his big head.

"So what did you do?"

"I took him by the hand and walked him home."

"Let his mother sort it out?"

"I suppose that's what I was thinking but, do you know, once in a while things have a habit of working out just fine. Guess who was at the house?"

"Donner and Blitzen? Rudolph?"

Instead of growling at my sarcasm, O'Reilly let go a guffaw that rattled the instruments on the stainless steel instrument trolley. "The next best thing. Samuel St. John Slattery was there sweeping the Browns' chimney." O'Reilly let go a mini-mushroom cloud from his pipe. "He was just about to climb his ladder when we arrived. 'What's up?' says he to the little lad. He just went on sniffling so I told Sam what the trouble was. I suppose I was hoping maybe Sam could say something to help. 'Is that fact?' was all he said, and he went up the ladder like a monkey up a pole."

"Right enough. The man has a heart of corn. You're not convincing me, Fingal."

This time O'Reilly did glower at me. "I will," he said. "There was me, both legs the same length, a little boy by the hand, still in floods, no sign of the mother, and Samuel St. John up on the roof. Then it happened." His frown vanished and was replaced by a smile so enigmatic that he could have posed for Leonardo da Vinci. "Sammy came back down, bent over the little lad, and held out a big black hand. The look on old Sam's face was one of complete awe. 'Look what I found up by the chimney,' says he, and opened his hand."

"And?"

"I watched the wee fellow. I've never seen anything like it. He rubbed his eyes, peered into the callused, sooty hand, and do you know what was there?"

I shook my head.

"A tiny golden bell. A sleigh bell. 'I wonder what this came off?' says Sammy. It was like the sunrise, the way the wee lad's face lit up. He looked at Sammy. 'You'd better have it,' says Sam, and gave the boy the bell. He tore off into the house yelling, 'Look, Mummy. Look what Santa's reindeer left on our roof.' Old Sam just coughed.

" 'How the hell . . .' I started to ask him. He stuck his hand into his trousers pocket and pulled out five or six little bells. 'He's not the first nipper I've seen like that. And you don't have to lie to them. Just let them draw their own conclusions. The poor little bugger is going to find out soon enough. Let him enjoy one more Christmas.'

" 'God, Sammy,' says I, 'you've a heart of corn.' "

I was so amazed I just sat there on the couch with, to use a graphic piece of Ulsterese, my eyes turned up like a duck in thunder.

Oh yes, I promised you a translation of other bits of my native tongue. Here you are. Airy tipsies: high winds. Slabbergub: a man with a foul mouth. Bit of a lig: a fool. Beelin': suppurating. Boggin': filthy. Boke: Throw up. And one more thing, in plain English: a merry Christmas and a happy New Year to all.

HOME IS THE SAILOR

AN IRISH COUNTRY DOCTOR STORY

AUTHOR'S NOTE

Since Tom Doherty and Associates first began publishing the Irish Country Doctor series in 2007 for a current total of seven novels with one in press, I have been overwhelmed by the number of kind letters that come to me through my Web site and as comments posted on Facebook. Readers have taken the characters in the books to heart and want to know more about them. A recurrent wish is for the works to appear more frequently. Like the title of the 1982 movie starring Jill Clayburgh, "I'm dancing as fast as I can" — for me, read, "I'm writing," and my publisher is doing his best, but it takes a while to write 140,000 words and to turn them into a paper book.

Sixteen thousand words do not consume as much time, and although this work has had all the technical attention paid to a paper book in terms of editing, design, and cover design, the Internet allows much more rapid publication.

In this long short story, for want of a better term, you will learn how the recent widower Doctor Fingal O'Reilly returns to Ballybucklebo after the Second World War. His attempts to reestablish his practice seem doomed until, in her usual understated but effective way, Mrs. Kinky Kincaid comes to the rescue.

Although this is not a giveaway — authors all have the same recurrent habits of needing to eat and find shelter — it is well priced and I hope will be regarded as a kind of gift from my publisher and me to help fill the gap before my first work about the Ulster Troubles, *Pray for Us Sinners,* a story of loss of faith and search for atonement, appears in June and *Fingal O'Reilly: Irish Doctor,* number eight in the Irish Country Doctor series, is on the shelves in October.

All the citizens of Ballybucklebo and I thank you for your loyalty, encouragement, and patience.

With my very best wishes,

PATRICK TAYLOR
Salt Spring Island,
British Columbia,
November 2012

1

FIRST IMPRESSIONS ARE
THINGS YOU DON'T GET A
SECOND CHANCE TO MAKE

Surgeon-Commander Fingal Flahertie O'Reilly, M.B., B.Ch., B.A.O., R.N.R., D.S.C., gave a third hard shove then kept his thumb firmly on the porcelain push of a bell that was mounted on a brass plate. "Get a move on," he said, and hunched his shoulders. It was nippy out here in the mid-February evening. His ship, HMS *Warspite,* had been placed in Category C reserve on February 1, 1946, and her remaining crew paid off. As soon as he had completed the formalities of his own demobilisation, O'Reilly had headed for the Liverpool cross-channel ferry to Belfast docks and then the train to Ballybucklebo. From there it had only been a short walk.

An Austin Ruby of early thirties vintage

451

rattled past the Presbyterian church on the other side of Main Street, part of the Bangor to Belfast road.

He heard a distant ringing and a woman's soft Cork brogue calling, "I'm coming, so. Take your hurry in your hand now."

He stepped back and regarded the familiar front of the big, old, three-storey house where he had been an assistant in general practice before the war had called him away on naval service for six long years. A steam engine whistled, coming from where the tracks of the Belfast and County Down Railway ran along the shore of Belfast Lough.

When he looked at the house again he saw ground-floor bow windows flanking a green-painted front door — a now-open green door wherein stood a solid woman in her late thirties. Fire flashed in her agate eyes as she squinted into the low sun. She dusted flour off her hands then stood arms akimbo. "You did make the bell sound like the last trump, bye. There's no need to —" She stepped back, smiling broadly with dimples coming into her cheeks. "Praise all the saints. It's yourself, sir." She stepped aside. "Welcome home at last. Come in, come in, come in, Doctor O'Reilly, sir. Come into the dining room and I'll make you a cup of tea and a plate of hot buttered barmbrack, so, before I see to your dinner. I've made roast rack of spring lamb with herb stuffing and caper sauce."

O'Reilly's tummy rumbled and his grin was vast. "By God that sounds like manna from heaven." After years of eating the efforts of Royal Navy cooks, often little more than corned beef sandwiches and cocoa when the ship was closed up at action stations, one of Mrs. Kinkaid's homemade meals would be bliss. "How are you, anyway, Kinky? I'm sorry I'm a bit late." On Monday, to let her know he'd be arriving Friday, he'd phoned Mrs. Maureen "Kinky" Kincaid, until recently housekeeper to the late Doctor Flanagan, to whom O'Reilly had been an assistant before the war. The estate had provided for her wages to be paid until the house and practice had been sold — to O'Reilly.

"Och, I'm grand, so, and it's better late than never, and I'm all the better for seeing yourself back here, sir." She beamed at him.

"It's good to be home." O'Reilly was very glad that she was now going to assume the same housekeeping role for him. He had, while the ship was still in Portsmouth, through his solicitor brother Lars, completed the purchase of the practice and the house and its contents from Doctor Flanagan's estate. It had taken every penny of O'Reilly's demobilisation gratuity and a sizable loan from the Bank of Ireland. It was, he thought, a blessing that Kinky had agreed to stay. With her knowledge of the locals she'd help him rebuild the practice, the patients of which must now be seeking their medical advice elsewhere. Doctor Flanagan had had no assistant before or after O'Reilly.

And neither would he, not for many years anyway. Apart from the need to pay off the loan, O'Reilly was looking forward to running a busy, single-handed practice and seeing a variety of patients and their ailments. He'd not delivered a baby for years and he'd always enjoyed midwifery. He wondered if he'd forgotten all he'd ever learned about diseases of women. Medicine on a battleship with a crew of more than twelve hundred healthy young men had largely been confined to treating accidental injuries — when in port the results of barroom brawls, hangovers, and venereal disease, and when in action, war wounds. He shuddered. He'd rather not think of those.

He cleared his throat. "It's been quite some time, Kinky," he said.

"A donkey's age, sir, but you do be back

so leave your suitcase and overcoat in the hall."

He took off his navy greatcoat, they'd allowed him to keep it, and hung it on the hall coat stand. He felt lucky to have been demobbed at last. British airmen in Ceylon had gone on strike this month to protest against the slow rate of their release from the armed forces.

"It's a grand tweed suit the navy did give you," she said. "Makes a change from a uniform. Now go you into the dining room, sir, and I'll only be a shmall-little minute, so." She left.

O'Reilly looked to what he automatically thought of as the port side of the house, then reminded himself he was on dry land now. This was the front parlour but had served old Doctor Flanagan as his surgery, what North American doctors would call their office. It didn't seem as if much had changed in there. Perhaps not, but he had. Six years of war service would change any man.

He went into the dining room. The furniture had come with the purchase of the house.

Same old high-backed chairs, long bog oak table, cut-glass chandelier, sideboard. Even the decanters were still there. He'd get a bottle of John Jameson's Irish whiskey tomorrow. He'd much prefer that to the navy's traditional tipple of Plymouth gin and Angostura bitters — pink gin.

The front doorbell rang. When he'd been an assistant here, it had been Kinky's job to answer. Business already? He hoped so. He waited, heard voices, one soft, Cork, female, the other male, raised, harsh, Ulster. "I don't give a tinker's toss if he's only arrived five minutes ago and he's getting his afternoon tea. His tea can wait. I want til see a doctor and I want til see him right now. Right now. It was in the *County Down Spectator* last week that a new quack was taking over here and I need til see him, so I do. Now. I'm a very busy man."

O'Reilly rose. He felt the tip of his boxer's bent nose grow cold, an indication that it was blanching, which was itself a sure sign that his temper was rising. He needed patients but not rude and demanding ones. He peered through the slightly open door.

Kinky, jaw set, arms folded across the top of her pinafore, stood four square in the front doorway. "I've told you, sir, the doctor —"

"I want him and I want him now. Now."

O'Reilly frowned. How dare this rotund little man in a three-piece blue serge suit and bowler hat speak like that to a woman? O'Reilly took a deep breath. Calm down, he told himself. You're dealing with civilians. You need to build up a practice. You can't treat them like naval ratings. And yet echoing in his head was the admonition of *Warspite*'s senior medical officer, Surgeon-Commander Wilcoxson, R.N., to a young Surgeon-Lieutenant O'Reilly, R.N.R., in 1939. *Never, never let the patients get the upper hand.* He opened the dining room door. "Can I help you, Mister . . . ?"

The man pushed past Kinky and came into the hall. "I dunno. Can you? Who the hell are you, anyroad?" The man squinted at O'Reilly. "Aren't you the young pup that worked with Flanagan before the war? O'Rourke or O'Rafferty or something like that?"

Struggling to keep his voice level, O'Reilly said, "I'm Doctor O'Reilly. Yes."

"Right. I'm Mister Albert Bishop. I'm a very important man round here, so I am."

"I'm sure you are," O'Reilly said in his most placatory voice while thinking about large fish, ugly ones at that, in small if not puddle-sized ponds. "What can I do for you?"

"I need to talk to you, and in private." He flicked his head dismissively at Kinky, who frowned, sniffed, and turned on her heel.

"Come into the surgery," O'Reilly said, overriding his intense desire to throw the man out. Some philosopher had made a crack about a long journey starting with the first step, and O'Reilly had a practice to build. He led the way. He pushed the door closed behind the man.

A swivel chair stood in front of a flat table that had served Doctor Flanagan as a desk. O'Reilly sat in the swivel, stuck a pair of half-moon spectacles on his nose, and waved at one of two simple, hard wooden chairs. "Have a seat."

Mister Bishop plumped himself down.

"And what seems to be the trouble?"

"I'm not sick nor nothing."

And you insisted on seeing me and you were rude to Kinky? O'Reilly told himself again to calm down. "Then what can I do for you?"

"You mind in 1939 we all had til get National Identity Cards?"

"Yes."

"Well, I've lost mine, and I need one to prove who I am," he shook his head, "as if everyone round here didn't know, so I can complete a big contract with the army at Palace Barracks outside Holywood. The stupid buggers that issue the cards say I've

458

til fill out this here thing." He slammed a government form on the table. "And I need a doctor's signature, so I do. Like on a passport application."

O'Reilly shook his head and said levelly, but with a touch of steel in his tones, "And for that you barged in here, were rude to Mrs. Kincaid . . ." Never mind not treating a physician with the courtesy custom demanded.

"I'm in a hurry, so I am." Clearly O'Reilly's attempted admonition had had no effect.

For a moment he ached to be back on *Warspite*. A naval rating who'd behaved like this man might have been up before the executive officer, before his feet had touched the deck, on a charge of insolence to a superior officer. Might have. O'Reilly prided himself that he'd never had to invoke naval law. A few well-chosen words roared in what O'Reilly thought of as his quarterdeck voice and an icy stare over half-moon spectacles had always quelled the most intransigent rating. But this Bishop was a civilian, and, O'Reilly reminded himself, he needed patients, and lots of them, if he was going to make a success of this practice. He took a deep breath. "Give it to me."

"Sign there." Bishop pointed.

O'Reilly did, recognising that he had lost the "upper hand." One day, Mister Bishop, he thought, either you are going to have to find a new medical advisor or you and I are going to rethink our doctor-patient relationship. "Here." He wondered what the fee was for signing forms. Perhaps Kinky would know. Doctor Flanagan, as far as O'Reilly knew, had handled the practice finances and had paid O'Reilly a salary.

"Right." Bishop rose and headed for the door.

"I beg your pardon," O'Reilly called at the departing back.

Bishop stopped, turned. "I never said nothing."

"Sorry. I thought I distinctly heard you say, 'Thank you, Doctor.' "

There was a small smile on O'Reilly's face as Bishop snorted, let himself out, and slammed the door.

O'Reilly headed back to the dining room to be met by Kinky, who had just delivered a tray of tea and hot buttered barmbrack. The scent of its spices was mouth-watering.

"There you are, sir," she said. "Eat up however little much is in it."

"Thank you, and Kinky?" He went to the tray and lifted a warm triangle of 'brack.

"Yes, sir?"

"What do I charge for filling in a form?" He bit into the wedge. Delicious.

"Lord bless you, sir, do not worry your head. Next time you see a patient there's a ledger on the table. Fill in the name and what you did. I send out the accounts every month."

"Really?"

She must have interpreted his relieved surprise as disbelief because she stiffened and said, "I have my School Leavers Certificate, so. I am not an unlettered woman."

O'Reilly swallowed his mouthful. "I never thought for one minute you were, Kinky."

"That's all right then." She smiled. "It's my job to leave you free for the doctoring."

"I appreciate that." Another mouthful. He'd missed Irish cooking.

"And will you be starting on Monday?"

"I will. I'm going up to Charles Hurst in Belfast tomorrow to buy a car, then I'm going down to Portaferry to see my mother and brother."

"Family does be important, so. Most of mine are still in County Cork near Beal na mBláth," she said wistfully.

"And you'll want to see them, I'm sure. I'll be able to give you time off soon, but I'll need you for a week or two first, Kinky. My mother has arranged for bits and pieces

461

she's been storing for me to be brought up here tomorrow. You'll need to let the movers in — I'll tell you where things are to go."

"That will not be any trouble, sir."

"And I'll certainly need you here on Monday on my first day as the principal here."

She smiled. "And I do hope you'll soon be busy for I remember how much you enjoyed your work when you were last here, so."

"I hope so too — and I do have to pay the bank."

"I'll be here to help, and the patients will come back and bring the fees with them, you'll see."

"I just hope they're more pleasant than that Bishop. I don't remember seeing him when I was here before, but he is a thoroughly unpleasant man."

She frowned. "Mister Bertie Bishop is an influential man here and he is a terrible one for bearing a grudge, so."

O'Reilly wondered if his parting shot had been altogether wise, but damn it all he was going to be the local GP and he'd be damned if anybody was going to ride roughshod over Kinky — or him. He'd never tolerated that kind of thing since the day he

462

used his newly discovered wicked right cross to flatten the school persecutor. O'Reilly had spent the last six years fighting one of the biggest bullies the world had ever known, and he'd be damned if he was going to let anyone get away with it here.

2

HOME THEY BROUGHT
HER WARRIOR

O'Reilly drove his black long-bonnetted
Rover 16 with all the flair of the pilot of
Warspite's Walrus observation seaplane. The
car was a second-hand 1945 model he'd
bought on the never-never, as hire-purchase
was called. He'd been lucky to get it. New
cars could take as long as a year to be
delivered and even used models were rare,
but those in some occupations, including
doctors, were given priority. The motor
industry was only now switching back to
peacetime production. "Poop-poop," he
shouted in what he thought might be a fair
imitation of Mister Toad from one of
O'Reilly's favourite books, *The Wind in the
Willows*. And he drove like Mister Toad.
Heavy on the accelerator and brake.

He passed elms and sycamores growing in

hedgerows. The great gaunt trees were leaf-less, reaching with bony fingers for a cold blue sky from which an occasional snowflake drifted. Black-faced ewes heavy with winter fleeces huddled in the corners of little fields bordered in drystone walls or blackthorn hedges while the lambs, seemingly oblivious to the cold, ran and bounced, full of the joys of spring. Lord, even if real spring was still some weeks away it was good to be back home in Ulster. There had been times in the last six years when it had seemed to him that, like the crew of the *Flying Dutchman,* he and his shipmates were doomed eternally to sail their great gallant ship through end-less growling seas. But he was home. At last. He roared out,

And it's home boys home, home I'd like to
   be
Home for a while in the old counteree
Where the oak and the ash and the bonny
   rowan tree
Are all growin' greener in the old counteree.

And in all of Ireland, his own old counteree, here on the shores of Strangford Lough, was the place he loved the best.

Overhead a skein of metallically honking Greylag geese drifted down a gentle wind heading for the islands of the lough that lay to his right. The peace washed round him and if he did hear gunfire, it would only be the report of a wildfowler's shotgun. A far cry from the islands of the Mediterranean Sea where he'd spent tumultuous parts of 1940, '41, and '43, or those of Puget Sound in Washington State where his old ship had gone because a German bomb had blown a great hole in her during the Battle of Crete. After being patched up as best the dockyard could in Alexandria Harbour she had passed through the Suez Canal for her long trip for extensive repairs and modifications in Bremerton Navy Yard and replacement of her worn-out main armament.

O'Reilly had mixed memories, some sad, some grateful, of Bremerton and the kindness of the Americans.

He sighed. He'd needed kindness, wounded as he'd been, still was, by the death of his wife, Deirdre, in the Belfast Blitz in April 1941. He must try to put it all behind him. Start a new life back here in Ulster. But it hurt. It hurt sore.

"Damnation." He stamped on the brake pedal. A rusty Massey Ferguson tractor was trundling toward him coming the other way. The horse trailer behind took up more than its share of the road and O'Reilly had to pull onto the verge. As soon as he was past he sank his foot and tore off, hardly noticing the lone cyclist who on the Rover's approach hurled himself and his bike into the ditch.

He turned on the car radio, fiddled with the dial, and found a BBC man's Oxbridge voice saying, "And finally in sports news; on Thursday in Paris the International Olympics Committee announced that the 1948 Games will be held in London." More fiddling before O'Reilly found the classical music he was looking for. He recognised Mozart's *Magic Flute* and let the cheerful sounds soothe him. He was able to manage a smile by the time he'd turned into the short drive up to Lars's home. O'Reilly'd been singing along with Papageno's *"Der vogelfänger bin ich ja"* and accompanying the performer's reed flute with a series of rising "tiddle-iddle-eyes —" and falling "pom-poms." He noticed a big Armstrong Siddeley near the house. Lars had warned Fingal of Ma's taste in motorcars. He parked to the final "pom-pom," got out, and crunched across the gravel to the front door where Lars and Ma stood smiling at him.

"Fingal, welcome home, son," Ma said, letting herself be engulfed in his hug. "Thank God you're safe."

"And sound," he said. "You're looking well." And she was, in her short tweed jacket and knee-length skirt.

"I do my best," she said, "but I'm afraid these wartime austerity fashions leave a certain amount to be desired." She laughed. "I think us ladies complaining about clothes rationing hardly compares with what our troops had to face."

He picked her up and spun her round. "God, it's good to see you, Ma."

"Put me down, Fingal." Her laughter filled the hall.

"I'm home, Ma. And it'll be a long time before I leave again." He set her down.

"Home is the sailor, home from the sea," Lars said.

"And the hunter home from the hill. 'Requiem.' Robert Louis Stevenson," O'Reilly said, and shook Lars's hand. "And how are you, big brother?"

"I'm grand, Finn, and very glad to see you. Come in."

He followed them into the hall. Something giving off a tantalising aroma was cooking somewhere. A large liver and white springer spaniel rushed up to greet him.

"Sit, Barney," Lars said, and the dog obeyed.

"Old Barney's still going strong," Fingal

468

said, noticing grey in the dog's muzzle.

"Remember when we used to go wildfowling with him? He was a great retriever."

"Still is," Lars said.

"Let me look at you again," Ma said. She frowned. "You've got older, Fingal," she said, "but you're still my handsome young son."

"It's been nearly six years and I think you need specs, Ma," he said, "but thank you." He was expecting to be ushered into Lars's spacious sitting room overlooking the narrows where the ripping tides had given the lough its Viking name, Strangfjorthr, the turbulent fjord.

Ma said, "That's a goose you can smell roasting." She glanced at her watch. "It'll be ready in about an hour. I've things to do in the kitchen. I know how long you've been gone, Fingal. There's so much to talk about, but why don't you boys give Barney a walk, go down to the Portaferrry Arms, and have a pint before lunch?"

"You sure, Ma?" Fingal said.

"Of course I am. I've waited this long, I can wait a bit longer. We can blether away to our hearts' content over lunch and in the afternoon. I've a feeling it might snow more heavily later so go on and enjoy yourselves before it does."

"Let me get my coat," Lars said.

"Do you know," said Fingal, "I don't think this place's changed one bit." He was striding beside his brother up the face of a low, rounded hill. Gorse bushes grew, spiny green and dotted with chrome-yellow flowers. Their almond scent was carried on the salty air. He sniffed. There was a more pungent aroma too. "You got a badger round here, Lars?"

Lars pointed to a burrow under a bank where brown bracken drooped. "Old Brock has his set in there. He'll be sleeping now. Leave it, Barney. Don't want him getting into a fight with the beast."

The dog, who had made a beeline for the burrow, now turned aside and began investigating the whins. Two rabbits bolted, ears back, scuts white and bobbing. Barney had been trained to know he was not allowed to chase flushed game. He sat abruptly and watched them go.

Overhead, small jackdaws and larger rooks that had flocked together cawed and flapped their way inland. A constant twittering was coming from a leafless blackthorn hedge and Fingal saw a flock of brightly coloured goldfinches take wing and whirl away across the field.

He strode alongside his brother across the little fields. When Lars asked a question, Fingal was, like most ex-service men, reticent about the details of his war. He was warmed by Lars's concern for Fingal's loss of Deirdre. Lars himself, bachelor solicitor and unable to volunteer because of flat feet, had lived out his war quietly here, keeping an eye on Ma, who'd been terribly busy raising money for the Spitfire Fund and working for a charity for unmarried mothers. No. Lars hadn't married. His disappointment over a judge's daughter in Dublin seemed to have put him off the fair sex for life, yet he appeared content to Fingal. Something to think about, because Fingal himself had no intention of becoming romantically involved. Certainly not for a while yet.

He followed Lars and Barney over a stile and onto the shore. A little past the tide's edge a heron, blue-grey, gangly legged, and with a pigtail of feathers hanging down behind, darted its head into the water and pulled it back, a silver fish wriggling in the bird's long beak. Across the narrow waters a vee of small geese with grey bellies, narrow white collars, and black heads flew up the lough.

"Atlantic brent geese," Lars said. "All the

way from Greenland and Spitzbergen to winter here. Probably heading up to the Quoile River."

"You always did know your birds, Lars," Fingal said.

"To shoot them. But you know, Finn, I'm beginning to think they need our protection. I haven't been out more than a couple of times this season. I'm thinking of joining the Royal Society for the Protection of Birds."

"Not until after next season, please," Fingal said. "You'd better be ready to go out once or twice with me. Unless you count my ship chucking everything she had from fifteen-inch shells to 0.5-inch machine-gun bullets at the enemy, I've not had a shot," he laughed, "for nearly seven years. I'd enjoy a day or two out with you for old times' sake, and," he said more softly, "it would make a nice change if no one's shooting back."

"I suppose it was pretty grim," Lars said.

Fingal took a deep breath. "It had its moments — but it's over, and I'm home, and I'm home to stay."

"I'd certainly say you're glad to be back," Lars said, picking up a stick and throwing it for Barney to retrieve.

"I am that." Fingal frowned. "And happy to be."

"Happy to be back, yes, but I'd say you don't sound completely happy, Finn. What's up?"

Fingal shook his head and waited for Lars to take the stick and throw it again. "Thank you for handling the conveyance of old Doctor Flanagan's practice, Lars."

"It was my pleasure, Finn."

"I'm excited about the practice . . ." He hesitated then said, "But I'm a bit worried. I haven't started work yet, but I just hope the old boy's patients come back. I'll see on Monday morning if anyone shows up."

"I suppose all folks starting a small business have the same worry. I know I did. We put our shingle up and pray they come." He clapped Fingal on the shoulder. "You'll be fine, Finn. I know you will because you're an excellent doctor, but don't be surprised if it's slow at the beginning."

"Thanks." Fingal warmed inside to his brother's touch and reassurance, but outside the snow Ma had warned them about had started and the air was as cold as a witch's tit. And tucked in a corner of his inner glow was a chilly worry that Lars might be wrong and the practice wouldn't grow. Forget it for today, he told himself. "It's getting bloody bitter," Fingal said. "Come on, big brother, call Barney in and we'll take Ma's advice and head for the Arms — but I'm buying you a hot half-un. It's too bloody cold for a pint."

3

IS OF HIS OWN OPINION STILL

O'Reilly looked at his watch. Ten o'clock on Monday morning and still no patients. He sat in the swivel chair in the surgery, rolling the top of his father's old desk up and down. It had been delivered on Saturday afternoon. Kinky, as he'd requested, had supervised the moving men in their placing of his few pieces of furniture and leaving packing cases of books in the upstairs lounge.

O'Reilly had spent Sunday afternoon arranging his volumes on the shelves there, wondering how he'd managed to accumulate so many, but then reading was amongst his foremost pleasures. He'd stood for minutes enjoying the sweeping views past the lopsided steeple of the Presbyterian church with its churchyard full of ancient tombstones and sombre snow-dusted yew trees. Looking farther over the roofs of the village to where gulls wheeled and swooped over the sand dunes, his gaze had taken in the calm, washed-out blue of Belfast Lough and in the dim distance the soft darker blue hills of Antrim rolling down to Carrickfergus and its brooding Norman castle. Only a single coalboat shoved her way steadily to the Central Coal Pier in Bangor Harbour, reminding him of a line in John Masefield's poem "Cargoes": "Dirty British coaster with a salt-streaked smoke stack." No yachts yet, but in the summer he knew the sailors would be out in force.

Later he'd asked Kinky to give him a hand hanging a photograph on the landing wall outside the lounge.

"And that does be your big ship, sir?" she'd asked when they'd finished.

"That's her," he said. "HMS *Warspite*. 'The Grand Old Lady.' " He adjusted the frame to be sure the picture was hanging straight. "The photo was taken when she was anchored in Grand Harbour, Valetta, in Malta."

Kinky leant forward to see better. "She does look a very powerful vessel, so."

"She was, Kinky, she and her four sister *Queen Elizabeth* class of battleships." He pointed to the eight fifteen-inch rifles, two each in X and Y turrets aft and two each in A and B turrets for'ard. "You see those big guns above the foredeck?"

"I do."

"The dispensary and sick bay where the medical staff worked were two decks below the most for'ard gun barrels. It was like the clap of doom when they were fired over our heads. Their shells weighed 1,950 pounds each, that's not far off one ton, and she could hurl them for fourteen miles."

"From here to Millisle down the Ards Peninsula, bye," Kinky said, and took her duster to the frame. "I can believe those guns would have made ferocious bangs, so. I've seen newsreel of battleships firing at France on D-Day," she looked him in the eye, "but the war does be over and you can settle down now and enjoy the nice peace and quiet of Ballybucklebo, so."

Peace and quiet? True enough, but things were a bit too quiet this morning. It wasn't that he wanted people to be sick, but he needed to work. O'Reilly drummed his fingers on the desktop.

That old piece held memories for O'Reilly of a much younger Fingal who all his life had wanted to study medicine. Father had been sitting at this desk in his study when Fingal had defied him back in '27, telling him, "I'm not doing nuclear physics." That stubbornness had led him into the merchant marine and the Royal Naval Reserve before he'd finally gone to Trinity College in Dublin to fulfil his dream. And that stint in the reserve had led to his call-up when war had broken out, a war that, as Kinky had remarked, was now over. And the Lord be praised. But now what he needed were patients in his surgery so he could get back to the kind of doctoring he loved.

He rose and for the umpteenth time walked back to the room that had originally been the scullery, but which Doctor Flanagan had used as his waiting room. Not for the first time O'Reilly scowled at the dismal, shiny, green-painted walls. He'd already decided to paper them with something more cheerful. Roses, he thought, roses would do very well.

The place was as deserted as a Protestant church on a weekday. He bent and lifted a tattered *Reader's Digest* from a heap of earlier editions, several *Women's Own* magazines, and some issues of a kiddies' comic book, *The Dandy Comic.* He smiled at the drawings of Korky the Cat on their front pages. As he was scanning the index of the *Digest,* the outside door opened and a young woman came in holding the hand of a little girl clutching a well-worn teddy bear. His first real patients. He didn't count Bertie Bishop. "Good morning," a smiling O'Reilly said. "I'm Doctor O'Reilly."

"I'm Kathy Dunleavy, Willie Dunleavy's wife."

"Are you related to Charles Dunleavy who owns the Black Swan?"

"He was my da-in-law. He's gone three years, God rest him. I married his son Willie five years back. He runs the pub now, so he does."

"Good Lord, the last time I saw your husband he was a bachelor kicking a ball around with his mates and looking for divilment." O'Reilly shook his head. "Anyway, what can I do for you?"

"I'm worried about wee Mary here."

"Let's see what we can do about that." O'Reilly led Mrs. Dunleavy and the child to the surgery and sat in his chair while she took one of the wooden ones and lifted Mary onto her lap.

"So, what seems to be the trouble with Mary?"

"The poor wee button's off her feed for the last couple of days, says she can't swallow right, and I think she's got a fever."

"Mmmh," said O'Reilly, already formulating his possible diagnoses. "Anything else?"

"No, sir."

"No convulsions, vomiting, diarrhoea? No pains anywhere? No earache? No sore throat?"

"No, sir."

At this time of the year he was probably dealing with acute tonsillitis, which could be a recurrent disease. "Has she ever had anything like this before?"

Mrs. Dunleavy shook her head.

He went and hunkered down in front of the girl so his eyes were at the same level as hers. "Hello, Mary."

She pulled the teddy bear closer and looked at him from big blue eyes, which he noticed were dull.

"Cat got your tongue?" He smiled and said to the bear, "And how old is your mistress?"

"He can't talk, thilly," she said. "I'm four."

"Are you now?" said O'Reilly. "You are a big girl."

That produced a little smile.

"Can I put my hand on your neck, please?"

She glanced at her mother, who nodded. "Yeth."

O'Reilly quickly examined her neck. He noted a few enlarged lymph nodes and her skin was warm. It was always tricky taking wee ones' temperatures so he'd settle for that inexact observation. The findings so far were in keeping with his thoughts. A couple more observations would confirm them. "Could you open wide and stick out your tongue?"

"Yeth." She did.

O'Reilly produced a pencil torch and shone it into her mouth. Small children always gagged if you tried to use a tongue depressor and he was confident he'd be able to find what he was looking for without one. "Say 'aaah.' "

He saw at once that the very back of the oral cavity, the fauces, were red and inflamed and that both tonsils were scarlet and swollen. There was no evidence of membrane formation so he could stop worrying about diphtheria or a rare condition called Vincent's angina, also known as trench mouth. "Thank you, Mary," he said. "You can close your mouth."

She did.

He patted the teddy on the head and returned to his chair.

"You've got tonsillitis, Mary," he said, but directed his remarks to her mother. "We'll have you better in three or four days."

"What do we treat it with, Doctor?" Mrs. Dunleavy asked. "My granny in Coalisland in County Tyrone uses a stocking filled with hot salt wrapped round the neck."

"Some folks here in County Down use hot potatoes instead of salt," O'Reilly said, "but do you think you could teach Mary to gargle?"

"Aye, certainly."

"Good, because I want you to get some aspirin. You'll not need a scrip. Break a tablet in half and crush one half up in warm water and have her gargle and then swallow the gargle. Do that every eight hours. Keep her in bed until I've seen her again and give her lots to drink. That should see her right in no time. If you are worried send for me." It was a great comfort to know that if simple measures failed he could always fall back on sulphas. Although penicillin had been available to the armed forces, it was not yet in use in civilian practice. The few doses he'd had on *Warspite* late in the war, like all the doses that had been stockpiled before D-Day, had all been produced in America from fungus taken from a mouldy canteloupe from Peoria, Illinois. "I'll pop in and see her in a day or two." And again in three weeks because there was always the risk of rheumatic fever or kidney disease developing if the infecting organism was a haemolytic streptococcus, but he'd not mention that.

"Thank you very much, sir. Say thank you, Mary."

"Fank oo."

As Kinky had instructed, he made a quick note in the ledger so she could send out the bill. Mary rose. "And Willy says the next time you're in the Duck the first pint's on him, so it is."

"I'll look forward to that." He followed them from the surgery and showed them out through the front door. The snow of Saturday had vanished. Whistling a few bars of Vaughn Monroe's latest hit, "Let It Snow," he walked back to the waiting room. His smile widened when he saw a middle-aged man wearing a bowler hat sitting on one of the chairs. "I'm Doctor O'Reilly," he said, "will you come with me?"

By the time they'd reached the surgery, the man, who was now setting his bowler hat on the second patient's chair, had already told O'Reilly his name. "I was given Hubert, but everybody calls me 'Wowser,' so they do. Wowser Ward. I'm connected with the Ward family, a bunch of highhee-jins. Lived in Bangor Castle. They gave thirty-seven acres to Bangor for a park, Ward Park, and one of their daughters married Lord Clanmorris from the west of

Ireland in 1878, so she did. Me? I'm forty-eight, I'm the foreman for Bishop's Builders, and I was a patient of Doctor Flanagan. I never seen you before the war because I thought you was too young, you know." He sighed. "But now? I heard you'd given Mister Bishop lip last Friday, but beggars can't be choosers, so they can't."

How flattering, O'Reilly thought, and grinned. He'd take no offence. A patient was a patient. After a short rummage in the desk drawer, he found the man's old record card. "And you live on Station Road. Number 12."

"Bingo," he said, "and if you look at my card you'll see what ailed me then and what ails me again, but worser now, you know. That's why I've come. I want it fixed the day. Right now if you can, sir. The bloody thing aches and aches all day unless I'm lying down." He unbuckled his belt.

O'Reilly put on his half-moons and read, *Tuesday, 11/Aug/42. Cold right groin abscess unchanged. Advised bed rest. May need lancing.* He whipped off his spectacles, whistled, and felt the hackles of his neck rising. Back in 1939, Doctor Flanagan had been puzzled by a rare local condition he called a cold groin abscess. Two of the cases he'd lanced in his surgery he explained to O'Reilly had

484

either, "Wind or shite in them and both patients died. It was most puzzling."

Not to the then-young O'Reilly. His senior colleague had been incising ruptures — inguinal hernias. No wonder he'd released bowel contents. Often such bulgings of the peritoneum through a weakness in the lower abdominal wall did contain small bowel. And after Doctor Flanagan's ham-fisted efforts, two of his victims must have succumbed to peritonitis following contamination.

"So you think you've a groin abscess?" O'Reilly said.

"Think? I'm bloody well sure. Doctor Flanagan knew his stuff, so he did." Wowser Ward was unbuttoning his fly.

The old doctor had certainly been convinced of his own infallability and had managed to persuade his patients of the same. Such was often the case with that generation of physicians. O'Reilly's attempt in '39 to suggest to Doctor Flanagan that these were hernias and not abscesses had been met with scorn and anger. And back then, death after surgery was, if not accepted, at least understood by the laity.

Now, with no real local reputation, O'Reilly was going to have to try to contradict the late and omniscient Doctor Flanagan for the sake of the patient. "All right, Mister Ward. Stand up and lower your pants."

The man did.

Even from where he sat O'Reilly could see a bulging in the fold between the belly and thigh on the right. "Cough," he said.

"Cough? It's my groin, not my chest's the trouble."

"Please?"

The man did, and O'Reilly had no difficulty observing a visible impulse under the skin. A hernia, no doubt, and one that should be repaired surgically. A third-year student could have made the diagnosis without any further examination. Its exact nature would need to be delineated by a surgeon but it was beyond the powers of a GP to fix. O'Reilly coughed and said, "I think I must tell you, Mister Ward, I believe medicine has moved on since Doctor Flanagan's day."

"How?" There was acid in the one word.

This was going to take diplomacy and tact, but if the Ard Rí himself — the High King of all Ireland — appeared and thought he could order O'Reilly to incise an inguinal hernia here in the surgery, his Royal Highness would have another thought coming. "Mister Ward, I believe that what you have is called a hernia and —"

"Why? *Her*nia? Amn't I a man? If it should be called anything, it should be a hisnia, and it's not nothing like that anyroad. It's a groin abscess and I want it fixed, Doctor." He shook his head. "You call sitting there and getting a fellah to cough an examination? Jasus, a horse trader would look more carefully at a horse, so he would."

"Mister Ward, I really want to get a second opinion from a specialist at the Royal Victoria Hospital." Two of O'Reilly's friends from Trinity, Charlie Greer and Donald Cromie, were surgeons there.

"Aye. Well. You can want. I've no time til be buggering about in Belfast, and them specialists cost a brave wheen of money, so they do. Why will you not do it here for me?"

"I'm sorry," said O'Reilly, realising that he was going to be sending away a dissatisfied customer. Better that than a dead one; although, oddly enough, if he acceded to the patient's request and that gloomy outcome occurred he was more likely to be forgiven by the locals than if he turned the man down. Never mind. The patient's health came first. "I wish you could under—"

The man and the colour in his cheeks both rose. He pulled up his pants and began to close his fly.

O'Reilly flinched.

"I understand that you're useless til me, Doctor."

"Lancing your hernia might kill you," O'Reilly said.

"Away off and feel your head." He buckled his belt, grabbed his bowler, headed for and opened the door. "Hernia, my aunt Fanny Jane. If you won't fix it, I'll just thole it, so I will, but just you wait till I put out the word you never even examined me properly, never mind put me right." Country patients had great faith in the powers of the examination — and of the X-ray. "I'm paying you nothing, neither. You don't know your arse from your elbow." He buckled his belt and slammed the door behind him as he left.

O'Reilly fished out and lit his pipe. He needed a minute to think. He'd been consulted three times and had only sent one customer away satisfied, and although Kathy Dunleavy was a nice young woman she'd hardly be rushing round telling the world how wonderful the newly returned doctor was. What he'd done for her Mary was routine. What would Bishop and Ward be saying and to whom? That neither had paid was not his real concern. The damage they might be doing to his reputation — he blew out a cloud of smoke — hardly bore thinking about.

Setting his pipe in an ashtray he walked back to the waiting room. Empty. No patients. Patience, he told himself and smiled. The words had the same Latin root, *patiens,* which meant "waiting" or "suffering," and both described what he was doing right now. He could only hope that by waiting a bit longer his worry, which in fairness could hardly be called suffering, would be over and his surgeries full. He brightened, remembering Kathy Dunleavy's parting remark. Maybe before supper he'd pop into the Black Swan, or Mucky Duck as the locals called their pub.

4

AND EVERYTHING IN ITS PLACE

The tips of O'Reilly's ears tingled after his short walk from Number One, past the maypole, and across the Main Street to its junction with Station Road, the corner site of the Black Swan Pub. In the icy, darkening evening, the snow that had stopped falling on Saturday had returned. The flakes were large and damp and barely lay on the pavement.

He heard the sounds of laughter and chatter even before he pushed through the pub's doors. Once inside he felt as if he'd walked into a wall of warmth coming from a blazing turf fire and a web of tobacco smoke from pipes and cigarettes. As he brushed flakes from and then unbuttoned his coat he waited for his eyes to become accustomed to the dim lighting.

The single, narrow room had not changed

since his last visit almost seven years ago. There was still sawdust on the plank floor, still the low black ceiling beams, and a few tables and occupied chairs in front of a long bar counter. Bottles of spirits on shelves behind the bar kept company with two barrels of the product of Mister Arthur Guinness and Sons, Saint James's Gate, Dublin, lying on their sides. Each had a brass spigot for drawing off the stout hammered into its bung hole near the bottom of the lower rim. A spile to regulate the release of carbon dioxide had been driven into the middle of each barrel at the top of its upper circumference.

O'Reilly's ears were assailed by a loud hum of men's conversation. Women were not permitted in public bars in Ulster, and the Duck boasted neither a snug nor a lounge bar where women could go — if escorted. Dogs, however, were allowed in, and O'Reilly noticed a border collie under one table, a lurcher — a collie greyhound cross much favoured by poachers for its intelligence and speed in pursuit of game — under another. Its owner had bright carrotty hair. Maybe, O'Reilly thought, one day he'd get himself a Labrador — but not until the practice was busier.

The rising and falling tides of noise

stopped as if a sluice gate had been closed, and he was aware of every eye being fixed on him. "A very good evening to this house," he said, but he might as well have been talking to a room full of deaf men for all the response he got. He'd seen Western films where a stranger comes to the town saloon and is ignored. It was often the setup for a fight scene — in Westerns and in the slums of Dublin where ruggy-ups, bare-knuckle fights, were commonplace, but not in a quiet little place like Ballybucklebo.

There was space at this end of the bar so he moved there, smiled at a big man in an army greatcoat and duncher — probably recently demobbed like O'Reilly — and took his place leaning on the bar top and putting one foot up on a brass rail beneath. He looked more closely at his companion. "You're Declan Finnegan," O'Reilly said. "I set a broken arm for you in '39. You were going to join the Tank Regiment when I left here for the navy."

The general level of conversation had risen to its previous levels.

"That's right, Doctor O'Reilly." Declan smiled. "And my arm mended rightly. You done a great job. And I was a tanker. I fought in Sicily and I drove a Cromwell tank in Normandy, so I did, but I was demobbed in late '45 and come home, you know. I heard you were coming back. It's good to have you here, sir, so it is. I wonder," he hesitated, "I wonder if I could ask you a wee doctoring favour, sir?"

O'Reilly hesitated. He generally refused such requests on social occasions and had no intention of letting his pub become an annex to his surgery. After all, he was on his own time here, but for just this once said, "Fire away." He'd get an opportunity sooner or later to make his position on pub consultations clear.

"What'll it be, Doctor O'Reilly?" a voice said from behind the bar counter.

O'Reilly turned to see the barman. Willie Dunleavy had packed on the beef since his soccer-playing days. He'd be about thirty. He wore a flowery waistcoat and his shirt sleeves were held up by satin-covered elastic garters.

"I mind my da, God rest him, who used to own this place, saying you were fond of your pint when you worked here before the war." He held out his hand. "Welcome back, sir, and thanks for seeing our wee Mary."

O'Reilly shook hands. "Thank you. I was sorry to hear about your father."

Willie shrugged. "Aye," he said. "Thon cancer's not nice, but . . . och . . ." He took a deep breath. "And will it be a pint, sir?"

"Please."

"You're on," said Willie, went to the two barrels, and started to pour.

O'Reilly turned back to Declan Finnegan. "You were going to ask a favour, Declan?"

"I wonder, maybe someday soon, if I could bring the missus til see you? We think she's pregnant."

"Of course, of course. Send her round about nine tomorrow."

"Fair enough."

"Fine."

Declan hesitated. "I'll come too," he said. "Melanie doesn't speak much English yet. She's learning, but —"

"Melanie? She's French?"

Declan nodded. "Aye. I met her in 1944, near Mont Pinçon. She'd volunteered to help the army doctors. I'd been wounded, only a toty wee scratch, like. I was back on my feet in time to rejoin my squadron and fight at Falaise and go the whole way to the Rhine River, but I never forgot Melanie Devereux, so I didn't. Her and me got married last May, after the war in Europe was over."

"Good for you both. More power to your wheels. And the French won't be a problem. *Moi, je parle un tres petit peu.*"

"Merveilleux," Declan said. *"Moi aussi."*

"And that's enough of the oul parley-voo from you, Declan Finnegan, so it is," Willie said with a grin. "Here's your pint, Doctor O'Reilly, sir, and like Kathy said, it's on the house. A wee welcome home. I hope you'll take a brave wheen more in here over the years."

"I'm beginning to think I will," O'Reilly said, hoping this and his easy conversation with Declan were more small steps to his gradual reacceptance in the village and townland. He lifted his pint, said, *"Sláinte,"* and took a hefty pull. "Mother's milk," he said, grinned, and fished out his pipe.

The Murray's Erinmore Flake tobacco was going well when it was time for his second pint and the one he bought for Declan Finnegan.

"I mind you was quare nor keen on the rugby football, sir," Declan was saying. "You should have a wee word with my younger brother, Fergus. He plays for the Bally-bucklebo Bonnaughts' Junior Fifteen."

"So you've got the club going again?" Most athletic pursuits had been interrupted by the war.

"Och aye. The marquis of Ballybucklebo's their patron. He's played for Ireland, you know."

495

O'Reilly felt a draught as someone opened the door, half-turned, and saw Bertie Bishop followed by Wowser Ward, of all people.

O'Reilly ignored them and said to Declan, "I did know about his Lordship's caps." O'Reilly had three of his own for representing his country, but it would be boastful to say so. Joining the club would increase the circle of his acquaintances — and possible patients — and put him back in touch with a game he loved. "I will join, Declan. How'd I get ahold of your brother?"

"He's no phone in his house. He's a jockey. Rides for the marquis. I'll tell him to come and see you, sir."

"Thank you."

O'Reilly glanced over. A table that he'd noticed upon arriving had been occupied by three obviously working-class men in dunchers and with mufflers wrapped round their necks, one man smoking a clay pipe. They now vacated their places in favour of the great Panjandrum and his friend. O'Reilly had a quick mental image of Mister Bertie Bishop saying, "I'm a very important man round here, so I am."

" 'Scuse me." A tall, narrow-faced patron pushed past O'Reilly to get to the bar and call an order. "Pint and a packet of crisps, please, Willie."

"Right, Archie."

O'Reilly had to think. Archie. Archie. Got it. "Hello, Mister Auchinleck," he said. The man shared a surname with a famous British general of Ulster stock who'd taken over command of the British Army in the Middle East after *Warspite* had left for Bremerton.

"Doctor O'Reilly. It's yourself. I hardly noticed you there. It's a bit dim in here. I heard you was coming back, so I did. Mrs. Kincaid's been putting the word around. If me or the missus or our wee lad get sick we'll come and see you, so we will."

Good for you, Kinky, O'Reilly thought. "The surgery's open every morning at nine o'clock," he said. He felt a tugging at his sleeve, turned, and saw Bishop. "Yes, Mister Bishop."

"I've not time for til come til your surgery. Bend you your head so I can whisper."

O'Reilly stooped to the shorter man, who said what he had to say.

No. Bloody well no. Declan's polite request had been one thing, this demand another entirely. This was a perfect opportunity to establish that unless someone was bleeding to death or having a heart attack, Doctor O'Reilly was off duty inside the Duck. "Certainly, Mister Bishop," he bellowed in his quarterdeck voice, which could be heard above a howling Atlantic gale. He paused. The falling of a pin would have been as noisy as the eruption of Krakatoa, so silent had the Duck become. "Just slip off your trousers and climb up on the counter so I can examine you." The falling of a single downy feather would probably have registered on the Richter scale. Silence hung until a clearly furious, puce-faced Bishop yelled, "My trousers? Here? Have you taken a fit of the headstaggers? Do you not know it's a feckin' pub!"

"Well, Mister Bishop . . ." O'Reilly had deliberately lowered his voice so that his audience would have to strain to hear. "I thought *you* didn't know. After all, you insisted on consulting me in here for something that can wait until the surgery opens tomorrow. I didn't think you'd mind being examined in here. But if it upsets you, I'll be happy to see you tomorrow. *Tomorrow.*"

Bishop spluttered. "By God, O'Reilly, you've a quare brass neck, so you have. Telling a fellah til take off his pants in public."

"I think," said O'Reilly, "the cervical alloy of copper and zinc is all yours." He turned back to Archie and Declan as a wave of laughter swept through the room. I've not made a bosom buddy, O'Reilly thought, but there is a limit. And for the moment, and

God bless Surgeon Commander Wilcoxson for his sage advice, the upper hand was back where it belonged. Nor would he be pestered in here in the future by other patients.

He glanced over to where Bishop and Ward had their heads together. Ward looked over at O'Reilly. The man's eyes were narrowed, his teeth clenched. He shook his fist and mouthed, "You wait, O'Reilly. Just you wait."

O'Reilly turned away. He had clearly offended two locals, but surely the laughter at Bishop's discomfiture signified that there was support for the newly returned doctor too?

"It's my shout, Doctor," Declan Finnegan said. "And well done putting Mister Bishop in his box. I'm sorry I asked you a medical question. I never thought —"

"You didn't ask me a question. You asked if you could bring your wife to see me. That's entirely different."

"Thank you, sir. Now, would you like that pint, and maybe one for you, Archie?"

O'Reilly shook his head and buttoned his coat. If Archie said yes, then the "my shout" circle would begin where everyone in the party had to buy a round. He smiled. "Maybe next time, Declan. It's time I was home."

Declan nodded. "I understand, sir." He lowered his voice. "See that there Bertie Bishop? His head's full of hobbyhorse shite, so it is." He spat into the sawdust. "Pay him no heed and never you worry, sir, me and Melanie'll be in first thing tomorrow."

O'Reilly smiled and said, "I'll expect you." And to hell with Bertie Bishop and Wowser Ward. O'Reilly hoped that the Finnegans would be the start of a steadily growing trade. "Good night to this house," he called, and was gratified by a few, although not everybody's by any means, "Good night, Doctor."

5

HAVE YOU NO BOWEL,
NO TENDERNESS?

O'Reilly pushed away his plate, empty save for a squeezed lemon slice. Not long before a pair of famous Craster kippers had lain, blissfully brown and seductively, steamingly scented. Utterly delicious. While drinking his second cup of tea, he finished reading a story in Tuesday's *The Northern Whig*. It seemed that fifteen alleged Soviet spies had been arrested in Canada. He wondered what they'd be spying on in that far cold country, tutted, put down the paper, rose, and crossed to the surgery.

He opened his doctor's bag, went to a cupboard, took out an ampoule of aminophylline, and put it into the bag to replace the one he'd used yesterday for a seven-year-old boy who was having a severe asthmatic attack. That home visit and a case of influenza had been the sum of the day's caseload. What had Lars said? "Don't be surprised if it's slow at the beginning." Slow? Glaciers moved more quickly. Still, O'Reilly thought, Declan Finnegan and his French wife were coming today. He headed for the surgery.

Declan and a petite but obviously swollen-bellied woman with glossy brown hair sat side by side. And across the room, perched like a gargoyle on a cathedral on one of the hard-backed chairs, was Albert Bishop. Before O'Reilly could even say good morning and invite them to come to his surgery, the man announced, "The Finnegans don't mind if I go first, O'Reilly." As Bishop strode past the couple, Declan raised his eyes to heaven and shook his head.

O'Reilly was sure Bishop had bullied his way past the Finnegans, but did not want to make a fuss about it — yet. He followed him along to the surgery, where Bishop had already seated himself. O'Reilly closed the door. "Good morning, Mister Bishop. I wasn't expecting to see you today." To tell the truth I was not expecting to see you ever after last night, O'Reilly thought, as he took the swivel chair. This was something he'd learned from Doctor Corrigan, his senior in general practice in Dublin. That not every patient and their doctor would get along. Sometimes it was better to come to the parting of the ways and have them seek medical advice elsewhere. He recognised that may have been at the back of his mind when he'd deliberately embarrassed Bishop last night.

"Aye, nor me you, but I've still not gone since I tried to have a wee quiet word with you. I've been seeing a Doctor Robbins in Bangor, but it's far too far to drive just because I'm bound. My missus, Flo, says she til me, she says, 'Go on, give O'Reilly a try.' I says til her that I tried to tell you on Monday night that I needed a strong laxative, but, no, you were too high and mighty to do me a favour, so you were. Sometimes my Flo does talk sense, but. Says she til me, 'O'Reilly worked here before. He never killed nobody then.' "

Now there was a backhanded compliment.

" 'And it'll take you an hour til drive til Bangor, see Robbins, and drive back. Go on, try O'Reilly.' So here I am. And it's your last chance with me, so it is. I've already heard you wouldn't treat Wowser Ward, so you'd better see me right or else."

O'Reilly frowned. "Or else what, Mister Bishop?" O'Reilly had been trained to understand that patients were not always as polite as they might be and to be prepared to make allowances, but this pompous little man didn't seem to recognise how close he was to being thrown out — physically. "Or else what?"

"Wowser and me'll put out the word you're no bloody good." He leant back, smiled, and folded his arms across his chest.

To give himself a moment to consider his reply O'Reilly fished out a pair of half-moon spectacles and perched them on his nose. Decision time. Could he afford to tell Bishop to go to hell, behave like that Anglo-Dubliner the Duke of Wellington and his famous, "Publish and be damned"? That would alienate this man when the practice was in an embryonic state. And how much harm could he and Wowser Ward do? Probably quite a lot. On the other hand, if O'Reilly simply ignored Bishop's rudeness and threats, he had no doubt that the man would proudly spread the word around that O'Reilly was so weak he couldn't beat the skin off a rice pudding, and he couldn't afford that either. Half a doctor's ability to treat lay in the esteem in which he was held by his patients. O'Reilly recognised that he was on the horns of what one of his naval patients had called a dilly-ma-ma.

But — but — he had to struggle to conceal

a grin. There was a way to appear to acqui-
esce but give Bishop a not-so-subtle message that Fingal Flahertie O'Reilly, Doctor
Fingal Flahertie O'Reilly, once called by an
old Dublin friend The Wily O'Reilly, was
not a man to be threatened — ever. "I see,"
he said levelly. "Then I'll have to make sure
you are treated properly, won't I?"

"That's more like it," Bishop said.

O'Reilly steepled his fingers. He'd learnt
long ago that the makers of patent laxatives
had taught the great public that their bowels
must move once a day. It wasn't true, but
such was the power of advertising. "When
was the last time you went?"

"Saturday morning, and that's three whole
days."

"I see, and has this kind of thing happened
before?"

"Aye, and Robbins gives me castor oil."
He screwed up his face. "Tastes like shite. I
thought you being younger —"

"I'm sure I do have something better for
you, but I need to make sure there's no
underlying disease. Have you any belly
pains?"

"Nah."

"No vomiting?"

"No, I've not boked. I'm rightly otherwise,
so I am. It's just I'm bound."

No pain, no vomiting, so no suggestion of anything obstructing the bowel. "Anything else bothering you?" Constipation if a symptom of something serious was invariably accompanied by other symptoms of distress, and Bishop looked the picture of overweight health.

"Are you deaf? I just told you. Not at all."

"I see," said O'Reilly, gritting his teeth and remembering Ward's anger at not having been examined . . . "I'd still better take a look."

It was a simple matter to examine Bishop's tubby belly, which O'Reilly did, finding nothing amiss. "All right," he said. "Get dressed." He went to his desk and found a prescription pad. His old teacher Doctor Micks had preached, *It may be dangerous to give a purgative but never to withold one.* Not in this case. Bishop appeared to have nothing physically wrong with him. There was nothing to worry about, O'Reilly was quite sure. He removed a fountain pen from an inside pocket, scribbled, and handed the prescription to Bishop. "Take that to the chemist. It'll do the trick."

Bishop took the scrip, scowled, and said, "Thank you. It had better work."

"It will," said O'Reilly. "I promise. Now," said O'Reilly, rising. "I'm sure you're a very busy man and in a rush." Not half the hurry you're going to be in after you've taken your medicine, he thought, hiding a grin.

"Aye. I am."

He took Bishop by the elbow, helped him stand, and began propelling him to the door.

"Take a teaspoonful of that as soon as you get home — and don't go out."

"Right."

"Good," said O'Reilly, letting Bishop out of the surgery. Only when the door was shut did he allow himself to chuckle. His prescription of *Tinct. Crotonis Oleum,* tincture of croton oil, was for the strongest purgative available. During the war, the U.S. Navy had added it to the alcohol fuel used in their torpedoes. The violent laxative effects were meant to discourage sailors from draining and drinking the fuel. It was also believed that a number of U-boat patrols from French ports had been abandoned because the French fishermen who supplied the German fleet had packed sardines in croton rather than olive oil. The effects on a U-boat's crew in a vessel with only two heads hardly bore imagining.

The self-important Mister Bishop was not going to enjoy himself today. He'd be spending a fair bit of it all alone in a small room. But he'd be hard-pressed to complain. He'd explicitly asked for a "strong" laxative and had demanded effective treatment. And he probably would have sufficient insight to recognise that messing about with Doctor O'Reilly was a less than smart thing to do.

He opened the ledger, noted, *B. Bishop. Consultation,* then headed for the waiting room where another patient, a young woman, had joined the Finnegans.

"Your turn, Mister and Mrs. Finnegan." He smiled at the newcomer. "I'll not be long."

Once in the surgery and with Declan sitting on one chair, his wife on the other, Declan said, "Good morning, Doctor O'Reilly. This here's Melanie, so it is."

O'Reilly made a little bow. *"Enchanté, Madame Finnegan."*

She smiled, but her torrent of heavily Norman-accented French overwhelmed O'Reilly. *"Je m'excuse,"* he said, *"mais moi, je parle Français comme une vache Espagnole. If faut que vous parleriez tres lentement, madame, s'il vous plaît."*

She laughed and said, *"D'accord, monsieur. Je comprend."*

"No harm til you, Doctor, but you done very good. And you do not speak French 'like a Spanish cow,' " said Declan, chuckling at the way native French speakers referred to those who hadn't mastered the language. "Not one bit. What you just done was set her at her ease that she can talk to you even if she does have to speak more slowly — and I'll help too." He turned to his wife, rapidly translated, and was rewarded with a beaming smile that lit up her ebony eyes.

"I'm sorry you got bumped," O'Reilly said.

"See that there Bishop?" Declan said. "He thinks he's no goat's toe, but he puts his trousers on one leg at a time just like ordinary people." He lowered his voice. "If you ask me, he's full of shite."

Not for much longer, O'Reilly thought, but said, "I am sorry you had to wait, and please explain that to Melanie and help me to ask her some questions."

With some of his own French and with Declan translating where needed, O'Reilly soon finished his history-taking and, after Melanie had climbed upon the couch, her physical examination. He'd noted that he was going to be looking after a twenty-three-year-old with no history of serious illness, who was today at about the twenty-sixth week of her first pregnancy and thus was due to deliver in late May. When he'd worked at the Rotunda in Dublin in the late 1930s, the master had begun to institute routine antenatal care aimed at trying to prevent stillbirth and foetal abnormality and screen women for high blood pressure. O'Reilly intended — when more started showing up — to follow that protocol with his patients. At least since 1936, with the advent of Red Prontosil, the first antibiotic, and since the war much better blood transfusion services, the risks of the two great killers of pregnant women, infection and haemorrhage, were being brought under better control.

In his very best French, O'Reilly, with Declan helping, explained that everything seemed to be fine, that he'd like to see her in a month, and to get hold of him if she was worried about anything.

"Merci, monsieur le medeçin. Je suis très content." And those deep eyes smiled at him again.

O'Reilly cleared his throat, then said, "There is one thing." Full obstetrical care was expensive and O'Reilly felt he had an obligation to warn Declan.

"Aye?"

"I'm afraid I'll have to charge you eight guineas," he rushed on, "but that includes

510

antenatal visits, delivery, and postpartum care." O'Reilly looked at his desktop. "I'm sorry."

"What the hell for?" Declan said. "For God's sakes, Doctor dear, the workman's worth his hire. I don't work for free. How much on account?"

"Four guineas, but we'll be sending out the bills at the end of the month."

"Fair enough."

"Thank you," O'Reilly said, and made an entry in the ledger. Not only did it allow him to keep his accounts straight, it would enable him when the time came to apportion to HM Inspector of Taxes his statutory thirty percent. And with the imminent introduction of Pay as You Earn, PAYE, this would, in O'Reilly's case, have to be paid monthly.

"We'll be running along, sir," Declan said, then, "*Viens,* Melanie, and she'll see you in a month, sir. And your Mrs. Kincaid told the ladies at the Woman's Union last night that you took special training in midwifery in Dublin too." He winked. "Never mind that ould git Bishop. I'll give you five til one Melanie isn't the only pregnant woman you'll be seeing soon, sir. You'll be sucking diesel before you know it, so you will."

O'Reilly accompanied the couple to the

front door and let them out, turned, and went back toward the the waiting room. "Sucking diesel?" That was a new one, but by the inflexion in Declan's voice O'Reilly reckoned it was akin to being on the pig's back or in clover. It was comforting for Declan to say so.

He headed back to the waiting room where another patient awaited. Perhaps things were looking up.

6

THERE ARE MORE THINGS IN HEAVEN AND EARTH, HORATIO

O'Reilly finished his roast pheasant and pushed his plate away. Somehow, despite Kinky's magic way with game birds, he had not relished his dinner. On Tuesday he'd hoped that things were looking up, but they were not. To be sure Tuesday had yielded two more patients after the Finnegans, but from Wednesday until today, Friday, he'd seen only another three, four if he counted a home visit yesterday to Mary Dunleavy. She and her family lived over the Duck, and after he'd reassured himself and her mother that Mary was well mended, he'd not been hard to persuade to have another pint with mine host. Willie had been more reserved than usual and had obviously had to steel himself before he'd been able to ask in a low voice, "Seeing lots of patients, Doc?"

O'Reilly had shaken his head. Willie's next words were indelibly imprinted.

"Aye, well no harm til you, sir, but thon Mister Ward was in here a couple of nights ago. He was telling everybody that you'd refused til treat him right, and that you'd near killed Mister Bishop. I telt him to shut his yap or I'd bar him."

O'Reilly had thanked Willie. And finished his pint.

It looked as if the damage had been done, and although O'Reilly's main reason for wanting the practice to expand was because he really enjoyed his work, there was no escaping the fact that the bank would be expecting his first loan repayment soon.

There was talk that the government was going to introduce a National Health Service by which all citizens would be insured and GPs would be paid monthly by a government agency so there would be no need for money to come between doctors and their patients. It couldn't be implemented fast enough for O'Reilly. He disliked the need to send bills, particularly to poorer patients, and was sure many of them avoided visiting a doctor because they simply could not afford to. Some found other ways round the difficulty.

He managed a smile. And once the practice did grow — if it did grow — he'd not object to gifts in lieu of cash. The chicken in return for a linament for a sore back, the brace of mallard instead of the surgery visit fee for a patient with acute conjunctivitis, and the lobster for strapping a sprained wrist he'd been given when he'd worked here before had been most acceptable.

On Wednesday, the father of a young, carotty-haired buck-toothed lad, Donal Donnelly, had offered O'Reilly a brace of pheasants to pay for his treatment of the boy's middle ear infection. The birds had almost certainly been "borrowed" from the marquis's estate, but taking a leaf from another sailor's book, O'Reilly had turned a blind eye. Slices of one of them with roast potatoes, seasonal brussels sprouts, and carrots had been his dinner that night.

The barter system appealed to O'Reilly and wasn't taxable, and as far as he was concerned what the eye didn't see the heart didn't grieve over. But until his debt was fully discharged, he did need hard currency too, and that would only come when he had full surgeries.

Kinky had used her best endeavours to bolster his reputation. The kind words of Declan Finnegan had been comforting, but his French-speaking wife was hardly in a position to shout O'Reilly's praises from the rooftops, at least in words comprehensible to the average villager. And he couldn't advertise. The General Medical Council, the disciplinary body of his profession, regarded that as unethical and could take away his licence if he tried to.

Bertie Bishop and Wowser Ward must have succeeded in blackening O'Reilly's name, of that he had no doubt, none whatsoever. Did he regret having given Bishop a laxative that if compared to usually prescribed ones was the atomic bomb of purgatives? Not one bloody bit. It might have been foolhardy, but O'Reilly had consciously decided to accept the risk. Bullies were bullies and had to be checked.

He rose, went to the sideboard, and poured himself a John Jameson. Sipping the Irish whiskey, he headed for the door, intending to go upstairs to the lounge and finish reading *The Captain from Castille*, one of last year's bestsellers.

The door opened and Kinky came in carrying a tray of polished silver. "Doctor O'Reilly," she said, "you do have a face on you like a Lurgan spade, as I've heard the locals say — although it would mean nothing in County Cork, so."

He shrugged and exhaled.

"Would you take it ill, sir, if your house-keeper was to ask you if everything is all right?"

He hesitated. O'Reilly was not one to cry on other people's shoulders, but tonight . . . "I'd not take it that way at all, Kinky," he said, and in truth he'd welcome a friendly person to tell his troubles to. His closest friends, Doctors Charlie Greer and Donald Cromie, both surgeons, were up in Belfast. His best naval friend from *Warspite* days, Tom Laverty, was a career naval officer and was God knew where, still on active service. "Will you sit down?"

She frowned. It wasn't commonplace for servants to sit down with their employers.

"Kinky," he said, "if I'm going to talk to you like a friend I'm going to treat you like one."

She blushed and said, "That does be greatly appreciated, so." She sat and put the tray on the table.

"Another thing," he said as he sat, "I got used to calling you Kinky when I was first here because that's what Doctor Flanagan called you. Would you prefer to be Maureen, or Mrs. Kincaid?"

"Lord bless you, sir, Kinky's just grand. My late husband, Paudeen Kincaid, God rest him, gave it to me as a nickname

517

because of how I used irons back then to curl my hair. It has a nice familiar sound, so. Kinky it is — but I appreciate your asking. It does be the act of a real gentleman. Now," she smoothed her apron, "can I offer a guess why you are upset?"

"Go right ahead."

"I knew from when you were here before the war that it wasn't the money you worked for. You were simply happy at your work."

"I've wanted to be a doctor since I was thirteen." O'Reilly shrugged. "Doctor Flanagan paid me well enough, I had my room here, and . . ." He grinned at her. "I had the best cook in all of Ireland feeding me."

"Go 'way out of that, sir," but her grin was one of enormous pleasure, "and be serious now. You are worried because not enough people are coming to see you, isn't that so?"

He pursed his lips and nodded. "True."

"And there are one or two who I'll not name who are blackguarding you round the village."

"How do you know?"

"Huh," she said, "there's precious little goes on here I don't know. Haven't I been here nearly twenty years and isn't everyone under that age one of Doctor Flanagan's

518

babies except for the ones delivered by yourself when first you were here?"

"Of course."

"And don't I know their mammies and daddies and grannies and grandpas?"

O'Reilly realised what an important source of information Kinky would be. "I don't suppose there is much goes on without you knowing."

"There is not. Now, would it help if I told you not to worry?"

He shook his head. "It would be a kindness, but how would you know? Have you heard something?"

"More seen." She leant forward and said very quietly, "Now, sir, it does be said in the village that I am a wise woman."

"And are you?" O'Reilly felt the hairs on his forearms bristle.

"From time to time I do find myself in a thin place."

"A what?"

"The old Celts believed that for some people in some places or times the gap between this earth and the other world becomes very thin and things can pass between. That is called a thin place. It can give some people, like my ma, it can give them the gift."

"Are you telling me you're fey, Kinky?"

She stared at a spot near infinity off to the left of the cut-glass chandelier, and her face became expressionless, her voice far away. "I was there last night, so."

The hackles rose on the back of his neck.

"I saw you in church. I saw people amazed. I felt —" She closed and reopened her eyes. "I knew all was well."

O'Reilly shivered as if a goose had walked on his grave. What was she trying to tell him?

"So, sir," she said in her usual voice, "it would give me great pleasure if you'd come to morning service with me on Sunday. It would not hurt for the villagers to see that you are a Christian gentleman."

With the cross of Jesus going on before.

O'Reilly bellowed out the last line of "Onward Christian Soldiers," a cheerful hymn with which the congregation had filled the barrel-vaulted nave of First Bally-bucklebo Presbyterian Church. Sunlight streamed through stained-glass windows. He inhaled the mustiness of two hundred years and the overpowering perfume of Old Spice aftershave coming from a man in the pew behind. Cissie Sloan, whom O'Reilly had seen for acne in 1938, finished with triumphal chords on the harmonium. She and her cousin Aggie Arbuthnot were two of Kinky's friends.

The service was progressing and so far none of the amazement Kinky had predicted had occurred.

As O'Reilly sat, his foot nudged the doctor's bag he had set on the floor when he had taken this pew. It had been a habit of both Doctor Corrigan and Doctor Flanagan to go nowhere without their bag. One never knew when an emergency might occur. He patted the left pocket of his jacket to make sure his stethoscope was there too.

He paid attention to the service. Today Mister Wilson, the septuagenarian minister, was being assisted by a young cleric, a Mister Robinson who, Kinky had told O'Reilly, had recently received the call to be taking over the parish when the older man retired in August. This morning Mister Robinson was to preach the sermon.

He ascended into a carved pulpit and began, "The text for today is from the Gospel According to Saint Mark, 12:31. 'Thou shalt love thy neighbour as thyself.' " He smiled down at Kinky. O'Reilly, who was sitting next to her, wondered if she'd persuaded Mister Robinson to use that text.

He half-listened and gazed ahead. When they'd arrived this morning, he had simply followed Kinky to her usual place three rows from the front, a place where, Kinky had solemnly assured him on their way to church, that when in good fettle preaching fire and brimstone, Mister Robinson's spits could be felt.

Bertie Bishop must not mind the salivary showers. His place was in the very front pew immediately facing the pulpit. He was accompanied by a dumpy woman wearing a pink cloche hat, presumably Mrs. Bishop. There didn't seem to be any little Bishops.

O'Reilly unobtrusively half-turned and stole another look over the congregation. Here and there were people he recognised, either from his previous time in the village or because he'd noticed them in the Duck, or, and he reckoned he could count them on one hand, because they'd recently been patients. There was Alfie Corry in a pew halfway down the nave adjacent to the aisle. The strapping unmarried farmer of, O'Reilly had to calculate — the man had been sixty-four in 1939 when he'd first consulted O'Reilly, so Mister Corry'd be seventy-one now. When O'Reilly and Kinky had arrived this morning to walk to their pew, Alfie'd greeted O'Reilly with a hushed "Nice til see you back, Doc."

At least somebody thought so.

And there was no mistaking Mister and young Donal Donnelly's carrotty hair. Archie Auchinleck sat farther down the nave beside an auburn-haired woman and a little boy of about Donal Donnelly's age.

O'Reilly'd not been surprised that the Finnegans weren't here. Finnegan was a Catholic name and the odds of finding a Protestant bride in rural Normandy would be pretty long indeed.

O'Reilly decided he'd better pay attention to the sermon.

"And where else better to love our neighbours than a little place like our own dear Ballybucklebo?"

Where else indeed, thought O'Reilly. Yet it is such a little place. Perhaps I should have found a practice in Belfast?

"Sweet Jesus, what's happened?" A woman's startled voice behind O'Reilly had stopped the sermon.

Another voice, "It's Alfie Corry. He's taken a wee turn. I'll run til get the doctor."

That was enough for O'Reilly. He leapt to his feet. "Excuse me, excuse me," he said, and forced his way along the pew and down the aisle. Fainted? The man had had a series of anginal attacks when he'd been here in 1939. O'Reilly shook his head.

As he pushed forward a man's voice said,

"The doctor's already here, you eejit. Bide where you're at."

The crowd parted to let O'Reilly get at Alfie Corry, who must have pitched sideways out of the pew to land on his back in the aisle. His face was dusky, his eyes open, but glazed, with their pupils dilated, and he was not breathing. Almost certainly the man had just had a fatal coronary thrombosis.

"Excuse me," O'Reilly said to a heavyset woman who wore a hat with pheasant tail feathers and who was taking the victim's pulse.

"I'm a first-aider," she said. "He's no pulse, you know. Could you try Holger-Neilsen artificial respiration, sir?"

"I'm sorry," O'Reilly said, "that's only for people who are nearly drowned. Now if you'd just — ?"

She needed no further bidding to move aside.

He unbuttoned the man's shirt and saw a farmer's chest, chalky white save for a tanned vee at the throat and upper chest. It was not moving. If he was right and the man had had a heart attack, there were no means of resuscitating such a patient nor any wonder drug to inject. Despite the accelerated progress of medicine brought about by the war, doctors were still helpless when it came to lethal heart attacks, and O'Reilly stifled a curse of frustration.

News of what had happened seemed to be spreading throughout the congregation by a series of loud whispers punctuated by, "Och, dears," and a, "Dear love, Alfie. Sound man. Sound man, so he is."

O'Reilly fished out his stethoscope, put the earpieces in, and clapped the bell over the left chest.

"Everybody wheest now," the first-aid lady said. "The doctor's trying til listen in, so he is."

Meanwhile, O'Reilly had felt in the angle of the jaw for the pulse of the carotid artery. There were no audible heart sounds and no pulse. O'Reilly fished out his pencil torch and shone it into each of the victim's eyes. Neither pupil contracted nor, he bent his head to Alfie's mouth, was there any evidence of breathing. Poor Alfie Corry, looking like a stunned mullet, was dead. Dead as mutton. And there was no treatment. None at all.

O'Reilly blew out a long breath against pursed lips. It wasn't as if he was a stranger to death — by disease, natural causes, and accident in peacetime, of the young, but mostly of the old. And death by fire, scalding, drowning, hypothermia, bullets, and explosives in wartime. Senseless, bloody senseless, and the victims so pathetically young. And while O'Reilly had tried to steel himself, had become inured by familiarity, there was always regret when a fellow human died in his hands, a sense of failure.

He started to rise and heard a familiar voice saying, "I think poor oul Alfie's gone, so I do." Bertie Bishop, not to O'Reilly's surprise, had forced his way to the front of the rubbernecking crowd. His wife stood just behind him. Bertie was a man who had to be at the centre of everything. He'd not have been satisfied at a wake if he wasn't the corpse. "But then, you'd not expect O'Reilly to have saved him, would youse?"

No one else in the congregation spoke. O'Reilly stiffened, and for a moment wondered, was the lack of response in his favour or against him? He took a deep breath, and like the navy he'd served in when attacked, prepared to defend himself with every weapon he possessed. But then an idea pushed into his mind. "Kinky, bring my bag," he roared. "Your man's gone." And nothing, nothing O'Reilly could do could bring him back. And yet . . . He heard shuffling of feet as a passage was cleared for her.

"Here, sir." Kinky gave him the leather bag.

"Requiescat in pace," O'Reilly muttered, "and please forgive me for what I'm going to do." He hoped his conscience would forgive him too, but the late Alfie might just perform a vital service for the living Fingal O'Reilly. He ripped open the bag, found a hypodermic syringe, filled it from a bottle of whatever was nearest to hand — the label said "sterile water" — plunged the needle into Alfie's left breast over the heart, and injected one third of the contents of the syringe.

The stethoscope was still in O'Reilly's ears so he put the bell over Alfie's chest. O'Reilly put an entirely forced look of awe on his face. "Praise be. He's got a heartbeat." No one could gainsay that.

O'Reilly looked up at a sea of faces, many with hands over their mouths, all of the people with wide, staring eyes. He smiled, put the stethoscope back on the chest. "Och, no," he said, letting his feigned anguish show. "No. He's going again." Another third of the syringe was injected like the first and the bell reapplied. O'Reilly took a long count before he whispered, loudly enough for the nearest of his audience to hear, "It's beating again."

Even with the earpieces in place he heard a voice yell, "Somebody send for an ambulance." That was no bad thing. Unless Alfie had recently been under a doctor's care it was a statutory requirement that a postmortem examination had to be performed to establish the cause of death, so the departed would have to go to the hospital mortuary anyway.

O'Reilly listened again, and knowing the effect his next utterance would have in here loudly said, "Damnation," and injected the remaining sterile water. There was no need for any further explanation and by the loud "tch, tching" and "tut-tutting," he could hear, even though his word was disapproved of, the message had got through.

He waited and this time made a display of taking the wrist pulse and letting a tired smile play on his face. Once more, judging by the communal indrawing of breath, the message of another success had been clearly received.

O'Reilly waited for what he considered to be a reasonable time, never letting go of Alfie's wrist before frowning mightily, clapping the stethoscope back on the corpse's chest, deepening his frown, and shining his torch into the nonresponding eyes. O'Reilly shook his head ponderously, stood slowly still shaking his head, before taking a very deep breath and saying, "I'm sorry. I did my best. I couldn't save him."

Now what?

"Och, dear," and "God rest him," and "At least he went easy" rose above the murmuring.

"May I speak, your reverence?"

O'Reilly recognised Kinky's voice.

"Certainly, Mrs. Kincaid." Mister Robinson was now standing behind Bertie Bishop.

She climbed up on a pew and was facing the crowd. "You said some powerful things, Reverend Robinson, about loving your neighbour. I think there's nobody here —" She glanced at Bertie Bishop. "— who would disagree."

There was a murmuring of agreement.

"But I know some malicious things have been said about Doctor O'Reilly here. You heard one now about not expecting Doctor O'Reilly to have done any good, so." She fixed Bertie Bishop with a stare O'Reilly thought would have done justice to Balor the one-eyed Fomorian, whose gaze could turn men to stone.

O'Reilly saw Bishop's wife give him a ferocious dig in the ribs.

Kinky continued, "And you all know the saying about giving a dog a bad name. Now I mean no irreverence, your reverences, but we all know the story of how our Lord raised Lazarus from the dead."

There was a loud muttering of agreement.

"And didn't Doctor O'Reilly, who could have gone anywhere in the world such a good doctor is he, so."

O'Reilly did something he didn't do often. He blushed.

"Didn't he choose to come back to us here?"

More muttering.

"And while Lazarus was brought back once, didn't Doctor O'Reilly bring back poor old Alfie Corry three times?"

O'Reilly heard a number of "Ayes," and "Right enoughs."

"Not once, not once, but three times — *three* times? I think we do be very lucky and I think it's about time when any of you need a doctor that you remember what you saw here this morning." Kinky smiled at O'Reilly. "I'll say no more, so," she said, and clambered down.

"Thank you, Kinky," he mouthed and was going to say it aloud when a woman's harsh voice rang out, "See you, Bertie Bishop? See you, you great glipe?"

O'Reilly recognised Mrs. Bishop by her hat.

"See you and your 'That doctor what's come back is only a quack?' You were trying for til drive him away, so you were. You and that Wowser Ward. Pair of bollixes, so youse are."

Bertie Bishop glared at his wife. "Hould your wheest, woman." The man was blushing.

O'Reilly saw a number of the congregation look at Bishop and shake their heads before turning to smile at O'Reilly.

Bishop, dragging his wife by the hand, headed for the narthex and the way out.

O'Reilly took off his jacket and respectfully covered the dear departed's face. "Perhaps," he said, "some of you men could give me a hand to carry Mister Corry to the vestry to wait for the ambulance. Will that be all right, Reverend Robinson?"

"Please. I'll come too. Say a few words. Reverend Wilson, will you please get everyone else back in their pews. Perhaps a hymn? 'Amazing Grace'?"

There was no lack of volunteers to carry Alfie. His corpse was laid on a bench and covered with a minister's robe that was hanging in the vestry so O'Reilly could recover his jacket.

Everyone there bowed their heads as the minister prayed for the soul of the departed.

All joined in the "Amen."

From the church proper came

Twas grace that caused my heart to fear.
And grace my fears relieved . . .

And after a moment's silence in the vestry Mister Robinson said, "Thank you for acting so quickly, Doctor."

O'Reilly, knowing full well it had all been a charade for his own benefit, hung his head and muttered, "It's my job."

"Nevertheless . . ." The minister let the sentence hang and then said with a smile, "And I think under the circumstances," he glanced up, "He will forgive your little indiscretion, and bless your continuing work here among us."

"I'm sorry," O'Reilly said, could have kissed the minister, and inside was grateful he'd only said "damnation." He'd had a full naval repertoire to choose from.

"We'd best be getting back," Mister Robinson said.

"Aye, but," one of the men said, "that was quare nor quick thinking, Doc. Me and the rest of the lads here," he glanced round at the other three ruddy-cheeked men, all probably farmers, "hope you'll stay on like. Isn't that right?"

"Aye," said one, and held out a callused hand, which O'Reilly shook. "Thank you," he said, and in his heart also said, "I'm sorry, Alfie Corry, but thank you. And bless you, Maureen Kinky Kincaid. Bless you. Bless you." Things looked like they were going to be all right after all, and he remembered Lars's recent quotation, "Home is the sailor, home from the sea." For Fingal Flahertie O'Reilly, recently Surgeon Commander, R.N.R., D.S.C., and now simply Doctor O'Reilly, this town and these people who would become his patients were his home — and always would be.

AFTERWORD:

BY MRS. MAUREEN KINCAID,
LATELY HOUSEKEEPER TO
DOCTOR THOMÁS FLANAGAN
NOW IN THAT CAPACITY TO
DOCTOR F. F. O'REILLY

We're back from all that excitement at the church now. I thought Mister Wilson did a fine job of getting everyone calmed down after poor Alfie Corry passed. The Reverend Robinson even finished the service. I was pleased to see how many of the congreation said kindly things to Doctor O'Reilly after. I think he need not worry anymore about his future here, so I told him as much.

Says he, "Kinky, I think you are right about the future, I thank you, and I'm in your debt." Then he surprised me when he went on, "And I want to be further in. I don't want a part of the past to suffer either. I meant it when I said you were the best cook in Ireland . . ." the ould soft-soaper, "but I'd hate to think of your recipes getting lost to posterity."

"So what would you like me to do?"

"Could you please start writing them down?"

"I will," says I, and here I am, pen in fist, getting the recipe for the first dinner I made for him when he came back after serving on that big ship where he had only men cooking for him, the poor soul. I hope you'll enjoy my roast rack of lamb too, so.

ROAST RACK OF LAMB WITH HERB STUFFING AND CAPER SAUCE

2 racks of trimmed lamb
Salt and pepper to season
1 teaspoon chopped rosemary
2 teaspoons of mild-tasting mustard (Dijon)
1 teaspoon of fresh herbs (mint, parsley, and thyme)
1 tablespoon breadcrumbs

Preheat the oven to 200° C/400° F/gas mark 6.

Heat a large roasting pan in the oven. Season the lamb and rub over with a little butter and some chopped rosemary. Place in the pan and cook for about 18–20 minutes or longer if you like it less rare.

Remove from the oven and coat the outside with a mixture of the mustard, crumbs, and herbs. Crisp under a hot grill for 2 to 3 minutes, making sure not to let it burn.

Stuffing

75 g/2 $\frac{1}{2}$ oz./$\frac{1}{3}$ cup butter
2 shallots, chopped small
75 g mixed herbs (mint, parsley, and thyme)
50 g/2 oz./$\frac{1}{4}$ cup chopped dried apricots
100 g/3 $\frac{1}{2}$ oz./$\frac{1}{2}$ cup breadcrumbs

Melt the butter in a pan over a gentle heat. Add the shallots, herbs, and chopped apricots. Cook gently for about 5 minutes, stirring frequently so as not to let it burn. Then add the crumbs and keep warm till needed.

Caper Sauce

50 g/2 oz. butter
1 tablespoon flour
1/2 cup lamb stock
50 ml/$\frac{1}{4}$ cup cream
Juice of half a lemon
3 tablespoons capers
1 tablespoon chopped parsley
Salt and pepper

Place the butter in a saucepan and cook gently until it browns slightly and smells slightly nutty. Remove from the heat and work in the flour. Cook for a minute and whisk in the lamb stock, cream, and lemon juice with the seasoning. Simmer gently for about 5 minutes and add the chopped parsley and capers.

Himself thinks this is a grand feast altogether, so, and likes me to serve it with buttery mashed potatoes, brussel sprouts, and mashed and mixed carrots and parsnips.

GLOSSARY

In all the Irish Country books I have provided a glossary to help the reader who is unfamiliar with the vagaries of the Queen's English as she may be spoken by the majority of people in Ulster. It is a regional dialect akin to English as spoken in Yorkshire or on Tyneside, American English used in Texas or the Bronx, or Canadian English in Newfoundland or the Ottawa Valley. It is not *Gaeilge,* the Irish language. It is not Ulster Scots, which is claimed to be a distinct language in its own right. I confess I am not a speaker.

Today in Ulster (but not in 1946 where this book is set) official signs are written in English, Irish, and Ulster Scots. The washroom sign would read *Toilets, Leithris,* and *Cludgies* respectively.

I hope what follows here will enhance your enjoyment of the work and unravel some of the mysteries of Ulsterspeak, although, I am afraid, it will not improve your command of Ulster Scots.

anyroad: Anyway.

away off and . . . : Go away, or you are being stupid. Often succeeded by **feel your head** or **chase yourself.**

bar: Refuse admission, as from a public house.

barge: Force your way through a crowd. Verbally chastise.

barmbrack: Speckled bread. (See Kinky's recipe, *Irish Country Doctor* p.340)

bide (where you're at): Stay (where you are).

boke: Vomit.

bollix: Testicles (impolite). May be used as an expression of vehement disagreement or to describe a person of whom you disapprove.

bonnaught: Irish mercenary of the fourteenth century.

bonnet: Hood (when applied to a car).

both legs the same length: Standing about uselessly.

bowler hat: Derby hat.

brass neck: Chutzpah. Impertinence.

brave: Large or good.

brave wheen: Large number of.

but: Ulster folks have a habit of putting "but" not at the beginning of a sentence but at the end.

capped/cap: A cap was awarded to athletes selected for important teams. Equivalent to a "letter" at a University.

cracker: Excellent.

crisps: Potato chips. In 1946 there was only one flavour and the salt came in a little bag of blue greaseproof paper.

currency: In 1946, well prior to decimilisation, sterling was the currency of the United Kingdom, of which Northern Ireland was a part. The unit was the pound, which contained twenty shillings, each made of twelve pennies, thus there were 240 pennies in a pound. Coins and notes of combined or lesser or greater denominations were in circulation often referred to by slang or archaic terms: half-penny (two to the penny), threepenny piece (thruppeny bit), sixpenny piece (tanner), two-shillings piece (florin), two-shillings-and-sixpence piece (half a crown), ten-shilling note (ten-bob note), guinea coin worth one pound and one shilling, five-pound note (fiver). In 1946 one pound bought nearly three U.S. dollars.

demob: Demobilise. Be honourably discharged from the armed forces. Ulster was an anomaly in the Second World War. Unlike the rest of the United Kingdom there was no conscription there. Ulster members of the peacetime reserve forces like the Territorial Army, Royal Air Force Volunteer Reserve, and Royal Naval Reserve were called up to fight, but all other Ulstermen, and indeed Irishmen, like RAF fighter pilot Paddy Finucane, were volunteers.

desperate: Immense, or terrible.

divil: Devil.

divilment: Mischief.

donkey's age: A very long time.

dote/doting: Something (person or animal) adorable/being crazy about or simply being crazy (in one's dotage).

duncher: Cloth cap, usually tweed.

eejit: Idiot.

face like a Lurgan spade: The turf-cutting spade particular to the town of Lurgan and surrounds was longer than most, so, having a very long face.

feck, and variations: Corruption of "fuck." Its scatalogical shock value is now so debased that it is no more offensive than "like" larded into teenagers' chat. Now available at reputable bookstores is the *Feckin' Book of Irish . . .* a series of ten books by Murphy and O'Dea.

feel your head: See **away off.**

ferocious: Extremely bad or very upsetting.

fey: Having the gift of second sight.

git: Corruption of "got," a short form of "begotten." Often expressed as "hoor's (whore's) git" or bastard.

give lip: Be cheeky or insulting to.

glipe (great): stupid (or very stupid) person.

go 'way (out of that): I don't believe you, or I know you are trying to fool me.

head (nautical): Lavatory.

headstaggers: A disease of sheep where a parasite invades the brain causing the animal to stagger and fall.

highheejin: Upper-class person.

HMS: His/Her Majesty's Ship.

hobbyhorse shite: Literally sawdust. Rubbish.

hot half un: Measure of spirits, usually whiskey, to which is added sugar, lemon juice, cloves, and boiling water.

hould your wheest: Keep quiet.

kipper: A butterflied and gutted herring, pickled or salted and cold smoked, usually over oak chips.

knows his onions: Is very knowledgeable about.

more power to your wheel: Words of encouragement.

no goat's toe: Has a very high and usually misplaced opinion of oneself.

no harm to you: An expression used prior to delivering bad news or disagreeing with the person being addressed.

no mission: Hopeless.

on your bike: Forceful "go away."

put in his box: Taken down a peg or two.

quare: Queer. Used to mean very strange, or exceptional.

R.N./R.N.R.: These letters following a name indicate either Royal Navy for someone who has joined in a career capacity or Royal Navy Reserve for merchant seamen who volunteered for extra training with the Royal Navy during peacetime and who, in times of emergency, were liable for call-up to active service.

scrip: Prescription.

see: See you, him, me. Drawing emphasis to the person "seen." It does not actually mean that they are in sight.

shit: Verb.

shite: Noun.

shout: In a bar, the person named's turn to buy.

shut your yap: Shut up.

so (so it is): Much used at the ends of sentences for emphasis in County Cork. (The same in Ulster.)

soft-soaper: Flatterer.

sound (man): Reliable or very good (man).

stunned mullet: To look stupid, surprised, or absolutely out of touch. A mullet is an ugly saltwater fish.

sucking diesel: Hitting paydirt. Probably in reference to siphoning tractor fuel.

telt: Told.

thole: Put up with. Suffer in silence.

thon (der): That person or thing (over there).

thran: Bloody-minded.

tinker's toss/damn/curse: Tinkers were itinerant menders with tins of pots and pans. Their attributes were not highly prized.

to beat Ban(n)agher: Far exceed realistic expectations or to one's great surprise.

toty: Very small.

turn: Faint.

warm: Have lots of money.

wee: Small, but in Ulster can be used to modify almost anything without reference to size. A barmaid, an old friend, greeted me by saying, "Come in, Pat. Have a wee seat and I'll get you a wee menu, and would you like a wee drink while you're waiting?"

wee man: The devil.

well mended: Recovered from a recent illness.

wheen: An indeterminate number.

wheest: Shut up or be quiet.

wind: Bowel gas.

you know: Verbal punctuation often used when the person being addressed could not possibly be in possession of the information.

your man (I'm): Someone either whose name is not known, "Your man over there? Who is he?" or someone known to all, "Your man, Van Morrison."

you're on: I will do what you ask or I accept the wager.

youse: You plural.

ABOUT THE AUTHOR

Patrick Taylor, M.D., was born and raised in Bangor, County Down, in Northern Ireland. Dr. Taylor is a distinguished medical researcher, offshore sailor, model-boat builder, and father of two grown children. He is the author of the beloved Irish Country novels, beginning with *An Irish Country Doctor*, as well as *Pray For Us Sinners* and its sequel, *Now and in the Hour of Our Death*, a duology centered around The Troubles. He now lives on Saltspring Island, British Columbia. Visit him at www.patricktaylor .ca.

The employees of Thorndike Press hope you have enjoyed this Large Print book. All our Thorndike, Wheeler, and Kennebec Large Print titles are designed for easy reading, and all our books are made to last. Other Thorndike Press Large Print books are available at your library, through selected bookstores, or directly from us.

For information about titles, please call:
(800) 223-1244

or visit our Web site at:
http://gale.cengage.com/thorndike

To share your comments, please write:
Publisher
Thorndike Press
10 Water St., Suite 310
Waterville, ME 04901